"If you were half a man, Pierce, your wife never would have gotten away with our heiress."

Adam Monarch faced his son, his fury a palpable thing. "You would have found a way to take care of her."

Griffen Monarch captured a butterfly and ever so softly stroked its velvety wings. He smiled to himself, agreeing with his grandfather, plucking off the creature's wings, one by one. His father was soft. And weak. Griffen had modeled himself after his grandfather; he let nothing stand in his way.

"I want my granddaughter back," Adam continued. "The future of Monarch's depends on her. I don't care what it takes. I don't care if you spend our entire fortune getting her back. I would do anything to get her back. *Anything.*"

Griffen swept away the pieces of the butterfly. "Do you mean that, Granddad? Would you do...anything to get her back?"

Adam looked Griffen dead in the eye. "Yes, I would."

Griffen nodded. "I'll find her, then. I'll bring her home, back to the family. And she'll never go away again."

Dear Readers,

The question I'm asked most often about being a writer is where my ideas come from. The truth is, they come from lots of different places and experiences, some of them most unlikely! The idea for *Fortune* came when I cracked open a fortune cookie and found a warning inside.

It read: *Be Careful What You Wish For...It Just Might Come True*.

I'd heard that saying all my life, but for some reason, as I stared at that fortune-cookie warning, my writer's imagination took off. Are there consequences for having your every wish come true? Do we sometimes wish for the very thing that starts a dangerous chain reaction and sends events spiraling out of our control?

Thus *Fortune* was born, a story about just such a scenario, and one that I hope will keep you on the edge of your seat from the first page to the last.

If you like *Fortune*, I hope you'll look for my next novel, *Shocking Pink*, due out in February 1998. It's another story whose idea sprang from a real-life experience—but that's for another letter.

Best to you,

P.S. I love to hear from my readers.
Write to me at P.O. Box 8556, Mandeville, LA, 70470 U.S.A.

ERICA SPINDLER

FORTUNE

MIRA

ISBN 1-55166-268-X

FORTUNE

Copyright © 1997 by Erica Spindler.

MIRA and the star colophon are trademarks of MIRA Books.

Printed in U.S.A.

For three women it has been my incredible good fortune to
call friends:
Jan Hamilton Powell, Terry Richards McGee
and
Karen Young Stone

Acknowledgments

My heartfelt thanks to the following people for helping me bring *Fortune* to life:

Huge thanks to Roxanne Mouton of Mignon Faget Ltd., for walking me through the jewelry-making process, from design concept to finished piece, and for patiently and thoroughly explaining the workings of a jewelry production studio.

Thanks, too, to the incomparable Mignon Faget, for allowing her staff to take time out of their busy day to make my tour possible, and to the staff themselves for answering my questions and putting up with a stranger peering over their shoulders while they worked.

Thanks to my sister, Stacie Spindler, for showing me the "real" Chicago and for her enthusiasm and support.

Big thanks also to the guys at Calvin Klein Camper Sales for letting me roam freely through their trailers; to Linda Weissert for the on-the-spot information about Pittsburgh; and to Drs. Leslie and Bill Michaelis for giving me a crash course in veterinary medicine.

And, as always, thanks to my agent, Evan Marshall; my editor, Melissa Senate; and the entire MIRA Books staff, particularly Dianne Moggy and Amy Moore.

Part I

Butterflies

1

Chicago, Illinois,
1971

Sunlight spilled through the nursery's floor-to-ceiling stained-glass window, painting the floor the color of rubies, emeralds and sapphires. Installed in 1909 to herald the first Monarch baby to occupy the Astor Street mansion, the window depicted a hovering angel, golden wings spread, her expression beatific as she guarded the children below.

Since that first Monarch baby, the angel had protected sad few children. One tragedy after another had befallen this family, a family desperate for daughters, one seemingly doomed to watch bitterly as other families grew and multiplied.

Two weeks ago that had changed. Two weeks ago Grace Elizabeth Monarch had been born and come home, to this nursery and its waiting angel, to this desperate family. She had changed everyone's life forever.

But no one's more than her mother's.

Madeline Monarch slipped into the nursery and crossed to the cradle and her sleeping daughter. She gazed down at her, love and a sense of wonder welling inside her. She reached out and stroked her baby's velvety cheek, and the infant stirred and turned her head toward Madeline's finger, sucking in her sleep, looking for a nipple.

A lump formed in Madeline's throat. She was so beautiful,

so incredibly...perfect. She still couldn't quite believe Grace was hers. Madeline bent her head close to her daughter's and breathed in her baby-soft scent. It filled her head, and she squeezed her eyes shut, nearly drowning in its sweetness.

What had she done to deserve her? Madeline wondered. Why had she been singled out for such a stroke of good fortune? Even Grace's birth had been like a miracle. She had rocketed into the world, nearly painlessly and at a speed that had taken even Madeline's veteran obstetrician by surprise. Madeline's water had broken and less than an hour later there had been Grace, howling and red-faced but unbelievably, incredibly perfect.

Madeline shook her head slightly, unable to fully trust her sudden luck. But how could she? She had never done anything well, or easily, before. No, Madeline was one of those people destined to make mistakes, to choose poorly and to be hurt time and again.

In truth, the moment before the nurse laid Grace in her arms, Madeline hadn't believed that anything in her life would ever be easy, or painless, or without flaw. She hadn't believed that she was worthy of true love, of real devotion; she had thought she would go through life reaching for that elusive emotion but always coming back empty-handed.

The next moment had changed all that. Grace had changed it. Madeline loved her daughter almost more than she could bear. And Grace loved her back, the same way. Unconditionally. Completely.

Madeline threaded her fingers through her daughter's silky dark hair. Grace needed her. Grace loved her. Madeline found that truth to be heady and shattering, but absolutely, positively the best feeling in the whole world. She would do anything, battle anyone or any evil, to protect her daughter.

If necessary, she would give her own life.

Madeline heard a sound at the nursery door and turned. Her six-year-old stepson, Griffen, stood there, his gaze fixed intently on the cradle, his expression strange, at once fascinated and wary, drawn and repelled. She breathed deeply though her nose, fighting back a feeling of resentment at his intrusion. Fighting back the distaste that left her longing for a drink of clean, sweet water.

She scolded herself for both her thoughts and her reaction to him. Griffen needed her, too. She had to remember that.

Yet even as the thought ran through her head, she acknowledged that something about her husband's son unsettled her, something about him affected her like an icy hand to her back; it had from the first.

It wasn't his appearance or demeanor. He was an uncommonly beautiful child. Bright, polite, at times even sweet. He didn't seem to affect anyone else the way he did her. So why, when she looked into his eyes, couldn't she suppress a shudder?

Madeline knew why. Because she was different; because she saw in a way others didn't. All her life she had been troubled by uncannily accurate "feelings" and "visions"—about people, about events to come and about ones past. For as long as she could remember, she had been embarrassed by her ability. She had learned to manage the visions by ignoring them. Over time they had become less frequent and less vivid.

No longer. Like everything else in her life, pregnancy and motherhood had changed that. Grace had changed it. Now her sixth sense, if that was even what she should call it, neither rested nor would be ignored, as if the hormones raging through her body had kicked on a switch she didn't know how to turn off.

. And her extra sense warned her that there was something wrong with Griffen Monarch. Something terribly wrong.

Madeline chastised herself. Maybe she was the one with the problem as her husband and Adam Monarch, her father-in-law, insisted; maybe all those hormones were affecting her judgment, her sense of reality and balance.

She swept her gaze over Griffen, guilt pinching at her. His

own mother was dead three years now, the victim of an "accidental" overdose of sleeping pills and booze. Madeline knew it couldn't have been easy for him, growing up with a grandfather obsessed with having a female heir, a grandmother driven to the point of near madness by seven late-term miscarriages and a father who hadn't the understanding or the patience for the needs of a young child. Then, as if those things hadn't been enough, she had been introduced into the mix.

And now he had a sibling to deal with, a sibling who had stolen whatever attention and affection this austere household had to offer.

Poor child, Madeline thought, mustering resolve if not warmth. She would try harder. She would be a good stepmother to the boy. She *would* learn to care for him.

Madeline smiled and motioned him into the room. "Come in, Griffen. But quietly. Grace is sleeping."

He nodded, and without a word to her, tiptoed into the room. He crossed to stand beside her and gazed silently at his half sister.

Madeline studied him a moment, then returned her gaze to Grace. In the past eighteen months, Madeline had come to understand just how deeply troubled a family she had married into. In fact, she had begun to fear that marrying Pierce Monarch had been another of her mistakes. He was not the man she had thought him to be—he was withdrawn, inflexible and, she had discovered, mean-spirited. So mean-spirited that she had wondered how she could not have seen it before.

Madeline frowned. She wasn't being truthful with herself. She knew why she hadn't seen it. She had been blinded by the Monarch name. By their wealth, their status in Chicago. She had been awed by Monarch Design and Retail, the jewelry-design firm started in 1887 by Anna and Marcus Monarch with the money they had inherited from their parents. Within a matter of only a few years, the brother and sister team had created a firm whose works rivaled Tiffany's in beauty, quality and originality.

Madeline recalled the many times previous to meeting Pierce Monarch that she had wandered through the Michigan Avenue Monarch's, aching to possess one of the impossibly extravagant, utterly fabulous pieces, a brooch or necklace or ring. Just one piece, she had wished. Any one at all.

Her wish had come true.

Oh, yes, she had been blinded by all that the Monarchs had and were. After all, she was a woman with no family and no pedigree, a woman Pierce had plucked off the sales floor of Marshall Field's and transported here, to the old stone mansion in the heart of the city's Gold Coast, to what she had thought of as a dream come true.

But the dream had the qualities of a nightmare.

She shook her head. That was over now. Here was Grace, a savior of sorts for the Monarch clan; already Madeline felt a lightening in the atmosphere of the house, a celebratory mood that affected all, even the household staff.

"Baby Grace is so pretty."

Startled out of her thoughts, Madeline looked down at the boy, her heart melting at his awed expression. Rather than being jealous of his new sister, he seemed fascinated by her. He seemed to adore her.

How could she think such awful things about her stepson when he looked at Grace that way?

Madeline smiled. "I think so, too."

"Grandfather Monarch says baby Grace has the gift."

Madeline's smile froze. "The gift?" she repeated.

He nodded. "The one the Monarch girls get. The one my great-great-grandfather Marcus saw in his sister and used to make our fortune. That's why Grace is so special. That's why we must always keep her close to the family."

Although only parroting words he had obviously heard many times before, something almost fevered in his expression chilled her. "Grace is special because she is, Griffen.

Not because of some…gift. Besides, just because only the girls in the family have been the artists so far doesn't mean that someday one of the boys won't be.'' She smiled and tapped him on the end of his nose with her index finger. ''Maybe you.''

''No.'' He frowned and shook his head, looking adult and annoyed with her stupidity. ''Grandfather says only the girls. That's the way it's always been. It's why Grace is so important.''

Only the girls. Madeline shuddered and rubbed her arms. ''Honey, Grace is just a baby. She might not have this…gift.''

''She has it. Grandfather says so.''

She frowned. ''And your grandfather knows everything?''

''He's the smartest person in the whole world. I'm going to be just like him when I grow up.'' Griffen moved his gaze back to Grace. ''Can I touch her?''

Madeline hesitated, then nodded reluctantly. ''Only lightly. Like this.'' She demonstrated, ever so gently stroking Grace's silky dark hair.

Griffen watched carefully, then mimicked her actions. After a moment, he drew his hand away. ''She's so soft,'' he said, looking up at Madeline in surprise. ''How come?''

''Because she's brand-new.'' She nudged the cradle and it swayed. ''When she gets a little bigger, I'll let you hold her.''

Again he mimicked Madeline's actions, nudging the cradle, making it swing. ''How much bigger?''

''A little bigger. Newborns are very delicate. They can be easily hurt.''

For several minutes, they said nothing, just stood side by side, rocking the cradle and gazing at Grace. Then Griffen looked up at Madeline once again. ''I'm going to marry her when I grow up.''

''Who, honey?''

''Baby Grace.''

Madeline laughed softly and ruffled his dark hair. "You can't, sweetheart. She's your sister."

Griffen said nothing. One moment became several, then he narrowed his eyes, the intensity in them taking her aback. "I will," he said softly, fiercely. "I will if I want."

Madeline's vision blurred, then cleared. *She saw a dark, white forest and blood spilling across a gleaming floor. She heard a silent scream for help, and saw small arms flailing against larger ones.*

A squeak of terror slipped past Madeline's lips. She blinked, and she was once again in her daughter's sunny nursery, once again staring into her stepson's cold, angry eyes.

Fear choked her. She fought it off, fought off the premonition and its chilling image. Drawing herself up to her full five-foot height, she frowned at him. "You cannot," she said sternly, though her voice quivered. "A brother cannot marry his sister. Not ever."

His face pinched with fury. "I will," he said again, grabbing the top rail of the cradle. "No matter what you say!"

He pushed as hard as he could. The basket swung wildly, almost capsizing. Madeline cried out and sprang forward, though it was too late. Grace was thrown against the side of the basket, her head against the wooden slats. The infant screamed.

Madeline scooped up her howling daughter and cradled her against her chest, rocking her and cooing, trying desperately to comfort her. Trying just as desperately to comfort herself. She shook so badly she could hardly stand. Grace was all right, she told herself. Just frightened; just a bruise.

It could have been worse. Much worse.

Blood spilling across a gleaming floor. A desperate cry for help.

She lifted her gaze. Griffen had retreated to the doorway and stood there watching her, his expression smug. Self-satisfied.

As she met his eyes, he smiled.

Madeline's knees gave. She sank to the floor, clutching Grace tightly to her chest. She shook, but not with fear. With the truth.

Griffen meant his sister harm.

Grace would never be safe around him. Never.

2

Madeline stood at her bedroom window, heart pounding, mouth dry with fear. She watched Pierce and Adam, engaged in conversation in the driveway below. Both men were dressed for a day of business; they had been standing in the driveway, their cars idling, for just over ten minutes.

Madeline checked her watch again, swore softly, then returned her gaze to her husband and father-in-law. She squeezed her eyes shut and willed the men to finish their discussion and go.

Her silent plea didn't move them, and she flexed her fingers, frustrated. Anxious. Why had they chosen today for a lengthy chat? Why today, when every minute counted? Every second?

She had everything planned. Adam was leaving for a buying trip; in moments Pierce would head to work; he had a cocktail reception to attend tonight and a racquetball match after that. The housekeeper did the marketing on Wednesdays, it was Nanny's day off. Grandmother Monarch was quite ill and hardly ever emerged from her suite of rooms. Griffen was in school.

Today was the perfect day to run away.

Her stomach fluttered. Nerves. Disappointment. In herself, in her husband. He refused to see the truth about Griffen, about the boy's intentions toward Grace. In the five years since the incident in the nursery, Madeline had countless times shared her fears, her premonitions about Griffen, with her husband and father-in-law. They had called her excitable. She was overreacting, they'd said. She was a neurotic, hysterical mother. They had even suggested that she was jealous of the boy.

Jealous! Of Griffen? Of the time he spent with Grace? It was worse than ridiculous. It was insulting.

Without support from the family, she had been forced to watch Griffen's bizarre attachment to his sister grow. He became alarmingly jealous when she ignored him or chose to play with another child, or even a toy, or pet. He followed Grace; he was possessive of her time, her attention. Madeline had caught him gazing with pure hatred at other children, at Nanny, at her, for heaven's sake.

But those had been nothing compared to what had come next.

Grace's favorite toys destroyed, sometimes mutilated. Her kitten bludgeoned to death.

Griffen on top of Grace, holding her down, one hand covering her mouth, the other up her dress.

Even now, months later, the horror of what she had stumbled upon, caused her stomach to turn. He had not been playing a guileless child's game with his sister. They had not been wrestling, as he had claimed with an innocent, beautiful smile.

Madeline had gone to her husband and her father-in-law; she had told them what she'd seen. She had begged them to believe her, had pleaded with them to trust her. Not only for Grace's sake, but for Griffen's, too. The child needed counseling.

Not only had they not believed her, her father-in-law had threatened her. If she didn't cease this madness, Adam had warned, he would take Grace away from her. She was unbalanced, he had told her. Her delusions about Griffen, about being able to see the future, were unhealthy for the youngster. Any judge would see that.

Adam had struck her then, sharply, across the mouth. The force of the blow had sent her reeling backward, into a wall. Pierce had stood silently by, watching his father, allowing it to happen without even a murmur of protest.

Madeline brought a hand to her mouth, remembering, holding back a sound of pain. Any affection, any last, lingering warmth she had felt for her husband had died in that moment. And in that moment, she had begun hating him. Hating him so much, so ferociously, that she had been able to taste the emotion.

It had tasted like acid. It had eaten at her like acid.

It still did.

All these months, she had controlled her feelings. Because she'd known she couldn't afford another of her "mistakes," because she'd understood that this time it was Grace's life at stake. Grace's well-being.

With the Monarch power, money and connections, Adam could make good his threat to take Grace away from her. He could do it without even breaking a sweat.

Then her daughter would have no one to protect her. No one who saw the truth about Griffen.

So Madeline had begun the elaborate charade—pretending to be smitten with her husband, acting the part of devoted, adoring wife, the part of the perfect Monarch daughter-in-law. She had claimed to both men that she'd had a sort of epiphany, telling them that they had been right—she had been overreacting about Griffen.

She didn't know what had gotten into her, she'd told them. She didn't know why she had been so excitable. She had told them she was sorry, that she was embarrassed by her behavior.

Pierce had fallen for it right away; Adam had taken longer.

She had begun planning her and Grace's escape.

Pierce looked up suddenly, catching her staring at him. He narrowed his eyes—with suspicion, with realization. Her heart stopped, then started again, thundering in her chest until she had to fight to catch her breath. He knew, she thought, completely panicked. Dear God…he had found her out.

What did she do now?

Madeline fought her panic. He didn't know. He couldn't. He didn't even suspect. She had been very careful. That morning, as a bit of insurance, she'd even submitted to his hands and mouth, she had submitted to his every demand, no matter how abhorrent to her. She had moaned and writhed and sighed, knowing that he would go off to work content and cocky. Knowing that he wouldn't give her another thought all day. All the while she had wanted to wretch; her skin had crawled at his touch.

But she would do anything to protect her daughter. Anything. This plan had to work. It had to.

Madeline forced an adoring smile and waved. Then for good measure, she blew him a kiss. He smiled, the curving of his lips confident to the point of arrogance, then returned to his conversation.

She backed away from the window, relief flooding her. He didn't know. Neither did Adam. She and Grace were safe.

For now.

Madeline spun around, thinking of the past months. She had lived in fear, she had spent every waking moment walking a tightrope between acting as if nothing was wrong and protecting Grace, between appearing unconcerned about Griffen and being too terrified even to sleep, lest he use that opportunity to sneak into Grace's room and violate her.

Living that way had taken its toll. She was tired and on edge. She had lost weight, so much that people had begun to comment. There had been times, as she paced the floor during the middle of the night, that she had wondered if she was crazy. If she was delusional, as Pierce had said.

But those times were few; they didn't last long. She would recall Griffen's expression when he looked at Grace, would recall the coldness of his eyes, the cunning of his smile, and she would know she wasn't crazy.

Everyone else was blind.

Madeline crossed to the bed, bent and peered underneath—her suitcases were there, where she had left them, waiting. Hers was packed, Grace's empty. As soon as Pierce was gone, she would remedy that.

Madeline stood, glanced around the room, mentally ticking off her few options, reassessing her decision. She had no family to go to and had lost touch with all her old friends. Even her once-best friend, Susan, who she had been so close to that she had believed them soul mates, had slipped out of her life. She had no nest egg to fall back on and no means to support her and Grace. Pierce had seen to it that she had no financial independence; everything she had, Pierce either gave her or she signed for.

Adam's sister, Dorothy, was sympathetic, but only to a point. Dorothy's allegiance would always be first and foremost to the Monarch family and the family business. And Dorothy, like the others, was obsessed with the notion that Grace had the gift, obsessed with the belief that Grace would one day succeed her as the artistic genius behind Monarch Design.

Having no other option, Madeline had pawned her engagement ring—Pierce thought she had taken it in for cleaning—and used the money to buy a car. A late-model Chevrolet, a junker compared to the Mercedes sedan she usually drove. But it had low mileage and the woman from whom she'd bought it had sworn it was absolutely dependable.

Madeline had parked it a dozen blocks away, in a transitional neighborhood where it wouldn't scream that it didn't belong. Everything was in place.

Madeline checked her watch, then twisted her fingers together. *Dammit, when were they going to leave?* Every moment counted. Because every moment meant another moment's head start before Pierce and Adam realized what she had done.

As if in answer to her silent plea, Madeline heard the slam

of car doors. She raced to the window in time to see Adam and Pierce drive off.

Finally! Heart in her throat, she flew to the door, into the hall and down the stairs. At the foyer she stopped, forcing herself to appear calm on the off chance someone was about. She made her way to the study, closing and locking the door behind her.

She leaned against the door, letting out a breath she hadn't even realized she held. She drew another. Across the room hung a small, exquisitely rendered landscape. Behind it, a wall safe.

She stared at the painting, working up her courage. For four months she had used every excuse to be in here when Pierce opened the safe; she had even used an insatiable need for sex, all in an attempt to learn the combination. She had watched, she had listened and counted and prayed.

And she had learned it, number by excruciating number. Or she thought she had.

Dear God, please let me have the right numbers. Don't let me be wrong.

Madeline crossed to the painting. She swung it away from the wall. Her hands shook. They were clammy, slick with sweat. She spun the wheel to the first number, then the next and next. She grasped the handle and pulled.

It didn't open.

She almost cried out in disappointment, physically biting back the sound. Without money, she couldn't go as far as the corner. Without money, there was no way she could get Grace away from here, no way she could hide and protect her.

Stay calm, Madeline. Take a deep breath and try again.
She did.
The safe opened.

Light-headed with fear and relief, she reached inside. She moved aside a black velvet pouch emblazoned with Monarch's "M" logo, counted out five thousand dollars, enough, she thought, to get her and Grace far from here and settled, until she could find a job.

She stuffed the bills into one of her cardigan's deep pockets, then moved the pouch back to its original position and started to close the safe door. Her gaze landed on that black velvet bag.

What was in it?

On impulse, she opened the bag and dipped her hand inside—and pulled out a fistful of sparkling, fiery gems. Diamonds, rubies and sapphires. She caught her breath, stunned. By their beauty. By their heat. For even though they were cold against her palm, their fire made them hot.

What were they doing here? she wondered, selecting a particularly large, brilliant stone and holding it up to the light. Why weren't they in the store's vault, where they belonged? There they would be both safer and fully insured. It didn't make sense. Adam and Pierce were nothing if not shrewd businessmen.

Madeline frowned at her own thoughts. She didn't have time for this; what Pierce and Adam did with the store's property wasn't her concern. It never had been. She dropped the stones back into the bag, then shoved the bag back into the safe.

Take them.

The thought raced into her head, and with it a feeling, sharp, overwhelming—that she would need them, that Grace would need them. Madeline shook her head, denying the thought, the feeling. She was overwrought and anxious; she wasn't thinking clearly. If she took the stones, Pierce and Adam would be that much more determined to find her. They would have that much more to hold against her in a court of law.

She swung the safe shut, made sure it was locked, turned and started out of the study. Halfway across the room she stopped, frozen, blinded by an indistinct but chilling image. *She saw snow. And blood spilling across a gleaming floor.*

She saw the twinkle of gems and the glitter of ice. Her mouth went dry; sweat beaded on her upper lip. *She saw dark water sucking someone down, swallowing them whole.*

She began to shake. *Take the gems. Take them now.*

With a cry of pure terror, Madeline spun back to the safe, reopened it and grabbed the pouch. She slammed the safe shut and as quickly as she could, twisted the dial, then eased the painting into place.

She couldn't turn back now.

Clutching the pouch to her chest, she ran from the library. Hysteria tugged at her; she fought it. She had to stay calm if she was to protect Grace. Today she was taking the first step, but every day after would prove as much of a challenge.

No one was about. Madeline supposed the housekeeper had already left. She made her way up to the nursery. She crossed to Grace's bed.

"Baby," she murmured, shaking her daughter gently, "sweetheart, it's time to get up."

Grace whimpered and rolled over, crushing her favorite teddy bear to her chest. Madeline shook her again. "Come on, sweetie, we're going on a trip. Time to wake up."

Grace yawned. She cracked open her eyes. Her lips curved up. "Hi, Mommy."

Madeline's heart turned over. She never got enough of hearing her daughter call her that, never got enough of that sweet, baby voice or the way the little girl looked at her— as if Madeline were the most important, the best, person in the world.

She loved Grace so much it terrified her. She prayed she was doing the right thing.

"I need you to dress, baby. Your clothes are right over there." She pointed to the rocking chair, where she had laid out her daughter's garments. She saw that her hand shook. "Can you do that for me?"

Grace nodded and sat up; she stuck her thumb in her

mouth—a habit Pierce couldn't abide—and eyed her mother. "Mommy's upset."

"No, honey. Just rushed."

"Where are we going?"

Madeline hesitated. What could she tell her daughter? That she planned to drive until she could drive no more, her only goal to put as much distance between them and the Monarchs as possible? Hardly. Instead, she tapped Grace on the nose. "It's going to be so much fun. Just you and me."

"Not Daddy?"

Madeline shook her head. "He has to work."

Grace accepted her explanation without question or murmur. The truth was, Grace and Pierce weren't especially close; he was always busy, and when he did have time for Grace he was critical—she was too loud, too messy, she didn't pronounce words correctly. He hardly ever hugged or kissed her; he always spoke of her in terms not of love but of value. To the family. To the business.

"Not Grandfather or Grandmother?"

Madeline shook her head. "Nope."

Grace curved her arms around herself. "Not brother?"

"Not brother," Madeline answered sharply. *Never brother.* "We're going to have such fun, just you and me."

"Okay." Yawning again, Grace climbed out of bed. "Clothes over there?"

"That's right, honey." Madeline went to the nursery door, stopping when she reached it. "You get dressed. I'll be right back, then I'll help with your socks and shoes."

"Thanks, Mommy."

Madeline squatted and held out her arms. "I think I need a hug."

Grace trotted over. She wrapped her chubby little arms around Madeline's neck and squeezed. Madeline hugged her back, hard.

"I love you, sweetheart. More than anything. I always will."

"Me, too. More than anything."

Madeline kissed her, then stood. "I'll be right back. Get dressed."

Madeline ducked into the hall, glancing at her watch again as she did. Time was slipping by. Too much time. She had to put as much distance between her and this family as she could, as fast as she could. When Pierce and Adam realized what she had done, they would use their every resource to find her.

She ran to her and Pierce's bedroom. There, she raced across to the bed and, getting down on her hands and knees, yanked the suitcases out from under. With trembling fingers she unlocked hers, looked it over to make sure nothing had been moved, then tucked the pouch of gems inside. That done, she snapped the case shut, stood and bent for the bags.

Pierce knew.

The thought came to her suddenly, with it an overwhelming feeling of dread. A sense of foreboding. She looked over her shoulder, half expecting to see him standing behind her, the expression in his eyes murderous.

The doorway was empty.

Even so, a shudder moved up her spine. *He knew. Dear Jesus, he knew.*

But how could he? She shook her head. If he did, he would have disturbed the contents of her suitcase. He would have confronted her.

She had to get a grip, she told herself, hoisting up the bags. She had to keep her wits about her—for Grace's sake. And her own. If Pierce caught her, she didn't know what he might do.

He might even kill her.

Madeline took a deep, calming breath. Twenty minutes from now she and Grace would be on the road, and on their way to starting a new life, one free of this unhappy, twisted family. Everything was going according to plan.

After peeking into the hall to make sure no one was about,

she returned to the nursery. Grace was dawdling, having gotten distracted in the bathroom.

"Mommy, I brushed my teeth really good. For a long time, every tooth."

Madeline took another deep breath. Losing her cool with her daughter would not hurry her. "Good girl," she said with elaborate calm. "Come on now, we have to hurry."

Grace trotted back into the room. "Why?"

Madeline held out Grace's jumper. "Why what?"

"Why do we have to hurry?"

"Because we do." Madeline's voice rose; she heard the edge of hysteria in it. She fought it back and smiled at her daughter. "I'll help you dress."

She did and within minutes Grace was ready to go. Madeline sat her on the rug next to the packed suitcase, handed her her favorite toy, then started filling Grace's suitcase, throwing in clothes and toiletries and toys, only the essentials and a few of Grace's favorites.

A knock sounded at the nursery door. Madeline swung toward it, heart thundering. The knock came again.

"Mrs. Monarch? I'm leaving for the market, is there anything special you need?"

The housekeeper. She hadn't left yet.

As if reading her mind, the woman said, "I got hung up on the phone with the plumber. They're sending someone by this afternoon. Is there anything you need?"

Madeline struggled to find her voice. She opened her mouth, but nothing came out.

"Mrs. Monarch? Are you all right?"

Madeline heard the question, the concern in the other woman's voice. Panic pumped through her; if she didn't answer, the housekeeper would come into the nursery. "I...I'm fine, Alice. And no, there's nothing I need. You...you go on, we're just fine."

"All right, Mrs. Monarch. Oh, Mr. Monarch's office

called, looking for him. Apparently, he forgot something and is on his way home.''

Pierce? On his way home?

Madeline struggled to breathe evenly. She thanked the woman, reminded her that she and Grace would be gone to the zoo all afternoon, then waited several moments to make sure the housekeeper had left before she jumped into action.

How long? she wondered, completely panicked. How long until Pierce walked through that door? She turned back to Grace's suitcase and did a quick inventory. She would just have to leave the rest; they would have to make do. There was no time. No time.

''Mommy!'' Grace squealed with delight. ''Look!''

Madeline swung around in time to see Grace emptying the pouch of gems into her lap.

With a cry, Madeline leaped across to her daughter. ''No! Bad girl!'' She snatched the pouch from Grace's hands. The jewels flew, scattering across the wooden floor.

For one moment, Grace stared blankly at her, as if in shock. Then she burst into tears.

Madeline hardly ever raised her voice with Grace. She could count on one hand the times she had yelled at her.

''I'm sorry, honey. Daddy wanted us to have the pretty stones for our trip. But they're very special, we mustn't play with them.'' She hugged her daughter. ''It's all right, sweetheart. Come, help me pick them up. Can you do that?''

Still whimpering, Grace nodded and together they retrieved the stones, put them back into the pouch, the pouch into the suitcase, Madeline painfully aware of each passing moment. She snapped the case shut, locked it this time, then did the same to Grace's. ''Come on, sweetie, time to go.''

The nursery door opened. Madeline swung toward it and froze. Not Pierce on his way home, she realized. The other Mr. Monarch. Worse, much worse.

Adam took in the scene before him, realization crossing

his features. His face went from passive to enraged. "Going somewhere, Madeline, dear? On some sort of a trip?"

Madeline wetted her lips. "This isn't what it looks like. It's—"

"Going on a trip," Grace chirped up, happily playing with her baby doll. "Daddy can't come. He has to work."

"You lying, conniving bitch." Adam took a step toward her, his expression murderous. "So this is what you've been up to. This is why you've been such a perfect little wife. So agreeable, so helpful. You've been planning to steal my granddaughter."

Madeline took a step back, heart thundering. "She's my daughter, Adam. *Mine.*"

"Pretty stones," Grace said. "Daddy sent pretty stones for our trip."

Adam looked at Grace, drawing his eyebrows together in question, then back at Madeline. "You're not taking her any-where."

"You can't stop me." Madeline jerked her chin up and stiffened her shoulders. "I have to protect her. I've tried to tell you about Griffen, I've tried to make you—"

"Griffen's her brother!" Adam's face mottled with rage. "He's my grandson. A Monarch, for Christ's sake!"

"But he's unbalanced!" she cried. "He's dangerous! You have to see it! You have to believe—"

"Believe what?" he demanded. "The delusional ravings of a woman who believes she can see the future? Please."

"I told you what I walked in on! I didn't imagine that. He was holding her down, he had his hand—"

"Shut up!" he shouted, nearly purple with rage. "You're the one who's unbalanced. You're the one who needs help." He advanced on her, flexing his fingers. "Let's get this straight. I don't give a fuck if you leave, you crazy bitch, but you're not taking my granddaughter."

"I have to protect her. You can't stop me."

"I can. And I will. She belongs here, she belongs to Monarch's."

"She's not property!" Madeline cried, putting herself between Adam and Grace. "She doesn't *belong* to the family business. For God's sake, she's a person!"

He shook his head, calm suddenly, his eyes burning with a fanatical light. "She has the gift, Madeline. You know I can't let her go. You know I won't."

Madeline took a step backward, frightened. "Adam," she said, trying to reason with him, "be realistic. How do you know she has the gift? She's just five years old. How can you be so certain—"

Because he was crazy, she realized. Obsessed with Monarch's. Obsessed with the notion that a "gift" was passed from one generation of Monarch daughters to the next. Twisted by the belief that without Grace, without the one with the gift, Monarch's would crumble.

Dear God, he was as disturbed as Griffen.

She pushed past him, intent on grabbing Grace and running; he caught her arm and spun her back toward him, his expression contorted with rage and hatred. "You're not going anywhere, Madeline."

She yanked free of his grasp. "The hell we're not. You'll hear from my lawye—"

Adam struck her. His fist connected with her cheek; stars exploded in her head. With a cry of pain, she stumbled backward. She hit the edge of the dresser, and the Mother Goose lamp crashed to the floor.

"Mommy!"

Adam snatched Grace up and started for the nursery door. She began to howl and kick. "Mommy! I want my mommy!"

Madeline dragged herself to her feet, though her head felt as if it might explode with the movement. "You're not taking my daughter from me!" She launched herself at Adam's back, clawing at him, digging her fingernails into the side of his neck.

With a grunt of pain, he loosened his grip on Grace. She dropped to the floor. Adam swung around and struck her again. Madeline flew backward, hitting the side of the bed, falling across it. Even as she struggled to sit up, she saw him advancing on her.

He meant to kill her.

With a cry, she struggled to her feet. He knocked her back again; then fell on top of her, closing his hands around her neck. "You demented bitch. Did you really think you could get away with this? Did you really think you could take our girl away from us?"

Madeline clawed at his hands, trying to free herself. She twisted and turned and kicked; he was too strong. She heard Grace's hysterical sobbing and her father-in-law's grunts of exertion. She heard her own silent pleas for help.

Her lungs burned; the edges of her vision dimmed. Above her the beatific face of the stained-glass angel gazed down at her. The angel that guarded the children. The angel that had been unable to guard her child.

Madeline flailed her arms. Her right hand connected with the cut-glass vase on the nightstand by the bed. The leaded-glass vase that had been a baby gift from a family friend. The one she kept filled with pink tea roses. She closed her fingers around it and swung. It connected with the side of Adam's head. He grunted with pain and eased the grip on her neck.

Oxygen rushed into her lungs; they burned and she gasped for air. She swung the vase again. This time when it connected she heard a sickening crack. Blood flew. Grace screamed.

Adam got to his feet. Red spilled down the side of his face and across his white dress shirt. He brought a hand to the side of his head, meeting Madeline's eyes, his expression disbelieving. Then, as if in slow motion, he fell backward, hitting the floor with a heavy thud. Blood splattered Grace, who was still screaming, one piercing shriek after another, like a burglar alarm gone berserk.

Madeline stumbled to her feet and across to Adam. He lay completely still, face deathly white, blood pooling around his head, matting his dark hair. She had killed him. Dear God, she had killed Adam Monarch.

She reached out to him, intent on checking his pulse, then stopped, realization hitting her with the force of a blow. Her vision, the one from the library earlier and the one from five years before. *Blood spilling across a gleaming floor.* Madeline brought her hands to her mouth. *Glittering ice and freezing water, a body being sucked down.*

It wasn't over.

With a cry, she snatched her hand back. She had to go, now; before someone discovered what she had done. Before Grace was taken away from her.

Madeline scooped up her daughter, grabbed the suitcases and ran.

Part II

The Traveling Show

3

Lancaster County, Pennsylvania,
1983

The countryside gently rolled. It was lush and green and fertile. Nineteenth-century farmhouses nestled amidst those rolling hills; corn silos and windmills dotted the landscape, horse-drawn buggies the roads.

It was picturesque. Quaint and beautiful. Every day tourists flocked to Lancaster County to soak up the atmosphere and to relive—if only for an hour or two—the ways of an earlier century.

Seventeen-year-old Chance McCord had experienced all of living in the nineteenth century that he could stand. Quaint and picturesque made him want to puke. He feared if he spent one more day in this all-for-one, one-for-all, plain-ways hell, he would go completely, fucking out of his mind.

Chance strode across his sparsely furnished bedroom to the open window, stopping before it and gazing out at the evening. He wanted to wear his blue jeans. He wanted to listen to rock'n'roll and watch TV. He wanted to hang out with his friends—hell, or anyone else who thought and felt as he did. Dear God, he even longed for school. The Amish didn't believe in schooling for children his age. By sixteen, Amish children were fulfilling their duty to the family and community by working on the farm. He had been fulfilling his duty for a year now; damn but he hated cows.

Chance braced his hands on the windowsill and breathed

in the mild, evening air. A year ago he wouldn't have believed it possible to long for the big, rambling high school in north L.A. where he had always thought of himself as a prisoner. He wouldn't have believed it possible to wish to be sitting in first-period English with old man Waterson droning on about some poet who had died long before the birth of the electric guitar.

Now, Chance knew what it was to be a prisoner.

If he didn't escape, he would shrivel up and die.

It wasn't that his aunt Rebecca—his mother's sister—or her husband, Jacob, were bad people. Quite the contrary, they were good ones—to a fault. They had taken him in when his mother had died and his wealthy father—if Chance could even call him that, he had never even acknowledged his existence—had refused to take him. They had made room for him in this house, though with four children of their own it hadn't been easy.

And it wasn't that they hated him, though it often felt like it. They simply had their beliefs, and those beliefs were ironclad. They expected him to believe, and live, as they did.

He couldn't do that. It wasn't in him.

Chance began to pace, feeling as he often did, like a caged animal. They had buggied to town today, he, Uncle Jacob and Samuel, his aunt and uncle's ten-year-old son. There, Chance had seen it. A traveling carnival, complete with a Ferris wheel and a fortune-teller. A traveling show, the kind whose troupe went from town to town, the kind of show Chance didn't even know existed anymore.

An opportunity, he'd thought. Maybe.

While Jacob had been completing his business, he had looked it over, taking Samuel with him. When Jacob found them, he had been furious, though he hadn't raised his voice. The things he had said to Chance had hurt, though Chance had hidden it; the things his uncle had left unsaid, the way he had looked at Chance, had cut him to his core.

Later, Chance had heard his aunt and her husband arguing.

Chance crossed to the window, looking toward town. In

the distance he could see the faint glow of the carnival's neon light. Frustration balled in the pit of his gut. Regret with it. He had brought tension to this house, had brought friction— between his aunt and her husband, between the children and their parents, the family and a community that didn't like or trust outsiders.

He was an outsider here.

He always would be.

Chance rested his forehead against the windowsill, thinking of freedom, thinking of traveling from town to town with no one telling him what he could think or how he should act.

A traveling show. An opportunity. A way out.

His heart began to pound. He didn't fit in here, he never would. The feeling wasn't a new one; he had never fit in, had always been an outsider, even with his mother in L.A. But he had big plans, dreams that he intended to make reality.

His mother. As always when he thought of her, her image filled his head. He pictured her pretty face and smile, remembered the faraway look she so often had, recalled her habit of staring into the distance just over his right shoulder. With her image came a tightness to his chest, a pinch, an ache. Chance fisted his fingers against the smooth, cool glass. Connie McCord had longed for so many things, things life had kept beyond her reach, things death had denied her ever obtaining.

They wouldn't remain beyond his reach. He knew what he wanted, what he needed and deserved. He would grab it with both hands. He would not end up like his mother, always disappointed and unfulfilled, always on the outside looking in.

He would not die without having obtained all that he desired.

Chance swung away from the window. He would make his dreams a reality. Starting now, this moment. Somehow, he would find a way.

A traveling show. The chance, the opportunity he had been waiting for.

The time had come to go.

4

Marvel's Carnival was a seedy, tired affair, one of the last of its kind, a dying breed. Forty years prior, before the proliferation of high-tech, big-bucks amusement worlds like Six Flags, Marvel's had been in its heyday. Part amusement park, part circus, the carnival and its troupe traveled from town to town during the summer months, staying a few days or a week, then moving on.

These days, a carnival like Marvel's was in less demand than during that glorious heyday. Now the troupe only traveled to small rural areas. Places with little access to big, fancy theme parks, places where the kids—young and old— were hungry for something to do, some way to fill the long summer nights.

Marvel's gave them plenty to do, plenty to gawk at. The fire-eaters and snake charmers were a big favorite with the preadolescent crowd, the teenagers gravitated toward the rides and games of chance, the adults to the food, acrobats and contortionists. Everybody loved the fortune-teller, especially this summer, as the show's owner had managed to snare a really good one.

Claire Dearborn—known as Madame Claire on the circuit—was the real thing, the genuine article, not a scam artist or slick fraud like most of the other sideshow acts. If Abner Marvel had had any doubts about that when he'd hired her, those doubts had quickly disappeared as word spread and the towners began lining up to have their fortunes told.

Abner Marvel, one of the last of the born-and-bred showmen, had quickly given the woman and her daughter their own trailer and raised the cost of a five-minute reading from two dollars to five. Additional time could be purchased, of course. At a premium.

In twelve-year-old Skye Dearborn's opinion, her mother could make a lot more money with her ability than she did working for this third-rate, traveling fleabag, but the one time Skye had suggested it her mother had said she liked traveling with Marvel's and that money didn't buy happiness.

Skye supposed she liked the traveling, too, but she didn't follow the bit about money and happiness. From what she had seen of life, rich folks seemed a whole lot happier than poor ones.

Skye ducked out of her and her mother's trailer and headed toward the midway. Living accommodations for the entire troupe, the trailers were positioned on the northern-most edge of the lot, as far as possible from the activity of the show. Even so, she could hear the carousel's calliope and the screams of delighted terror coming from the Screamin' Demon, the show's rather modest roller coaster.

She and her mother were traveling with Marvel's for the summer; come fall they would settle somewhere, some little town where her mom would get a job at the local diner or drugstore and where she would go to school. Skye made a face. School sucked. She hated everything about it except art class, and some of the schools she had gone to had been so small and backward they didn't even have art. Then it totally sucked.

In truth, whether the school had art or not never really mattered, 'cause she and her mom never stayed in any one place too long. Just about the time she had gotten her reputation as a smart-mouthed troublemaker good and fixed, they would move on. Skye could count more than a dozen schools she'd attended in the last couple of years.

She and her mom had been traveling this way for as long as she could remember. Her mom said they were nomadic adventurers; Skye kind of thought they might be criminals or something. All the moving around, to her mind, just didn't add up.

Skye frowned and kicked at a discarded Coke can. Still half-full, the beverage spewed out, splattering her shorts and T-shirt. Making a sound of annoyance, she swiped at the drops of cola. If only her mom would tell her the truth. The few times Skye had confronted her, her mother had denied keeping anything from her; she had denied having any secrets.

She was lying; Skye was certain of it. She had the feeling that her mother was running, that she was constantly looking over her shoulder. That she was always afraid.

And that made Skye afraid, too. Her mother was all she had.

She climbed over the rope barricade that circled the perimeter of the show and separated what was called the front yard from the back yard, the towners from the troupers. Up ahead lay the midway, with its bright lights and raucous laughter, its frenetic mix of music, games and tasty treats. The rides flanked either side of the midway; the sideshow tents—including her mother's—were located at its far end.

Skye didn't have a set job with the troupe, but helped out as she was needed, filling in for troupers who were ill, helping set up and tear down, but mostly, she worked as a sort of shill on the midway, drumming up business for the various games of chance.

A "sort of" shill because Marvel's was a one-hundred-percent Sunday-school show—no overcharging or short-changing customers, no rigged games. Skye had played each game about a million times; she knew the trick to winning at each, so she made it look easy. So easy, in fact, that as she walked away, arms full of prizes, folks lined up, eager to win one of the big stuffed toys.

As Skye stepped onto the midway, the scent of popcorn hit her in a mouthwatering wave. Nearly 8:00 p.m., the carnival was in full swing, the midway packed, even for a Saturday night. Skye moved her gaze up, then down, the aisle of game booths, noting that most were busy.

All except the quarter toss.

She ambled over, stopped at the booth as if sizing it up, then dug in her pocket for a quarter. "What do I do?" she asked Danny, an obnoxious zit-face of a boy who seemed to have made tormenting her his life's work. But still, this was business. She had to get along with him for the good of the troupe.

He sidled over. "See those platforms there?" He pointed at the three levels of platforms topped with round pieces of thick, slick glass. She nodded. "Just toss your quarter. If it lands and sticks to the low platform, you win a small prize, the middle platform a medium prize, and the high platform a grand prize."

"That's all?"

"That's it." He grinned slyly. "Easy as pie."

Skye tried, deliberately missing twice for the sake of realism. The third time, she expertly flipped the coin so it would land flat on one of the glass tops.

It did, and she clapped her hands together. "I won!" she squealed. She swung, as with excited, disbelieving delight, toward the people in the aisle behind her. "I won! I can't believe it!"

"Here you go, little lady," Danny said, and handed her a stuffed parrot. "You wouldn't like to give it another try, would you? And go for one of the grand prizes. You seem awful good at this."

"Sure." Skye grinned. "I'll try again."

A handful of quarters later, she walked away from the now-crowded booth, her arms loaded with stuffed toys. She went to the supply wagon to dump them—she never kept what she won, that wouldn't be right—then skipped back to the midway for some more fun.

A commotion at the concession stand caught her attention.

A teenager stood at the front of the line, clutching his stomach and holding out a half-eaten hot dog.

"This made me sick," the boy said loudly. "I think it's bad or something."

Skye inched closer to get a better look. She saw Marta, a big woman with steel gray hair and a personality to match, eye the boy suspiciously. "What do you mean, it made you sick?"

"Sick. You know." He groaned and clutched his stomach, then doubled over as with cramps. The people behind him in line stirred and moved backward. He raised his voice a bit more. "Isn't it against the law to serve rotten meat?"

"We don't serve rotten meat," Marta said, her voice shrill. "We're very careful."

"Smell it." He held it out. "It smells rotten."

Marta leaned away, her face twisting with distaste. "I don't want to smell it. If it's a problem, I'll give you back your money. Or another hot dog."

"Another hot—" He moaned. "I want to talk to the owner or manager or something. This isn't right." He doubled over, groaning. "If I die, it's going to be your fault."

The line stirred again; several people turned and walked away. Someone said something nasty about carnivals. Skye frowned, studying the boy. He looked kind of weird. His jeans were strictly high-water, his hair cropped unevenly, as if done by hand with a pair of kitchen shears. The front of his T-shirt was emblazoned with the name of a rock group that hadn't been popular in a year, and instead of tennis shoes, he wore some kind of funky work boots.

Weird, she thought again. This kid wasn't for real. He was trying to scam Marta, no doubt about it. She had seen a hint of a smile tug at his mouth as he bent over the last time. Skye cocked her head, indignant. But why? What did he hope to gain?

Money, no doubt. She folded her arms across her chest, disgusted. The lengths some people would go to for money.

"Abner Marvel's the owner," Marta was saying, obviously anxious to get rid of him before he tossed his cookies. "You can probably find him at the little top. That's the sideshow tent." The woman pointed. "At the end of the midway. If he's not there, try the main ticket booth."

Still clutching both his stomach and the hot dog, the kid turned and hobbled in the direction she'd indicated.

Skye narrowed her eyes. She made it her business to know everything that went on at Marvel's. She knew what all the members of the troupe were up to, including who was doing what and with whom. A person couldn't burp on the lot without her finding out about it.

She meant to get to the bottom of this, too. Nobody was going to pull a fast one on Marvel's, not if she had anything to say about it.

She started after him, keeping him in sight but keeping her distance, too. After he had gone some distance, he straightened, glanced back at Marta and the concession stand, then smiled. A moment later, he tossed the hot dog into the trash can and started walking again—this time both upright and quickly.

Skye made a sound of triumph. She knew it, the creep was up to something.

"Hey! Brat-face!"

Skye stopped and glared over her shoulder at Rick, the kid who ran the shooting gallery, a particularly odious creature. When she and her mother had first joined Marvel's, he and a couple of his equally gross friends had tried to scare her by locking her in the fun house after closing. Instead of scaring her, he'd made her mad. When one of the roustabouts discovered her and let her out, she'd found Rick and popped him square in the nose, bloodying it. He had never forgiven her for that. But he'd never tried to scare her again, either.

She propped her fists on her hips. "What do *you* want?"

"I gotta take a break."

"So take it. I'm busy."

"Marvel sent Benny to cover the coaster for a while. If I don't get to the john, I'm going to piss on one of the customers. Get over here."

Skye looked at the mystery kid's retreating back, then at Rick. She sniffed. "Do you always have to be so gross? You're disgusting. Find somebody else."

"If you don't get your ass over here, I'm gonna beat the shit out of you."

"Yeah, right. I'm so scared." She cocked her chin up. "Pretty clever, the way you sneaked off the lot last night to meet that girl. Hardly anybody saw you. Except me. What do you think Marvel would say about that?"

His face turned beet red. He glanced at her, and shoved his hands in the back pockets of his blue jeans. "You're such a little twit. I wish you'd fall off the face of the planet."

"And you're a brainless butthead."

"You're just jealous 'cause no boy's ever going to want to sneak out to meet you. You're probably a queer, you act more like a boy than a girl."

For a moment, Skye couldn't find her breath. Her eyes burned and her chest ached. Horrified, she struggled for a comeback, struggled to keep Rick from seeing how much his comment hurt.

She tipped her chin up again, as much for show as to keep it from wobbling. Why should she care if Rick thought she was ugly and unlovable? So what if he thought she was a...queer. He was gross and stupid, and she hated him.

"You better watch it," she said, "or I'll get my mom to put a curse on you."

Rick snorted with amusement, but only after a moment's telling hesitation. Showmen were notoriously superstitious. They believed in bad luck and gris-gris and witches. And the truth was, her mother's ability scared them silly. They thought that, somehow, if Madame Claire could see their future—which she could—she could also change it. For the worse.

Because of that, they kept as far away from Madame Claire as possible.

Skye grinned. Silly, superstitious delinquents. It didn't work that way, of course. But if they wanted to believe it did, that suited Skye just fine. Her mother wasn't interested in being one of them, and Skye liked being able to yank their chains every once in a while. Sometimes a girl needed a little threat to hang over a bully's head; it was a way to even the odds a bit.

Skye knew using the other trouper's fear of her mother's ability that way didn't make her too popular, but that was tough nuts. She was used to not being liked, to not having friends. Besides, when she and her mom left, she wouldn't be leaving anyone behind. Goodbyes were a real bummer.

But detest Rick or not, she was part of the troupe. And he needed her help.

Skye took one last look at the direction the mystery kid had disappeared, sighed and turned back to Rick. "Go already. But hurry back. I've got things to do."

5

Chance had taken one last glance behind him—the woman at the concession stand appeared to have forgotten all about him—and tossed the remainder of his perfectly edible hot dog in the trash.

This had to work. Abner Marvel had to give him a job.
He had no contingency plan.

Chance wiped his damp palms on the thighs of his newly resurrected blue jeans. He had dug them, a T-shirt and the remainder of his pre-Lancaster County things out of storage, dressed, packed, then written his aunt and her husband a note. Then he had headed out into the night to hitch a ride.

From there he had winged it. The food-poisoning routine had been a last, desperate attempt to find a way to get to the carnival's owner. Before he had come up with that scheme, he had asked a half-dozen carnival employees who the owner/manager was and where he could find him; each time, his inquiry had been met with surliness and suspicion. All had told him the same thing—no jobs available.

Then he had realized his mistake. He had done it all wrong—to get to the owner he needed something better than the truth, he needed a scam.

If there was one thing people understood, it was liability. If nothing else, Chance had learned that from his father. The bastard had considered Chance a liability. And nothing else.

Thus the rotten-meat routine had been born.

Determination swelled inside him. Confidence with it. Chance shifted the strap of his duffel bag, inching it higher on his shoulder, and picked up his pace, anxious to secure his future.

Chance made his way down the wide, crowded midway. People streamed around him, laughing with each other, jostling him as they passed. Garish pink, green and yellow neon lights illuminated the moonless night. The scent of popcorn made his mouth water. Rock music blared, a different song from every dizzily spinning ride. Carnies called out lewd greetings to one another; with each revolution of the hammerhead and tilt-a-whirl, girls screamed. The sounds blended together creating a strange, at once ugly and exciting mix.

A group of rowdy teenagers pushed past him. One of the girls giggled and glanced back at him, but not in admiration, Chance knew. He had grown taller in the year he had been imprisoned at his aunt's, his shoulders had broadened, his chest thickened. Consequently, his denims were too short, his T-shirt too tight; he hadn't even been able to get his feet into his old Nikes, so he'd been forced to wear his farm-boy work boots. He looked like a total nerd.

Chance stiffened, straightening his shoulders. Not for long, he vowed silently. He was going places; he was going to be somebody important. Someday, girls like those would look at him and wish, pray even, that he would look back.

Up ahead he saw the little top, as the woman had called it. Actually, there were several tents of varying sizes at the end of the runway. Chance decided to try the one dead center first. It was empty save for a man sweeping trash from ringside. Chance hesitated a moment, eyeing the burly man. It seemed doubtful that this was the carnival's owner, but he might know where Abner Marvel was.

Chance moved farther into the tent. He cleared his throat. "Excuse me, I'm—"

"The next show's not for an hour," the man said, not glancing up. "Come back then."

"I'm not here to see the show." Chance swaggered toward the man. "I'm looking for the boss."

"That so? The boss?" Chance earned a glance. The man's face could only be described as battered. It looked as if his head had once played ball to someone's bat and the exchange had left his entire face pushed in.

"That's right. You know where I might find him?"

The man swept his gaze over him, head to foot, real leisurely-like. He was built like a gorilla, thick and strong, and he was looking at Chance as if he might want to flatten him. No doubt it had been his pleasure to have flattened many punks in his day.

"You already did," he said.

"You're Abner Marvel?"

At the obvious disbelief in his tone, the man's mouth twitched. "None other. And who are you?"

"Chance McCord." Chance held out his hand, but the man ignored it, going back to his sweeping.

"What can I do for you, Chance McCord?"

"I'm looking for a job."

"Figured as much. What kind of job you looking for?"

"Any kind."

"Figured that, too." The man eyed Chance again, sizing him up once more, his expression openly doubtful. He arched his eyebrows. "You eighteen?"

"Just last month," Chance lied. He would turn eighteen in October.

"Funny, I'd have guessed you to be younger than that."

Chance squared his shoulders and stuck out his jaw. "Well, I'm not. And I'm a hard worker."

"Your parents know you're here? They know you're wantin' to run off and join the carnival?"

"I don't have any parents." Chance cocked up his chin. "I've been living with my aunt."

The man cleared his throat, turned his head, spit out a wad of phlegm, then looked at Chance once more. "She know?"

"She doesn't have to. I'm eighteen."

"So you said." Mr. Marvel shook his head. "What makes

you think you can handle a job with my show? The boys here have been around. They play pretty rough.''

"So do I. I've been around.''

"Right.'' He spit again, this time with flourish. "You Amish?'' He pronounced the word with a short A.

"My aunt is. I'm not.''

"And I take it you don't have any carnival experience?''

"No, sir.''

The man shook his head again. "Look, kid, I've seen a whole lotta shit during my years on the circuit. A whole lotta ugly shit. Been in the business as long as I can remember, my old man was a showman, his old man before him. I got this place from them. It's in my blood. But if it wasn't, I'd be outta here.'' He snapped his fingers. "Just like that.''

He looked Chance in the eye. "There're lots of other things a boy like you can do with your life. Go do one of 'em. Go home. Go back to the farm. I don't need any help.''

"I need a job.'' Chance took a step toward the man, not too proud to beg. "I have to have one. I'll work hard. You'll see.''

"Everybody with my troupe works hard. Sorry, kid.'' The man spit another wad of phlegm, this time directly into the pile of swept trash. "Maybe next year.''

He turned and walked away. Chance stared after him, stunned, disbelieving. Just like that, and he was screwed. *Back to the farm with you, kid. Back to hell on earth.*

"Wait!'' Chance hurried after the man. "I'll do anything, the dirtiest most low-down job you have. Just give me a chance.''

Abner Marvel's ugly face actually seemed to soften. He shook his head. "Look, kid, I've got nothin'. No jobs. I'm sorry.''

"But...somebody might quit tonight,'' he said, grasping at straws. "They might get fired. It's good to have an extra person, just in case.''

"Can't afford a 'just in case.''' The momentary sympathy

Chance had seen on the man's face was replaced with annoyance. "Look, nobody quits midseason. Nobody in their right mind, anyway. We come all the way up here to God's country from our winter quarters in Florida, and none of my boys wants to get caught without a way back. And the only thing that'll get one of this crew fired is drinking, fighting and hittin' on the local jailbait. None of my boys been doin' that either, at least not that I've seen. They know better. Is that plain enough for you?"

He jerked his thumb toward the door. "Go on now. Get lost. I've got things to do."

This time Chance did not follow Abner Marvel. The carnival's owner had made it clear that he was not going to give Chance a job.

Unless one suddenly opened up. Unless a miracle happened.

A miracle.

Chance narrowed his eyes. There had to be a way. He wasn't going to be like his mother and spend his life wishing for the things he didn't have, the opportunities that had never come his way.

Sometimes in life, you had to make your own opportunities. Your own miracles.

His mother hadn't understood that. He did.

Chance turned and headed back out to the midway. He wandered the wide aisle, aware of each minute ticking past. Tonight was the carnival's last night in Lancaster County. Tomorrow would be too late.

From the shooting-gallery booth to his right, Chance became aware of arguing. He shifted his attention to the two carnies working it. One was taunting the other with a tale of a sexual exploit—with the girl the other wanted.

"You see this, asshole?" The uglier of the two boys held up a plastic sandwich bag he'd dug from his back pocket. "When Marlene gets a look at this, you won't have another chance with her. So you better remember what she tasted like, 'cause that's the only taste you're going to get.''

The second boy guffawed, ''Yeah, right. Like *one* joint is really going to impress her.''

Several players stepped up to the booth, and the first boy tucked his bag behind the wooden ticket box. Chance watched the two as they helped the players, noting how, as each moved by the other in the booth, they delivered surreptitious blows, jabs and obscenities to the other.

Chance eyed the boys, an idea occurring to him. The two had been drinking; Chance was certain of it. Their tempers were short, their inhibitions dulled by drink. If the bag and joint disappeared, the first boy would blame the second and a fight was sure to break out.

Of course, if he got caught, they would beat the crap out of him and he would be tossed off the carnival lot. But if he didn't...

This might be his only shot. He had to take it.

He watched. And waited. The opportunity presented itself—in the form of the fought-over Marlene. Personally, except for the pair of awesome hooters covered by a severely overextended tube top, Chance didn't see what all the fuss was about.

While the two teenagers fell all over themselves, completely ignoring their crowded booth to compete for the girl's attention, Chance reached over the partition and snatched the bag and joint. Heart thundering, he stuffed it into his right front pocket and moved as quickly as he could away from the booth.

But not too far away. He had to be around for the fireworks.

They weren't long in coming. As soon as Marlene walked away, the two boys began bickering over who she liked best. Moments later, Chance heard a howl of rage and a shouted obscenity.

''Motherfuckin' asshole! Where is it?''

"Where's what?"

"My bag, you asswipe." The outraged carny advanced on the other, fists clenched. "Give it back."

"I don't have your stupid little prize. I'm the one who doesn't need it. Remember?" He smirked at his rival, then turned away. "Jerk."

With a howl of fury, the first teenager leaped onto the back of the other. "Give it back or I'll beat the shit out of you!"

"Get off me, you son of a bitch!" The kid threw his rider, turned and swung a fist. It connected, and the first boy stumbled backward, then righted himself and charged like a bull at the other boy. He caught him dead in the ribs and the two went careening backward into the booth's shanty-style wall. It toppled. A woman screamed. A child began to cry. The two carnies rolled on the ground, tangled with each other in a death grip, shouting obscenities and delivering blows as best they could.

"That's enough!"

The bellow came from Abner Marvel as he charged around the side of the booth directly across the midway, a baseball bat in hand. With him were two other men, as big and burly as Marvel, also wielding bats. How the old showman controlled his rowdy crew was obvious, and Chance took another step backward.

"Get up! Both of you."

The boys immediately broke apart and scrambled to their feet. One's nose was bloodied, the other's eye had already started to purple and swell. From the way the teenagers cowered, Chance suspected that Abner Marvel wouldn't hesitate to take a swing with that bat.

A trick he had probably learned from his father.

"He stole from me!" The first boy pointed accusingly at the second. "He deliberately stol—"

"I didn't take nothin'! He's just jealous 'cause Marlene—"

"Shut up!" Abner Marvel bellowed, his face crimson with

rage. "Both of you. Pack your things. I've taken all I'm going to from you two, you're out of here!"

The two rowdies' expressions went slack at the news, then in unison they began begging to keep their jobs. The old carny didn't budge. "You're out," he said again, this time calmly. "You know the rules about fighting. Now get, before I decide I have to use this." He slapped the wooden bat against his palm. "Stop by my trailer and collect your pay on your way off the lot."

Chance didn't even wait until the two ousted boys skulked off, to jump forward. "Mr. Marvel! Wait."

Abner Marvel stopped and turned, his face fixed into a fierce scowl.

"I couldn't help hearing what happened," Chance said quickly, all too aware of Marvel's beefy fist curled around the baseball bat. "It looks like you might need...I mean, it looks like a position has suddenly...opened up."

"That it does." Marvel narrowed his eyes. "You have a point?"

"Yeah." Chance held the man's intent gaze, never wavering or breaking eye contact. "I'm your man."

Marvel reached into his breast pocket and pulled out a cigar. He bit off one end, spit it out, then lit up. Through a cloud of noxious smoke, he studied Chance.

"In the carnival," the showman said after several moments, "you're either with-it or you're a towner. A rube. A sucker. There's a term in the trade, called the First of May. You have any idea what it means?"

Chance scrambled to come up with a reasonable guess. "The beginning of the carnival season?"

"It means rookie. Outsider. Rank beginner. It means you have to prove yourself before you're accepted. You won't be with-it until you do. Initiation can be...rough."

Chance squared his shoulders. "I've had to prove myself before. I can handle it."

"And I won't be able to protect you," Abner continued, puffing on the cigar. "These boys will eat you alive."

"You can't scare me off." Chance took a step toward him. "I need this job. I need it bad. If you give it to me, I'll work my ass off for you. I'll do the job of both those losers. You'll see."

Marvel laughed, the sound deep and rusty. "I'll be damned. You're one cocky piece of work, aren't you?" He took off his hat and wiped his forehead. "The job of two, you say? I'd like to see that, I really would."

"Give me the job and you'll see it."

"If you get caught drinking, you're out. If I catch you fighting or fucking with paying customers, you're out. Leave the local jailbait alone. No second chances."

"I won't need one."

"You have to bunk in a trailer with five other roustabouts. If you can't hack it, it's not my problem, you're out."

"I can hack it."

"What did you say your name was?"

"Chance McCord."

"I'll tell you this, Chance McCord, you've got guts." Marvel gave him one final, measured glance, then a smile touched his mouth. "What're you standing around for? There's work to be done. You can start by cleaning up this mess."

6

Skye sat cross-legged on her mother's bed, her sketch pad laid over her knees. She moved her charcoal pencil across the page, enjoying the feel of the pencil in her hand and the soft, scratchy sound it made as the tip rubbed against the paper.

She smiled to herself, enjoying the quiet, this moment alone with her art. Their camper trailer didn't afford many moments alone. Though luxurious compared to the ones the majority of the other troupers occupied, the trailer had exactly two interior doors—the one to the tiny lavatory and the one to this bedroom, located at the back of the camper. In the open area up front was the kitchenette, a booth-style dinette and a couch that folded out to make a bed.

Usually Skye took the couch. But not always. Sometimes they shared the bed, other times her mother offered to sleep on the couch.

Skye missed having her own space. Not that she was accustomed to a palace, or anything. But they had never lived in quarters this tight before; they had never had to travel this light before. Storage inside the camper was limited to two narrow wardrobes, one built-in chest of drawers and several cubbyhole-type compartments.

This summer, her big box of art supplies was a luxury.

Skye cocked her head, studying the image taking shape before her—a monarch butterfly. Skye moved the pencil again, this time automatically, quickly and with certainty, as if her hand possessed a will of its own. The image grew, changed. Within moments she had transformed one of the butterfly's wings into an ornate, curvy letter.

The letter "M."

Skye stared at the image, the letter, heart thundering against the wall of her chest, beating frantically, like the wings of a butterfly against the sides of a glass jar. Skye recognized the "M"; she had drawn it hundreds of times before, the first time three years ago. She recalled the day vividly. She had been in art class; her teacher had commented on it. Skye remembered feeling breathless and sort of stunned. She remembered staring at the "M" and thinking it both beautiful and ugly, remembered feeling both drawn and repelled.

The way she felt now.

Skye sucked in a deep, shaky breath. She had been drawing the image ever since, sometimes repeating it over and over, until she had filled the entire page of her sketch pad.

Why? What did it mean?

"Skye? Honey...are you all right?"

At her mother's voice and the rap on the bedroom door, Skye looked up, startled. "Mom?"

Her mother opened the door and stuck her head inside. "I've been calling you for five minutes. It's almost time for lunch."

"Sorry. I didn't hear you." Skye returned her gaze to the image. "I'm almost done. I'll be there in a second."

Instead of returning to the kitchen, her mother crossed to stand beside her. She gazed silently down at the tablet, at the ornate butterfly, and Skye stiffened. She didn't have to glance up to know that her mother's expression was frozen with fear, stiff with apprehension.

It always was when Skye drew the "M."

Skye swallowed hard, fighting the fluttery, panicky sensation that settled in the pit of her gut, fighting the beginnings of the headache pressing at her temple.

Skye moved her pencil over the page, starting on the other wing. Within moments, the drawing was complete.

Still her mother stood staring; still she said nothing.

Her mother's silence gnawed at her. It hurt. Skye had asked her about the "M" about a million times. Her mother always answered the same way—she said she had no idea why Skye drew it.

Skye brought her left hand to her temple. *If that was true, why did her mother act so weird about it?*

Her mother touched Skye's hair, lightly stroking. "What's wrong, honey?"

She tipped her head back and met her mother's eyes.

"I keep trying to remember where I saw this 'M.' There has to be a reason I'm always drawing it. There has to be."

"I can't imagine, darling." Her mother smiled, though the curving of her lips looked forced to Skye. "It's just one of those things."

"One of those things," Skye repeated, then frowned and returned her gaze to the sketch pad. "That doesn't make sense."

"Sure it does." Claire shrugged. "You saw the monogram somewhere and remembered it."

"But where?" Skye balled her hands into fists, frustrated, hating the darkness of her memory and the feeling of help-lessness she experienced every time she tried to remember.

Like now. Skye drew her eyebrows together, searching her memory for a recollection of anything before kindergarten, for a glimmer of where she had been born or of her father. They were linked to the "M"; she was certain of it.

But how?

She dropped her face into her hands, head pounding. *Why couldn't she remember? Why?*

"Sweetheart, please..." Her mother sat on the edge of the bed and gathered her hands in hers. "It doesn't matter. It doesn't. Let it go."

But it did matter. Skye knew it did. Otherwise she wouldn't find herself drawing that letter again and again.

"I can't," she whispered, tears flooding her eyes. "I want to, I really do. But I just...can't"

Her mother put her arms around her and drew her against her chest. "I'm so sorry. So very sorry."

"It's not your fault." Skye rubbed her forehead against her mother's shoulder, the pain behind her eyes intensifying. "Are you proud of me, Mom? Are you glad I'm...I'm the way I am?"

Her mother tipped her face up and looked her in the eyes. "How can you even ask, Skye? I'm more proud of you than you can imagine."

But not of her artistic ability, Skye thought, searching her mother's gaze. Her mother wished she didn't like art so much, that she wasn't so good at it. She wished her daughter would never pick up a drawing pencil again.

Why?

Skye whimpered and brought a hand to her head.

"It's one of your headaches, isn't it?" Claire eased Skye out of her arms and stood. "I'll get your medicine."

A moment later her mother returned with two white tablets and a glass of water. Skye took them, then handed the half-full glass back to her mother. Past experience had taught them both that if they caught the headache early enough, Skye could beat it. If they didn't, the pain could become nearly unbearable.

"Thanks, Mom."

Claire bent and kissed the top of Skye's head. "Why don't you lie down for a minute. I'll finish making lunch, then come see how you're feeling."

Skye caught her mother's hand. "Will you stay a minute? And rub my head?"

"Sure, sweetie. Scoot over."

Skye did and her mother sat on the edge of the bed and began softly stroking her forehead. With each pass of her mother's hand, Skye's pain lessened. Each time she stopped, it returned, full force. And with it the questions that pounded at her.

"Feel a little better?" her mother asked.

"A little. Mom?"

"Yes, sweetheart?"

"My dad didn't want me, did he?"

Her mother caught her breath. "What kind of question is that? Of course he wanted you."

"You don't have to lie to me. I know how it works. You probably didn't even know who my father was."

"That's not true! Of course I know who—"

"Then why aren't there any pictures of him!" Skye caught her mother's hand, desperate, the pain blinding. "And why won't you talk about him?" She tightened her fingers. "Please. Just tell me, Mom. I won't cry. I'm not a baby anymore."

For long moments her mother said nothing, just gazed at the floor, her expression troubled. Finally, she met Skye's eyes once more. "He wanted you, Skye. I promise you that. But we can talk about this later. You need to rest—"

"No! Mom, I want to talk about it now. Please." Skye squeezed her mother's fingers. "If he really wanted me, where is he? What happened to him?"

"What happened to him?" her mother repeated, her voice sounding high and tight. She freed her hand, stood and took a step backward, toward the door. "I told you before. He's dead."

"Yes, but...how? What happened?"

"It was an accident." Her mother reached the door. "I've told you that before, too."

"What kind of accident was it? A car crash? A fire?" Skye lifted herself to an elbow and gazed pleadingly at her mother. She saw her mother's hesitation, her wavering, and pressed her further. "Where did it happen? Was I there? Were you?"

For a moment her mother said nothing, then she cleared her throat. "It was very ugly. I don't want to talk about it. Maybe someday."

Her mother was lying to her, hiding something. But what? And why? A lump in her throat, Skye shifted her gaze to her sketch tablet and the curvy "M."

Why wouldn't her mother trust her with the truth? What could be so ugly that her mother...

"Did someone kill him?" she asked, eyes widening. "Is that it? Was he...*murdered?*"

Her mother made a sound, squeaky and high. She shifted her gaze, as with guilt, and Skye's heart began to pound. "Was it the mob? Is the mob after us, too?"

"Don't be silly." Claire smiled stiffly. "It was an accident and nothing—"

"That's why we're always moving, isn't it?" Excited, Skye sat up and pushed her hair away from her face. "Just like in the movies, we're on the run from the mob!"

"That's enough, Skye!" her mother's voice rose. "I don't want to hear any more of this ridiculous talk. Do you hear me? No more."

Tears flooded Skye's eyes, and she flopped back to the mattress, rolling onto her side and turning her back to her mother. "Forget it. Just go away. After all, *I need my rest.*"

Claire sighed. "Your father wasn't a nice man, honey. And his family..." Her words faltered, and she drew what sounded to Skye like a careful breath. "I'll only say that I'm glad they're out of our lives forever. That's why I don't like to talk about them."

Heart pounding, Skye turned and looked at her mother. "What do you mean, he wasn't...nice? Did he, you know...did he hit you?"

Her mother hesitated, then nodded. "Yes."

"Oh." Skye caught her bottom lip between her teeth, the pressure in her head almost unbearable. "Did he...hit me?"

"No. But—" She bent and cupped Skye's face in her palms. "When we were with him, I was afraid for you."

Skye swallowed hard. "Is that why you won't even tell me where I was born?"

"Yes. I—" Claire sighed again and bent her forehead to Skye's. "Trust me, sweetheart. When you're older, I'll tell you more."

"Promise?"

She nodded, then smiled. "Our soup's probably boiled over by now. I'd better check it."

Skye caught her mother's hand. "Mom? Do you ever wonder what it'd be like to have...you know, a real family? To live in one place and not..."

Her words trailed off at the sadness in her mother's eyes.

"Yes," Claire answered softly. "Sometimes I wish that with all my heart. This isn't the life I wanted for you. It's not the way I wanted you to grow up." Her eyes filled with tears. "I didn't have—"

Her throat closed over the words, and she cleared it. "I didn't have that growing up and I always thought how nice it would be."

Her mother had been an orphan. Skye couldn't imagine that. She couldn't imagine not having her mother. She would die without her. Feeling guilty for having brought up the subject, she hugged her. "I'm sorry, Mom. I'm sorry I bugged you about...you know."

"Yes, I know." Her mother stroked her hair again. "Sometimes the truth hurts, baby. Sometimes it's better not to know the truth."

Skye tipped her head back and met her mother's eyes. Something in them, something dark and terrifying, made her tremble. "What is it, Mom? What do you see?"

Her mother pressed her lips to her forehead. "It's only the past. And the past can't hurt us as long as we make it stay there. Will you help me?"

Skye nodded, suddenly afraid. Of being alone. Of the past

and the future. She clutched her mother. "Don't ever leave me. I don't know what I'd—"

"Shh." Claire kissed her again. "Silly baby. I would never leave you. You're my whole life. Didn't you know that?"

Skye relaxed and smiled, remembering a game they had played when she was little—when she had still believed in monsters and bogeymen and things that breathed heavily in the dark.

Every night before bed, she had asked her mother the same thing: *Would you fight the monsters for me?* And every night her mother had searched out and destroyed the evil things for her. Only then had Skye been able to sleep. Only then had her nightmares retreated.

She tipped her face up to her mother's and smiled, still remembering. "Would you fight the monsters for me?"

"The biggest and the badest. Always." Claire smiled softly. "I love you, sweetheart."

Skye hugged her tighter, nesting her head against her chest, though she knew she was too old to do so. Suddenly, miraculously, her head didn't hurt. "I love you, too, Mom. More than anything."

7

Claire closed the bedroom door behind her, then leaned against it, her knees weak. She brought a trembling hand to her mouth, shaken, relieved. Afraid.

How long could she continue to keep the past a secret from Skye? How long before her daughter simply demanded to know everything? Today, Skye's wild imaginings had touched uncomfortably, even dangerously, close to the truth.

Claire shut her eyes and breathed deeply through her nose. There would come a time when she would no longer be able to put off her daughter with transparent evasions and vague promises. Today had proved that time was almost here.

She shook her head, shuddering. *Monsters.* What Skye didn't know, what she must never know, was that her mother had already faced and fought the monsters for her, that she had looked squarely into the eyes of evil and had seen the future. Skye's future. Her own.

And she had run. As fast and as far as she had been able.

But not far enough to stop her daughter's curiosity, her questions. Not far enough to be finally free of fear.

Claire pressed the heels of her hands to her eyes. She was tormented by nightmares of huge, dark and distorted birds stalking her daughter. Some nights she awakened bathed in a sweat, heart thundering, certain she would find Pierce standing above her. Or worse, that she would awaken to find that he and Adam had swept Skye away while she slept.

For Adam was very much alive.

And he was searching for them. Still, after seven years, he hadn't given up.

He wouldn't, Claire knew. Not ever.

Claire dropped her hands and pushed away from the door, heading back to the trailer's kitchenette and the soup she had left unattended on the range. The smell of scorched food hung in the air. The tomato soup had boiled over, the red liquid a vivid splatter across the white enamel top.

Claire stared at the pool of red, her mind spinning back to the morning she had run away with Skye, seeing Adam's blood spilled across the wooden floor, the splatters of red on her daughter's white pinafore.

And hearing her daughter's howls of fear.

When she had first realized that Grace had no memory not only of the awful events in the nursery but of anything of her life as a Monarch, she had thanked God. Her daughter had gone to sleep and awakened without a memory—though Madeline hadn't understood that at first.

No, at first she had thought her daughter was in a kind of shock, but as several days passed without her mentioning her father, the events in the nursery or home, Madeline had begun to suspect the truth.

Too afraid of being found out to see a doctor about Skye's condition, Claire had done some research at the library of one of the towns they passed through.

There, she had learned that sometimes, when something was too awful, too painful to deal with, the brain simply chose to forget it, to reject the unpleasantness and go on as if nothing had happened. Repressed memory, the book called it. Though Claire knew she wasn't qualified to make a diagnosis, she believed that's what had happened to Skye. She had simply, on a subconscious level, chosen to forget.

Though grateful, initially, Claire had been worried by her daughter's repressed memory. And frightened. But Skye had seemed so happy; she had acted so…normal. As if she didn't have a care in the world.

That had changed in the last few years. It had changed with the emergence of that damned "M." Skye's subconscious had let that image push through to her consciousness.

Remember, Skye, it seemed to say. *Remember.*

And with the "M" had come Skye's questions. Her discontent with Claire's evasive answers. Her headaches.

Claire brought a hand to her throat. *Dear God, what was she to do? How could she continue to keep the truth from her daughter?*

The soup bubbled over again, sizzling as it hit the electric coils. Claire jumped at the sound, startled out of her thoughts. She grabbed a pot holder and took the pan from the burner, then turned off the heat.

The soup had made a mess, charring the burner and the pan underneath the coils. Claire turned to the sink for a sponge, wet it, then began cleaning up the mess, her thoughts still on Skye and their future.

She couldn't tell Skye the truth, no matter how much she hated lying. At least not yet. She couldn't, for Skye's own safety. When she was older, when she could really understand what kind of people the Monarchs were, what kind of person Griffen was, then she would tell her. Maybe.

Claire began to mop up the worst of the soup. Today, Skye had offered her an easy solution. Why hadn't she taken it? If she had told her she didn't know who her father was, that Skye was the product of a one-night stand, her daughter's questions would have stopped.

Why hadn't she taken that easy out. Why?

Claire sighed. Because she hated lying. She had told so many of them over the past seven years—to Skye, to school principals, to employers, co-workers. The fabrications made her feel sick, deep down inside. They made her feel small and cheap.

Today, something had stopped her from telling Skye that lie. For, even as she had told herself to take the out, she hadn't been able to bring herself to do it. It would have been a big lie, one that would have been irreversible, with far-reaching consequences.

She supposed she wanted to have her cake and eat it, too.

But for now, her inability to commit to either the truth or a lie left her daughter with questions. And fantasies, some of them wild and romantic. She would have to tell her something soon. She would have to make up something safe. Something that would satisfy Skye's curiosity forever.

It broke Claire's heart. She hated being dishonest with her daughter, but she feared the truth more. The truth had a name. It had a face. It had evil intent.

Claire closed her eyes and pictured Adam as she had seen him that last day, flushed with fury, eyes bulging as he tried to squeeze the life from her. She pictured Griffen, remembering the way he had followed Grace around, the way he had stared possessively at his sister; she pictured him holding her baby down while he violated her.

The monstrous dark birds hovered over her.

Claire's eyes popped open and she realized she was panting, her heart pounding. They were after her; Aunt Dorothy had told her so. Even if she hadn't, Claire would have known by her dreams; her premonitions and visions.

She left the mess on the stove and began to pace. It had been Aunt Dorothy who had told her Adam was alive. Three months after she had run away with Grace, her premonitions had started. So, she had called Aunt Dot. Claire had told her nothing but that they were all right—not the names they had taken nor the direction they had gone. Dorothy had begged her to come back. She had told Claire of the depth of Pierce and Adam's fury and of their quest to find Grace. But she hadn't mentioned the missing gems. Not then or in any of their conversations since.

Claire had found that strange. She still did.

The gems. Many times she and Skye had been desperate for money, but she had been afraid to try to sell the stones. She had no idea how or where such a transaction would take place, but more, she had feared that Pierce would be able to trace her through their sale.

Claire crossed to the dinette, to the storage compartments located under the bench seats. She lifted out a carton of cookware, then dug carefully through it until she found what she had hidden there. A six-inch-square, antique cherry-wood box.

Claire looked over her shoulder, then unlocked it with the key she wore around her neck. Nestled inside was the pouch of gems. She'd had no reason to think it might be gone, but she breathed a sigh of relief anyway. They were her insurance policy, though against what she didn't know.

She opened the pouch, dipped her hands inside and moved her fingers through the cool, smooth stones. As she did, she was assailed with the strongest sense that the gems were important, that they would someday help her. That they would help Skye.

She curled her fingers around the stones, absorbing their heat, their vibrations. Images assailed her, of the dark and of cold. Of ice and of a bird of prey stalking, stalking…

Claire made a sound of fear and released the stones. They slipped away from her, the frightening images with them. She closed the pouch, tucked it back into the box, then locked the box.

Someday, she thought again, someday, somehow, those stones would save Skye's life.

8

Chance tipped his face to the bright, cloudless sky, squinting against the sun. Sweat beaded his upper lip and rolled down the center of his already slick back. Not even 8:00 a.m. and already hellfire hot. Appropriate, as his first couple of days with Marvel's had been hell.

His first day, the troupe had traveled to Zachary, a town a hundred miles east of Lancaster County. As far as metropolitan pools went, the town of Zachary, Pennsylvania, was about the size of the average spit. Not quite the kind of opportunity Chance had been looking for, but just the type of town that appreciated a show like Marvel's.

No sooner had the drivers positioned the trucks and trailers on the lot than the skies had unleashed a flood. No matter, in anticipation of clear skies later and a heavy opening-night crowd, the troupe had gone to work. Rides needed to be positioned, tested and inspected, booths set up and tents raised.

Chance hadn't had much choice but to acclimate, and to acclimate fast. The rain had turned the low-lying patch of ground into a mud stew, thick, black and viscous. Some places the mud had been so deep, it had seeped over the top of Chance's work boots. After that, with every step he'd taken, the goo squished between his toes.

Once the worst of the downpour had let up, Chance had begun hauling and spreading bales of straw. He'd worked until his muscles quivered, and he bowed under the weight of the wet bales. But still, he'd kept on. He had promised

Marvel that he would do the job of two, and he meant to keep his word.

The sky had finally cleared; the customers had come, the night with them. Then Chance's initiation into carnival life had really begun. As Marvel had warned, these boys were rough, coarse and brutal. Brutal in a way he had not been exposed to before. And they were loyal, blindingly loyal. To each other, to the show. And even to Marvel, though he ruled them with a baseball bat.

The others blamed Chance for their friends' expulsion, though Chance knew they didn't suspect the real part he had played in the two getting fired. He was a towner to them, an outsider. The one who had taken the place of their trusted buddies.

In the last two days, Chance had been harassed; he had been threatened. He brought a hand to his swollen and bruised right eye. He winced even as his lips twisted into a half smile. He supposed he should be grateful—the boy who had given him the shiner had also promised to slit his throat while he slept. Yet here he stood, throat intact.

Chance untied the bandanna from around his neck and dipped it into a barrel of cool water, one of many Marvel kept constantly filled for his employees to refresh themselves. Chance drenched the bandanna. He was going to have to earn the other guys' respect. Unfortunately, he knew of only one way to do it—beat the crap out of somebody tough. These boys weren't unlike L.A. street kids—violence was the one thing they understood and respected.

Chance brought the drenched fabric to the back of his neck and squeezed, sighing as the water sluiced over his shoulders and down his back. He could handle it, and anything else that was dished him. For, despite it all—the heat and mud, the exhausting work and the other boys' animosity—Marvel's was his way out.

And nobody was going to screw it up for him. Nobody.

"I saw what you did."

Chance swung around. A scruffy-looking girl stood a couple of feet behind him, arms folded across her chest, head cocked to one side as she studied him. Her dark hair was pulled back into a high, untidy ponytail; her eyes were an almost uncanny blue.

He arched his eyebrows. "Excuse me?"

"I saw what you did," she said again, obviously pleased with herself. "The other night, at the hot-dog stand. I heard what you said."

"Yeah?" Pretending disinterest, he sent her a dismissive glance. "So what?"

"You were scamming Marta, weren't you? To get this job."

Damn kid was too smart for her own good. Too smart for him to even think about trying to deny it. He shrugged. "So? What if I was?"

"Aren't you worried I'll go to Mr. Marvel?"

"Why should I be? You're just a snot-nosed kid. Besides, what's the big deal about a bad dog?"

She huffed with annoyance, sounding very adult. "I am not a...*snot-nosed* kid. I'm twelve."

"Twelve? Gee, that old?" Amused, he turned his back to her. He bent, splashed water over his face, then straightened and retied his bandanna.

"Okay, you're right. Mr. Marvel wouldn't care about *that*. It was a pretty cool scam. But the other one would really piss him off."

The other one? Chance swung to face her, narrowing his eyes. "What are you talking about?"

"You know. Benny and Rick. The shooting gallery, your trick, their fight." She lifted her chin as if daring him to tell her she was wrong. "Mr. Marvel would fire you if he knew about *that*."

Chance swore under his breath, then met her eyes. "Interesting fairy tale, kid. But I don't have time for kiddie stories right now." He moved past her. "See you around."

She followed him, skipping ahead, then swinging to face him once more. "It's not a fairy tale, and you know it."

"Is that right? And what makes you such a big authority on everything?"

"I make it my business to know everything that goes on at Marvel's."

"And I'm sure your mother's real proud. Now, could you please get lost? I've got work to do."

He started off again; again she stopped him. "When I saw you at the concession stand, I thought you were up to something, so I followed you. I saw the whole thing."

"Yeah? Well, it's my word against yours, kid. And I don't know what you're talking about."

She tilted her head back and laughed. "Don't look so worried. I hated those two guys. They were total pigs. I'm glad they're gone." She leaned conspiratorially toward him. "Your secret's safe with me."

Just what he wanted, to be in cahoots with a snot-nosed, busybody twelve-year-old girl. *Just great.*

"Look, kid," he said, "you want to buzz off? Like I said, I've got work to do." He headed in the opposite direction; she followed him.

"My name's Skye."

"Whatever."

"My mother's Madame Claire." At his blank look, she frowned. "You know, the fortune-teller."

"Is that supposed to mean something to me?"

"Not if you don't care about a curse being put on you."

"I'm really worried."

"She can do it. She made one kid's hair fall out."

He laughed. "And I bet she turned another one into a frog."

"Laugh now. You'll see."

"You're terrifying me, really. See you around."

He turned and started for the supply tent. She hurried after him, and he muttered an oath. *What was with this kid? What did he have to do to get rid of her?*

"If I ask her to put a spell on you, she will."

He made a sound of annoyance, stopped and swung to face her. "So, you're saying your mom's a witch?"

"No. She's a fortune-teller."

"A Gypsy fortune-teller?"

"No." The girl propped her hands on her hips and sucked in a quick, frustrated-sounding breath. "She's just a fortune-teller."

Amused, he mimicked her, making an exaggerated sound of frustration and placing his hands on his hips. "Witches put curses on people. Fortune-tellers tell the future. Gypsies do both, at least in the movies. Of course, I don't believe in that stuff. In fact, I think it's all a bunch of crap, so why don't you get lost?"

She ignored him. "Where'd you get the black eye?"

"None of your business." He started off again.

"I bet it was one of the other guys." She screwed up her face as if deep in thought. "My guess is Max or Len." She cut him a glance. "But, probably Len. He's a real badass."

Chance supposed he would call Len that. He was the blade-happy bozo with dibs on his throat.

"They're all pissed at you," she continued, "because you took Rick and Benny's place."

"Yeah, well, that's tough shit. They'll get over it."

She smiled. "Good thing they don't know what I know." He glared at her, and she smiled again. "I didn't mean anything by that. I told you I wasn't going to tell, and I'm not."

This was just getting better and better. He stepped up his pace in an effort to shake her.

"I'll tell you what to do about those creeps," she said, hurrying to keep up. "Just give 'em a good pop." She nodded for emphasis. "They'll respect that."

He scowled, annoyed that she, a goofy kid, was saying

the same thing he had thought only moments ago. "What do you know? You're just a kid. And a girl, at that."

"So what? Girls can know anything boys can."

"Right," he drawled.

"They can!" She lifted her chin, practically quivering with twelve-year-old indignation. "You know, I've been around. Besides, you don't see any black eyes on me, do you?"

He stopped so suddenly she collided with his back. Exasperated, he turned to face her. "Is there some reason you've decided to single me out for torture?"

She laughed. "I like you, Chance. You're funny."

Funny to a twelve-year-old girl. Wow. Another great life accomplishment. "I'm out of here, kid." He started walking away.

"I'll go with you."

"I'd rather you didn't."

She ignored him. "Really, Chance, you can't let those guys push you around." She tucked a hank of hair that had escaped her ponytail behind her ear. "I meet a lot of smart-asses in school. A lot of tough-guy types."

"I'll just bet."

"I'm the new kid a lot, and you know what that means."

He stopped and faced her again. "You seem intent on telling me this."

"I am."

"So do it, little-miss-know-it-all. Then leave me alone."

"You don't have to be so grouchy." She cocked up her chin. "You have to be smarter and tougher. If they give you any crap, just give it back double. That's what I do."

"And I'm sure you're very popular."

"With the principal." She shrugged. "It's cool."

"I'll think about your advice. Okay?" Chance saw a couple of his bunk mates across the way, and he scowled, not wanting them to see him conversing with a kid. "Now, for the last time, will you please buzz off?"

This time, when he walked away, she didn't follow or call out. Relieved, he took one last glance over his shoulder, just to make sure. She stood alone, looking out of place in the midst of all the activity around her; she looked lonely.

For a moment he almost felt sorry for her, then he shook his head. If the kid was lonely, it was because she was a know-it-all pest. Let her mother, the witch-Gypsy-fortune-teller worry about her, she wasn't *his* problem. His lips curved up at the thought of actually being responsible for a kid like that. Forget sugar and spice, that girl was nothing but piss, vinegar and trouble with a capital T.

The farther away from her he stayed, the better.

9

The kid did not give Chance the opportunity to keep his distance. For the next week she dogged his steps. Morning, noon or night, it didn't matter where he was or what he was doing, he could turn around or look up and there the know-it-all little pest would be, grinning at him. Asking questions, giving advice. Offering to help him, no matter what he was doing at the time.

He didn't know why she was so interested in him; he didn't care. Besides annoying the crap out of him, the kid was making things even more difficult for him than they already were. He was barely holding his own with the other roustabouts, as it was; now, because of her kiddie crush or whatever it was, he was the butt of their jokes, as well. He had heard the jeers of the other guys as he passed, their snickers, the little ditty they chanted every time he was near enough to hear.

Skye and Chance, sitting in a tree, k-i-s-s-i-n-g, first comes love, then comes marriage, then comes little Skye riding in the baby carriage.

They all thought it very funny. A laugh-riot. He was not amused—not with their ditty or her interest in him. He was going to have to put an end to this. And soon.

The pest in question plopped down onto the picnic-table bench beside him and smiled. "Hi, Chance."

He didn't look up. "Go away."

"Whatcha doing?"

Chance scowled and tossed his fork back onto his plate. "I *was* eating my breakfast."

"Don't let me stop you." She drew up her knees and propped her elbows on them. "I ate in our trailer early."

He wiped his mouth with his napkin and stood. "Good for you."

She popped up. "I'll go with you."

From across the tent, he saw two of the sideshow performers watching them, their expressions openly amused. One of them winked at him and began mouthing some words. Chance had a pretty good idea what those words were.

Skye and Chance, sitting in a tree...

He gritted his teeth. "Look, kid, what do you want?"

"I came to help you set up your booth. I thought you—"

"Go help somebody else." He picked up his tray and carried it to the bus-station.

She scurried after him. "Wait. You know, it's Saturday, and I thought you might nee—"

"I don't." Turning his back to her, he scraped the last of the unappetizing bacon and eggs into the trash then set his plate and utensils in a dish tub, his tray beside it. Without even a glance back in her direction, he hurried from the tent and out into the bright day beyond.

She followed, catching up in moments and tugging on his sleeve. When he met her gaze, she indicated his bruised cheek. "I see those creeps nailed you again."

"It's no big deal."

She shook her head, screwing up her face in disgust. "Those guys make me sick."

"Yeah, well, life's rough all over."

She skipped along beside him. "I tried to tell you before, if you'd just give 'em a good pop they'll leave you alone. Or, you could go to Mr. Marvel and tell him."

"Gimme a break."

"No, really. You could."

Chance stopped and glared down at her, exasperated. "Are

you enjoying this, kid? Is this fun for you? Ruining my life? Making me the laughingstock of the show? How many times and ways do I have to ask you to leave me alone before you actually do?''

"I'm not trying to ruin your life." She shook her head, her expression hurt. "We're friends, and I only wanted to hel—"

"You're not helping. And we're not friends."

"We could be."

"No, we couldn't!" *Enough was enough. He had tried to be nice, but he'd had it.* Hands on hips, Chance faced her, looking her straight in the eyes. "I'm an adult and you're a kid. We have nothing in common. In fact, I don't even like you. You're a know-it-all and a pest. I tell you what, I'll give you five bucks to go ruin somebody else's life for a while."

Her eyes filled with tears, and she took a step backward. She opened her mouth as if to say something, then shut it again without speaking. He muttered an oath, feeling like a total heel. She was just a kid, for Pete's sake.

"Hey, I'm sorry. I'm sure you're a perfectly okay kid and all, it's just that I'm—"

"Well, well…what do we have here, fellas? The farm boy and his little girlfriend."

Shit, Len and his band of hick-thugs. Chance turned around slowly. The boy and his group stood just beyond the little top, their expressions twisted into amused sneers.

Len placed his hands on his hips. "And just look at the two of them, standin' there all cozy. Isn't that *too* sweet?"

The group of boys howled. Chance took a step toward them, fists clenched. "Go to hell, asshole."

The group oohed in unison. Len laughed. "I think they make a real cute couple. You like 'em young, farm boy?"

Skye took several steps forward. "That's so gross! You guys make me sick. You ought to be ashamed of—"

"Shut up, Skye!" Chance caught her arm and dragged her

back toward him. Her help was the last thing he needed; he would never live it down. He faced the group, eyes narrowed. "Get out of our way."

The boys spread out, circling them, blocking their way in every direction. Len smiled slyly. "Make us."

Chance felt a flush start at the base of his neck and move upward. Marvel's rules be damned, he had taken all the crap he was going to from these losers. He wasn't walking away until they backed down or he'd killed somebody.

"I said, move."

The group hooted, and Len cocked his head to the side. "She the only piece of ass you can get, farm boy?"

Chance took a menacing step toward the other boy, adrenaline pumping through him. "You want to say that again?"

Len, too, took a step forward. "And if I do?" he mocked. "What're you going to do about it? Ask your little girlfriend to beat the shit out of me?"

"No. *I'm* going to beat the shit out of you." Chance clenched his jaw and waved the boy forward. "Come on. You first."

Chance held Len's gaze, unflinching. The other guy was older, bigger and meaner—plus he had three of his delinquent cronies to back him up. Chance didn't care. He had reached the point of no return. He might go down, but not before he inflicted a little pain of his own.

Len hesitated; Chance waved him forward again. "Come on, asshole. Let's rock 'n roll. If Marvel catches us, we're both out. But what the hell? I'm game."

He saw the other boy waver, weighing his options. Len might be big and dumb as a stump, but he wasn't ignorant of his options. If Marvel canned him, Len knew he was up shit creek without a paddle.

Chance smiled grimly and waved his opponent forward. He almost had him. One more minute and—

"Leave Chance alone!" Skye flounced forward, placing

herself between him and Len. She propped her fists on her hips and lifted her chin. "He hasn't done anything to you. I think you're just jealous because he's got—"

"You to protect him," one of the guys jeered.

The group howled so loudly they nearly drowned out her sputters of indignation. Chance wanted to die. He was certain he would. He made a desperate grab for her. "Skye, don't—"

She shook him off. "What you're doing is just plain mean. You guys make me want to puke!"

That brought a fresh wave of amusement. A couple of the roustabouts laughed so hard, they doubled over.

"Tough guy has to have his little girlfriend protect him. We're *so* scared!" They were all but hysterical with laughter. The boys began clucking their tongues, taunting Chance.

"Pussy," Len said laughing. "Pussy needs a little girl to protect him."

"That's not nice," Skye shouted. "You should be—"

"Shut up!" Shaking with rage and embarrassment, Chance grabbed a handful of Skye's T-shirt and dragged her backward. "I can fight my own battles!"

"Come on, then," shouted Len, and the circle of teenagers tightened around them. "Let's party, farm boy."

Just then, Abner Marvel came around the corner, bat in hand, expression murderous. The group froze. "What the hell's going on?" he bellowed, slapping the bat against his palm. "We all on break here, or what? Did we forget it's Saturday and the show opens in less than an hour?" He slapped the bat again. "Did we?"

The group scattered. Marvel caught Chance's arm as he started past. "I'm watching you, McCord," he said. "I'm watching you real close."

Chance swallowed hard. "Yes, sir."

"You'd better learn to fit in, because you're running out of time."

"That's not fair!" Skye cried. "It wasn't Chance who—"

Marvel's face mottled. "And you, little miss, you stay out of business that doesn't concern you. You're going to get somebody hurt. Understand? I don't want to have to go to your mama, but I will."

Without another word, he walked away. Chance watched him a moment, then turned to Skye. "Get the hell away from me." He all but spit the words at her.

"You should be grateful I—"

"Grateful! Don't you get it? You don't help. You make things worse. For me and everybody else."

"I do not! You're just saying that because—"

"I'm saying it because it's true." He grabbed her shoulders and forced her to meet his eyes. "If you hadn't stuck your big nose in, I would have won that fight. I almost had him."

"He would have beat your ass. And you know it!"

"You don't know anything. Get lost."

He started off; she followed. "At least I'm not mean," she said, running to keep up. "At least I don't—"

"Look!" he shouted, stopping so suddenly she plowed into his back. "You're ruining my life. I want you to buzz off, scram, get lost. I can't be any plainer than that."

"Make me."

He glared at her. "What did you say?"

"You heard me. It's a free country, and if I want to follow you I will." She folded her arms across her chest and cocked up her chin. "And you can't stop me."

"Like hell," he muttered, so mad he felt as if the top of his head was going to pop off. "Like hell."

He closed the distance between them, picked her up and swung her scrawny little body over his shoulder.

She squealed in surprise. "What are you doing?"

"Getting rid of you. Once and for all."

"Getting rid of me? Put me down!" She tried to kick her feet, but he had her legs anchored at the knees. "I said, let me go!"

He kept walking. She pummeled his back with her fists, landing a few good blows to his ribs. "That hurt!" he shouted. "Cut it out!"

"Not until you put me down."

"I asked you nicely, you didn't listen. Now I'm taking you home. Where you and all babies belong...with their mommies."

She made a sound of outrage. A moment later, he felt her teeth sink into his back. She'd bit him! He couldn't believe it. "You are a spoiled brat!" He smacked her on the bottom, hard. She howled. "Bite me again, you little shit, and I'll hit you again. Harder this time."

He could tell by the way she tensed that she was thinking about it, weighing her options. She must have decided against it because he went unbitten, though she seemed to double her efforts to wiggle free.

He finally reached the trailer she shared with her mother. He pounded on the door. When Madame Claire opened it, he dumped her red-faced daughter at her feet. "Keep your little brat away from me. Do you hear? Keep her away."

Madame Claire—a pretty woman who looked nothing like the devil-eyed witch the other boys portrayed her to be—moved her surprised gaze from him to her daughter. "I don't understand, what... Skye, have you been bothering this boy?"

"No, Mom, I—"

"Yes, Mom," he interrupted. "Skye has been bothering this boy." He glared at mother, then daughter. "She's been following me around. Today, she nearly got me killed. Keep her away from me."

"I was only trying to help." Skye looked beseechingly at her mother. "Really, Mom. I didn't mean to make trouble."

"But you did, anyway." The woman looked down at her daughter, obviously angry. "Get inside. Now."

"But, Mom—"

"Now!"

The girl obeyed, but not before sending her mother a petulant look. The fortune-teller turned to Chance. "I'm sorry. Skye is a bit strong-willed."

"That's what you call it. I call it spoiled. And selfish. Keep her away."

He turned and started off. The woman stopped him. "What was she trying to help you with that almost got you killed?"

"That's none of your business."

"Some of the other boys gave you that shiner, didn't they?"

"What if they did?"

The woman's lips lifted. "Skye always roots for the underdog. She can't stand to see other people being mistreated. I think it's because she's been the underdog so often."

"That's her problem. I don't need any help."

"I can see that." Her gaze seemed to see much more than his surface bruises as it settled on his face—she seemed to see clear to his soul. He shifted uncomfortably.

"There's nothing wrong with needing help," she said softly.

"I don't need help." He scowled as ferociously as he could. "Especially hers. Just keep her away from me."

He took a step backward, then with a final glare, swung in the direction he had come.

"I'll tell your fortune for free, if you'd like. To repay you for your trouble."

He looked over his shoulder at her. "No, thanks. I already know what my fortune is. I don't need some sideshow huckster to tell me."

She arched her eyebrows. He sensed, rather than saw, her amusement. "Really? Are you a clairvoyant?"

"I don't need to be." He tipped his chin up, daring her— or the whole fucking world, for that matter—to defy him. "I know what my fortune is, because it's in my own hands. And I know I won't let myself down."

"And you're the only one who won't. Is that it?"

"That's right." He folded his arms across his chest. "I suppose you're going to tell me differently?"

"Not me. Life's rough all over."

Something in her knowing expression grated. He narrowed his eyes. "Screw you. Leave me alone."

Again he turned and started to walk away. Again she stopped him, though she spoke so quietly he could hardly make out what she said. Even as he told himself to keep walking, he swung to fully face her. "What did you say?"

"Forgive the man with the long beard and plain ways, he was only doing what he thought best."

She was talking about his uncle Jacob. Prickles ran up his spine. *How did she know about him?*

A trick, he told himself. She had looked him over; she probably knew about the circumstances of his coming on at Marvel's and had figured out his background. People like her, who made their living tricking people, were adept at putting two and two together in a convincing way.

Hell, considering that they had been in the heart of Amish country, it wasn't even that good a trick. He told her so.

She simply smiled. That small, knowing smile bugged him, and he stiffened, angry. Defensive. "You, lady, are a fraud, your powers are no more than a parlor trick. A side-show gag. In life what you see is what you get. Period."

At his own words, his mother's image filled his head. With it, thoughts of her and all the things she had seen and wanted. All the things she had never obtained.

As he looked at Madame Claire, he thought—believed in his gut, startlingly—that she knew exactly what he was thinking. That she, too, could see his mother as clearly as he did.

The hairs on the back of his neck stood up, and he backed away, understanding now why all the other troupers steered clear of Madame Claire. Understanding her power over them.

"Just leave me alone," he said finally when he had found his voice. "And keep your brat daughter away from me, too."

10

Skye sat cross-legged on the bed, her sketch tablet before her, open to a drawing in progress. It was a drawing of a toad—an ugly one with warts and a distorted face. He was cowering before another creature, a princely, handsome frog, one complete with bulging muscles and a gold crown.

Skye selected an emerald green pencil and carefully added a few final strokes of color to her handsome frog. She had been working on the drawing for days. It was for Chance. A peace offering. An apology.

The toad was Len. The frog Chance.

And she was the pesky little fly, buzzing around his head.

Skye frowned, remembering the way she had acted and the things he had said to her. In truth, in the past week she had thought of little else.

You're a know-it-all and a pest. You're ruining my life. I want you to buzz off, scram, get lost.

Make me. It's a free country, and if I want to follow you I will.

Skye moaned, her cheeks hot. How could she have acted that way? How could she have been such a jerk? Such a spoiled brat, just like he'd called her?

Skye moved her gaze over the drawing. She had only wanted him to like her. She had only wanted to be his friend.

She still did.

Tears stung her eyes and she tossed the colored pencil back into her box. She hated that. She hated that she cared what he thought about her. That she wanted him to like her.

She had never given two flips what anybody thought about her before, and she didn't like the way caring made her feel.

Really crappy. Like something that had crawled out from under one of the show's Port-o-lets. Ugly and unlikable. No, she corrected herself. Unlovable.

That's what she was—unlovable. The only person who had ever loved her was her mother. Even her father, despite what her mother said, hadn't loved her. He hadn't wanted her.

Skye squeezed her eyes shut, fighting the tears. The other day, after Chance left, she had told her mother everything. And her mother had sided with Chance.

That had hurt. Her mother had always sided with her before; she had always championed her daughter—even times when Skye had landed in the principal's office. Skye had believed she always would.

That, more than anything her mother had said, made Skye see how badly she had behaved.

Skye drew her knees to her chest and pressed her face to them. She *had* been a bossy, little know-it-all pest. A big creep, she thought, her chest aching.

She didn't like *her* either.

But she still liked Chance. She still wanted him to be her friend.

He wasn't like the other boys with Marvel's. He was smarter, for one thing. He worked harder, he didn't drink or smoke pot or chase the local girls. And he always smelled good, even when he was working. She hadn't figured that one out yet; the other boys sometimes smelled so bad she wanted to retch.

She liked his smile and the way he laughed. She liked the way he had faced down Len and his gross, toady friends— like the hero in a story would. Cool and kind of smart-alecky. As if he wasn't afraid, not one bit.

She sighed. He was the coolest boy she had ever met.

Straightening, Skye cocked her head to the side, assessing

her drawing. She labeled the toad, frog and fly, then, giggling, wrote at the bottom:

Frogs rule, toads drool. Or, once a toad always a toad.
I promise I'll never act so stupid again.

That done, she rolled the drawing and secured it with a rubber band, wrinkling her forehead in thought. Now, how did she get it to Chance? She could slip it into one of his pockets or leave it someplace he would be sure to find it. That way, if he didn't like it or if he was still mad at her, she wouldn't have to face him.

Skye shook her head. She was a lot of things, but a chickenshit wasn't one of them. No, she would wait for the perfect moment to approach him. A moment when he was alone but not working, a moment when she didn't think she would aggravate him. The moment when he would be most likely to forgive her. She would hand him the drawing and hope for the best.

That moment arrived two days later, at just past 7:00 a.m. Since the carnival didn't open till noon on Sundays, most of the troupers slept in. But not Chance. She saw him leave the deserted mess tent, screwed up her courage and followed him.

"Chance?"

He stopped and turned to her. He didn't look exactly pissed to see her, but he didn't look happy, either. Her cheeks heated, even as she fought the urge to look away in total embarrassment.

She held out the rolled drawing. "This is for you."

"What is it?"

"A drawing. I..." She stubbed her toe into the dirt, wishing she had taken the chickenshit way. "I acted really...dumb. I'm sorry."

He unrolled the drawing, stared at it a moment, then lifted his gaze to hers. "I'm the frog?"

She nodded, heart in her throat. "Len's the toad."

A smile tugged at his mouth. "That's cool."

"Thanks. I just…I…" Her words trailed off. "Gotta go."

She turned and started off, feeling like about the biggest nerd on the face of the planet. *So much for their being friends. So much for—*

"Hey! Kid? I have a question for you."

She stopped and looked over her shoulder. "Yeah?"

"You really think I look like a frog?"

She didn't know how to answer. She thought he was the coolest, cutest boy ever. But she couldn't say *that*. She stared at him, cheeks on fire, totally, completely tongue-tied.

He grinned. "Lighten up, I was just teasing. I like the drawing. Thanks a lot." He tucked it into his back pocket. "See you around, kid."

11

Skye awakened with a start. Heart pounding, disoriented, she moved her gaze over the dark bedroom. Something had awakened her, some sound. Like a person clearing their throat or a lock clicking into place.

"Mom," she whispered. "Is that you?"

Silence answered her. Skye lay back against the pillows, drawing the sheet up to her chin. She had probably been awakened by a sound from the road just beyond the lot, or by a dream she had already forgotten. Sure. It had happened before.

Skye twisted to glance up at the window above her head. She had left it open to let in the nonexistent breeze; she saw that the nearly starless sky still wore the deep black of midnight. From outside came the sound of crickets and cicadas, but little else. It was late, so late that even the rowdiest of the roustabouts had gone to bed.

She lay back against her pillow once more. *Go to sleep, Skye.* It was nothing. She closed her eyes and tried to relax. Even as she did, her head filled with thoughts: of Chance, of her mother's jumpiness of late, and of what the end of summer would bring.

She rolled onto her side, then onto her back again, focusing on thoughts of Chance. She had been careful not to pester him. She would stop by to say hi, but she wouldn't hang around offering advice and stuff. If he was busy, she left him alone. And she *never* tagged after him, though she had wanted to.

Little by little, things had changed between them. He didn't get that annoyed look on his face anymore when he saw her; he had stopped telling her to scram. He even smiled at her, once in a while.

Not that she thought he *really* liked her or anything, but she didn't seem to bug him anymore. She supposed he had just gotten used to her; maybe in the same way the other troupers seemed to have gotten used to him.

Secretly, she hoped he had decided she wasn't a know-it-all, spoiled brat. Secretly, she hoped he did, at least, kind of like her. That, she had decided, would be about the coolest thing that had ever happened to her.

Skye sat up and turned on the bedside light. She retrieved her sketch tablet from the floor and flipped through the pages, stopping at the drawing of him she had done a week ago. Her favorite thing to do was sit and draw while he worked a game booth. She drew all sorts of things, but a lot of the time she drew him; this was the drawing of him she liked most.

In it, he looked out at the horizon, at nothing, yet the seriousness of his expression suggested he saw something, something important. She touched the drawing lightly, careful not to smudge the pencil. She traced her finger along the line of his strong jaw, then across his high cheekbone.

He liked her art. He thought she was good. Really good. He had told her so. And he hadn't laughed when she told him she was going to be an artist someday, that she was going to be famous.

Skye's cheeks burned as she remembered telling him that. Afterward, she had wished with all her heart that she could take the words back, but he had been really cool about it. He had told her to keep believing in herself. He had said that someday her belief in herself might be all she had to hang on to.

Skye drew her eyebrows together, recalling his expression. He had looked so determined. And so alone. Swallowing hard, she glanced back at the drawing of him and tilted her head to the side as she studied it. What was he looking at? she wondered. When he stared off in the distance that way, what did he see?

She would never know. Like her mother, Chance had secrets.

Chill bumps raced up her arms. Suddenly, the trailer was too quiet, the night too black. Suddenly, Skye was afraid. She moved her gaze around the room. The shadows in the corners seemed darker, fuller, as if they hid someone. Or something.

Something cold. Evil. Something that watched her.

With a squeak of terror, Skye threw aside her sketch pad, scrambled out of bed and out of the room. Her mother had taken the foldout that night. She would let Skye curl up with her; she would protect her from the dark things.

But her mother wasn't there.

Skye stared at the empty couch, heart pounding. "Mom," she whispered. Then louder, "Mom!"

Her voice resounded in the empty trailer. Her mother was gone.

She was alone.

The sound that had awakened her, Skye realized. The sound of their front door snapping shut. The sound of her mother leaving.

Her mother leaving. Skye thought of all the times they had picked up in the middle of the night and moved on. She thought of the things they had left behind each time—furniture, her toys, their food, no matter how full the refrigerator or pantry.

Maybe this time her mother had decided to leave without her. Maybe this time she had decided that it would be Skye she left behind.

Skye couldn't breathe. She curved her arms around her middle, fighting hysteria. What did she do now? What did—

Her mother always took their clothes. Always. Heart in her throat, Skye raced back to the bedroom. She yanked open the narrow wardrobe, then each of the drawers in the built-in chest, riffling through the contents—her mother's underwear, her favorite blouse, the housecoat she had worn so much the fabric was nearly transparent in places. Nothing was missing.

Nothing except her mother.

Skye wandered back to the open couch. She sank onto its edge. As she did, paper crackled. Frowning, she stood and dug under the rumpled bedding and pulled out a section of newspaper.

She flipped on the light to get a better look. It was the front page of the *Philadelphia Inquirer,* two days old. She stared at the newspaper, something tugging at her memory. That's right. Her mother had picked up the paper at the Laundromat the other day. Skye remembered her taking a section of the paper with her when they'd left.

Skye screwed up her face in thought. After that, her mother had begun acting weird. Jumpy and distracted. Short-tempered.

She quickly scanned the page's headlines: *Reagan Sets Foreign Policy; Train Derails Outside City, Four Killed, Dozens Hurt; Jewelry Designer To Host Benefit; Mob Boss Set…To…Testify.*

Mob boss. Skye's legs began to shake, and she sank to the edge of the bed, rereading that last headline again, then the article accompanying it. The article detailed the start of the grand-jury investigation into allegations made against the head of the East Coast's most notorious crime family.

She had been right. Her mother was on the run from the mob.

Maybe what she had heard hadn't been the sound of her mother leaving, but the sound of her being taken away.

Taken away.

With a cry of terror, Skye jumped to her feet and ran to

the bedroom to dress. She would get Chance. He would know what to do; he would be able to help her. She pulled on her denim cutoffs and a T-shirt, folded the piece of newspaper and stuffed it into her pocket, then raced out into the night.

Skye made it to the trailer he shared with the other guys, and not wanting to wake anyone but Chance, went around to the back side, to the window nearest his bunk.

She grasped the razor-thin ledge and stood on tiptoe. "Chance," she whispered. "Wake up. It's me. Skye."

From inside she heard a rustle of bedclothes and a moan. She waited a couple moments, then tried again. "Chance, wake up. It's Skye. Wake up, please."

A minute later his face appeared at the open window. He looked as if he was still asleep. "Kid?" He passed a hand across his face and yawned. "What are you doing out this time of night?"

"I need your help." She hugged herself hard. "I don't know what to do!"

"What are you talking about?" He eased up the screen, stuck his head farther out and looked around. "It's awfully late. Does your mom know you're ou—"

"She's gone!" Skye cried. "I woke up...I don't know why, except I thought I heard a sound. But it was really quiet...and all of a sudden I had this feeling and...and I was really scared." Her teeth began to chatter, and she rubbed her arms. "So I went to curl up with her, and she was...her bed was..." Skye burst into tears.

"Oh, geez. Don't cry..." He glanced over his shoulder, then back at her. "Hold on. I'll be right out."

A couple minutes later, Chance emerged from the trailer. Skye stumbled toward him. "What am I going to do, Chance? How are we going to find her?"

Chance put an arm around her. "Come on." He led her away from the trailer, to a grassy spot by a scrubby-looking tree. They sat down, facing each other.

Chance caught her hands and rubbed them. "You're getting all upset about nothing. She probably went for a walk."

"In the middle of the night?"

"Here you are, and it's the middle of the night. I bet she couldn't sleep and decided the night air would help."

Skye shook her head, wiping roughly at her tears. "But she's never done that before! I know she hasn't."

"How can you be so sure? Maybe every other time you just didn't wake up."

Skye caught her bottom lip between her teeth. "At first I thought maybe she'd left me for good. But her clothes are all there. But now I...I think she might have been kidnapped."

"Kidnapped?" he repeated, a smile tugging at his mouth. "Skye, don't you think that's just a little far-fetched?"

"No. Look at this." She leaned forward and dug the folded newspaper page from her pocket. She held it out. "Here."

Chance took the paper, unfolded it, then met her eyes. "What exactly am I supposed to be looking at?"

She reached around him and pointed. "This, about the mob guy."

Chance read it, then shook his head. "You think this has something to do with your mother?"

Skye nodded, tears welling again. "I found it on the sofa bed. She must have been reading it and now...and now she's...gone."

She started to cry again, but softly this time. "What am I going to do, Chance? I don't have anybody but her."

He scooted forward, put his arms around her and patted her back. "Look, kid, your mom didn't run away and the mob hasn't kidnapped her. She went for a walk. Or to meet a friend."

"She wouldn't do that." Skye pressed her face to his chest, the beginnings of one of her headaches pushing at her.

"Besides, you don't understand. I think she's...that we're...I think we're in some sort of trouble."

"What sort of trouble?"

Skye rubbed her temples. "I don't know. She won't tell me. But we're...always moving around. We pick up in the middle of the night sometimes and just...go. Don't you think that's weird?"

For a moment he was silent, and Skye tipped her head back to meet his gaze. "Chance? You think it's strange, too, don't you?"

"What I think doesn't matter. Ask your mom."

"I did. She says we're nomadic adventurers."

He made a sound of amusement. "Sounds about right, kid. More right than the mob being after you."

"It's not funny!" She stiffened. "She won't tell me where I was born or what my father's name was. She says he's dead, but that's weird, too. If he's dead, why won't she tell me about him?"

"I don't know, Skye. She must have her reasons."

Skye moaned, the pain in her head intensifying. She pressed her hands to her temples and squeezed her eyes shut, battling it.

"What's wrong?"

"I get headaches. Bad ones." She drew in a sharp breath. "I'm okay."

"Yeah, right. Come on, I'm walking you back. You need some aspirin or something."

"Wait!" She grimaced as pain knifed through her skull, and her vision blurred. "Did your mom keep that kind of stuff from you? Stuff about your dad?"

Chance laughed, the sound rough. "Hell, no. I wish she had, though. My father was a real prick." He stood and pulled her gently to her feet. "Come on. I'm getting you home. I'll bet your mom's there, waiting for you. She's probably worried sick."

12

But Claire wasn't there. Chance stood in the center of Skye and her mother's obviously empty trailer, working to hide his dismay, trying to decide what he should do next. Skye was beside herself, hysterical with worry, her headache nearly unbearable.

Even so, she refused to take her headache medicine, because she said it sometimes made her sleepy. She told him she was afraid to go to sleep. Finally, by promising he wouldn't leave until her mother returned, Chance convinced her to take two of the tablets and lie down.

He sat on the floor beside the bed, the space so small he barely fit. He forced a breezy smile, all too aware of the time that had slipped past. "It's going to be all right, kid. Any moment your mom's going to walk through that door. And boy, are you going to feel silly then."

She searched his gaze. "What if she doesn't?"

"She will."

"Where's your mom?"

He hesitated a moment, feeling her question like a punch to his gut. "She's dead."

"Oh." Skye drew her eyebrows together. "What happened? I mean, was it an accident or—"

"She got sick," he said roughly. "And then she died."

"Oh." An awkward silence stretched between them. After a moment's hesitation, she cleared her throat. "Chance?"

"Yeah?"

"What's it like? Being without a mother?"

"I don't think about it much. Not anymore, anyway."

Tears flooded her eyes, and he knew she was thinking about her mother, thinking that she would never see her again. He leaned toward her. "It's bullshit, Skye. She's going to be home any minute."

"But wha'if she's not?" Her words slurred slightly, and he knew the medicine was kicking in.

"She will be."

Her eyelids fluttered. "Don't...leave me. You promised."

"Yeah, I know. I promised, and I won't."

Within moments her eyes closed and her breathing became deep and even. He stayed beside the bed, anyway, watching her while she slept. Silly, sweet Skye. She liked to play the tough kid, the invincible one. But that wasn't the way she looked now. She looked young. And soft. And lost. He lightly touched his index finger to her cheek, then drew his hand away, surprised by the rush of tenderness he felt for her.

He'd never had a brother or sister, though once upon a time he had wanted one. Someone to share things with, someone to belong to when his mother didn't have the time—or inclination—to belong to him.

That had been a long time ago. So long he had almost no memory of it anymore. He'd been lonely, he supposed. Ages ago, back when he had needed people to make him happy. To make him feel safe.

He unwedged himself and crossed to the door. There, he stopped and looked back at her. What she had told him earlier, about her and her mom picking up and moving in the middle of the night did sound weird. But the mob? No way. That was just too Hollywood.

No, Claire was probably trying to stay a step or two ahead of the bill collector. She had probably refused to tell Skye anything about her father because she didn't even know who he was.

Ugly but true. Too ugly, he supposed. Too true to tell a little girl who loved her mother.

After one last glance at Skye, he went to the front of the camper to wait. He sat. He paced. He checked—and re-checked—his watch. The minutes ticked past. Still Claire didn't show.

He shook his head. She probably had a boyfriend and had sneaked off to fuck her brains out.

Even as the thought filtered through his head, he acknowledged to himself that it didn't ring true. He didn't know why. He didn't know Claire well, hardly at all, in fact. She could be a raving nympho, for all he knew.

But he had seen the way she looked at her daughter. He had seen how much she loved Skye. Nothing meant more to Claire than her daughter, and certainly not some small-town, back-lot fuck. Maybe he was being naive, but he didn't believe Claire would leave her daughter alone to go do that.

Then, what had she left her alone to go do?

Even as the question registered, he heard her at the door. A second later, she stepped into the kitchen, saw him and stopped dead.

"Hello, Claire."

She looked past him, toward the back of the trailer where Skye slept, then back, her expression alarmed. "What are you doing here?"

"I think the question is, why weren't you here?"

"I went out for a walk. I couldn't sleep and—"

"It's the middle of the night!" He jumped to his feet. "Jesus, Claire, Skye was scared to death. She came to get me, she was so scared."

Claire paled. Her hand went to her throat. He saw that it trembled. "I'm sorry. Like I said, I couldn't sleep, and I…" She turned her head toward Skye's bedroom. "Is she asleep?"

"I think so. She took a couple of those headache tablets,

but only after I promised her I'd stay. She was afraid to be alone.''

Tears flooded Claire's eyes. "Thank you, I'll... I need to see her. Excuse me.''

Chance thought about leaving, then decided against it. Something didn't sit right with Claire's explanation. Skye was right, her mother acted as nervous and jumpy as a cat. She was afraid of something. Or someone.

Chance took a seat at the dinette and waited. From the bedroom, he heard the sound of muffled voices. And of tears, though whether Skye's or her mother's he wasn't sure. Maybe both.

Several minutes later Claire reappeared. She looked shaken. "I can't believe I... I didn't think she would wake up. She's always been a sound sleeper and...''

Her voice trailed off. She met his eyes. "I need a drink. You want a beer?''

"Sure.''

She went to the mini-fridge and took out a couple of beers. As she opened the door, a shaft of light speared through the dark kitchen, illuminating her expression. Something was wrong. Definitely.

She handed him a bottle of beer. "Glass?''

He shook his head. "This is fine. Thanks.''

Without another word, she slipped into the booth across the table from him. She took a swallow of the beverage, her gaze on a place somewhere over his right shoulder. He was reminded so vividly of his mother he winced.

He shook the thoughts off and narrowed his gaze on Claire. "What the fuck's going on?''

Startled, she swung her gaze to his. "Pardon me?''

"You don't add up. Neither does Skye. Why are you traveling with this two-bit outfit?''

"Why are you?''

"It's a way out. It's not permanent.''

"It's not permanent for us, either. It's just for the summer."

"Same question still applies." He brought the bottle to his lips, tipped his head back and drank, his gaze still on hers.

She looked away first. "What question was that?"

"Please, give me a little more credit." He set the beer sharply on the table. "Why are you here? You don't belong. You're too..." He cocked his head, studying her, trying to put his finger on what it was that had bothered him about her all along. "You're too classy. These people are rough, they're a breed all their own. You have other options."

"Maybe I like it."

"That's bullshit."

"Thank you for helping Skye." She slid out of the booth and crossed to the door. "Good night, Chance."

He met her eyes but didn't stand. "Skye thinks you're on the run from the mob."

She caught her breath. "That's ridiculous."

"Is it?"

"Yes."

"She brought me the front page of a newspaper. On it there's this bit about a mobster set to testify day after tomorrow in Philadelphia. She found the newspaper on your bed and put two and two together. Is she right, Claire?"

"No." She shook her head for emphasis. "Not even close."

He gazed speculatively at her for a long moment. "Then, what is close?"

"This is none of your business, you know. I'd appreciate it if you left now."

"It became my business tonight. When you weren't here."

"I made a mistake, Chance. I shouldn't have left her alone. It won't happen again." She opened the door. "But thank you for your concern."

He slid out of the booth and crossed to her. "Skye thinks you're in some sort of trouble. She's thinks you're running from something. Or someone. If not the mob, Claire, who? Skye's father?''

She opened the door wider, then motioned out with her half-full bottle. ''I'd like you to leave now.''

''Fine. My pleasure.''

As he moved past her, she caught his arm, stopping him. ''I love my daughter, Chance. More than anything. I'd move heaven and earth for her, I'd face the most unspeakable evil to save her. And that's all you need to know.''

Something in her expression told him that she had already faced the unspeakable for her daughter. But that didn't change what had happened tonight. He looked her square in the eye. ''I'm sure you do love her, but she thought you either ran away or were taken away. And she was really scared. I think you need to face that. I think you need to deal with it.''

She dropped her hand. ''Good night, Chance.''

He took her invitation to leave, turning back to her when he had cleared the stairs. ''You know, Claire, Skye doesn't buy what you've told her about her father. She doesn't buy that you pick up and move in the middle of the night because you enjoy it. Frankly, I don't buy it, either.''

13

The weeks slipped by. June became July; the Fourth came and went. The initial days of August brought both blistering heat and, unbelievably, the first tinges of fall's golden hues. Marvel's had traveled from Pennsylvania, through West Virginia, up to Ohio, and was now deep into small-town Indiana. From Indiana, the show would head south, winding its way through the Deep South on its way back to winter quarters in Florida.

Chance planned to be long gone before then. As would Claire and Skye, he knew. The question was, who would be the first to leave.

It didn't really matter; either way, he would miss them.

Over the past weeks, the three of them had become friends, forming a kind of family. Chance supposed sharing that strange, emotion-charged night all those weeks ago had, on some level, connected them, for after that they had slipped into a familial role. They helped each other, they kept each other company, they filled the empty hours between gigs together. Chance took many of his meals with them, and always breakfast, as that was the one meal they all had at the same time during show runs.

Most mornings he would wander over to their trailer on the pretense of saying good morning, and Claire would offer him coffee and eggs. It had gotten to be a kind of joke with them, about how his morning stroll always ended up in a home-cooked meal.

In truth, he liked to check on them in the mornings, just

to make sure they had made it through the night, to make sure that one or both of them hadn't disappeared. For, as the weeks had passed, Claire had seemed to become jumpier, more nervous. She had lost weight; her eyes had taken on a hollow, hunted look.

And as those weeks had passed, Chance had come to believe that Skye was right about her mother. She was in some sort of trouble; she and her daughter were on the run from something. Or someone.

He wondered who. He wondered where Claire was from and what had happened to Skye's father. Though when he did, he reminded himself that they, like his stint as a carny, were only temporary. He reminded himself that Marvel's was only a means to an end; their friendship only a way to fill a few hours.

In truth, he was glad he didn't know more about the mother and daughter, glad that Claire didn't offer up personal information the way she did eggs and bacon in the morning. Because then he would feel compelled to share himself with them, then he would feel closer to them.

He preferred his isolation. He preferred some distance. He had never belonged, not anywhere or with anyone. He never wanted to worry about having to say goodbye.

Chance alighted from his trailer and tipped his face to the turbulent gray sky, the early-morning sun obliterated by the approaching storm. The weather forecast called for rain across the entire region for the next thirty-six to forty-eight hours. An extensive line of slow-moving thunderstorms, some possibly severe, was headed their way. The night before, Marvel had told them all to hold on to their butts, it looked like this one was going to be a doozy. For the first time in a decade, he'd ordered an early teardown. Depending on how the weather played out, they would either batten down the hatches and sit tight or pick up and try to outrun the weather.

Either way, the next few hours were going to be a real bitch.

"Chance!" Skye ran toward him, eyes wide. "Did you hear about the weather? A twister touched down in Fulton!" She skidded to a halt, then fell into step with him. "I can't believe it."

He cut her an amused glance from the corner of his eye. "You're awfully charged up this morning."

"It's just so exciting! That twister touching down and all."

"You're right," he teased, "we could all be killed in the blink of an eye. That *is* exciting."

Ignoring his sarcasm, she skipped out in front of him. "Do you think Marvel's going to have us haul out early?"

Thunder rumbled in the distance, and Chance shook his head. "All these trailers on the road? No way. I think we're here for the duration."

As they walked the rest of the way to her and her mother's trailer, Skye kept up a constant flow of excited chatter. Her mother was making her favorite for breakfast, French toast; she mentioned that damned twister three more times and shared some gossip she'd heard about Len and a girl back in Florida. Then she mentioned that her mother had had a nightmare the night before.

"A nightmare?" he repeated. "What about?"

"I don't know, but she screamed. And when I ran in to check on her, she was all sweaty and out of breath." Skye pursed her lips. "She has nightmares a lot, but lately…lately they seem to be worse."

Chance wanted to ask Skye more, but they had arrived at the trailer. They stepped inside just as Claire set a heaping plate of French toast in the middle of the table.

"'Morning," she said, turning back to the range. "Get it while it's hot. You know where the coffee is."

Skye didn't need to be told twice; she grabbed a plate, piled on several pieces of toast and drowned them in Aunt

Jemima's. Chance took his time. He poured himself a cup of coffee—a taste he had acquired in the past two months—took a seat at the table and filled his plate.

"So," Claire asked, "what do you think? Are we going today or staying?"

"Skye asked me the same thing." He poured syrup over his toast. "Staying, I'm certain of it. It would be too dangerous to be on the road."

"I agree." Claire sat across from him. "Better safe than sorry."

She speared a piece of toast with her fork; Chance noticed that her hand shook. He shifted his gaze to her face, and made a sound of concern. She looked like hell.

He told her so, and Claire laid her napkin in her lap. "I'm fine. I just haven't been sleeping well, that's all."

"I told him about your nightmares," Skye said around a mouthful of food. "I told him you had one last night."

"It's no big deal. Really."

Claire met his eyes, then motioned toward Skye and shook her head. He nodded, understanding that she didn't want to talk in front of Skye.

Twenty minutes later, after sending Skye out for an updated weather report, Claire turned to Chance. "I need a favor."

"Sure. What's up?"

"I need you to watch Skye for a while. Tonight, after she's gone to sleep."

"After she's gone to sleep?" he repeated, the hairs on the back of his neck standing up. "What's going on?"

"Nothing."

"Right."

"No, really. It's nothing, I just—"

He caught her hand and looked down at her nails. They were raw, bitten to the quick. He met her eyes. "You practically jump out of your skin every time someone speaks. You're constantly looking over your shoulder, and you're not sleeping. I don't have to be a fortune-teller to know something's wrong."

She snatched her hand away. "You're not a fortune-teller."

"Exactly my point. You want to tell me what's going on? Maybe I can help."

For a moment he thought she was going to feed him the same line of bullshit she usually did. She opened her mouth, then shut it again. Turning away from him, she crossed to the sink and stared out the small window above it.

"I wish you could help," she said softly. "But you can't." She swung to face him. "I have to go into town. I have to make a...phone call, and I...I don't want to leave her alone. Especially with the storm."

"Why can't you take her with you, Claire? Who're you calling? Skye's father?"

"No!" She shook her head for emphasis. "No."

"Last time, that night you disappeared, is that where you were? Making a call?" She shifted her gaze, and he had his answer. He held out a hand to her. "I know you're in some sort of trouble, Claire. And I'm pretty sure it has something to do with Skye's father."

"Well, you're wrong. It has nothing to do with him." She caught his hands. Hers were like ice. "I need your help. I need you to do this for me. Will you? Yes or no?"

"Claire—"

"Yes or no? It's important, Chance."

He hesitated, not at all certain he was doing the right thing, then nodded. "What time do you want me here?"

14

Claire had asked Chance to come at ten-thirty. She checked her watch, thankful to see it was almost that now. She could hardly think for the terrible sense of urgency, of impending disaster, pressing in on her. She had to call Dorothy. Now, tonight. She had no more time, she felt that keenly, with every bit of psychic ability she possessed. She and Skye had run out of time.

Shuddering, Claire glanced toward the back of the trailer, at the closed bedroom door. Skye was asleep and had been for better than a half hour. Still, Claire worried about her waking, worried about how she would explain where she was going if she did.

The wind buffeted the camper, rocking it; several particularly strong gusts seemed to actually lift it off the ground. She crossed to the door and peered out, struggling to see through the driving rain, feeling suffocated in the tiny trailer. She thought back to her last call to Dorothy, to the way she had sounded—distracted and nervous. Guilty, even.

Claire froze, searching her memory. After seeing the bit in the newspaper about Monarch's having hosted a charity benefit in Philadelphia, she had, on impulse, called Dorothy. But she hadn't told the woman anything that would give them away. Had she? She'd been just as careful as always.

Claire checked her watch again. *Ten-thirty. Finally.* She collected her rain slicker and car keys and went to the door to wait. She had unhitched her car from the back of the trailer before the rain started; after lunch she had darted into town and filled up its gas tank. While there, she had bought a sack of nonperishable food for the car and two gallons of water. Her and Skye's duffel bags were in the camper, stuffed into the storage compartment above the dinette. The pouch of gems was already tucked into her duffel, just in case. She couldn't chance forgetting them.

That she and Skye might be leaving the carnival tonight was a very real possibility.

It all depended on what Aunt Dorothy said. It all depended on Pierce.

Claire drew in a deep, shaky breath. Even if Dorothy reassured her, she might choose to leave, anyway. The advent of the school year wasn't that far off; if she and Skye left now, it would give them more time to get set up someplace. That would be good for Skye, it would be good for her, too.

She had laid the groundwork for her and Skye's departure with Marvel already: she'd told him that they had friends nearby, and if he didn't mind they would wait out the storm with them. She'd told him that she had asked Chance to watch their camper while they were gone, because of the storm. Marvel hadn't asked any questions, he had merely nodded and muttered something about wishing he could wait out the storm elsewhere, as well.

Claire rubbed her arms, chilled. She couldn't go on this way, not knowing, unable to sleep for the nightmares, for the horrible feeling of doom that hung over her and dogged her every waking moment.

Last night the nightmare had been particularly vivid. The monstrous dark bird had nearly had Skye, its great, sharp talons had closed around her. Claire had snatched her daughter away, a moment before the longest of the talons had pierced her daughter's heart.

Claire had awakened out of breath and drenched with sweat. And she had known, just as she had known every time in the past, that Pierce was close to finding them.

He had never been so close before.

Chance arrived. They spoke little, though the silence between them was heavy with her anxiety and his unasked questions. For one moment, she considered telling him the truth, sharing her fear. The desire to lean on someone, to have someone support her, even if only a boy, was so strong it took her breath. It had been such a long time since she'd had someone to lean on, someone to be strong for her.

But in the end, she knew she could depend on no one but herself. It had always been that way; she feared it always would.

Promising Chance she would be back as quickly as she could, she headed out into the storm.

The trip to town took nearly three times as long as usual because of the wind and driving rain. She had planned to call from the pay phone in the tavern; she hadn't planned on the place being so crowded. It seemed the entire town of Ridely had decided to wait out the storm drunk.

Claire picked her way through the crowd, heading for the back of the bar and the phone. A woman stumbled over to her and grabbed her arm, though Claire wasn't sure whether to get her attention or to steady herself. The woman reeked of booze.

"You're that psychic, ain't you? From the carnival?"

Several people turned, and Claire averted her face. The last thing she needed was to have a roomful of people able to confirm having seen her.

"Please, leave me alone."

"Aw, come on." The woman swayed. "Tell my fortune. I need to know if that big stud over there is gonna take me home tonight." She laughed and winked at Claire. "I could use a little premonition, you know."

That's precognition, Claire wanted to shout. Instead, she leaned closer to the drunken woman. "Leave here, now," she whispered. "I see something terrible happening to you here."

The woman paled. "Here?"

"Yes. You must hurry. Tell no one you saw me."

The woman backed away, eyes wide.

"And don't drive drunk," Claire added, "just in case I'm wrong about where I see the terrible thing happening."

"I live just around the corner."

"Good. Go. Now!"

The woman turned and ran, stumbling, bumping into people, earning their glances of amused disgust. Feeling almost sorry for the woman, Claire went to the phone. She hated doing that, but she couldn't chance the woman making a scene.

A stool was positioned in front of the phone; Claire moved it out of the way and after depositing a fistful of change, she dialed. Dorothy answered on the third ring.

"Dot, it's me. Madeline."

"Madeline? Thank God! I've been hoping and praying you'd call. You must come home. You must! If you do, I know he'll go easier on you. I know he will."

Claire's stomach sank. She knew the answer to her next question, but she asked it anyway. She had to. "What's happened?"

"He's found you."

A squeak of terror raced to her lips. Claire's knees gave and she sank to the stool.

"Tonight, we all had dinner at the Astor Street house. Pierce was positively preening. He told us that a private investigator had found you. He said that within twenty-four hours Grace would be returned to the family and to Monarch's, where she belonged. He said you were so close he could smell your stench."

Claire squeezed her eyes shut, battling for breath. It was her every nightmare coming true; her every fear being realized.

"There's more. He said he has everything in place and that you're going to pay for what you did. That you deserved whatever you got." Dot's voice rose to a hysterical pitch.

"He said you would never see Grace again. Never! I tried to reason with him, but he wouldn't listen."

Claire bowed her head, paralyzed by what she was hearing. *The monstrous dark bird was almost upon them. She had been right. She should have trusted her premonitions and gone, weeks ago.*

"It's my fault, Madeline. All my fault. I didn't mean to hurt you or Grace. I really didn't. I only wanted you and Grace home, where you belong. I thought Pierce would bring you home and we'd all be a family again. It's all I wanted."

Dorothy's words registered, and Claire straightened. "What are you saying? You didn't know where I was. You didn't—"

"Your last call, about the paper. Since you'd seen an article about the benefit, I figured you must be somewhere in the Philadelphia area. Then, while you were talking, someone yelled at you and I...I..."

Now Claire remembered. While she had been talking, a man had wanted to use the phone. He had been loud and insistent. He had called her carnival scum. How could she have been so stupid?

"I thought I would help all of us," Dorothy continued. "I never believed Pierce would carry through on his threats, after all you're Grace's mother. She needs you and I...I..." Her voice trailed off miserably. "Come home, Madeline. Please."

"How could you, Dorothy?" she whispered. "You know why I ran. I told you about Griffen. I told you what he...did. He means Grace harm, he—"

"You're wrong about him, Madeline. You always were. He's grown up, going off to college in a few weeks. He's responsible and so handsome. Girls love him, Maddie. If what you thought was true, do you think girls would flock around him the way they do? Please, just come home. It's not too late. I'm sure, if you did return of your own free will, Pierce and Adam would forgive and forget. Grace belongs here, with her family. With Monarch's.''

Claire only half heard the last, her mind racing, scrambling to think of a way out of this, a way to escape.

"Madeline? Are you still—"

"Does he have pictures of Grace?" she asked, interrupting, a thought occurring to her.

"What? I don't—"

"Does he know what Grace looks like?" Claire gripped the receiver tighter. "Does he?"

"I don't think so. Because Griffen asked. He wanted to know what she looked like and Pierce said he didn't. But why do you—"

"Griffen," Claire interrupted, cold racing over her. "He was at dinner."

"Of course."

The line crackled. "He said he's anxious to have his sister back. He's been waiting for her, he said. He loves her, Madeline. He could never hurt her, he—"

Claire hung up the phone, her world crumbling around her. She never should have trusted Dorothy, she was given to fits of emotionalism and poor judgment. And she was a Monarch, after all. To her, the family and the family business were everything. *Everything.*

And Dorothy, like everyone else, hadn't believed her. She hadn't seen Griffen's obsession as dangerous; she hadn't witnessed the scene in the playroom; she hadn't seen Griffen's expression as he hurt Grace.

It had been like looking into the face of pure evil.

Claire began to shake. Pierce was close. So close he could "smell" her. They would take Skye away from her. Easily. She might even go to jail. She probably would.

Who would protect her baby then? Her head filled with the image of what she had stumbled upon all those years ago. Griffen holding Grace down, his hand over her mouth to silence her cries for help. His other hand up her dress. Inside her underwear. Touching her, violating her.

Claire brought a fist to her mouth, holding back her sound of horror. Griffen had not changed. She knew he had not. Dorothy's words had said it all—he was anxious to have his sister back. He had been waiting for her.

She had to run. They had to run.

But they would be looking for her. Claire dropped her head into her hands. Except for her hair color and cut, she had changed little in the seven years she had been gone. And although Skye looked completely different, they would recognize them together. They would be looking for a mother and daughter—*her* and a daughter.

Together, because of her, they would recognize Skye. But apart...

If she left Skye, if she went on without her, Skye would be safer.

Claire shook her head, not believing what she was thinking. She couldn't leave Skye. How could she live without her baby, even if only for a few weeks.

But if Pierce got her, she would never see her again.

Susan. The image of her oldest friend popped into her head. Though as different as two people could be, they had been as close as sisters, growing up. From the first grade on, they had seen each other through both triumphs and heartaches, through the upheavals of youth and the giddy fears of early adulthood.

Pierce had put an end to that. She and Susan had fought over Claire's decision to marry Pierce; Susan had warned her about Pierce, she had said awful, ugly things about him, things Claire hadn't been able to accept. Hurt and feeling betrayed, Claire had accused her friend of being jealous and bitter.

Susan had been right, of course. Claire should have known. Susan had always been right. Where she, Claire, had struggled through school and made one poor choice after another, Susan had sailed through both school and life.

Pride had kept Claire from calling her friend when she had realized the truth about her husband and marriage, it had kept her from calling her for help when she ran with Skye.

Until about a year ago. Claire had awakened one morning to realize that pride was a silly, stupid thing and that she needed her friend, that she wanted to talk to her. She had located Susan through her parents, and called. It had been like nothing had ever happened between them. They had both cried, so happy to talk to each other.

Claire had told her everything. *Everything.* About Pierce's abuse and threats. About Griffen's obsession with his half sister and the horror she had witnessed. She had told her about Adam's nearly strangling her, and of how she'd escaped. Susan was the only person in the world who knew who Claire and Skye Dearborn really were.

It had been so good to talk to her again, so good to have someone she could share her fears with. Since then, they had spoken several times. Each time, Susan had begged Claire to come live with her. She was an English professor at St. Mary's College in Notre Dame, Indiana. She would help her, she promised. And if Pierce found them, she would help Claire fight him.

Claire had declined each invitation. She had been too afraid. Susan didn't understand the power of the Monarch family. She didn't understand the lengths they would go to have their girl back.

And her friend didn't understand the depths of Griffen's dark obsession. No one did but Claire.

"Lady, you paying rent on that stool, or what? I gotta use the phone."

She looked over her shoulder at the dripping-wet, red-faced man who stood behind her. "Sorry," she murmured, sliding off the stool. "It's all yours."

Claire made her way to the bar, got a glass of wine then

returned to the phone. The man was still talking, so she took a seat at the empty booth adjacent to it. She sipped the slightly sharp cabernet, her hand shaking so badly some of the wine sloshed over the side. She sipped again, then sagged against the booth's ripped vinyl back. She couldn't do what she was contemplating. Leave Skye? Even if only for a few weeks? How could she bear to be without her?

What other option did she have?

Claire closed her eyes, thinking again of Susan. Susan was the one person she knew well enough, the one person she trusted enough, to leave her precious baby with.

Susan would help her. If she asked her to come for Skye, if she asked her to keep her—hide her—for a while, she would. Claire could give Pierce and his private investigator the slip. She could run tonight, in the height of the storm's fury; she had already laid the groundwork for her and Skye's disappearance. Everyone would think that they had gone together. Of course they would. When Pierce's P.I. showed up, Chance could point them in whatever direction she had asked him to.

She dropped her head into her hands. If Pierce caught them, he would take Skye away from her. He would take Skye back to that dark, joyless place. Skye would be at Griffen's mercy.

The monstrous dark beast was almost upon them.

The red-faced man hung up the phone and walked away. Claire took a gulp of her wine, screwed up her resolve, stood and crossed to the telephone. She deposited some change, dialed Susan's number, then said a silent prayer that her friend was home.

The phone rang once, twice, then three times. *Answer, Susan. Please answer.* And then she did, her voice thick with sleep.

"Susan, it's me."

"Madeline?" Claire could almost hear her come awake. "What's wrong?"

Claire took a deep breath, dangerously close to tears. "I need your help."

"You've got it."

Claire glanced over her shoulder, then turned her back to the crowded room, hunching over the phone's mouthpiece. "Pierce has found us. He'll be here...soon. He means to take my...he means to take—"

Her tears spilled over so violently she couldn't speak. Her friend waited out her tears, allowing her time to compose herself enough to finish. "He means to take Skye away from me. He means to see to it that I go to...jail. He said I would never see her again."

"My God, Maddie, what can I do?"

"I need you to come get Skye. I need you to keep her for me, for a little while. I'll give them the slip. I'm their only link to her."

"I'll leave now, Maddie. Don't worry, your daughter will be safe with me. I'd die before I'd let that bastard get his hands on her."

15

Chance opened his eyes. Claire stood in front of him, dripping wet, visibly shaking. He blinked, realizing that he must have fallen asleep. "Claire?" he said, glancing around the trailer, dark save for the intermittent flashes of lightning from outside. "What time is it?"

"I need your help," she said, ignoring his question, squatting in front of him, taking his hands. Hers were as damp and as cold as death. "Please, Chance."

He straightened, fully awake now. He searched her gaze, a sinking sensation in the pit of his gut. Something terrible had happened. "What is it?" he asked. "What's wrong?"

"I need you to watch Skye for...for a while longer. Please, I—" Her words dissolved into tears. She bent her head to their joined hands, her shoulders shaking with the force of her sobs.

"My God, Claire, what's—" He drew in a ragged breath. "Of course I'll watch Skye. Go do what you have to do. I'll stay."

"You don't understand." She lifted her tear-streaked face to his. "You don't understand. He's coming. He's almost...I have to go."

She looked lost. Devastated. Chance closed his fingers around hers. "Who's coming? Where do you have to go?"

"There are some people after us. They mean us harm. They mean *Skye* harm." She struggled, he saw, to compose herself. "Tonight I learned that they're close."

"I don't understand...what do you mean they'll hurt

Skye? Who?'' He sucked in a sharp breath, alarmed. ''Claire, this sounds a little nuts. You're exaggerating, right?''

She shook her head, her teeth chattering. ''If they...find us...I might never see Skye again. They'll take her away from me. And they'll...there's someone who'll hurt...he's hurt her before.''

''How close are they?''

''Very close. I don't know what I...what I—''

Tears choked her, and she released his hands, stood and went to the window. Outside, the storm raged, vivid jags of lightning ripping through the night sky. She hugged herself, rubbing her arms as if to ward off the cold.

She turned to face him once more, her expression bleak. ''They could be here tomorrow night. I'm hoping the weather slows them up. I need to put as much distance between us as I can.''

''Jesus, Claire.'' He crossed to her. ''Who are they?''

''I can't tell you.'' She caught his hands again, begging. ''You're safer not knowing. Skye's safer. You have to trust me on this. Please?''

He nodded, and after drawing in a shaky breath, she continued, ''I have to go away. Now. Tonight. I have to go as far and as fast as I can. And I—'' She tightened her fingers on his. ''I have to go without Skye.''

''Without Skye,'' he repeated. ''I don't understand how—'' But then he did, and he took a step backward, shaking his head. ''Oh, no. You're not leaving her with me. No way.''

''It would only be for the rest of the night and a few hours tomorrow morning. A friend's coming for her. Someone I trust completely. She's already on her way. She'll be here by 10:00 a.m. tomorrow. Maybe sooner. Please, Chance. I have no one else to turn to.''

''I still don't understand. Why not take Skye with you? Or meet this woman halfway?''

"These people have pictures of me. But not of Skye. And it's Skye they want. It's Skye they'll hurt."

"Son of a bitch. Claire, I...this isn't a small thing. This isn't—" He swung away from her, wishing he could think straight. Wishing he could block out her desperation, block out the way she looked at him, like if he didn't help her she would be lost. "You can't be serious about this, you can't mean to go...without her. You can't."

"Skye's all I have. She's in danger. I have to protect her, even if it means—"

Her throat closed over the words, choking them off. She cleared it and took a step toward him. "I'm begging you, Chance. I have no one else to turn to. Skye has no one else. They're almost here."

He brought the heels of his hands to his eyes. This felt wrong, somewhere, deep down, in the pit of his gut. But he didn't know what to tell her to do instead. He didn't see what other choice she had.

He sighed and faced her once more. "What's your plan?"

"I leave now, tonight. I slip out during the storm, tomorrow my friend Susan comes for Skye. I'll rendezvous with them later, when I know it's safe. It'll probably only be a couple of weeks."

"What if something goes wrong? What if this Susan doesn't show up? What if these people show up before she does?"

New fear shot into her eyes. She shook her head, as if denying the possibility. "They won't. They can't. And I trust Susan completely. I've known her all my life, she won't let me down." Claire drew in a deep, uneven breath, catching his hands once more. "Will you do this for me, Chance? Will you do it for Skye?"

He looked into her eyes, knowing he couldn't refuse her. She needed him; she had no one else. It would be for only a few hours.

He nodded and her breath caught on a sob. She brought

his hands to her mouth. "Thank you, Chance. Thank you, I—" She drew away from him, looking almost frantically around her. "I have to pack now. I have to go as soon as I...I have to go."

"Wait." He caught her arm. "What about Skye? When are you going to tell her?"

She wasn't going to. Even as Claire's eyes flooded with tears, he shook his head. "You can't do this. You can't leave without telling Skye. I won't let you."

"I have to. If I wake her, I won't leave without her. I won't be able to, and she...she won't let me. I have to do this, Chance. I have to. For Skye."

He saw how close to falling apart she was. One nudge and she wouldn't be able to go. One nudge and she would take Skye with her.

He couldn't give her that nudge. Claire's desperation was real; her terror was real. He was afraid for Skye.

Feeling helpless, he watched as she took an empty duffel from the storage space above the dinette, then went to the wardrobe, located right outside Skye's closed door. She quietly and quickly took out her clothes, folded them and shoved them into the bag. From there she went to the bathroom for her toiletries, then the built-in chest for some folded clothing items. It took her less than ten minutes to pack.

"I have a couple of boxes in the outside storage," she said, fastening the clasps on her bag. "I'll get them on my way out."

She scrawled a name and phone number on a piece of paper and handed it to him. "It's Susan's number, just in case you...need to reach her. She'll always know where I am."

She carried the duffel to the door, dropped it and turned to him. Her eyes were bright with tears, and when she spoke, her voice shook. "Don't tell anyone what's going on. Not anyone. I've already told Abner that Skye and I were waiting out the storm with a friend. I had to have an explanation for unhitching my car. I told him you were watching our trailer through the storm."

She took a deep breath. "Keep Skye hidden until Susan gets here. If someone besides her comes looking for us, lie. Tell them what I told Marvel. Tell them Skye and I left together. Tell them anything but the truth.

"After Skye's gone, and safe with Susan, go to Marvel and tell him we didn't return from our friend's. Early tonight was the last time you saw us. Understand?"

"Yes."

"Tomorrow morning, have Skye pack. It'll take her mind off...you know." She hesitated at the door, looking back toward the bedroom and Skye. "Oh, God...I don't know if I can do this."

"Then don't, Claire. Please. I'll help you."

"You are helping me. And I have to. For Skye. Pierce is—" She bit back the words. "I'm going to miss you, Chance."

This was goodbye.

He stared at her, realizing that truth, stricken. "Claire...God, I...I'm never going to see you again, am I?"

"Oh, Chance." She put her arms around him. "I'll never forget you."

He hugged her back, choked, eyes burning. "I won't forget you, either."

She clung to him. "Take good care of my baby. Tell her how much I love her."

"I will. I promise." He squeezed his eyes shut, hating the way he hurt. "Can I...is there some way I can convince—"

"No. She'll be safer this way." Claire stood on tiptoe and pressed her cheek to his, hers wet with tears. A moment later, she released him and retrieved her duffel. She opened the door, then looked back.

"Thank you," she whispered. "Tell Skye that I...tell her I'll see her soon. And that I love her more than anything in the world. Tell her that. Don't forget."

"I won't, I promise."

He watched helplessly as she propelled herself into the storm. As the rain swallowed her, he took a step forward, feeling as if there was something more he needed to say. Something he should say, something that would convince her to stay.

But it was too late. She was gone.

16

Chance didn't sleep for the rest of the night. He couldn't. He sat beside Skye's bed, watching her and worrying. He didn't know how he was going to break the news to her; he didn't know how he was going to handle her heartbreak.

But he didn't have a choice, not anymore. He would help her through these next hours, then he would say goodbye to her. Just as he had said goodbye to Claire. He drew deeply through his nose, working to ignore the pinch in his chest. The feeling of loss. He would miss them, though he wished with all his heart that he would not. He would think of them, wonder about them, forever.

When Skye awakened, she awakened with a smile. She was surprised to see him, but not afraid. "What are you doing here?" she asked, looking toward the window, to the gray stormy day beyond, then at him. "Did I oversleep?"

Chance told her then. Simply, clearly and with as little emotion as possible, hoping that his lack of emotion would soften the blow of his words.

It didn't. She stared at him, her expression reflecting the horror she felt at his words, the stunned disbelief.

She shook her head, her eyes wild. "You're lying! My mom wouldn't leave me! She wouldn't!"

"It's only for a little—"

"No!" Skye scrambled out of bed. "Mom!" she shouted, running for the front of the trailer. "Mom!"

She stopped for a moment, her expression panicked, then

turned and raced back to the bedroom, to the wardrobe. She yanked it open.

And saw that it was only half-full. Her mother's clothes were gone.

With a cry of terror, she tried the chest of drawers next. She pulled each open, riffling through what was left, panting and whimpering.

Her fingers stilled. She lifted her face to Chance's, her expression bleak, brokenhearted. "She left me?"

"She was afraid. She said you would be safer this way. She said—"

"No." Skye backed away from him, shaking her head. "It can't be true. My mom would never leave me. She said she wouldn't!"

Skye bumped into the closet door and collapsed into tears. Not knowing what else to do, Chance put his arms awkwardly around her, feeling a million miles out of his depth. "It's going to be all right, Skye. Just stop crying, and I'll tell you everything."

"Let me go!" She struggled against his grasp and, breaking free, ran for the door. "I'm going after her! And you can't stop me!"

But he could. He caught her a moment before she reached the door, dragging her against his chest, wrapping his arms around her. She fought him like a wild thing, thrashing and flailing her fists and feet. He tightened his arms, holding her as closely as he could, folding his body over hers, immobilizing her so she couldn't hurt him or herself. Holding her so tightly that she would know that he was there and that she wasn't alone.

Eventually her fury and hysteria became wails of despair, the wails after a time becoming heartbreaking whimpers. They sank to the floor. He held her in his lap, smoothing her tangled hair, murmuring sounds of comfort, ones that felt awkward and unfamiliar on his tongue.

Finally, quietly, he told Skye what her mother had told

him. All of it, sparing no detail. He shared with her, too, her mother's fear and desperation, her absolute love.

When he had finished, Skye looked up at him. "I was right, wasn't I? About the bad people?"

Chance nodded. "Your mother didn't want to leave you. She was afraid for you. She said you would be safer here first, then with her friend."

"This isn't forever." Skye whispered the words once, then again. "She hasn't really left me."

"No." He pushed the damp tendrils of hair away from her face. "She told me to tell you how much she loved you. More than anything, she said."

"Then why—" Skye bit back the words, though they hung in the air between them.

Then why didn't she take me? How could she have left me behind?

"She didn't want to," he said again, softly. "She didn't think she had a choice. Come on now. Your mom wanted me to help you pack." He helped Skye to her feet. "Susan, that's your mom's friend's name, should be here before too long. Your mom thought by ten."

Skye hung back, looking scared. "Do I know her?"

"I don't know." Chance frowned, trying to recall all that Claire had told him. "Your mother said she trusted her completely. She said she had known her all her life."

"Well, I don't know her. I've never met any Susan."

"Maybe you just don't remember?"

"Maybe." She took a deep, quivering breath. "Are you coming, too?" She saw his answer in his expression and made a sound of fear. "I don't want to go with her. I don't know her. I want to stay with you."

"I trust your mother," he said gently. "Do you think she would let you go with just anyone?"

"No. But..." She caught her trembling bottom lip between her teeth. "But I want you to go, too."

"I like you, too, kid," he teased, hoping to get a ghost of a smile out of her. "I promise to write if you will."

Her eyes flooded with fresh tears. "That's not funny!"

"I'm sorry." He caught her hands and rubbed them between his. "I don't blame you for being scared. If this Susan seems like a weirdo or pervert or anything, I won't let you go with her. I promise. All right?"

"But...why can't you go, too? You're my friend and I...I...don't want to go with her."

A lump formed in his throat, and he swallowed against it. "Because I can't, Skye. It's time to move on." A tear rolled down her cheek, and he caught it with the tip of his index finger. "Besides, this doesn't mean we'll never see each other again. Right?"

She nodded, though he saw that her chin trembled.

He smiled again. "Come on, kiddo, we've got to get you ready to go. Susan could be here any minute."

17

Chance and Skye waited. Claire's friend didn't arrive. Not that first morning or the next. He tried the number Claire left and got an answering machine. Afraid to leave a message, he had hung up, a ball of uneasiness in the pit of his gut.

Something had gone wrong.

Luckily, the storm had lasted a full twenty-four hours and did a fair amount of damage to the show, the worst being to the generator truck when lightning struck nearby. Since then, everyone had been scrambling around, making repairs, too busy to worry about whether Madame Claire and her daughter had returned.

Until a private investigator showed up, anyway, looking for them, asking questions and giving his card to everyone he spoke to. Eventually he was directed to Marvel, who brought him by the trailer.

Chance faced the two men, his heart thundering, his mouth dry. He pealed off exactly what Claire had asked him to, speaking mostly to Marvel, only reluctantly agreeing to answer the investigator's questions.

As he responded to the man's questions, he kept telling himself to go slow and not to fuck up. Claire and Skye were depending on him.

"So," the investigator was saying, "you haven't seen the woman or her daughter since the other night?"

"No, sir." Chance slipped his hands into his front jeans pockets, acutely aware of Skye hiding in the narrow wardrobe in back. "Like I said, Claire asked me to stay here and watch the place. She and Skye were going to stay with some friends.''

"Do you know where those friends live or their names?''

Chance shook his head. "She never said. I didn't think it was a big deal.''

"And you expected them to come back?''

Chance lifted his shoulders. "Well, yeah. They said they would be. I didn't think anything of it until this morning. I mean, the rain's stopped, so, you know, they should be back. So I checked around, and their stuff's gone.''

The investigator studied Chance a moment through narrowed eyes. Chance found something slimy about the man. And cold. He didn't like him, and he sure as hell wasn't about to turn Skye over to him. "You didn't think to check their stuff before this morning?''

"Nope? Like I said, I expected them to come back.''

"Of course," the P.I. said sarcastically. "After all, you were good friends.''

"That's right.''

"But they didn't tell you they were going to take off? Even though you were *good* friends? Funny.'' When Chance just stared stonily at him, the P.I. looked over at Marvel. "Mind if I take a look around?''

Marvel bristled, obviously not liking the man any more than Chance did. "Yeah, I do mind. The woman and her daughter are gone. Just like the kid said.''

"And you don't find that a little unusual?''

"Not in this business. Now, if you don't mind, this is private property and the kid here needs to get to work.''

"Sure thing." The P.I. handed Chance his card. "If you see either of them, I'd appreciate a call. There'd be a thousand dollars in it for you.''

"A thousand bucks?'' Chance widened his eyes, as if awed. "Wow, what'd they do? Rob a bank or something?''

The man laughed. "Nothing like that. A lawyer hired me

to find them. About an inheritance. These are two very rich gals. They'll thank you for calling me.''

Yeah, right. Chance wanted to puke at the bald-faced lie. Claire was scared out of her wits because someone wanted to give her money?

"If I see either of 'em, I'll call you first thing," he said, pretending to study the card. "I sure could use a thousand bucks. Yes, I could."

Chance caught Abner Marvel's eye. He saw that the old showman thought about as much of the P.I.'s story as he did. He also saw that his helpful-hayseed act might be stretching the limits of believability just a bit.

But Marvel didn't call him on it, not then or after the P.I. left. "No wonder they call those guys private dicks," the showman said, stuffing the card into his pocket. "He sure was one."

Chance forced a chuckle. "Do you think he was, you know, telling the truth about Claire and Skye having inherited money?"

"Could be," Marvel said after a moment, thoughtfully. "Seems kind of weird, though, someone being so anxious to give away money that they hire a high-priced P.I." Marvel looked Chance square in the eye. "What do you think?"

"Could be true. Though Claire never mentioned any kind of family money." Chance shifted his gaze away guiltily. Something in Marvel's expression told him that his boss knew something was going on, that he knew Chance wasn't telling him everything.

Marvel cleared his throat. "Repairs to the gennie are just about done, I figure we'll be heading out at first light. If you want to stay the night here, it's okay. Claire and Skye still might be back."

"Maybe."

"If not, I'm going to need the trailer for somebody else."

Chance's heart sank. "Yes, sir. I'll be out first thing."

"There's a crew at the gennie now, I could use you there. I'll walk over with you."

Chance nodded. He hated leaving Skye, he knew she was probably frightened. But there was nothing he could do about it. Taking one last glance toward the back of the trailer, he followed Marvel out the door.

For the rest of the day, Abner Marvel's final words rang in Chance's ears. He expected Chance to clear out of the trailer; he would be moving someone new in, probably in the morning.

He had to make a decision about Skye. And he had to do it fast. Before morning. Claire's friend wasn't coming. That was clear. But what to do with Skye was not.

His choices left him pretty much scared shitless.

All day he had thought about it, going over the situation, his choices. He and Skye couldn't continue with Marvel. She was a minor. Once Marvel discovered her presence, he would be forced to call Social Services, or maybe worse, that private dick.

The man had left a card with just about everyone, giving each the inheritance/reward story along with it. If any of the troupers saw Skye, they would kill themselves in an effort to get to the phone. Hell, Len and his cronies would sell their souls for a lot less than a thousand dollars. They probably already had.

Chance pulled the P.I.'s card out of his pocket. It was pretty fancy-looking—on heavy paper with raised letters and metallic ink. The dick had been dressed pretty slick, too, with shiny leather shoes and a watch that had looked like real gold. The guy's card said the firm had offices in Chicago, Dallas and Los Angeles. Whoever had hired him was paying his firm good money.

Oh, yeah, this dick was costing someone big bucks.

Chance frowned. He had thought Skye's theory about the mob pretty silly the first time she had told him about it. Now he wasn't so sure. Could the mob be after Claire and Skye? If not them, who?

Chance ran his thumb over the card's raised, gold letters. He couldn't turn her over to the P.I. or allow one of the other trouper's to do it, either.

That left only one choice. Take Skye and run.

But if he and Skye left the carnival, her mother wouldn't be able to find her.

If she even wanted to find Skye. Chance hated the thought, but as much as he wanted to deny it, he couldn't. Not completely, anyway. What if this whole thing was an elaborate scam on Claire's part? A way to dump her daughter?

He frowned. No way. If that had been the case, and Claire wanted to be rid of her daughter, she could have simply left. Simply let the P.I. find Skye.

No. Claire had been afraid. She had been terrified. For Skye. Claire loved her daughter more than anything—he believed that with every scrap of his being. She would never abandon her; she had believed her friend would come.

But something had gone terribly wrong. Susan wasn't coming. Chance swallowed hard, trying to stay calm, to coolly and rationally consider all his options. He kept coming back to the same thing. He had promised to watch out for Skye. He had promised to keep her safe.

He wouldn't leave her. He wouldn't break his promise.

Skye was frightened. And despondent. He had watched her grow more of both with each passing hour. Though they hadn't discussed it, she knew Susan wasn't coming. She was young and frightened, but she wasn't stupid.

The time had come to discuss it. Even though Skye was only twelve years old, they had to make this decision together. He had to give her a choice.

That night, he talked to Skye. Honestly. He laid their cards—her cards, really—on the table. He wanted her to understand her situation. It was her life at stake, her future.

He gave her two choices. They ran together, tonight. Or

they waited for Susan, or Skye's mother, as long as they could, then went to Mr. Marvel for help, taking the chance of Skye being turned over to Social Services or the private dick.

Skye understood. She made her choice.

That night, while everyone slept, Chance and Skye slipped away.

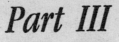

Part III

Birds of Prey

18

Fall came early to Horizon's End. Summer, it seemed to those who endured her long and bitter winters, made a brilliant but fleeting appearance, only to be swallowed by the cold once again.

True to form, only August fifth, and already browns, golds and oranges had begun to steal across her landscape. The nights had already dipped into the fifties and the day's zenith brought the mercury to a mild seventy-nine degrees. That wasn't to say there couldn't be another heat wave; one August had delivered seven straight days of ninety-plus-degree heat. That summer the weekenders, those who owned the million-dollar cottages that dotted the shore of Lake Horizon and who came from the city to escape just such heat, had complained bitterly. The locals had simply smiled.

Eighteen-year-old Griffen Monarch sat on the sweeping patio of the Monarch family's summer home, his father and grandfather's conversation swirling around him. Built and designed by a student of Frank Lloyd Wright's, the house emulated Lloyd's famous Falling Water at Bear Run. With an abundance of glass and natural stone, it crouched atop a hill that overlooked Lake Horizon, like a jewel nestled amongst the evergreen, maple and birch trees. A stone retaining wall circled the patio and beyond; except for a long grassy slope of land that led to the lake and dock, the surrounding property had been left wild. That property stretched a mile in every direction; the Monarchs' nearest neighbors were a good half mile beyond that, both similarly outfitted summer homes.

The family had come here every August of Griffen's life, to escape the choking heat and humidity of the city, to escape the crush of sweaty bodies and short tempers. The only thing that differentiated this summer from all the others was that in two weeks Griffen would leave for Evanston, Illinois, and his first semester at Northwestern, where he would study business, of course. In four years, after he had graduated with honors—which he hadn't a doubt he would—he would take his place as an officer of Monarch's, eventually replacing his father as president.

Eyes closed, Griffen rested his head against the chair back, the perfect blue sky and pillowy clouds reflected in the lenses of his Ray•Bans.

He smiled to himself, his thoughts drifting to his plans for later, a date with a local girl he'd met just that morning at the Pack and Post in town. She was a real hayseed honey, but what she lacked in culture and education she made up for with an ass and pair of knockers that had just begged for a squeeze. He intended to give them what they begged for.

Some girls were just built to fuck.

Life had been good to Griffen; he acknowledged that. He didn't waste time on humility. Modesty was for losers. He was handsome and athletic and could have—and had had—any girl he wanted. He was brilliant, school had been almost pathetically easy, and any doors that couldn't be opened with his brains, charm or good looks, he had only to say the name Monarch, and open they did.

He had everything he desired, save for one. The thing he desired most.

His half sister. His Grace.

A butterfly landed on the arm of his chair. Ever so

carefully, Griffen closed his hand around the delicate creature, trapping it. He stroked its velvet-soft wings a moment, then systematically plucked them off, thinking again of his half sister.

Not a day went by that he didn't think of her, not a day that he didn't plan for their reunion. For they would be reunited. He didn't have a doubt about that. It was inevitable, destined to be.

He narrowed his eyes. He hated that bitch Madeline for taking her from him; he hated his father more for letting her do it, hated him for his weakness. That day seven years ago, when he had returned home from school to learn that Madeline had stolen his Grace away, he had made a promise to himself—that someday, somehow, he would make both Madeline and his father pay for their stupidity and selfishness.

Smiling to himself, he rolled the still-twitching butterfly between his fingers. His body stirred. Sometimes, when he was fucking another woman, he would think of his revenge or picture his reunion with Grace, and he would pop off, right away, his orgasm almost unbearably intense.

Perhaps it would be that way tonight, with his milk-fed date.

His smile faded. But it might be the other way, the way it was when he couldn't picture it, and he would be left unfulfilled. And angry.

Those times his need to punish became so strong it burned in the pit of his gut. Those times he lost sight of all but the heat of his hatred.

At the mention of Grace's name, Griffen opened his eyes, though he didn't straighten. His father was whining about how it wasn't his fault that Madeline and Grace had gotten away again. Griffen curled his lips in distaste. Pierce whined like a girl. Or a baby. It made him want to puke.

Just as did his father's ineptitude. Grandfather was right

to be angry. Furious. He was right to chew him out. Only a few nights ago they had celebrated Grace's certain return. Then his father had come back, tail tucked between his legs.

The P.I. had lost them again.

"For Christ's sake!" Pierce exploded, swinging to face Griffen and motioning toward the mangled butterfly. "Do you have to do that? Jesus, I would have thought you'd have outgrown that."

Griffen laughed and swept the pieces off the table. Predictable. When confronted, Pierce turned his anger on someone else, anyone who might be near—a member of the household staff, an employee, his son. Griffen found that tactic as weak and pathetic as everything else about his father.

"Outgrown it, Dad?" he murmured, his lips curving up. "And I would have thought you'd have found Grace and Madeline by now. It's been seven years."

His father's face mottled with rage. "Someone keeps tipping them off. It wasn't my fault they slipped out of our grasp again."

Griffen eyed his father with contempt. "Not *our* grasp, Dad. Yours. Your wife, your daughter. You're the one who let them get away in the first place."

"Who did it?" Pierce said angrily, turning back to Adam. "Who tipped Madeline off? That's what I'd like to know. If it was Dorothy, I swear I'll—"

Adam cut him off. "It wasn't. She's the one who found them in the first place. If not for her, we wouldn't have had any leads at all."

Pierce scowled. "She's a soft, old fool."

Like you, Father. Griffen looked at his father, smiling thinly. "Maybe no one tipped them off. After all, Madeline's a psychic. Isn't that what you're always telling us? Maybe she *predicted* your detective's arrival."

Pierce flushed at Griffen's sarcasm. "Don't discount

her ability. That might be closer to the truth than you think.''

Griffen snorted with disgust. ''Oh, please, Dad. Now you're trying to blame mumbo jumbo for Madeline and Grace having again slipped through your fingers.''

When Pierce started to retort, Adam slammed his fist onto the tabletop. ''Stop it, both of you! I've had enough. I never want to hear mention of Madeline's so-called ability again. We three are the only ones who know about her delusions, and I want to keep it that way. The last thing we need is the press getting hold of that ridiculous piece of tripe and blowing it out of proportion.''

Adam stood and strode to the stone retaining wall and for long moments looked out at the lake. Without turning, he said, ''We need to stop assigning blame and start figuring out what we're going to do. I want my granddaughter. I need her. Monarch's cannot continue on its present course.''

He did turn then and Griffen saw his anger, his frustration. He bristled with it. ''The International Design Festival in Milan was a joke. We won nothing! Not even an honorable mention! Dorothy is slipping. Her designs are passé, dated.'' He swung around and pinned Pierce with his angry gaze. ''My sister has lost her edge. So what, Mr. President, do you propose we do?''

Pierce shifted nervously, then cleared his throat. ''I've done some checking around. There are a number of people available—''

''People?'' Adam repeated slowly. ''Available for what?''

''Designers. Gifted designers. Ones who could...'' Pierce cleared his throat again. ''Marcel Louckes from Tiffany's. Annessa St. Pierre from—''

''No. Never.'' Adam strode across the patio, stopping before Pierce. Adam was the picture of health, robust and fit. He had kept his body strong and his mind keen. Adam Monarch did not let anyone or anything stand in his way.

Unlike his own father, Griffen thought contemptuously. His father was soft and weak. Only forty-one-years old and he had already suffered a major heart attack. Always afraid, he carried those silly little nitroglycerin tablets around with him.

Griffen despised him. He had modeled himself after his grandfather. Like Adam, he, too, would let nothing or no one stand in his way. Especially not his pitiful excuse for a father.

Adam towered over Pierce, his fury an awesome, palpable thing. "Don't ever again suggest hiring an outsider to be lead designer for Monarch's. We will never do that. Never! Do you understand?"

Pierce jerked his chin up. "What other choice do we have? Tell me that. We—"

"We get our fucking girl back! That's what. Jesus, you make me sick."

Pierce launched to his feet, two bright spots of color dotting his cheeks. "How do you know Grace even has the gift? How? We haven't seen her since she was five. And even if she came home today, how do you know that she would agree to work for Monarch's someday? We know nothing about her. Madeline could have ruined her. Poisoned her mind against us."

"Monarch's is her destiny. She would see that. And if, at first, she didn't, we would convince her. There are ways of convincing, you should know that. How much stock do you think she'll put in what her mother told her, when her mother is in jail? I think she'll grow quite accustomed to living in luxury, to having anything and everything she desires. She'll be quite willing to be one of us. In fact, by the time we finish with her, she'll hate her mother for taking her away from all this."

Adam bent to look Pierce directly in the eye. "As for

the Monarch gift, she has it. I know she does. And so do you."

"I'm trying," Pierce said, his small burst of defiance wilting. "I have tried. I divorced Madeline. I married again, I had another daughter."

"A daughter who's dead now. Because that drunk of a wife of yours was too busy taking calls to watch our girl in the bath. Not that Grace could have been replaced. She had the gift. I saw it even at five, just as my father saw it in Dorothy when she was five."

Griffen stood and crossed to the retaining wall, to the place his grandfather had stood only moments ago. Several sailboats skimmed across the lake, their bright sails billowed out in the stiff breeze. His grandfather was right; Grace couldn't be replaced. She was special. She had *the* gift. He, too, had seen it.

Grandfather had tested her. Simple tests, the way Dorothy had been tested at the same age. He had taken Grace to the studio and store, he had allowed her to choose both gems and finished pieces, he had provided her with many choices and closely monitored what items she was drawn to and what patterns and shapes and colors she put together.

She had always gone to the best, she had put items together in a uniquely beautiful way. And she had already been drawing at five. Not the scribblings and stick people of most children her age, but with tremendous detail and skill. Just as Dorothy had at the same age.

Griffen had read that Picasso's father, an artist and teacher himself, had been so overwhelmed by his thirteen-year-old son's talent that he had given young Pablo his palette and brushes and vowed never to paint again. Some things did not need to be taught and learned, some things were inborn. Some things were a gift.

Grace was Monarch's gift, its fortune. *His* fortune.

"If you were half a man," Adam was saying, "Madeline never would have gotten away with her in the first place. If you were half a man, you would have found a way...any way, to take care of her. And Grace would be with us now.

"I want my granddaughter," he continued. "I want my heir. I need her. *We* need her. I don't care what it takes, do you hear? I don't care if you spend our entire fortune getting her back. I would do anything to get her back. *Anything.*"

Griffen swung to face the two men. "Do you mean that, Granddad? Would you do...anything to get her back?"

Adam looked him dead in the eye. "Yes, I would."

Griffen nodded. "I'll find her, then. I'll bring her home, back to the family. And she'll never go away again."

Part IV

Chance and Skye

19

Nowhere, Indiana,
1983

Chance and Skye's initial hours on the road were harrowing. Skye said little, just doggedly kept pace with him, never straying more than a few inches from his side. The first time he'd had to go to the bathroom, she had become almost hysterical, quieting only after he'd repeatedly promised that he wouldn't leave her.

She had stood right outside the gas station's rest-room door, whimpering, holding on to the doorknob, he knew, because every so often he would hear it rattle. As he stood there relieving himself and listening to that pitiful sound, reality had hit him, and hit him hard. Skye was a child. She had no one to take care of her now, no one but him. He was totally responsible for her—he had to make sure she had food and shelter and sleep, he had to protect her from those who might try to hurt or use her.

The responsibility was awesome. It was sobering.

In the safety and shelter of the carnival camper, he hadn't grasped the consequences of running away with her. His choice had seemed more clear-cut, his decision less of a challenge. He hadn't understood.

Now he did. Now, too late, he wondered if he had made a hasty decision and a big mistake. Now he really was scared shitless.

That first night, they slept under a train trestle, huddled

together, warding off autumn's early chill and midnight's darkness. Although exhausted, Chance couldn't sleep. His mind raced from one worry to the next, one frightening what-if to another.

Skye, too, couldn't sleep, he knew, though she didn't stir or speak. She simply clung stiffly to his side, as if frozen with fear.

Chance rested his head against the concrete support and shut his eyes. What the hell had he been thinking when he had decided to do this thing? How could he take care of a kid? He had no job, no place for them to live. He could hardly take care of himself, let alone a twelve-year-old girl.

Jesus, help him. He knew of only one way out. Call the man who had come looking for Skye. Call the number on the card the P.I. had given him, the card he had kept—just in case.

Even as he considered it, Chance pictured Claire's expression as it had been that last night—white with fear, eyes wide with panic. He recalled her voice, her desperation. Her pure terror.

She couldn't have faked that. She couldn't have.

He wouldn't call that number. If he did, he might be sentencing Skye to a fate worse than this one.

But how much worse than this?

He had no way of knowing. Chance released a pent-up breath, resigned to what he had to do. He would take care of them both. He could do it. He had to.

Luckily, he had saved most of what he had earned working at Marvel's. It would hold them for a while; they wouldn't go hungry.

Not yet, anyway. His money, he had seen already, would go fast. He and Skye were going to have to settle someplace; he was going to have to get a job. He didn't want to wait until they were dead broke to do it, either.

Once they were broke, they would be completely vulnerable.

Skye whimpered. The small sound tore at his heartstrings, and he lowered his gaze to her. She was probably thinking of her mother. Wondering where she was. Wondering why she had left her.

Chance wondered, too. He felt certain that something terrible had happened to Claire's friend, he feared something may have happened to Claire, too, though he probably would never know what. And neither would Skye.

He shifted, stretching his cramped legs. Skye cried out and clutched at his arm.

For a moment, he felt smothered, trapped. In that moment, he was angry—at Skye, himself, the world. He had left his aunt's to make his future, his fortune. Now he was saddled with a twelve-year-old, and his future looked bleak, fortune an impossibility.

He breathed deeply through his nose, shaking off the feeling. If he was saddled with anyone, he had done it to himself. They wouldn't be together forever; she wouldn't be a child forever.

But for now, she was. And she needed him.

"I'm not going anywhere," he murmured. "Just trying to get comfortable."

She nodded and pressed herself into his side, her teeth chattering. He put his arm around her. "I'm not going to leave you, Skye. I promise."

She was quiet a long time, then she stirred and tipped her face up toward his. "What are we going to do, Chance? Where are we going to go?"

"I don't know, kid. We're just going to have to play it by ear."

She nestled her head against his chest; he felt her shiver. "I'm scared."

He didn't blame her for being afraid. He was, too. He bent and pressed a kiss to the top of her head. "I know. But you don't have to be. I'm going to take care of you, Skye. I promise. I'll take care of you."

20

Twenty-four hours after leaving Skye in Chance's care, Claire began calling Susan. At first, when she couldn't reach her, she wasn't too worried. After all, she figured, the drive from Notre Dame to Ridely was a long one, made worse by the bad weather. No doubt Susan had stopped somewhere along the way to wait out the storm.

But by the end of the second day, when she still couldn't reach her friend, she began to panic. She called early in the morning, before hitting the road. She tried at noon and at three; she tried at suppertime and again at 11:00 p.m. Still no answer. The last time she tried, an automated voice informed her that the number she had dialed was no longer in service.

Something had gone wrong. Terribly wrong.

Claire hung up the phone. Change clattered into the coin return. Around her, the sounds of the truck stop faded and her head filled with the sound of her daughter's voice, calling her.

Skye needed her. Wherever she was. Whoever she was with.

She had to go back. Now. As fast as she could.

Heart pounding, mouth dry with fear, she turned and ran for her car, ignoring the curious stares of the diners as she raced past them. She reached the car, unlocked it and scrambled inside. She rummaged around on the passenger-side floor, shoving aside empty foam cups and take-out bags, searching for her atlas.

Finding it, she opened the book to the map of Indiana. Susan was a professor at St. Mary's College in Notre Dame, Indiana, all the way up at the top of the state. Knowing that and wanting to lead Pierce as far away as she could from Skye, Claire had driven a zigzag path south, going to St. Louis first, then to Memphis, and on to Nashville. She had reached Atlanta the night before. Now she had to make it back in the shortest time possible.

Claire studied the map for several minutes, then set it on the seat next to her, dropped the car into Reverse and peeled out. The way she figured, driving straight through, she was talking about a ten-hour trip. She could be in South Bend by five that evening.

Claire made better time than she had hoped, and pulled into Susan's quiet college neighborhood just after four. Moments later she located Susan's street, then house number. She parked in front, flew out of the car and up the walk.

She rang the bell, then pounded. "Susan!" She pounded again with the side of her fist as hard as she could. "It's me. Please, open up. Susan!"

"Hello there. Can I help you?"

Claire swung in the direction the voice had come. A woman stood on the porch of the house next door, looking at her, her expression worried.

"Thank you," Claire answered, struggling to remain calm. "If you could help, I'd be so grateful. Really."

Claire hurried toward her, crossing the lawns that separated the two homes, knowing she must look half-wild to the other woman. She hadn't changed or bathed in thirty-six hours and she couldn't remember the last time she had brushed her hair. Indeed, the woman looked as if she wanted to disappear back inside her house.

But she didn't, and Claire stopped before her. "I'm trying to reach my friend Susan Willis. It's important and I... That is her house, isn't it?"

The woman cleared her throat. "Yes, but she's not... home."

"Have you seen her, then?" Claire clasped her hands together. "Please, it's an emergency."

"I'm sorry, but..." The woman looked away, then back, her eyes bright. "I'm so sorry, but Susan's...Susan's dead."

"Dead?" Claire repeated, her world rocking. "You can't be serious. You can't...mean... Dead?"

"It was a car accident. Four or five nights ago. I don't know, it was such a shock, I...I lose track of the days. The weather was so awful that night. A drunk driver hit her head-on. I'm so sorry."

Claire stared at the woman. *It couldn't be true, Susan couldn't be dead. Not Susan. Not her sweet friend. Her confidante, her—*

What about Skye? Had Skye been with her?

Claire brought a hand to her head, dizzy suddenly. Her legs felt rubbery, weak. She swayed.

"Oh, dear, let me help you." The woman hurried off her porch and down to Claire. She took her arm. "Come. Sit down. You've had a shock."

Claire let the woman lead her to the front porch, to the big wicker rocker there. She sank into it, then curving her arms around her middle, bent double, rocking and moaning.

Her best friend. Her only friend. Gone. Dead.

Skye. Her baby. Dear God, let her be okay.

"I'm so sorry," the neighbor murmured, her voice shaking. "We all loved Susan. She was such a nice person...you don't look so good. Let me get you a glass of water. I'll be right back."

Claire caught her hand, stopping her. She tipped her face up to the other woman's. "Was she...was Susan...alone?"

"Alone?" the woman repeated, wrinkling her eyebrow. "Why, yes. She was south of here, near Culver, though Lord only knows why." Her voice thickened. "She died instantly."

Claire dropped her head into her hands, weak with relief, feeling guilty for it. Susan was dead because of her, because of the favor she had asked of her. But still, she was relieved. *Susan had been alone. It had happened before she'd reached Ridely. Before she had collected Skye. Thank God, thank...*

Claire lifted her head, realization dawning. But that meant that Susan had never come for Skye. A whimper of fear escaped her. That meant Pierce could have her daughter. He probably did.

Claire held her stomach, feeling sick. And if somehow, miraculously, he didn't...Skye could be anywhere. With anyone.

Claire jumped to her feet, still holding her middle. "I have to go," she whispered. "Thank you for...thank you."

"Please—" The woman touched her arm. "You don't look so good. Stay a minute. Let me get you some water."

"I can't." Claire drew in a deep, shaky breath. "Thank you for your kindness, but I have to go. My daughter is...she's..." Claire met the woman's eyes. "I have to find my daughter."

21

The lights of the midway spun crazily around Claire. Even the wild, blaring music couldn't drown out the sound of her thundering heart. In the desperate hope that Chance and Skye were still traveling with the carnival, she had sought it and Abner Marvel out.

Now she faced the old showman, trembling so badly she could hardly stand. "Where's Chance?" she asked, her voice quaking. "I have to find him, Abner. It's important. It's—"

"He's gone. A week ago now." Abner frowned. "At least that's when I think it was. I went to talk to him about you and your little girl, that's the last I saw of him."

Claire caught her breath, battling tears. *Gone. But if Chance was gone, where was her daughter?* She cleared her throat. "When you saw him, did you see...was Skye with him?"

Abner wrinkled his forehead. "He told me Skye was with you, Claire. He told me you two left together, the night of the storm. He told everybody that."

"I know, that's what I..." She struggled to keep from falling apart. "So, you didn't see her?"

"I can't help you, Claire. I'm sorry."

She curved her arms around her middle, crumbling. *Where was her baby?*

"A man was by, lookin' for you and Skye, though. Right before Chance took off. A P.I. He left his card."

Claire lifted her gaze. "A private investigator?" she repeated, fear sour on her tongue. "What did he want?"

"Like I said, he was looking for you two. I kept his card, just in case you came back around. I figured you'd be interested." He took the card out of his wallet and handed it to her. "I told him you and your little girl had left. Together. Chance told him the same thing."

Claire stared at the card, hand shaking. She recognized the name of the investigative firm. They were very well known in Chicago, top in their field. Adam Monarch had used them before, things to do with the business.

"He said you'd inherited some money, Claire. Big money. He gave 'bout everyone around here a card and said there'd be pay for anyone who found you for him." Abner looked her square in the eye. "A thousand dollars, Claire."

She nodded, understanding the warning, understanding that he knew as well as she did that she was in deep trouble. She glanced over her shoulder, double-checking to make sure no one was around, searching her memory for any of the show folk who had seen and recognized her.

"I'm real sorry you're havin' troubles, Claire. You were the best fortune-teller I ever had."

She caught his hands, begging. "You won't tell anyone you saw me, will you? You won't tell anyone that Skye and I are not together? Please? It's important, Abner."

"I didn't see you." He squeezed her hands, then dropped them. "Good luck."

"Thank you," she whispered, backing away. "For everything."

"Claire?" She stopped and looked back at him. His expression was grim. "I hope you find your little girl."

She nodded, her throat closing over anything she might say. In truth, there was nothing to say. She had to find Skye. She simply had to.

22

Chance and Skye fell into a regular rhythm of living. They traveled together as brother and sister, going from place to place, stopping wherever Chance could find work, living and sleeping wherever they could afford—usually in cheap boardinghouses or even cheaper by-the-week motels.

Most of the places they lived scared Skye. They were dirty. They smelled. The people who lived around them looked like the kind of people her mother had always told her to stay away from. Sometimes, while Chance worked and she was home alone, she would huddle under her blankets and listen to the sounds of the building—the scurry of creatures in the walls, the cries of unattended infants, the deep, frightening voices of the men who came and went at all hours of the day and night.

Those times it seemed a million years instead of a few short months since she had felt safe, since she had been with her mother and protected. It seemed longer ago still that she had stood up bravely to Len and his gang at the carnival, taunting them. She had been so cocky. So confident and unafraid.

Now she was scared of everything.

But of nothing so much as losing Chance.

Skye drew the worn, stale-smelling blanket to her chin. It was rough and scratchy, but it kept her warm. It comforted. And after some of the places she had slept in the last couple of months, she appreciated both of those things more than she had ever imagined she could.

She moved her gaze around the shabby motel room, avoiding the dim corners, not wanting to speculate what might be lurking in there. Chance had found temporary work—about a week's worth, the man had said—with a mason. For the past two days, he had left at dawn, and returned home at dark with a bag of take-out hamburgers and French fries. Both days he had been too exhausted to do more than eat, shower and fall into bed.

When he left in the morning, he ordered her to stay inside with the door locked. She was not to answer the door for anyone or to venture out. Chance feared her being picked up by the police or Social Services. After all, kids were supposed to be in school during the day, and she would stick out like a sore thumb on these small-town streets. He worried, too, about drug dealers or pimps getting their hands on her, he worried about her being abducted.

She shuddered. Those things terrified her, too, but not nearly so much as the fear that one day Chance wouldn't come home for her. That he, like her mom, would decide that life would be easier without her.

Tears stung Skye's eyes; they choked her. Her mother had promised she would never leave her. She had said she loved her more than anything. Her mother had called Skye her whole life. But she had left her alone. She had left her behind.

Skye drew her knees to her chest and pressed her face against them, the pain almost unbearable. She missed her mom. She wanted her to come back. She wanted to be able to undo whatever she had done that had caused her mother to stop loving her.

She tried to believe what Chance had told her, tried to believe that her mother had left because she had been afraid for her daughter's safety. And sometimes, on a good day, when she managed to forget for a time, she almost did believe it.

But most days she figured her mom had just decided to

leave her behind. The way she had left so many places and jobs behind.

Without a backward glance.

Skye's throat filled with tears and her chest hurt, hurt so bad she could hardly breathe. She tightened her arms around her drawn-up knees and rocked back and forth, fighting the tears, not wanting to cry. Not wanting to hurt anymore.

She was sick of both. And of being alone. Of being scared all the time.

But she couldn't seem to stop, no matter how much she wanted to.

From beyond the thin wall behind her bed came the sound of arguing. She jumped as she heard a man's shouted curses and a crash, then a woman's cry of pain. There came more swearing, more sounds of blows and cries of pain. And then silence, deathly white silence.

Skye covered her ears with her hands. She wanted to go home. She wanted her mom to put her arms around her and tell her everything was going to be all right, that it had all been a bad dream. She wanted her mom to love her again.

Skye's tears came then, and she cried, cried until she was dry, until she hadn't the strength to even whimper. She fell back against the pillows and gazed numbly up at the cracked and pitted ceiling. She had no home. She had no mother, not anymore. There were no loving arms to hold her, no soft comforting voice telling her everything was going to be all right.

Chance was all she had. She had to hold on to him; she had to make him love her the way her mother had not, so much he would never leave her behind.

She would, she promised herself. Somehow, she would.

23

True to her promise to herself, Skye worked on making certain Chance wouldn't leave her. She kept their room perfectly clean. She drew pictures and made cards for him. When he got home at night she was happy instead of sad. She let him watch what he wanted on TV. She didn't complain, make demands or pester him.

She hadn't even reminded him that today was her birthday.

He had remembered, anyway. That morning, before he had left for work, he had wished her happy birthday and promised to be home early today with a surprise.

Skye climbed out of the bathtub, dried off, then dressed, slipping into her best-fitting, least ragged pair of blue jeans and her newest sweater. She smiled. He had remembered. That must mean he was starting to like having her around, it must.

Maybe it even meant he was starting to love her.

Skye gazed at herself in the cloudy mirror, pushing away the thoughts of her mother and of birthdays past that pressed at her. Pushing away memories of presents and cake and of being made to feel like a princess. Those memories only made her sad, and she didn't want to be sad. Not today.

Maybe not ever again. And especially not around Chance. She forced a bright smile. She hardly ever cried anymore, and never when he was around. And she always tried her hardest not to cling.

That was the hardest part, because she was still afraid. Sometimes she woke up in the middle of the night, heart pounding, drenched with sweat, certain that she was alone, that Chance had run away and left her behind.

She didn't confide her fears in him, she hadn't told him about the nightmares she'd been having. She didn't want him to know. So, when she awakened that way, she would lie as still and as quiet as she could, tuning into the darkness and listening for his breathing. And when she finally heard it, she would know that everything was okay.

And the nights she couldn't hear it, she lay awake, terrified, wondering what she should do, lay awake until morning or until exhaustion took her against her will.

Skye began combing her wet hair. Badly in need of a cut, it was snarled and took several minutes to completely comb through. Finally done, she braided it into a single braid down her back and fastened it with a rubber band.

A moment later, she heard Chance call her name. Skye flew out of the bathroom and out to meet him, stopping a moment before she threw her arms around his waist. She beamed up at him instead. "You made it home early. Just like you said."

"Of course I did. After all, it's a special day." He reached into his coat pocket and pulled out a wrapped package. "Happy birthday, Skye."

"Oh, Chance!" She hugged him hard. "Thank you, thank you!"

He laughed and freed himself. "Hey, not so fast. You haven't even opened it yet. And I warn you, it isn't much."

"It doesn't matter." She snatched the present, wrapped in last Sunday's funny papers, and held it to her chest. "I can't believe you got me something. I can't believe you remembered today was my birthday."

He shook his head. "What kind of buddy would I be if I forgot your birthday or didn't get you a present? Well, aren't you going to open it?"

She laughed and darted across to the bed, then plopped onto it. She should savor opening it, she knew. Take her time. Instead, she tore the paper away greedily, squealing with delight when she saw what was underneath—a box of pastels.

"The lady said they're really good ones," Chance murmured. "Professional quality."

Tears pricked Skye's eyes, and she reverently lifted the lid off the box. Setting it aside, she trailed her finger over the row of neatly wrapped square sticks.

"They're beautiful," she said, her voice thick. "I've always wanted some of these. Mom always...she always said I was too young."

"Not anymore. Hey, you're thirteen now." He sat beside her. "Try one."

She selected a pink, a delicious rose hue, and rubbed the tip along the back of her hand. It was soft, velvety and vibrant. A world different than the cheap ones she usually worked with, ones that were hard and gritty, their color chalky and dull.

She lifted her gaze to Chance's, a tear spilling over and rolling down her cheek. "Thank you. I love them."

He caught the tear with his thumb and shook his head. "Don't go getting mushy on me. Remember your reputation, you're a tough-as-nails tomboy. Besides, we've got a party to go to."

"A party?" She sat up straighter, excited. "Whose party? Where?"

"Yours, dope. And you'll know where when we get there." He ruffled her hair, then caught her hands and pulled her to her feet. "Come on."

First he took her to the Pizza Hut nearby and told her to order whatever she wanted. She chose the biggest pizza on the menu, loaded with all her favorite toppings. When they had stuffed themselves, they walked down the block to the arcade. She had eyed it dozens of times, but they'd never had the money to blow on video games and pinball.

Chance found the money tonight. They played every

game, from Pac Man and Asteroids to air hockey and Foosball.

Finally, exhausted, they walked back to the motel. There, Chance had one more surprise for her. A Hostess Ho-Ho that he covered with thirteen candles. It looked like a torch when they were all lit.

Skye made a wish and blew them all out. Chance didn't ask her what she had wished for, though she suspected he knew.

She wanted what she used to have. She wanted her mother to love her.

Thinking of her mother, tears flooded her eyes. She looked away, feeling like an ungrateful brat. "I'm sorry," she whispered.

"For what?"

"This." She sniffled, then giggled, though the sound broke on a sob. "I don't know why I'm crying, this has been the best night of my life."

"I'm glad you liked it, kid. I know it's been..." He cleared his throat. "I wanted you to have a good birthday."

"I did, Chance." She rested her head against his shoulder. "I really did."

"So how does it feel to be a big thirteen-year-old now?"

She thought about it for a moment. So much had happened in the past months, she didn't know if she was different, older and more mature, or if it was just her life, not her, that had changed.

Finally, she shook her head. "I don't think I'm any different. Just the same old Skye."

He chuckled. "Good. 'Cause I think the same old Skye is kind of nice."

She rested her head on his shoulder, happy and tired and full. She yawned. "Chance?"

"Hmm?"

"You're the best friend I ever had."

He was quiet for a moment. Then he bent and planted a

light kiss on the top of her head. "Thanks, kid. That means a lot to me."

Skye didn't realize until much later, as she lay awake, unable to sleep for her jumbled thoughts, that he hadn't told her she was his best friend. In fact, that he hadn't said he liked her at all.

24

Claire stood atop the Fort Pitt Bridge, the lights of Pittsburgh in the distance, the water of the Ohio River below.

She gazed at the dark, swirling water, despondent. Thirteen years ago today she had held her baby daughter in her arms for the first time. She had gazed at the pink-and-white bundle, her tiny Grace, and had known real love for the first time.

That day, that moment, had been the happiest of her life. And this was the most bleak.

Claire lifted her face to the midnight sky, cold, black and starless. The wind caught her hair, whipping it around her head; it tore at her thin coat. Her face and hands burned from the cold, she ached with fatigue.

A fitting night to die, she thought. Cold and ugly and black. Even the stars had not come out to say goodbye.

Tears choked her. Claire breathed deeply, forcing air into her lungs, breathing an effort. Thirteen years ago she had made a promise to her baby daughter, she had promised to cherish and protect her, to shield her from harm. Motherhood had been the only thing she had done right; Grace had been the only thing worth living for.

But even that, she hadn't done right. She hadn't protected her daughter. She hadn't loved her enough. As usual, she had made one mistake after another. She had failed.

And now her daughter was lost.

A sob rose to Claire's throat, though she didn't release it. No one could hear her, there was no reason not to cry. But she found herself pathetic enough without her tears; in a way, holding back her grief was the only thing she had left to hold on to.

That and the gems. Claire clutched the pouch to her chest, against her thundering heart, thinking of the past, desperate months. She had gone from one small town to another, showing Skye's picture, asking anyone and everyone if they had seen her daughter. If they had seen Chance.

Claire believed they might be together, but they could be anywhere. Or, they could be nowhere.

For no one had seen them. In the three and a half months she had been searching, she'd had not one lead. Not one glimmer of hope. It was as if Skye and Chance had fallen off the face of the earth.

She knew Pierce didn't have her because she had called Dorothy, who, of course, thought that mother and daughter were still together. Pierce had made no more progress than she. For that, at least, she could be grateful.

But she wasn't. Because now she lived with another, worse fear—that her baby, her sweet Skye, was dead.

Pain took Claire's breath. Though she struggled with the fear, working to deny it, what could she think? Her visions had stopped. Her nightmares. The monstrous bird no longer stalked her or her daughter; she no longer heard her daughter's cries for help in her head.

She saw only blackness now. A yawning dark pit of nothingness.

Claire stepped up to the guardrail, eyeing the catwalk on the other side. She curved her fingers around the railing, readying herself. She would never find her daughter. She had accepted that. She had no money, no way to finance a search.

She couldn't go on living without searching. She couldn't go on without hope.

Claire gazed down at the water again, her vision blurring. Death would be sweet. Perhaps in death, she could continue her search. Perhaps as spirit she could find her daughter and watch over her. Protect and cherish her as she had promised all those years ago.

Or perhaps, like now, there would be nothing. Just the end. Just a cold, black nothing.

Claire took the pouch from around her neck and opened it. She had allowed the gems, the premonitions and feelings she'd had while holding them, to keep her going for months now. Skye needed the gems, she had told herself. The gems would someday play a part in saving her daughter's life.

And if the jewels were to help Skye, she and Skye would be together again. She had grasped on to that hope like a lifeline, clutching at it until her heart had been numb.

The time had come to let go.

Claire climbed over the guardrail and onto the narrow ledge beyond. She curved an arm around the railing for support and dipped her hand into the pouch. She planned to drop the stones, one by one, into the water. And when they were gone, she would follow.

She curled her fingers into the stones. As they had felt all those years ago, they were both hot and cold against her fingers, smooth and sharp, vibrating with a kind of pure energy.

A hysterical laugh bubbled to her lips. Ironic, those visions she'd had of icy water and of someone being sucked under for the final time—that someone had been her, all along she had been previewing her own death.

She closed her eyes and imagined it—the cold, the black, her lungs burning. Her desperate, instinctive fight to save herself.

Then, finally, the sweet oblivion.

Happy birthday, Grace. I love you.

Forgive me.

She scooped up the stones, making a fist around them. She held them out over the water. As she began to open her hand an image came upon her, so suddenly and vividly it took her breath.

She saw a man. And a young boy. Unspeakable horrors. Claire's knees buckled. She crumpled, grabbing on to the concrete support, hanging on for dear life. *Trees were all around. She sensed rather than saw a place, dark and fecund...cramped. She heard a cry of pain. A plea, helpless and terrified, for help.*

Hurry. She had to hurry. His time was running out.

The visions moved through her head, hammering at her, one after another. With the images came pain, real and gut-wrenching, ripping her wide, leaving her panting.

And then, as suddenly as they had come upon her, they were gone. She opened her eyes, realizing she was crying, her cheek pressed to the metal railing, her fist still closed around the gems.

She drew a ragged breath. This was another's child. One she recognized. She had seen his sweet face—on TV and the front page of the *Post-Gazette*, on flyers taped in storefront windows and stapled to trees and telephone poles.

And he was alive. For now.

Claire dragged herself to her feet. He needed her.

It would be enough.

25

Being thirteen did change Skye. In the weeks and months that had passed since her birthday, her contentment of that night had disappeared, replaced by a restlessness she'd never experienced before. She longed for something she couldn't name and was frustrated to the point of tears that she couldn't have it. She found herself happy one moment and sobbing the next, found herself gazing into the mirror alternately admiring her looks and despairing over them.

And she found herself wishing Chance would see how grown-up she had become, wishing he would start treating her like a real girl, instead of a pesky little kid or a baby who needed to be protected.

Suddenly, being Chance's best friend wasn't enough. Drawing and watching TV and waiting all day for him to come home wasn't enough. Not anymore.

Skye stood at the door of the trailer Chance had rented for them to live in, gazing out at the bright spring day. March had come in like a lion and, true to the old saying, was going out like a lamb. The six inches of snow they'd gotten only a week ago had already melted. Sunshine spilled through the trailer's tiny windows, thrown open to let in the warm breeze, a balmy sixty-eight degrees.

The town of Boyton, Illinois was, no doubt, kicking up its heels and celebrating the end of winter, Skye thought bitterly, gazing out at the perfect day. Of course, she wouldn't know. Because she was trapped inside this stupid, gray trailer.

Chance had found steady work at a small grocery store in town. The manager had directed him to a friend who had a furnished trailer for rent; the same man had had a car for sale, a fifteen-year-old Chevy Impala. The guy had taken two hundred dollars for it. Now they had wheels.

Skye knew Chance found it liberating, but it hadn't changed her life one bit. She was still stuck inside this ugly box, looking out at the rest of the world.

Skye began to pace. Frustrated. Bored. Angry with Chance for making her stay locked up all the time, furious with her mother for leaving her behind.

She wanted to go out. She was sick and tired of being alone. Of being trapped inside, like a butterfly in a jar.

It wasn't fair. Chance got to go out. Chance got to see people, and not just at work, either. Twice in the past week he had gone out with friends after punching out for the day. She had been alone even longer on those days; she had sat and wondered who he was with, and wishing she was out too. She had been angry. And jealous.

Skye stopped in front of the open door and gazed out through the screen, locked tight. It wasn't fair, she thought again. And she was sick of it.

But Chance refused to be reasonable. He didn't see how much more grown-up she was than when they had left Marvel's. She let out her breath in an angry huff. He treated her like a little baby. Ruffling her hair. Chucking her on the chin. Calling her kid and pest.

Why couldn't he see how grown-up she was? Why?

Skye resumed pacing. She saw him as an adult, and he wasn't *that* much older than she was. He was only eighteen, for Pete's sake. There was only five years between them.

His image filled her head and she ached, deep inside, ached in a strange way, one she didn't understand. She only knew she wanted him to see her as a grown-up. As a real girl, not a pesky little kid.

Screw it, she decided defiantly. Chance wasn't her boss. He wasn't her parent or even her brother. And if she wanted to go out, she would.

Grabbing her windbreaker and the key to the trailer's front door, she headed outside.

Skye's first foray into the great unknown went well. So well, in fact, she made it a daily ritual. Every morning, as soon as Chance left for work, she gathered together her art supplies, a jacket and something to snack on, and off she went.

Freedom was delicious. Heady and exciting. She felt alive again, for the first time in as long as she could remember. Everything felt new, too. Special and bright and wondrous. She imagined that she felt the way a baby might, seeing and exploring things for the first time.

Most days, like today, she took her sketch pad to the park, found a pretty spot and sat and drew for a while. After that, she just wandered. She'd had a few close calls; one with a mother in the park, one with a clerk at the corner drugstore where she had stopped in to buy a Coke. Both times she had come up with a neat and convincing lie for why she wasn't in school.

Chance she hadn't had to lie to. He didn't suspect a thing.

Skye stood, dusted off the seat of her jeans and tucked her tablet under her arm. Today it was too pretty to sit and draw; today she felt like exploring.

She did just that, following paths she hadn't noticed before, going deeper into the park, farther away from the most populated areas. As she crossed over an old stone bridge, she noticed a group of teenagers below. It looked as if they were just hanging out, and as Skye gazed down at them, one of the boys looked up. He was cute, really cute. Their eyes met. He smiled. Her heart did a funny little something, like a somersault, and she caught her breath. She sort of smiled back—she was so flustered, she wasn't quite sure what she did—then hurried over the bridge.

The boy was waiting for her. She made a sound of surprise and stopped in her tracks, uncertain what to do.

"Hi." He smiled and took a step toward her. "I saw you up on the bridge, so I decided to come meet you."

"Oh." She folded her arms across her chest. "Hello."

"My name's Kevin. My friends call me Kev."

She swallowed hard. "I'm Skye."

"And I'll bet your friends call you Skye."

She laughed, relaxing a little. "You guessed right."

"You going someplace?"

"Not really." She shrugged. "I'm just hanging out."

"Me, too." He gestured toward the path. "You wanna walk?"

"Together?"

"Yeah." He grinned. "Together."

"Okay."

They started off. "I haven't seen you around before," he said. "You new in town?"

She glanced at him, then away. *He was so cute.* "I've been around awhile. I live with my brother. He works at Taylor's grocery."

"What about your parents?"

She hesitated a moment, searching for the right answer, then lifted her shoulders. "They're…gone."

"Hey, that's cool. I'm on my own, too. A whole bunch of us are."

Skye didn't know whether to believe him or not. And she wasn't sure why he was being so nice to her. Boys usually weren't.

"How come you're not in school?"

She stiffened. "Why aren't you?"

He laughed and held up his hands, palms out. "Hey, be easy. You don't see me in school, do you? In my opinion, it's a total waste. Why don't we sit over there?" He pointed toward a bench under a big maple tree. The tree was only beginning to leaf out and as they sat beneath it, the sun filtered through the branches, warming them.

She unzipped her jacket. "It sure is a pretty day."

"Sure is."

She felt his gaze on her and embarrassed, laced her fingers together and looked at her toes. "I hate the snow. Too cold."

"It was pretty gruesome this year." He dug in his jacket pocket and pulled out a pack of Marlboros. "Smoke?" She shook her head and he lit one for himself. He inhaled, then blew out a long stream of smoke and looked at her. "How old are you, Skye?"

"Fifteen." She cleared her throat, her cheeks heating at her lie. "I just turned in November."

"No kidding? I just turned seventeen in November. What date's yours? Birthday, I mean."

"The sixth."

"Mine, too." He put his arm around her shoulders. "We must be soul mates or something."

Soul mates. She liked the way that sounded. She liked the way he looked her in the eye and smiled when he talked to her. As if he thought she was special and mature, not some pesky little kid.

And she liked the way he put his arm around her shoulders, though it made her feel weird—warm and tingly and sort of nervous, but in a good way.

He laughed again and flipped his half-smoked cigarette into a puddle. "Come on." He caught her hand and stood, bringing her to her feet with him. "I want to show you something."

She held back, nervous. "What?"

"It's a surprise, but you'll really like it. I promise."

"I don't know, I...I need to be home soon."

"Aw...come on, Skye. Don't be a wimp." He tugged on her hand again and flashed her a breath-stealing smile. "It won't take long."

Skye thought of Chance. He would not like her talking to Kevin this way. And he certainly wouldn't have approved of Kevin's arm around her, though it had been perfectly okay.

Chance wouldn't approve? she thought. Chance wasn't her father; it was none of his business what she did. She had absolutely no reason to feel guilty. He just didn't want her to have any fun at all.

She pushed the guilt away, and smiled up at Kevin. "Okay, but I really do have to be back home in an hour."

It turned out that what Kevin wanted to show her was a sort of home for runaways, a big old Victorian house on the outskirts of town. Kevin told her that it had been abandoned for years, and insisted that if she would look past the rotting floor and crumbling walls, she would see that it was a really cool place.

Skye decided he was right. But it wasn't the house itself that she thought was neat, it was the other kids there. Kevin introduced her around, telling everyone she was fifteen. The group was pretty well split between boys and girls, and everybody was nice to her, really nice. They didn't question her age or her being there; in fact, she had never felt so welcome before. She liked the feeling. She liked it a lot.

When she had to leave to go home, Kevin walked her part of the way. He wanted to walk her the whole way, but Skye was afraid that somehow Chance would find out. And that was the last thing she wanted. If Chance found out about Kevin or her other new friends, he would keep her from seeing them again.

And she wanted to see them again. Especially Kevin.

"I'll go on from here," Skye said, stopping at the bridge where they had met. "It's not far."

"Are you sure? I don't mind walking you the rest of the way."

"No. I don't want to take the chance that my brother... He's a little overprotective."

"That's cool." Kevin caught her hand. "Will you come by tomorrow?"

"I don't know. I—"

"Please?" He curved his fingers snugly around hers. "Pretty please?"

She caved. "All right, if you really want me to."

"I do." He leaned closer, so close she saw the flecks of gold in his brown eyes. "You sure are pretty."

She blushed and averted her gaze, flustered by his words and by the way he was looking at her. "I'm not," she murmured.

"You are. Skye?" She returned her gaze to his, her heart stopping at the look in his eyes. "If I tried to kiss you, would you let me?"

Skye stared up at him. She wanted to say yes, wanted to so badly she ached, but she couldn't find her voice. Finally, afraid he would change his mind, she simply nodded.

With a small laugh, Kevin kissed her. His lips brushed lightly against hers, once, then twice. Skye thought she had died and gone to heaven.

"I'll see you tomorrow, right?"

Skye blinked, embarrassed as she realized she had been standing there frozen, her eyes closed, lips still slightly parted.

She took a step backward, mortified. "Right. Tomorrow."

"Great!" He backed away, laughing. "See you then, Skye."

She watched him jog off, then with a giggle of pure delight, hugged herself. She had friends, she realized. She had a *boyfriend*. A real boyfriend who had held her hand and kissed her.

Feeling as if she had wings on her feet, she raced back to the trailer.

26

From that day on, Skye spent every minute she could with her new friends. They laughed and talked; they went to the park and the mall and just hung out at The House, as they called the old Victorian. The other kids had discovered her ability to draw, and they had all begged her to draw them. Skye had been happy to comply; their interest in her art made her feel special.

But the best thing about the days spent with her friends was being with Kevin. He paid more attention to her than to anyone else. Most of the time he was either holding her hand or had his arm around her, and even when one of the other guys wanted him to go do something with them, he stayed with her. Skye had caught some of the other girls looking at her, their expressions strange; but Skye decided they were just trying to figure out the same thing she was—what he saw in her. Kevin was way too cute to be interested in her, but he acted as if he was, anyway.

She decided she must be about the luckiest girl in the whole world.

It hadn't taken Skye long to realize how her friends got by—they panhandled and shoplifted, and everyone shared with everyone else. Like a big family.

At first, knowing they stole things had made Skye uncomfortable, as did their smoking and drinking. Then she figured that as long as she wasn't actually doing that stuff herself, she wasn't doing anything wrong.

In truth, the way her friends lived seemed exciting to Skye, a lot more exciting than being cooped up alone all day, a lot more enjoyable than doing without until she and Chance scraped up enough money to buy whatever it was they needed.

But what she envied even more about her friends' lives was that no one ordered them around, telling them what they could or couldn't do. No one treated them the way Chance treated her, like a baby, like a stupid little pest who couldn't take care of herself.

Most days, she didn't even want to return to the trailer. Several times she had fantasized about not going back and had waited until the last possible second to leave The House, then had hurried home, arriving only moments before Chance.

He seemed to have noticed nothing out of the ordinary about her behavior. In fact, Skye had begun to believe he never looked at her at all.

But then, he was probably too busy looking at and thinking about that other girl, Skye thought, scowling into the bathroom mirror. That Cindy he worked with. Chance had told Skye about her. She was a checker at the grocery, a beautiful blonde, he had said. A couple of times, they had gone out for a quick beer together after work.

Skye brushed her teeth, furiously wielding the brush, thinking of what Chance had said about the other girl. Skye rinsed and spit, then rinsed again. That done, she reached for a towel, then stopped and turned back to the mirror. She studied her face. Oval-shaped, a nice nose and a mouth that was a bit too big; cheekbones that could be higher.

She leaned closer to the mirror. Her eyes were her best feature—bright blue, surrounded by dark lashes. Lashes that matched her eyebrows and hair.

She pushed her hair away from her face, tilting her head this way, then that. She wasn't pretty, not the way *Cindy* must be, but she wasn't gross, either. She wasn't ugly.

She let her hair fall, her frown deepening. Why didn't

Chance like her? Why didn't he think she was…beautiful? Like that Cindy girl?

She knew he didn't, because of the way he treated her, like a stupid kid. She knew it, too, by the way he looked at her, not with admiration or awe or even as if she was a girl, but with a kind of humor. A kind of *tolerance*.

She bristled, thinking of it. Kevin thought she was pretty. He thought she was sexy. Kissable. So why didn't Chance?

Skye closed the bathroom door and faced the long, narrow mirror attached to its back. She peeled off her nightshirt, then stared at herself. Stared hard.

Her breasts were depressingly small—no more than two tiny mounds tipped with pink. She touched them lightly and her nipples puckered up, tight and sensitive, the way they did when she was cold. She made a sound of surprise and ran her fingers over the sensitive pebbles again, liking the feeling, being almost superaware of them.

Cheeks burning, she moved her hand lower, across her rib cage—she was so thin she could count each rib—then lower still, to her waist. She drew her eyebrows together, studying her body. Was it her imagination or was her waist smaller than it had been? It seemed to dip in, her hips to flare out. She fitted her hands at each side of her waist, uncertain, then turned to the side, then the back, straining to see her reflection over her shoulder.

Her hips definitely flared, she thought, surprised, pleased. They hadn't done that before; she was certain of it. She had always been as straight and narrow as a board.

She faced the mirror again, hesitated a moment, then eased her underpants over her hips and down, then stepped out of them. Standing naked in front of the mirror made her feel funny, guilty and nervous. She had seen herself naked, of course, but she had never…deliberately looked at herself this way. And she had never stopped to wonder what others thought about her body or about how she looked compared to other girls. In truth, she had never really cared—not about how she looked, or about what others thought.

Now she did. Now she ached for people to think she was pretty. To think she was…sexy. Like the girls in the magazines and on TV.

Skye lowered her gaze, her cheeks burning. She was growing hair *there*. She wasn't sure how she felt about it; she knew it was part of becoming a woman, but it made her feel…weird. And it looked strange, kind of gross.

She touched herself there, then jerked her hand away, mortified. Good little girls didn't touch themselves, not deliberately. Her mother had told her that.

But her mother was gone. And she wasn't a little girl anymore.

Defiantly, she touched herself again, keeping her eyes fixed on her face in the mirror. She trailed her fingers across the surface of the V between her legs, over the sprinkling of crisp hair.

Goose bumps raced up her torso; her nipples puckered, aching. Skye caught her breath at the sensations. She touched herself again, her head filling with thoughts of Kevin, of his lips on hers, his body pressed close, so close against hers.

She closed her eyes and slipped her fingers between her thighs, stroking herself more. She was slick. And warm. Her heart began to pound; her breath quickened.

Skye moved her fingers back and forth. Suddenly, it wasn't Kevin she pictured in her head. It was Chance. Chance's hands. Chance's mouth. A sound escaped her, low and wrenching, as if she hurt. But she didn't hurt. She ached, in a new way, in a way that at once delighted and terrified her. In a way that felt both wrong and right.

She moaned and dropped to her knees, doubling over.

Stars exploded in her head.

Skye realized she was crying. She realized, too, what she had done to herself. What had happened. She curved her arms around her middle and squeezed her eyes shut, wishing for her mother, feeling young and scared and alone. More alone than she had ever felt.

Skye pressed her face closer against her knees. Why was this happening to her? Why was she changing? She didn't want to change; she didn't want to think about Chance in *that* way.

She wanted to go back. To the way she had been before her mother had gone away, to the way she had been the night of her thirteenth birthday. She had been so happy that night. Everything had seemed so right.

Now everything felt wrong. Now nothing seemed to fit.

Skye squeezed her eyes shut tighter, longing to be held and loved, the way her mother had once held and loved her. She longed for someone to assure her everything was going to be all right, that *she* was going to be all right.

Maybe if she wished hard enough, Skye thought, hurting, maybe then she could go back to the way she had been. To before, when Chance had been her best friend and everything had been good between them, to the time when everything had felt right.

But even as she wished as hard as she could, Skye knew that Chance could never be her best friend again. Today her feelings about herself and him had changed forever.

She and Chance could never go back.

27

That night, Chance didn't come home alone. He brought that Cindy girl home with him.

Skye glared at the other girl, hating her on sight. She had long, curly blond hair, blue eyes and a pretty, pink mouth. And breasts. Serious ones. Ones that made what Skye had look like anthills.

Skye narrowed her eyes and folded her arms across her embarrassingly small chest. At least *she* didn't laugh like a hyena, Skye thought. At least *she* didn't toss her head when she talked like some sort of demented, bubbleheaded Barbie doll.

Chance introduced Skye as his kid sister. As if that wasn't bad enough, he told her to take a couple slices of pizza and get lost.

Kid sister! Skye fumed silently. *Get lost?* She faced him, angrily jutting out her chin. "What if I don't want to? You can't make me."

Cindy giggled; Chance's mouth dropped. "What did you say?"

"I said, you can't make me."

"Oh yes, I can. Don't push me, Skye." He lowered his voice and leaned toward her, not stopping until they were nose to nose. "I would hate to embarrass you by *spanking* you in front of Cindy. But I will. Now, I said to get lost."

Furious, Skye spun away from him. She stomped across to the kitchen, got her pizza and a drink, the entire time slamming and flinging and generally being as loud and obnoxious as she could be.

Chance whispered something to Cindy, who giggled. Skye gritted her teeth and marched to the bedroom, slamming the door shut behind her.

She flopped onto the bed and gulped down her pizza. It wasn't fair. How could he bring that hyena-girl home with him? How? This was her home, and she didn't want that girl here. Didn't she have any say about anything at all?

Skye decided she hated Chance. Despised him. The only one she hated more was that stupid girl.

Skye went to the door, cracked it open and peeked out, expecting to see the two eating and talking. Instead, they were cuddled up together on the couch, nearly in each other's lap. They were talking softly and nuzzling each other.

Then, as she watched, Chance kissed Cindy. Not the way Kevin had kissed her, but deeply, with his whole mouth. Indeed, it was as if he was kissing her with his whole body.

Skye swallowed hard, unable to tear her gaze away. Chance tangled his hand in Cindy's hair, cupping the back of her head, bending her backward, pressed tightly to her. They broke apart, then came together. Again and again.

It was just as she had fantasized today, Skye realized, her cheeks hot. Only it wasn't *her* Chance was kissing. It wasn't *her* Chance was touching.

Skye squeezed her hands so tightly into fists that her short nails bit into her palms. She shook her head, telling herself to make a sound to break them apart, or to lower her eyes, but she couldn't find her voice, she couldn't force her gaze away.

Chance moved his hands to Cindy's ample chest. He cupped and stroked; with a husky murmur of satisfaction Cindy eased out of his grasp and yanked her short sweater over her head.

Her bra was pink and lacy; her breasts spilled slightly over the top. Skye folded her arms across her own chest, aching to look like Cindy, to have a pretty pink bra and breasts that spilled over it.

Chance touched Cindy's breasts, then cupped them, whispering something Skye couldn't make out. They kissed again. And again.

Then he kissed *them.*

Breathing hard, fighting tears, Skye jerked her gaze away. She hated Cindy, Skye decided. She hated her completely. She wished she were dead.

And she wasn't going to put up with this a minute longer.

Skye flounced out of the bedroom. The couple sprang apart, Cindy with a cry of embarrassment. The girl grabbed her sweater and clutched it to her chest.

"Oh, excuse me," Skye said, snickering. "Did I interrupt something?"

"Dammit, Skye!" Chance jumped to his feet, his face red, "I told you to go to the bedroom. Now, get out of here."

She glared at him. "And I told you, I don't have to if I don't want to."

"You are such a brat. I swear, Skye, if you don't get lost I'm going to beat you!"

"Yeah, right. I'm really scared."

Cindy yanked on her sweater and stood. "Maybe I should go."

"No, Cindy. Wait." He caught the girl's hand. "Let me talk to—"

"Yes, why don't you leave," Skye interrupted him, sending the other girl a venomous look. "I don't want you here."

"Shut up, Skye."

He took a menacing step toward her; Skye held her ground, jerking her chin up. "Let her go. She's just a slut."

Cindy gasped. The veins in Chance's neck bulged.

"I don't have to take this." Cindy grabbed her purse and started for the door.

"Cindy, wait." Chance hurried after her. "I'm sorry.

She's only a kid and I...I don't know what's gotten into her. She's not usually like this. I don't—''

"Forget it." Cindy flung the purse over her shoulder. "I'm not going to stick around and take that from some snot-nosed kid. I'm out of here."

"I'm not a snot-nosed kid!" Skye called after the girl, pleased with herself, certain the hyena-girl wouldn't be back. She brushed her hands together. Good riddance to bad rubbish.

Skye's satisfaction was short-lived. Chance came back inside, slamming the trailer door behind him, his expression murderous. "Thanks a lot!" he shouted, advancing on her, hands curled into fists. "I was having a good time. Thanks for blowing it for me."

"Well, I wasn't having a good time." Skye hiked up her chin. "So I got rid of her."

"She'll probably never talk to me again, and it's all because you decided to become the kid-sister-from-hell." He stopped before her. "I really liked her."

Skye snorted with contempt. "What *exactly* did you like about her? Her big boobs? Or her bottle-blond hair?" She sniffed. "I bet those boobs are as phony as her hair."

Chance stared at her as if she had sprouted horns. He shook his head. "What's gotten into you? Where did you learn to talk like that?"

"Wouldn't you like to know?"

"I'm going to spank you, you little brat."

Skye didn't give him the chance. She launched herself at him, wrapped her arms around his neck and kissed him hard, trying to emulate the way he had kissed Cindy.

Chance stumbled backward, his hands closing around her upper arms, pushing her away. "Skye, what the—''

"I can kiss, too," she murmured. "I'm a girl." She tightened her arms and tried to kiss him again.

He tore himself free, ripping her arms from around his neck. He wiped the back of his hand across his mouth, his expression disgusted. "You're just a kid. How could you…that's…gross. Don't ever do that again. Ever."

Skye stared at him, realizing what she had done, realizing how he had reacted, his brutal rejection sinking in completely.

She took a step backward, going hot, then icy, clammy cold. She disgusted him. He thought kissing her was gross. He thought she was a gross, disgusting little kid.

"I hate you," she said. "I hate you!"

Bursting into tears, she turned and raced to the bedroom, closed and locked the door, then flung herself across the bed.

She heard him swear. A moment later the trailer's front door slammed shut so hard the trailer rocked.

28

The next morning Chance left for work without saying goodbye to Skye. He didn't know what to say to her, and even if he had, he didn't trust himself to actually look her in the eye and speak to her. He couldn't stop thinking about what had transpired the night before—about the horrible way she had acted, the things she had said to Cindy, then to him, but most of all, he couldn't stop thinking about the way she had flung herself against him and kissed him.

He shuddered, remembering. What had she been thinking? Holy shit, she was just a kid. She shouldn't even be thinking about those kind of things, let alone…let alone acting on them.

He sliced open a case of canned soup, then set it on a loading cart. He frowned and split open another case. She had completely surprised him. Never in his wildest dreams had he thought about kissing her. It wasn't right. She was like his sister. His kid sister.

Chance let out a long, frustrated breath. His response had hurt her feelings, but what had she expected? Jesus, it *was* gross. He couldn't have Skye kissing him. He couldn't have her thinking *that* kind of stuff about him. Surely last night had been a freakish, one-time thing. She had seen him and Cindy making out, she had been jealous and had wanted him to pay attention to her instead. She had thought she had to do *that* to get his attention.

He never should have sent her to her room. He should have let her hang out with him and Cindy. After all, the poor kid had been alone all day. If he'd let her hang out with them a while, she wouldn't have felt left out and Cindy would still be talking to him.

He stacked another case on the cart, slamming it down so hard the cans shook. Damn but he had been having a good time. Until Skye had pulled her little-sister-from-hell routine, anyway.

Cindy. Damn. She had been teasing him for weeks now, flirting, then backing off, coming on to him again, then backing off again.

He had been horny enough to bust. So, when she had suggested coming over to his place, he hadn't thought about anything but getting his hands on her. And those few minutes when he'd actually had his hands on her had been pure bliss.

Of course, now Cindy thought he was a creep-geek and refused to even speak to him. He might as well live in the past, because he was damn sure the future didn't hold another taste of Cindy Ferguson's chest.

Just fucking great.

Chance made a sound of disgust and checked his watch. *Noon, finally.* He tossed down the box cutter and headed for the time clock. He would grab a sandwich from the deli department, then head home to check on Skye. Just to make sure she was okay. Just to make sure she didn't do anything dumb.

And if he could find the right words and a way to get her to listen to him, he would apologize for hurting her feelings, then firmly explain the facts of life to her.

They didn't have *that* kind of a relationship. They never would. Period.

He punched out, grabbed a couple of turkey sandwiches and a bag of chips from the deli, and headed outside. As per employee regulations, he had parked at the very back of the lot. Taylor's grocery was a small affair, just like the town of Boyton. It was located on the corner of the original downtown square, an area now populated mostly by businesses and transients.

Most of Boyton's families had moved to the eastern edge of town, into one of the several subdivisions that had sprung up in the last five years. A sleek new supermarket, at least three times the size of Taylor's, had sprung up with them. Old man Taylor had hung on by offering specialty and home-made items that a chain supermarket could not. He also made it a point to know the name of everyone who shopped at his store, whether they came in to pick up a quart of milk on the way home from work or to do their weekly shopping.

He was a smart man. Chance had learned a lot about earn-ing customer loyalty from watching him.

Chance started toward his car, unwrapping the first sand-wich and eating as he went. A commotion from across the street caught his attention. Bev, the owner of one of the three dress shops in Boyton, was on the sidewalk in front of her store, waving her fist and shouting something at a group of teenagers.

Chance took another huge bite of his sandwich, polishing it off. Street kids. Runaways. Chance shook his head. Boyton had a collection of them, they came into the grocery store in big groups. When they did, Taylor had everybody quit what they were doing to follow them around, certain they were stealing him blind. Since Chance had started on, however, they'd only caught one kid. He had been trying to make off with a bag of cookies, a package of bologna and a loaf of bread. The bread had been his downfall. It had slipped half-way out from under his coat when he was walking out of the store.

As he watched the commotion, one of the teenage girls swung in his direction. Chance stopped dead. The girl looked like Skye. He shook his head, squinting. But it couldn't be Skye. She was home.

A boy put his arms around the girl and kissed her; and the blood began to thrum in Chance's head. It couldn't be Skye, he told himself again. It wasn't. He jogged the rest of the way to his car, unlocked it and slid inside, tossing his sandwich and chips onto the seat beside him.

It couldn't be. But if it was, he was going to kill her.

He drove toward the group of kids, slowing when he neared them, hitting the breaks when he saw that it was, indeed, Skye. He gripped the steering wheel, fury taking his breath. She wasn't home and safe; she had sneaked out, she was with this group of hoodlums.

And from the way that scummy boy had his hands all over her, she had been doing this for some time.

He would kill the boy first. Then it would be Skye's turn.

Chance reached across the front seat and rolled down the window. "Skye!"

She stopped and turned to him, the color draining from her face.

"Get in the car. Now!"

When she didn't move, he swore. "Get in the goddamned car, Skye! Now!"

The boy with her turned and flipped him the bird. Chance saw red. He slammed the car into Park and hopped out. He flew around the vehicle, fists clenched. The kids scattered, though not too far; they wanted to watch the show.

He grabbed Skye's arm and dragged her toward the car.

"Let me go!" She struggled against his grasp. "You're hurting me."

"Good. You deserve it."

"Hey! Who the fuck are you!" Though the boy shouted the words bravely, he didn't make a move toward Skye.

Chance yanked open the car door and shoved Skye inside, then swung to meet the boy's eyes. "I'm her brother. You see her again and you're a dead man. Got that?"

Not waiting for a response, Chance slid into the car and dropped it into gear, hitting the gas and burning rubber as he did. He flexed his fingers on the steering wheel, struggling to get a grip on his fury. He was so mad he felt as though the top of his head was going to pop off. "How long have you been lying to me, Skye? How long have you been sneaking out of the house to be with those…people?"

She glared at him, then turned her face to the window.

"Dammit, Skye! How long?"

"None of your damn business."

"Son of a bitch. That long?"

The light at the next intersection had changed and he hit the brakes, then looked at her, shaking with the force of his anger. "Well, I hope you had a chance to say goodbye, because you will *not* be seeing them again. You got that, little girl? Starting now, whatever you've been doing is over."

"They're my friends!" she shouted, swiveling to face him. "You can't tell me what to do. You can't tell me where I can go and who I—"

"The hell I can't. I'm telling you." The light changed and he floored the accelerator. "You won't see them again. You'll do what I say. Period."

They drove in angry silence for several minutes. When the entrance to the trailer park was in sight, she turned to him again, hands balled into fists. "I hate you," she said, all but spitting the words at him. "You're a pig. I wish I'd never met you."

"You don't own the market on that one, you little monster." He swung into the trailer park, taking the corner so fast the big old car fishtailed. "I didn't realize how much I liked you as a know-it-all pest until now. I should spank you."

"You'd like that, wouldn't you? You pervert."

"It seems to me, *I'm* not the pervert." They reached their trailer, he whipped into a parking space, spitting up gravel and dust as he did. "Or have you forgotten last night?"

Her eyes filled with tears and she flung herself out of the car, tripping, then righting herself and running for the trailer door. He followed her, catching her before she could get it unlocked. Grabbing her shoulders, he shook her. "Is that boy the one who's been giving you ideas? Is he? He was all over you. Jesus, Skye—''

"At least Kevin thinks I'm pretty." She wrenched her shoulders free. "At least Kevin likes to kiss me."

"I should have known," he said softly, sickened at the thought of that hoodlum touching her. "I kept wondering at things you were saying, the way you were acting... It's those kids. They're turning you into what they are. Thieves and drug-heads. Gutter trash."

"They're not that way! Kevin's not. They're my friends, and I—''

"I forbid you to see him again. Do you hear me?" Chance took a step closer to her, crowding her against the door. "I forbid you to see any of them again."

"What about you and the hyena-girl? How come you can make out, but I can't? Tell me that? The way you two were going at it, I'm surprised you didn't fuck her right there!"

Chance took an involuntary half step backward, stunned. He couldn't believe the words, the thoughts, that were coming out of Skye's mouth. He couldn't believe this was the same sweet girl who had clung to him and cried, the same girl who had called him her best friend.

He gazed at her, remembering the way she had been, an almost wrenching sense of loss moving over him. He wanted that girl back.

He feared she was gone forever.

"First off," he said softly, evenly, "I don't want to hear you talk that way again. Ever. Second, I can date because I'm eighteen. I'm an adult. You're thirteen and—''

"And a kid. Is that what you were going to say?"

"Yeah, I was."

"Well, save it. I'm not a baby!" She swung back to the trailer door, got it unlocked and stumbled inside.

He followed her in, slamming the door behind him. "Then stop acting like one."

"You're not my brother. You can't tell me what to do."

"You're right, I'm not." Chance crossed to stand before her, bending so that they were nose to nose, so angry he shook. "And I don't have to take care of you, either. I'd like a life, too. You think I want to work all day for this?" He gestured around the room. "I have no friends, no social life. I have no future. Not with a rock around my neck. Not when I'm trying to take care of a brat kid who isn't even my sister."

She took a step back, her face white and pinched. "What's that supposed to mean?"

"If you want to be with those kids, with your sleezy-ass boyfriend, go on. If you don't care if you end up in the gutter, then neither do I. But if you go, don't come back. 'Cause I won't be here. You got that? I'm going to get my-self a life."

"I hate you."

"You've said that before, kid. It's getting really old. If you hate me so much, take off. I gotta get back to work. So I can make the money, the money that pays for this dump."

He strode to the door, yanked it open, then turned back to her. She looked lost and alone, standing there, eyes wide and bright with tears, arms curled protectively around her middle. She looked like the little girl he had known and cared about. The one he missed.

He steeled himself against pitying her. He didn't have the energy to feel sorry for her, he was too busy feeling sorry for himself.

He fucking hated this. Everything about this moment and the life they were living.

He met her eyes. "As much as you want to escape, Skye, so do I. Remember that the next time you're thinking what a prick I am."

29

For a long time after Chance left, Skye lay on the bed and gazed dry-eyed up at the ceiling, the things he had said to her running through her head, taunting her.

"I have no future. Not with a rock around my neck. Not when I'm trying to take care of a brat kid who isn't even my sister."

Skye rolled onto her side and drew her knees to her chest, denying the ache, the hurt squeezing so tightly at her that she had to fight to breathe. Chance didn't want her around. He didn't like her; he never had. To him, she was a stupid, pesky little kid. He wished she would leave, then he could be rid of her without having to be the bad guy.

She swiped impatiently at the tears that trickled down her cheeks, angry at herself for being so dumb, angry at him for not wanting her. Angry at her mother for not loving her, for running away and leaving her behind.

A sob rose to her throat; she battled it back. Fine, she thought, sitting up, pressing her fists to her eyes. Chance didn't want her? He wanted a life? Fine. She wouldn't hang around being a pest any longer. She would go where she was wanted.

She jumped out of bed and began throwing her things into her duffel—her clothing and toiletries, her art supplies. She reached for the box of pastels Chance had given her for her birthday, hesitated, then snatched them up defiantly and tossed them into her art bag.

She would forget Chance McCord, the way she had forgotten her mother. She hated them both. She wished she had never even known them. Skye wiped her nose with the back of her hand. She was going to go live with Kevin and the others. That was if, after the way Chance had treated them, they still wanted her around. If they didn't, well, she would figure out what to do then.

She stomped to the door, stopping when she reached it and looking back at the empty trailer. She pictured Chance's face and smile; she remembered the way he had held her when her mother left, recalled the times he had coaxed laughter out of her, remembered how good he had been able to make her feel, just by caring.

Her eyes flooded with fresh tears, and Skye called herself a jerk. He didn't care about her; he never had. He had made that clear today. He had only done those sweet things, had only been kind to her because he felt he'd had to. He wasn't her friend; he didn't even like her.

She was through being a rock around his neck. She was out of here.

Skye flung open the door and darted outside.

And ran smack-dab into Kevin.

He caught her arms to steady her. "Whoa, babe. Where's the fire?"

She dropped her duffel and threw her arms around him. "Kevin! I'm so glad to see you." She started to cry. "I hate my brother. He's such a jerk!"

"An asshole, you mean. A major, fucking asshole."

"Is that why you're here?" She tipped her face up to his. "Because you were worried about me?"

"Sure, babe. That's why." He smiled. "Never fear, Kev baby's here."

"I'm sorry he was so mean to you," she said, wiping her eyes. "I was afraid you wouldn't even talk to me after the way he acted."

"It's no sweat. It's not your fault he's an asshole." He grinned. "Got any brew in there?"

"I think so. Come on in." They went in and Skye got him one of Chance's beers from the fridge, telling him about her and Chance's fight and about her decision to run away.

"He said I was just a rock around his neck," she said, her voice thick. "He wants a life, he said." She brought the heels of her hands to her eyes. "Like I don't? Why can't he see that?"

She looked over her shoulder at Kevin, but he wasn't looking at her—he was studying the room. She wondered if he had even heard her.

"Kevin?"

He met her eyes. "Go on, babe. I'm here."

"So I decided to leave. I've got all my stuff in the duffel." She clasped her hands together, struggling not to cry. "Can I stay with you and the others? Like you said before?"

"Sure." He smiled. "You'll have to pull your own weight, though. Sometimes it's not easy. Sometimes you have to do things that you don't like. That's the cost of being on your own."

"I don't care. I'll do anything to get away from Chance." She swiped at her tears again. "Can we go now? I want to go."

"What's the rush? Big, bad brother's not due home for a while, right?"

"No, but I—"

"Let's chill then." Taking a swig of his beer, Kevin opened one of the kitchen cabinets, sifted through its contents, then went to another and did the same thing. Next he opened the drawer where they kept the silverware, then the storage space below the sink.

Skye frowned, watching him. She didn't like the way he was poking through her and Chance's place. It made her feel funny. She cleared her throat. "I have all my stuff, Kev. It's in my duffel."

"So?" He took another swallow of the beer.

"So…" She stuffed her hands into the front pockets of

her jeans, uncomfortable. "So everything else here belongs to Chance."

He met her eyes. "I thought you were going to pull your weight?"

"I am. I just—"

"So do it. There might be something here we can use."

"But..." Skye bit down on her lower lip. She had never seen Kevin act this way. He was usually sweet and attentive. He was usually so...understanding. So why didn't he see that she didn't like what he was doing? Why didn't he see how uncomfortable he was making her?

He began riffling through the fridge, then the freezer. She cleared her throat again. "I want to go, Kev."

"Hey, now, what's this?" He pulled a roll of bills out of the coffee can they kept in the freezer. "Bingo, baby, we struck it rich."

"Kevin, no!" Skye leaped forward, reaching for the roll. "That's the rent money. Chance needs that."

Laughing, he jerked his arm back, keeping the money from her. "Oh, no you don't. We need it, too."

Skye's heart began to thunder. She was mad at Chance; she hated him. But she didn't want to steal from him; it wasn't right, he needed that money to pay the rent. He had worked hard to earn it.

She shook her head. "Put the money back, Kevin. Chance needs it."

"I thought you hated him."

"I do, but—"

"No buts, babe. I told you, if you're going to be with me, sometimes you'll have to do things you don't like. Remember when I said that?"

She nodded, heart thundering. "I remember, I just...I just don't want to take Chance's money."

"You know what?" Kevin swept his gaze over her, his expression contemptuous. "I don't think you have the guts to be on your own. I don't think you have what it takes."

"I do! Really!" She held a hand out to him, pleading. "But if Chance doesn't have the rent, he'll get kicked out."

"You think I give a shit?" Kevin pocketed the roll. "Come here and let Kev baby make everything okay."

"No." She shook her head. "Not until you put the money back."

He crossed to stand before her. "If you care that much about it, maybe I will."

"Really?" She smiled, relieved. "You will?"

"Maybe." He grinned. "If you're really, really nice to me."

Her smile faded. "What do you mean?"

"You know what I mean." He opened his arms. "Come here."

She wanted to say no, but if she refused to kiss him, he wouldn't put the rent back. If she refused, he might not let her come live with him and the other kids. Mouth dry, heart pounding, Skye took a step toward him. He pulled her the rest of the way, closing his arms tightly around her. A moment later, his mouth descended onto hers, his open so wide she thought he was trying to swallow her.

Skye shuddered, but not with pleasure. She didn't like being in his arms. She didn't like his mouth on hers. It felt wrong, it tasted...sour. She kept thinking about the rent money, about how he didn't care that it belonged to Chance. She kept thinking about the things Chance had said to her, about her behavior, about the kind of people her friends were.

Skye's stomach rose to her throat. She longed to push Kevin away, to run. She tried to relax instead. She closed her eyes and leaned into him, wanting to feel the way she had the other times he'd kissed her. She squeezed her eyes shut, trying to recapture those feelings, the rubbery light-headed feeling, the tingle at her pulse points, the flutter of heat between her legs; she reminded herself that she liked kissing him.

But she didn't like it. She felt sick. And trapped. She couldn't breathe. Curling her hands into fists, she whimpered.

He muttered something she couldn't make out and dropped his hands to her bottom, squeezing and kneading. He had never done that before, and it scared her. She squirmed, but instead of letting her go, he used his grip to draw her more tightly against him, smashing his pelvis against hers.

Then he stuck his tongue into her mouth.

Skye gagged and tried to pull away.

"Relax, babe," he murmured against her mouth. "You're going to like this, I promise." He thrust his tongue into her mouth again.

Skye wrenched her mouth free, feeling as if she might throw up. "Kevin...don't. I don't like that. Let me go."

"Sorry, babe." He wound his hand in her hair and jerked her head back. "But you have a lot to learn, and Kev here is going to teach you."

He caught her again and dragged her against his chest. She fought him, kicking, trying to claw, to bite. Finally, hysterical, she wedged her arms between them and pushed free. When he made a grab for her, she slapped him as hard as she could.

His head jerked backward at the blow. He brought a hand to his cheek, his expression stunned, then furious. "Little bitch. Nobody hits me. Little cunt."

She scrambled for the door. He grabbed a handful of her hair and yanked her backward. She cried out, lost her footing and fell. As she hit the floor, her head snapped back against the linoleum, and she saw stars.

He threw himself on top of her, pinning her beneath him. Catching her hands, he dragged her arms over her head, and began kissing her, his mouth making slobbery paths over her face and neck.

She couldn't breathe. She could hardly move. He rotated

his pelvis against hers and she felt something hard poking at her, then realized in horror that it was his penis.

He was going to rape her.

No! Skye began to struggle in earnest then, thrashing and kicking with her legs, twisting her body, begging him to stop. The more she struggled, the more aggressive he became. He ripped her shirt. His free hand went to one breast, then the other, squeezing and pinching, making grunting sounds as he did. Sobbing, writhing, she begged him to stop. Instead, he shoved his hand into her pants and plunged his fingers into her.

She screamed. Only no sound came.

The dark thing was upon her.

A darkness settled over her, a fear like no other she could remember. Yet, she did remember. It clutched at her, smothering her, stealing her ability to think, to fight. She had been touched like this before; she had struggled like this before.

Her head filled with the memory—though the memory had no face or shape. It was dark. And frightening. The thing, the one that held her wanted to hurt her. To punish her.

It hated her.

She screamed then, the sound ripping past her mouth, shattering the quiet of the trailer. The grip that held her eased, for only a moment, and Skye clawed and scratched and kicked out, her foot hitting soft flesh.

The thing bellowed with pain, cursed, and fell on her again, knocking the breath from her lungs.

"No means no, asshole!"

Suddenly, Skye could breathe. Suddenly, she was free. Sobbing, she scooted backward until she ran into the wall. The trailer door was open, sunshine spilled through, cutting across two figures. Chance, she realized. He had come to save her; he had dragged the thing off her.

Not a dark, shapeless evil, she saw. Kevin. Chance had dragged Kevin off of her.

As she watched, Chance's fist smashed into Kevin's face.

Blood flew; the boy went sailing backward, crashing into the wall, hanging suspended for a moment like a rag doll on strings, then sliding down the wall into a heap.

A moment later Chance was by her side. "Skye, sweetheart, are you all right?" He touched her face and arms, moving his hands gently over her, his expression frantic. "When I came in and saw...him—"

He choked on the words, and Skye began to cry. She put her arms around him. "I was so sca—scared. He forced me...he said...if I wouldn't...then he—"

"It's all right, baby. It's all over."

But it wasn't. Kevin was on his feet. He had a knife. Skye screamed Chance's name.

Her warning came too late. Chance swung around, fists clenched. As if in slow motion, she saw Kevin lunge forward, saw the glitter of light on metal as the blade slashed across Chance's middle.

Chance stumbled backward, a hand to his chest. A scream pierced the quiet; her scream. Blood seeped between Chance's fingers, staining his white T-shirt.

"Nobody flips me off," Kevin said, advancing on Chance again. "Nobody threatens me, got that?"

"No!" Skye leaped to her feet and threw herself at Kevin's back. She clawed and kicked; she pulled his hair and dug her fingers into the side of his neck. The knife slipped from his fingers and clattered to the floor; he swung around, catching her in the shoulder with his fist, knocking her backward.

Both Chance and Kevin dived for the knife. They struggled, rolling together on the floor. Kevin's hand closed around the blade's handle, Chance slammed his elbow on the other boy's right shoulder. Kevin's hand opened, releasing the knife, and Chance lunged for it. A moment later, he rolled to his feet, the weapon clutched in his right hand.

He stood over Kevin, panting. "Now who's the big man? Huh?" Chance kicked the other boy. Skye jerked at the sound of Chance's foot connecting with flesh. Crying out, she brought her hands to her ears.

"She's only thirteen, you son of a bitch. She's just a kid." He kicked Kevin again. Moaning, Kevin rolled onto his side, arms curved protectively around his middle. "I could kill you now, you piece of shit. I swear I could."

She had never seen Chance this way, had never seen anyone this way. His face was white and tight with fury, the veins in his neck bulged, his taut form radiated a frightening energy.

He *could* kill Kevin, she realized, making a sound of terror. He could do it.

He kicked the boy again. This time the force of the blow lifted Kevin off the floor.

Skye stumbled to her feet. She went to Chance and put her arms around him. He tried to shake her off, but she clung to him. "Don't, Chance," she pleaded. "Don't...please. You can't. Let him go. Please...please."

Kevin was blubbering like a baby, begging Chance not to kill him as he inched on his belly toward the door.

As she held Chance, as she begged, she felt the violence slip away from him. The fury. He began to tremble, his teeth to chatter. Turning, he wrapped his arms around her.

Skye buried her face against his chest. It was sticky from his blood; it smelled musky. He had been hurt, because of her. He could have died. What would she have done if she had lost him? What would she have done if he hadn't come home?

"I'm sorry," she murmured over and over. His blood stained her hands, her ripped shirt, her cheek where she pressed it to his heart. "It's my fault, everything...my fault. I didn't mean it. Don't hate me, Chance. Don't leave me. Please...I'll do anything you say. Just don't ever...leave me."

But Chance said nothing at all.

He just held her.

30

Chance sat on the bed and watched Skye while she slept. Her head rested in his lap; she clung to him even in sleep. He touched her cheek and the ugly bruise that marred it. Emotion choked him, and he looked quickly away.

He had scared himself today. When he had seen that son of a bitch on top of her, he had gone nuts. He had wanted to kill the slimy bastard, had wanted to so badly, he had all but tasted it.

If not for Skye stopping him, he would have.

Chance shifted and winced, his hand going to his chest and the bandages that covered the long cut that ran diagonally across it. He probably should have had stitches, but stitches were a luxury they couldn't afford.

Especially now. Kevin had left with their rent money in his pocket.

Skye hadn't remembered until too late.

He had been angry, but not with her. With Kevin, their situation, with himself for not having been able to protect her. Especially that.

Thank God he had come home. Old man Taylor had taken one look at him and told him to punch out and not come back until he got a grip on himself. Chance had tried to reason with his boss, but Taylor had been insistent. Thank God. If he had listened to Chance, if he had relented and allowed him to come back to work...

Chance couldn't think about that now. If he obsessed over

all the things that could have happened, he would drive himself crazy. As it was, he might never sleep again.

Chance brought the heels of his hands to his eyes, and wished the four over-the-counter pain relievers would hurry and offer him some relief. His head throbbed; the cut burned.

His heart hurt more than either of those.

He loved Skye. He had realized just how much when he had come home to find that piece of shit trying to rape her. She was his family, his sister, his best friend.

He bit back a moan, gritting his teeth, the pain almost unbearable. His feelings for Skye didn't change the fact that they couldn't go on this way. Skye couldn't. She needed to go to school, to have friends, a regular family and a real life. The life of a thirteen-year-old. If nothing else, the events of the past days had proved that.

He needed a life, too. The one he wanted, the one he had promised himself he would have.

Chance breathed deeply through his nose, fighting the regret and doubt that ate at the edges of his determination, his certainty. He forced himself to focus on what had happened today, on what had been going on—unbeknownst to him—for weeks now; he imagined the future. Her future. His.

And what he imagined looked grim.

He squeezed his eyes shut, then reopened them, knowing the time had come to face the truth, to face what had been inevitable from the first.

He had to find a family for Skye. He had to leave her behind.

31

Michael and Sarah Forrest were kind people, former flower children who had gotten left behind as the sixties had progressed into the seventies, then had become dinosaurs as the seventies had become the eighties.

Sarah was a crafts artist, a jewelry maker, who taught adult-education classes at the Northern Illinois University there in Dekalb, Illinois, and sold her wares at crafts shows and local boutiques; a woman given to wearing round wire-rimmed glasses, like those favored by John Lennon, and long, flowing caftans. Michael was a farmer, a soft-spoken man with a quick smile and an aversion to both the government and all forms of violence.

Chance had found them through a want ad in the *Dekalb Farming News*. Michael had advertised for a summer field hand, someone with experience, someone who would work for a small wage plus room and board. He had, no doubt, expected a student from the university to apply; he had gotten Chance and Skye instead.

The farm was a modest one, not much more than an old clapboard farmhouse surrounded by fields of sweet corn. But it was pretty. And picturesque. The house had a sweeping front porch, complete with a swing; a creek ran along the edge of the property, land which was dotted with flowering fruit trees and shady maples.

Sarah and Michael had taken him and Skye under their wing, accepting their story about being an orphaned brother and sister, with no questions asked. For the first time since leaving Marvel's, Skye, Chance knew, felt safe. She was happy here.

He, on the other hand, couldn't shake a growing urgency in himself, an urgency to get on with his life, the feeling that something was out there waiting and if he didn't get about going after it, he would be too late.

So, he had decided. Sarah and Michael were the ones. Sarah was crazy about Skye. She would be a good mother; Michael a good father. They had no children of their own, and Michael had confided to Chance that Sarah's inability to conceive had been heartbreaking for them both, but especially for Sarah.

Chance descended the steps to the farmhouse's basement, where Sarah had her jewelry studio set up. Sarah and Skye were working at one of the benches, heads bent together as Sarah showed Skye how to solder a finding to the end of a necklace. Skye was fascinated with what Sarah did and showed an amazing aptitude for it.

He smiled. They hadn't been there a week before Skye had begun nosing around the studio. Sarah had been only too happy to share her knowledge and equipment with Skye; she had been blown away by Skye's talent. He had watched Skye blossom under the other woman's attention and admiration.

He was doing the right thing. She would have a good life here. She would have a good life without him. He wasn't cut out to be a big brother; he didn't want the job, he wasn't good at it.

He hoped Skye would forgive him. He hoped she would understand. If not right away, then someday. Leaving her would be for the best, for both of them. Someday she would see that. She had to. He couldn't stand the thought of her hating him forever.

As if becoming aware of his presence, Skye looked up, breaking into a big smile when she saw him. He sucked in a sharp breath, realizing how big a part of his life she had become. Realizing how much he would miss her.

"Look," she said, holding up the necklace she'd been creating out of beads and pieces of pounded silver. "It's almost finished."

"It's beautiful." He smiled, looking at her rather than the necklace, thinking what a beautiful woman she would someday be.

"Sarah says I'll be ready to try the lost-wax casting process soon." Skye all but bubbled over with excitement. "Maybe even this week."

"Probably this week," Sarah corrected, gazing affectionately at Skye. "I think you're ready. Your progress has been amazing."

"Did you hear that, Chance? She said my progress has been amazing!"

"I heard," Chance murmured, his last doubts fading away. He was doing the right thing. Skye would thank him one day.

Now it was only a matter of how he would do it. And when.

32

Skye awakened with a smile. She sighed and stretched, loving the feel of the bedclothes around her. After some of the places she had slept over the last ten months, she would never take a real bed and real sheets and blankets for granted again. Never.

She turned her face toward the open window and the gentle, early-morning light. A whisper of a breeze stirred the antique lace curtains; it wafted across the bed, sweet and soft. Skye snuggled her cheek deeper into the feather pillow. The truth was, she loved waking up here, at Sarah and Michael's. She loved being here.

She and Chance had found a home.

They had found a family.

Skye curled up on her side, drawing her knees to her chest, listening to the song of a bird perched in the apple tree outside her window. The past two months had been so wonderful, she had almost forgotten the horrible events of those last days in Boyton.

Almost. For she would never be able to erase them completely. Even now, with her mind's eye, she could see the glitter of light on Kevin's knife as he had slashed out with it at Chance; she could see Chance's blood, brilliantly red, soaking through his white T-shirt. She could recall the way her heart had seemed to stop, her world with it. In that moment, she had feared that she had lost Chance.

Chance could have died. And she could have been raped; would have been if Chance hadn't come home when he did.

Because of her stupidity. Her childish defiance.

She had been everything he had called her. A rock around his neck. The thing keeping him from having a real life. A brat kid who wasn't even his sister.

Skye squeezed her eyes tightly shut, wishing she could forget, wishing she could block out those words forever. She couldn't; she had tried. They, like the image of Chance's blood seeping through his white shirt, seemed to be permanently fixed in her memory.

Those last days in Boyton had changed her forever. Just as they had changed her and Chance, something between them. She saw it in his eyes, heard it in his voice. She felt it in the air whenever they were together.

But they were here now, she thought, her lips curving up again. If they could go back to the way it had once been between them, it would happen here. With Sarah. And Michael.

Skye sat up and drew the sheet around her. Sarah thought she had real talent, she had said so. She had even taken her over to the art department at N.I.U. and shown her around. That's where Sarah had gone to college, and Skye had thought it the coolest place she had ever seen. Like a city of art.

Skye had watched some of the students work. They were the ones who were talented, she had told Sarah, intimidated. Compared to them, she had no talent at all. Sarah had only chuckled and reminded Skye that they were also much older and much more experienced than she was. Sarah said she thought Skye had more talent than any of them.

Skye reached across to the bedside table and picked up the pin she had cast just last night. It had been her first attempt at the lost-wax casting technique, and though still far from finished, she thought the pin the most beautiful thing she had ever created. Skye turned the piece—shaped like a butterfly—over in her hands. Today she would cut off the sprues and begin to file and polish it.

Skye drew her eyebrows together, recalling each of the steps she had to take to get the pin to this stage. First she'd had to make a wax model. She had taken great pains creating it, carving and smoothing, using a heated biology needle to get the butterfly just the way she wanted it. Next had come attaching the sprues—they provided the channels for the molten metal to flow to her pin—and mounting the sprued piece in a pipe flask.

Sarah had shown her how to mix the investment, a plaster-like material, then had shown her how to fill the mold with it, taking precautions to ensure no air bubbles settled near her pin. After the investment had dried, they'd burned out the wax in a kiln.

It had been technical, painstaking work. Tedious, even. But Skye had loved every moment of it, anyway. She didn't know why, but she had.

Skye ran her fingers lovingly over the silver, then brought it to her cheek. It was cool now, but she remembered the way it had looked, red-hot, glowing as if illuminated from within, remembered the way it had held heat, even after being cooled.

She shook her head. She didn't know which had been more exciting, releasing the spring on the centrifuge and watching as it threw the molten silver into the mold, forcing it into every nook and cranny of her pin, or breaking away the mold after it had been quenched in a bucket of water and revealing her pin, now cast in silver.

It had all seemed like magic to her.

Magic. She screwed up her face in thought. That's exactly what it felt like when she worked in Sarah's studio. As though she was making something special, magical. And there, she felt special, too. Free. Of everything but the moment and her pleasure in it.

In the jewelry studio, even her bad memories couldn't touch her.

Her mother's image popped into her head, clearly and in

a way it hadn't in a long time. With it came a sharp, bitter feeling of betrayal.

Skye frowned and rubbed her temple. Why had she thought of her mother today? Why, when she was feeling so good?

That morning she had awakened with a smile, too.

The morning her entire world had fallen apart.

Fear settled over her. Oppressive. Breath-stealing. Her heart began to thud, her palms to sweat. She pulled in a shaky breath, feeling the way she used to, when she would awaken in the middle of the night, certain that Chance was gone, that he, like her mother, had sneaked out in the night and left her behind.

No! Skye threw aside the covers and scrambled out of bed. Chance wouldn't do that. They were happy here. Everything was perfect now.

Skye grabbed her robe and darted into the hall, putting it on as she went. Chance's room was across from hers; his door was open, his bed made. He must be downstairs already.

Sarah was in the kitchen cooking breakfast. Skye heard her moving about; she smelled bacon frying. Skye leaned over the banister. "Sarah," she called, "where's Chance?"

Something crashed to the floor and broke. Sarah muttered what sounded like an oath. Skye frowned. Sarah never swore; she was the most even-tempered person she had ever known.

"Are you okay?" Skye asked, leaning farther over the railing, trying to see around into the kitchen. "It wasn't one of your grandmother's dishes, was it?"

When Sarah didn't answer, Skye ran down to the kitchen. There, she saw that Sarah had, indeed, broken one of the mixing bowls her grandmother had left her. She was on her knees, pancake batter everywhere. Skye hurried to help her clean up.

That finished, they stood. Skye looked around. "Where is everybody?"

Sarah hesitated. "Michael's outside. I better...call him."

She went to the screen door, pushed it open and rang the dinner bell, mounted on the wall just outside the door.

Skye frowned. "Sarah?" The other woman didn't look at her, and a knot of apprehension settled in the pit of her stomach. "Isn't Chance outside, too?"

Sarah sighed, then met Skye's eyes. "Skye, honey, why don't you sit down."

Skye shook her head. "Why are you looking at me like that? What's wrong?"

Michael came in from outside. He and Sarah exchanged unhappy glances. A sickening sense of déjà vu moved over her.

This couldn't be happening to her again. Dear God, not again.

Panicky, Skye looked from one to the other of them. "Where's Chance?"

"Honey, he's—"

"No." Skye took a step backward. "I don't want to hear this."

"I went to wake him this morning, and I...he's..."

Sarah looked helplessly at her husband. He cleared his throat. "He's gone, Skye. I'm sorry."

"It's not true. He went out last night," she said, desperate, searching for an explanation. "He...he must have stayed at a friend's. That's all."

"His things are gone," Sarah said gently, crossing to her, holding out a hand. "Honey, I'm so sorry."

Skye jerked away. "It's not true!" she said. "It's not!" Turning, she raced upstairs to Chance's room. She checked the closet first, then the chest of drawers.

Empty, they were all empty. Just as Sarah had said.

No note. No goodbye. Nothing.

Skye sank onto the bed, her world crashing in around her. At least her mother had left him with a lie to give to her, an empty platitude, a false I love you. He hadn't even bothered with that.

What had she expected? She had never been anything but a rock around his neck.

Skye didn't cry, though tears welled in her throat, choking her. She stared at her hands clenched in her lap. She hated Chance for this. She would never forgive him. Never.

"He'll be back, honey. He will."

Skye lifted her gaze to Sarah's distraught face. She stood in the doorway, Michael beside her, hand on her shoulder, a silent support. A cry of despair rose to Skye's lips; she held it back, but only barely. *He'd left her behind, just as her mother had, just as she had always feared he would.*

He hadn't loved her any more than her mother had.

"We've talked about it and..." Sarah took a deep breath. "Until he gets back, you can stay with us."

"He won't be back." Skye turned her gaze to the window and the brilliant summer day beyond. "He's gone for good."

Sarah took a step toward her. "Honey, he will. Surely, after all, you're his sis—"

"No," she whispered. "Everyone leaves me behind."

Part V

Fortune

33

For Chance, it had been love at first sight. He had taken one look at the Chicago skyline and he had known, instinctively and in his gut, that this was the kind of town where anything could happen, where a boy with nothing but street smarts and determination could make something of himself. It was an accepting city, a midwestern city that still believed in the old-fashioned work ethic and offered the hungry a version, Chance's version, of the American dream.

Chicago didn't put on airs. She wasn't pretentious like Los Angeles, not manic like New York or tied to convention like Boston or Philadelphia. She sprawled, a not always graceful mix of the old and the new, the super rich and the utterly poor, the energy of youth and the wisdom of age. It was a city of contrasts and homogenization, both reflected in her architecture, her neighborhoods, her people.

In the arms of this city Chance had felt alive and exhilarated. He'd felt unstoppable. Here, his past had fallen away from him and the future had opened before him.

Chance had spent his first days in Chicago exploring. He loved the way the shore of Lake Michigan rippled along the edge of the city and the way the Chicago River cut through her heart, like an arrow shot from Cupid's bow. He rode the El, browsed through the retail empires that lined the Magnificent Mile and visited the office towers that held seat to

Fortune 500 companies like Sears and Amoco. And when he visited those places, he made his wishes, his plans. He promised himself *someday.*

Within a week, Chance's first infatuation had become a deep, abiding certainty that in Chicago, if he worked hard enough, believed in himself enough, he really would make his dreams come true, he really could become anyone he wanted to be.

And he wanted to be one of those who held the money and wielded the power, one of those to whom all the right doors were open.

He began setting about making those dreams come true. The first order of business was finding a permanent place to live, the second, a job. He hadn't bothered applying for corporate positions he'd had no possibility of getting; and he'd had no desire to be stuck in some basement mail room where the only people he would encounter were others like himself. Nor was he so foolish as to think he could work his way up from there. Not in this lifetime, anyway.

He wanted to move up fast. He wanted to rub shoulders with the beautiful, the wealthy and educated. So he applied for a job as a doorman at the Ritz Carlton hotel.

There, he watched the wealthy. He noted the way they dressed and what they ate. He noted their labels, their manner of speech, the things they said to one another, verbally and with body language. He studied, he memorized. And at night he practiced what he'd learned, mirroring mannerisms, patterns of speech, facial expressions. On his days off, he shopped, though he rarely bought. He studied the merchandise that made these people *look* their part; he tried garments on, learning what worked on him and what worked together, learning where he could cut corners without anyone noticing.

When he had learned all he needed there, he left the Ritz, moving on to the Palm Court, a fashionable restaurant in the heart of the business district. He studied the executives, the CEOs and the up-and-coming movers and shakers. He learned what they ate and drank and wore; he developed the ability to read who the most important man at the table was and why.

He eavesdropped shamelessly. He learned the fine art of the deal while serving prime rib and grilled tuna with beurre blanc.

His quest became a kind of game, a competition with himself.

A competition he was determined not to lose.

Chance began grooming himself for success. Literally. He figured two things: to get a shot he had to look the part, and he wouldn't actually have to prove himself until the shot had come his way. Until then, all he needed was image and a good, very good, line of bullshit.

He enrolled in night classes at the University of Chicago. It seemed to Chance, from watching and listening, that everybody had something to sell—even if only themselves— something or someone they needed marketed or promoted. So, he signed up for every marketing, advertising and business class the university would let him take.

Chance realized quickly that he had a gift for understanding the mass market and for knowing what people wanted. He found that he understood not only how the system worked but how to make it work for him.

His professors described him as one of the best bullshitters they had ever had the pleasure to try to instruct. His fellow students either liked him a lot—or they despised him—for that same quality.

Inside two years after going back to school, Chance landed his first agency job. Within five years of that, he had worked his way up the corporate ladder, not stopping until he was named vice president of public relations and special events for Adams and Sloane.

Now, twelve years to the day since looking at the Chicago skyline and knowing that his future had finally begun,

Chance was celebrating his first day as president and CEO of McCord Public Relations and Special Events.

Nothing could stop him now.

Life was good.

Leaning back in his all-leather armchair—an extravagance his fledgling company couldn't afford but one he had indulged in, anyway—he brought his flute of champagne to his lips. He had his strategy mapped out. Tomorrow he would begin making cold calls; he would muscle or charm or finesse his way past receptionists and flunky assistants and into the seats of money and power. Once there, he would convince those powers to hire him.

Chance smiled to himself. He would call on every damn business in Chicago if he had to, he would call on them again and again, until someone gave him a shot. Until someone opened the magic door.

With a laugh of pure triumph, he held up his glass in a salute to the future. His plans began tomorrow. Today he would allow himself to bask in the pleasure of his achievement.

He swiveled his chair to face the window behind his desk. The sky was a perfect robin's-egg blue, the clouds fluffy and white. As he gazed at them, he thought of Skye. He often did, though he didn't regret what he had done. He had missed her, but he hadn't looked back, hadn't second-guessed his decision to leave her with Sarah and Michael Forrest. It had been the best for them both.

He wished he had been able to say goodbye. That hurt. It had bothered him. It still did.

Had she forgiven him? Was she happy? He had wondered both countless times over the years. Though he hadn't wondered if she was well. He knew she was. Somehow, in his gut. Skye was a survivor. They had always had that in common.

Once again, he lifted his glass in a salute. But this time to Skye, wherever she was.

34

"Skye! Wait!"

Skye stopped and turned. One of her fellow grad students, a woman named Roxy, hurried across the parking lot toward her. Skye lifted a hand in greeting and waited, though she was anxious to go.

Roxy reached her, slightly out of breath. "I just heard!" she said. "Way to go, girl. God, I'd kill to get into a show at the MOMA."

Skye hugged her books to her chest and smiled. She had received the news today that several of her pieces, including a rather experimental brooch, had been accepted into the Museum of Modern Art's prestigious Decorative Arts exhibit. Jewelry designers from all over the world had submitted pieces for possible inclusion in the show. Only a handful had been accepted, hers among them.

"I was pretty much blown away," Skye murmured. "Wildest-dreams stuff."

"You're going places." Roxy fumbled in her coat pocket for her pack of cigarettes. She found it and swore when she saw it was empty. She crumpled the pack and stuffed it back into her pocket. "A few of us are going out tonight. Come with us. To celebrate."

Skye shook her head. "Thanks, really, but I can't."

"Come on. It's Friday, for heaven's sake. You deserve a night out."

"I can't. Really. I have plans." Skye took a step backward, working to look apologetic. "Thanks anyway, though."

"Plans?" Roxy made a face. "With your studio and that big Moo mutt of yours, I'll bet."

"Guilty." Skye smiled. "And that's 'Mr. Moo Mutt' to you."

"You know what they say about all work and no play. You're going to turn into a very dull girl."

"Boring can be good, Rox. Believe me, adventure isn't all its cracked up to be." She took another step backward. "See you Monday."

Skye turned and walked away, aware of the other woman's speculative gaze on her back. Skye knew what the other grads said about her: that she was a snob, that she thought she was too good for them. They thought she was cold, unfriendly, serious to a fault.

None of those things were true, at least not in her estimation. She preferred to think of herself as focused, determined, motivated. She had worked damn hard to get here—so she could learn. Not to party, not to make friends. And certainly not to hop from one bed to another, in search of a nineties HIV-free version of Mr. Goodbar, which several of her fellow grads—and a couple of her professors—had seemed to think when they'd put the rush on her.

Instead of socializing, she buried herself in her creations and in the absolute wonder of this opportunity. If she had realized anything from her past, it was never to take anything—not people, situations or things—for granted. You could wake up one day, any day, and they would be gone.

So, she took the maximum number of hours her faculty adviser would allow her, absorbing as much as she humanly could. Her load left her little time for friends or partying.

She would rather spend her time with her art and Mr. Moo, anyway.

Skye climbed into her Hyundai, tossed her books into the back and started for home, stopping on the way to pick up her favorite Thai chicken and a bottle of wine. As Roxy had said, she should celebrate.

MOMA. She had made it into the MOMA. She shook her head, almost unable to believe it had really happened. For an artist, the Museum of Modern Art in New York was *It*. The best, the pinnacle; if she did nothing else in her life, she could still say her work had been shown at *the* Museum of Modern Art.

But she would do more, much more. Her inclusion in this important exhibit was only the beginning.

Home at last, Skye climbed the stairs to her third-story apartment, deposited her books, purse, packages and the mail beside the door, then retrieved her keys from her coat pocket and unlocked the door. Bracing herself, she swung it open.

As she did, Mr. Moo—so named because he was black and white and as big and clumsy as a cow—came bounding around the corner from the kitchen, charging toward her, one hundred and ten pounds of pure, unbridled joy. He launched himself at her—a habit she had not been able to break him of—though, in truth, she hadn't put that much effort into it— his front paws hitting her chest, knocking her backward several steps. He kissed her, not caring at all that he was sending slobber flying in all directions, then dropped to all fours and raced around her in dizzying circles.

Laughing, she dropped to her knees and hugged him. "I'm happy to see you, too, buddy. How about a walk?"

He barked twice, and she pointed toward the kitchen. "Go get your leash. Go on, get it."

He turned and bounded for the kitchen. Smiling to herself, she collected her things and followed. She and Moo had a lot in common. She had found him as a puppy, abandoned at the side of the road. She had taken him in, and he had been grateful. He loved her completely. But not as much, she often thought, as she loved him.

He was her best friend.

He was waiting in the kitchen for her, leash dangling from both sides of his mouth. She shook her head, amused at the way he stood there gazing at her with that hurry-up look in his eyes, his whole backside swinging with each wag of his tail.

"All right, all right. I'm hurrying." She dumped her stuff on the table, attached it to his collar and let him lead her outside.

Thirty minutes later, after Moo had taken her for an anything but leisurely walk, she fixed herself a plate of the Thai and a glass of wine, and sat with Moo on the floor in front of the couch. As she ate, she fed him bits of her meal and chatted with him about the events of the day.

"We'll have to call Sarah," she said to the dog, sipping her wine and feeling totally relaxed and deliciously satisfied. "To tell her about the show. She'll be tickled."

Skye rested her head against the sofa, smiling. The truth was, Sarah would be thrilled and proud.

Skye owed Sarah so much. It had been Sarah who had introduced her to jewelry making, Sarah who had convinced her she had talent and had encouraged her to use it. It had been Sarah, too, who had gotten her back into school, using her connections to get her into the local high school without a birth certificate, Sarah who had helped her secure the scholarship to the Rhode Island School of Design.

And it had been Sarah who had helped her through her devastation after Chance left her; Sarah who had showed her a reason to live, who had given her the *will* to live—by sharing her art with Skye, by allowing Skye to immerse herself in it, by showing Skye how to draw energy from it.

Without Sarah, she might not have made it. Without Sarah, Skye wasn't sure she wouldn't have simply curled up and died.

Skye wished she could love the other woman. She wished she could think of her as a mother, for she knew Sarah longed to be loved that way. For *Skye* to love her that way.

Skye believed she owed Sarah that.

So she had tried, tried as hard as she could. But she simply couldn't. Skye had seen, had experienced firsthand, what happened when you loved people. They let you down. They left you. No matter how much they promised they wouldn't.

They broke your heart.

And when they did, it hurt too much. She couldn't bear it again, she knew she couldn't. Twice had almost done her in.

Skye pushed away her plate and refilled her wineglass. She cupped the red wine bowl in her palms and brought it to her lips. The wine was warm and sturdy, with just a bit of a bite. She sipped, enjoying the flavor and the slightly numbing effect it was having on her senses. She knew she should stop now, before slightly numb became downright stupid, but it was Friday night and she had nowhere to go and no one to be with. So she would indulge herself tonight and pay the price tomorrow.

In life, it seemed, everything came with a price.

She set down the glass and turned to Moo. ''Ready for dessert?'' He barked, and she cracked open his fortune cookie. ''Hmm, it says here you're on your way to fame and fortune. Cool, Moo. Can I come?'' She fed him half the cookie, which he wolfed down, then the second half, which he also inhaled. Then she cracked open her own cookie.

Be careful what you wish for...
It just might come true.

Skye gazed at the fortune, amused. A warning? A fortune cookie with a warning inside? She shook her head. Moo got fame and fortune, and she got a warning? What was wrong with this picture?

She fed Moo her cookie, then sat back, studying the fortune, thinking about her wishes, her many wishes.

"Let's see," she murmured, going to the easiest, the most obvious first. She wished to be rich and famous, a designer everyone was talking about. She wished to be mentioned one day in the same breath with the likes of Paloma Picasso, Angela Cummings and Dorothy Monarch.

But she wasn't about to stop there. If she was wishing, she wanted it all, starting, she supposed, with the biggest—true love with the perfect man.

Skye laughed to herself, imagining him. He would be gorgeous, of course. Rich and successful, with a family who adored her.

But most important, he would love her almost beyond reason, so much, so completely, he would never leave her. Never. So much that she wouldn't be afraid to love him back. She wouldn't be afraid to give him everything—her heart and soul, her very life.

Skye brought her wine to her lips and sipped, growing dizzy as she imagined her perfect man, as she imagined how good it would feel to be loved that way. How good it would feel never to have to be alone again.

Her smile slipped as suddenly her head filled with thoughts of her mother. And Chance. And the secrets locked tight inside her.

Mr. Moo nuzzled up against her, his nose cold and wet. She turned her face to his, longing to block out the thoughts but knowing she could not. Her wishes, it seemed, past or present, sweet or bitter, all mixed together to make a big, hollow place inside her. A place that ached from wanting so badly for so long.

Skye gave in. Silly as it was after all this time, she wished to be reunited with her mother. And when that happened, she would learn it had all been a mistake, that a terrible twist of fate had separated them, that all these years her mother had been hunting for her, desperate to find her, heartbroken.

She would learn that her mother had loved her, after all.

Eyes stinging with tears she refused to shed, Skye shifted her thoughts to Chance. She had cried buckets of tears over him and her mother; she had left those tears behind long ago. She lifted her glass in a mock salute. She wished to see Chance again, but only to make him regret having hurt her, only to make him pay for having broken her heart. She wished that he would realize that all his dreams meant nothing compared to having lost her.

The wine tasted bitter suddenly, and Skye set it aside, regretting ever having started this ridiculous wish-inventory but wanting to finish it, anyway. Wanting to put it behind her, once and for all.

She shut her eyes and completed her list, wishing that someone or something would unlock the door to her past so she would know, finally, the secret of those first years of her life, the years, the things, her mother had never told her.

Because then, Skye was certain, she would at last feel whole.

Skye reopened her eyes and found herself staring at the fortune. She reread its silly warning, the beginnings of a headache pressing at the back of her eyes. How could her wishes be bad? she wondered, anger taking her breath. Why should they come with a warning?

She crumpled the bit of paper, stuffed it into her cardigan pocket and stood. If all of her wishes came true, she wouldn't care what happened to her.

She would be too busy being the happiest person alive.

35

Chicago, Illinois,
1996

Griffen gazed at the business card laid squarely on the desk before him. His assistant had handed it to him only moments ago, along with a stack of phone messages.

McCord Public Relations and Special Events
Chance McCord, President

Chance McCord. Griffen knew that name. He had heard it before, somewhere…in connection with something important. He drew his eyebrows together in thought.

His memory never failed him. He had nearly perfect recall—of people and faces, of dates and events. It was one of the reasons school had been so easy for him, it was one of the qualities that made him a formidable businessman.

He tested the name on the tip of his tongue, then stopped, his mind flooding with the memory. The last time his father had gotten a lead on Madeline and Grace's whereabouts, the private investigator had talked to someone, some carny-kid named Chance McCord.

A lead. Maybe. A link to Grace. Maybe.

His Grace. Griffen's heart began to thunder, his palms to sweat. It couldn't be, could it? They had never come close to finding Grace and her mother again. It had been as if they had fallen off the face of the planet. Even his grandfather had given up.

Griffen hadn't. As the years had slipped by, he had never doubted that he and Grace would be together again. He had known they would be. Some things were simply meant to be.

Griffen breathed deeply through his nose, working to contain his excitement. This could be nothing, it could be another dead end. But it could be what he had waited thirteen long years for—his way back to Grace.

"Mr. Monarch?" His assistant tapped on the door, then popped her head inside, visibly excited. "Paloma Picasso's on line one."

"Tell her I'll call her back."

The woman's mouth dropped. "Excuse me? Did you say—"

"I'm unavailable right now. I'll call her back."

"But we've...she's calling from...Beijing."

"I don't care how long we've been trying to reach her or where she's calling from." Griffen narrowed his eyes. "Tell her I'll call her back. Then come back in here, I need to talk to you."

She opened her mouth as if to argue, then shut it again, spun around and left the office. He watched her go, smiling to himself. It had taken several months, but his assistant had finally learned that he did not allow underlings to question his decisions. Not ever. And if she thought he was a prick—which she did—that was just too fucking bad. She could be replaced, the way he had replaced a half dozen other assistants.

A moment later she returned, two bright spots of angry color dotting her cheeks. "You needed to see me, Mr. Monarch?"

He held up the business card. "Tell me about the man who left this."

"What do you mean?"

"What didn't you understand about the question, Ashley? I want you to tell me about this Chance McCord."

She stiffened. "As I already said, he was making a cold call. He wanted to get in to see you, I told him that was impossible but I promised to see you got his card."

Griffen made a sound of impatience. "What did he look like?"

"Look like?" she repeated, flushing. "He was…handsome. Kind of boyish, like a California surfer. Light hair and eyes. Nice smile, dimples. I thought…he seemed smart. Ambitious. And he was hungry."

"His age?"

"I don't know, thirty. Thirty-two."

Griffen nodded and stood. "Don't go far. I need you to do something for me. But first, I have to get something from my father's office."

Without waiting for her reply, he left the room. Pierce Monarch's office was adjacent to his. He crossed the hall and entered the reception area, brushing by his father's secretary without a greeting, without bothering to ask permission to enter or to be announced. His father wasn't there; he hardly ever was anymore. His health had deteriorated to the point that, although still the official president of Monarch's, Griffen had been acting president for over two years.

He closed the door behind him, and went to his father's private files. Using the key his father would be furious to know he had, Griffen unlocked the cabinet and began leafing through the files, searching for the investigator's report from thirteen years ago.

He located it, then the information he sought. His memory hadn't failed him. There the name was, in black and white.

Chance McCord.

Griffen scanned the report. This Chance had been friends with Madeline and Grace, though he had known them as Claire and Skye Dearborn. That summer, the report said, the three had traveled together with the carnival, as a kind of family. The kid had denied knowing the mother and daughter's whereabouts, though the investigator had suspected the boy of lying.

There was little else of interest in the report, though the investigator had included a brief, general description of the kid and a fuzzy photograph taken from a distance with a telephoto lens.

Griffen stared at the report, at the photo, narrowing his eyes in anger. Grace hadn't needed to be family with some carny, low-life scum. She'd had a family. One that had longed for her.

A family her crazy bitch of a mother had stolen her from.

Sucking in a deep, calming breath, Griffen plucked the photo from the file. He studied it, doing some quick addition in his head. The age was right, the general description.

He pocketed the photo, slipped the file back into place, shut the drawer and locked the cabinet, then turned to find his father's secretary standing in the doorway, watching him, her expression openly hostile.

He smiled thinly and dangled the cabinet key from the end of his index finger, amused by the way she glared at him. "Can I help you with something, Mrs. Fitzpatrick?"

"No, Mr. Monarch. Can I get something for you?"

"Thank you, no. I've helped myself." He smiled, slipped the key into his suit-coat pocket and moved past her, stopping when he had cleared the door. He looked back at her. "You know, Mrs. Fitzpatrick, it seems to me, considering how little my father is in the office, that you might have something better to do than spy on me."

She flushed. "I only do what your father asks of me."

"How loyal. You're a treasure, Mrs. Fitzpatrick. When you call him, be sure to tell him I said hello."

She would, too. Griffen laughed to himself, imagining his father's face when she told him his son had a key to his precious files. The news just might give him another heart attack.

A son could only hope.

Griffen laughed again, feeling almost giddy. He had waited nearly thirteen years for this day. For something, any scrap of a lead, any clue, no matter how insignificant it might seem, anything that might help bring his Grace back to him.

Finally, that day had come. Finally, he had something to go on, something he could pin his plans on.

And nothing or no one was going to stand in his way.

36

The door was marked Interrogation #2. Outside that closed door, the noise level of the S.F.P.D. held at a level near mind-numbing. Inside that door it was quiet, deathly quiet save for the crackle of newspaper pages being turned.

The room was airless and smelled stale, like old cigarettes and dirty linen. It had no window that could be thrown wide to let in the fresh breeze, no window through which sunlight could spill, cleansing and invigorating with its healing light.

Someone had carved the words *Jesus Saves* on the top of the room's one table, a top scarred with cigarette burns caused by years of use by careless smokers.

Claire spent a lot of time in rooms like these, at tables like these, surrounded by old newspapers and other people's tragedies. She did so willingly, enthusiastically. For in these airless rooms she found her life, her reason to live.

Much had happened to Claire since that terrible day she stood atop the Fort Pitt Bridge and gazed down at the Ohio River, ready to take her own life. The visions that had bombarded her that day had involved a child she recognized, the victim of a much-publicized kidnapping. Claire had gone to the police; she, her visions, had led them to the boy, saving his life.

She had been helping police and families ever sense. Although she shunned all publicity, within police circles she had become quite renown. Missing children were her specialty, a fact she found painfully ironic—she helped others find their children, but she had been unable to find her own.

Though she had never stopped looking. Everywhere she went, she searched faces, hoping, praying, she would see the one she longed for. Whenever she was in a new city, she checked area phone books, scanned local newspapers and business directories, all in the irrational hope of finding her daughter.

But irrational or not, she had promised herself that she would never allow herself to sink to the depths she had visited that day in Pittsburgh, she had promised herself she would never again give up hope.

Claire took off her reading glasses and massaged the bridge of her nose. She had come here straight from the airport—she checked her watch—four hours ago. Yesterday she had been in Boston. Three days before that she had been in Braille, Florida, a small town near the Everglades.

She slipped her glasses back on and returned her attention to the papers before her. They were searching for a six-year-old girl, missing a week now. She had left her friend's house, just down the block from her own, and never been seen again. No leads, no witnesses. Nothing.

Claire brought a hand to her chest, to the gems she wore as a talisman around her neck and against her heart. After her visions on the bridge, she'd had a wearable container fashioned to hold them. She never took it off.

The gems were the key to her visions; she believed that. Just as she believed they had saved her life.

Just as she believed they would someday save Skye's.

"Ms. Dearborn?"

Claire turned toward the door and the fresh-faced officer who stood there, looking uncomfortable. "Yes?"

"Can I get you anything?"

She smiled. "Thank you. An orange juice if you can round one up. And please, call me Claire."

He returned her smile. "Can do. Anything else?"

"All the area phone books."

"You got it." He started backing out the door, then stopped, his smile disappearing. "Any...luck yet?"

"I'm sorry. Nothing yet."

"I hope you find her. If there's anything I can do, I...I know the family. They're good people.".

Claire nodded, understanding, feeling for this young man, for the child, her family. She didn't have the heart to tell him she feared it might already be too late.

"I'll try my best," she said instead, softly. "I promise, I'll do everything I can."

37

Griffen Monarch's call had come out of the blue. At least Chance thought of it that way, because although he had called on Monarch's Inc., he had never expected to get farther than a secretary.

Not yet, anyway. Not until he had proved himself with other, smaller accounts. Not until he had fought for it.

But the man himself had called. Griffen Monarch, unacknowledged acting president and heir apparent of Monarch's, Inc. Griffen wanted them to meet. To talk.

So, here he was. Chance neared the Monarch building and slowed his pace. Ahead of schedule, he used the extra moments to pull his thoughts together, to quell his rush of nerves, of excitement. He couldn't reveal either to Griffen Monarch. Just as he couldn't appear too eager. All would be the kiss of death. All would earn him nothing but the door.

Monarch's flagship store and corporate headquarters were located in the six-hundredth block of Michigan Avenue, appropriately dead center on the Magnificent Mile. Chance paused outside the store's oversize double glass doors. Surrounded by polished brass and weathered iron filigree, the doors had been designed by Monarch artisans nearly a century before. They, like the jewelry creations sold inside, had stood the test of time.

Chance lifted his gaze. Perched two stories above the door, a huge winged Nike, the goddess of victory, announced to all who passed under her that they had, indeed, arrived.

He certainly had. Chance smiled to himself. *This was the big time, McCord. Don't fuck up now.*

The uniformed doorman opened the door. Nodding, Chance moved through the hallowed portal and into the small, richly appointed store. Salespeople and clients alike spoke in reverent, hushed tones, tones more befitting a church or sanctuary. He supposed to some, Monarch's was like a church, this was where they came to worship at the altar of beauty, self-indulgence and wealth.

Chance had done his homework. In the forty-eight hours since Griffen Monarch's call, he had read everything he could get his hands on about Monarch's Inc. and its history.

He knew that the company had begun as a jewelry atelier and had grown into a multifaceted, international company. Monarch's Design and Retail, now only one of the company's many divisions, had ten Monarch's boutiques worldwide, otherwise distributing their creations to only a handful of the world's finest jewelers. They didn't oversell, purposely keeping their exposure limited. That the public could only obtain Monarch designs in a limited number of places added to the Monarch's allure. It made their wares more exclusive, more expensive and more coveted.

Though the company had diversified, from what Chance had learned, the jewelry division was the company's—and the family's—pride and joy, its crown jewel.

Chance glanced at the glass cases as he passed them, taking note of several exquisite pieces, moving toward the back of the store and the elevators that would take him to the third floor. He checked in at the receptionist's desk, then headed into the elevator and up. Griffen Monarch's assistant, Ashley, greeted him there, then escorted him to a waiting area, asked him if he would like a refreshment, then to take a seat. Mr. Monarch would be with him directly.

Chance declined both, preferring to stand and study the enlarged photographs that lined the walls of the room. Most were photos of Monarch's fabulous creations; several were of family members with celebrities who had patronized their store over the years. Richard Burton and Elizabeth Taylor, President Kennedy, Princess Grace of Monaco, among others.

"Chance McCord, I presume. And right on time. I like that."

Chance turned toward the man crossing the room. He had expected someone older, graying and distinguished. Instead, the man striding toward him looked to be close to his own age, more dashing than distinguished, and certainly not graying. He wore an Armani suit and a Cartier watch, he moved with the kind of confidence, the kind of unwavering belief in himself, that money alone could not buy.

No, that kind of self-assurance was the product of a lifetime of winning, a lifetime of every door being open, every opportunity there for the taking.

Griffen Monarch was the epitome of what Chance longed to be; he was the image of what Chance had been struggling to become.

"You presume correctly." Chance grasped the other man's hand and smiled. "And you must be Griffen Monarch. It's good to meet you."

"Call me Griffen. Come into my office. We'll talk."

The man's office was spare and uncluttered, yet exuded wealth, nonetheless. Perhaps because the few things that graced the walls and shelves, the few pieces of furniture that filled the cavernous space, were obviously expensive and most certainly rare.

Or, perhaps, it was the presence of the man himself.

They took a seat on the leather couch that dominated a conversation area at the center right of the room. Chance cleared his throat. "Thanks for seeing me."

"I took you by surprise."

It wasn't a question, and Chance smiled. "Yes. You could say that."

Griffen laughed. "Can Ashley get you a coffee, a Coke or something?"

"I'm fine, thanks."

"Let's go on, then." Griffen leaned back against the leather couch, completely relaxed. "Who is Chance McCord? That's what I want to know."

So Chance began, slipping easily into his verbal résumé. "Until recently, I was vice president of public relations and special events for Adams and Sloane. I worked on the Chicago Symphony, on Art at the Park, Chicago Fest—"

"I'm familiar with their clients. Why did you leave?"

"Two reasons." Chance leaned forward. "The first, I wanted my own business. I always have. I want to make it or break it, on my own. Second, the time was right. I'd gone as far as I could with Adams and Sloane. As you know, I'm sure, public relations and special events is only a tiny arm of Adams and Sloane. Advertising is the big gun over there. Someone from the PR arm wasn't going higher than V.P. of that division. Period. The same is true for most of the big agencies. No way was I going to coast for the next thirty years."

"Everybody's ambitious." Griffen made a dismissive gesture with his left hand. "What can McCord Public Relations and Special Events do for me?"

Griffen Monarch didn't play around; he cut through the bullshit and said exactly what was on his mind. Chance liked that, though it didn't allow him any illusions about how important this meeting was in the course of this man's day. When you reached Griffen Monarch's level, you didn't have to play nicey-nice anymore. At least not with people the likes of Chance McCord.

"First of all," he began, "we have to get Monarch's creations on celebrities. You've done some of that, but not recently and not near enough. The Oscars aren't that far off. I'd want to see key presenters and some—hell, all, if there was a way to arrange it—of the best-actress nominees wearing Monarch's jewelry.

"Second, I have a connection at *Vanity Fair*. When the right cover celeb came along, I'd use that connection to get them photographed wearing our stuff. We don't stop there. We contact the major designers, the hot photographers, the fashion editors and art directors for the big magazines. We want covers, we want exposure. We want the people with money to want to be seen wearing Monarch's jewelry."

Griffen Monarch appeared to have no reaction to anything he'd said. He played his cards close to the vest, as any good businessman would. His lack of response only fired Chance's determination more.

"For that matter," Chance continued, "why don't we get Adam and Dorothy Monarch on *Vanity Fair's* cover. Good God, the Monarch family is like American royalty. We need to increase awareness with the public of who Monarch's is and why it's so important. With its history, Monarch's should be an international household name, the way Tiffany's is."

Chance sat forward, excited now, his mouth damn near watering for the opportunity to sink his teeth into this account. "Why hasn't a coffee-table book been done on Monarch's yet? Tiffany's has had several. *Tiffany's 150 Years* was put out in 1987 and *My Time at Tiffany's* in 1990, to name two. That's great exposure; it increases the public's awareness of the company's importance. When that awareness goes up, so do sales."

Chance had gotten Griffen Monarch's attention now, he saw, by the subtle change in the other man's expression and posture. He looked less relaxed, more intent.

"Damn little has been written on the Monarch family in the last few years," Chance continued. "Why is that? I went back, researching. A society blurb here, a business or philanthropical mention there. It's damn little. And not near enough."

"How far back did you go?" Griffen asked suddenly, sitting forward.

"Eight years."

Griffen nodded and sat back again. "Good. Go on."

"Monarch's is a Chicago treasure. A natural resource. You're like the Sear's Tower or Marshall Field's Christmas tree. When someone comes to town, Monarch's should be on their 'must do' list. The way Tiffany's in New York is."

"And you can do that?"

"Yes. Though I'm not going to lie to you. It's a building process, some things will happen immediately, others take time before you see the cumulative effect. Monarch's has, in essence, been hiding its light under a bushel for years. My job is to get rid of the bushel and get people to see the light. Now, can I ask you a question?"

Griffen inclined his head. "Certainly."

"Why did you call me? You're with Price, Stevenson and Price. And happy, I hear."

"No specific complaints, I suppose." Griffen shifted. "A bit bored, maybe."

"Bored?" Chance repeated, arching his eyebrows.

Griffen stood and walked to the window that looked out over Michigan Avenue. Without turning, he murmured, "Ashley told me you seemed ambitious and bright. She thought you were hungry. Those are qualities I find useful."

"Useful? Interesting choice of word."

Griffen turned and met his eyes. Chance noted for the first time what an uncommonly brilliant blue the other man's were. Skye was the only other person he had known with eyes so blue.

"I think they're assets, Chance. When you have a fire in your gut to get somewhere, you usually do. The folks at Price, Stevenson and Price are fat and happy."

"And complacent."

"Yes. But they're also the biggest firm in the city, they have a lot of experience, a lot of connections."

"If you've got enough drive, you can make connections. True, I'm small, but I don't have a lot of overhead to charge you for. And I'd work my tail off for you. An account like Monarch's would be my top priority. Can you say the same about Price, Stevenson and Price?"

"That's the question of the hour." Griffen crossed to stand before him. He held out his hand. "I'll be in touch. Thanks for coming in."

Chance's heart sank. Just like that, the meeting was over, and he was out the door. He stood and grasped the other man's hand. "I'd love to do an in-depth analysis of your needs and put together a proposal outlining what McCord Public Relations and Special Events could do for you."

"Maybe. Like I said, I'll be in touch." Griffen walked him to the office door, stopping and facing him when they had reached it. "Do you like surprises, Chance McCord?"

Chance drew his eyebrows together, surprised by the question itself. He lifted a shoulder. "I suppose. Why not?"

"Why not, indeed." Griffen smiled. "I just might surprise you, Chance. We'll just have to wait and see."

38

Griffen did surprise Chance. Shocked the hell out of him, actually. Chance hadn't expected the other man to call. In fact, when he'd walked away from their initial meeting, he had wondered why Griffen had even wanted to see him.

Though he could have called out of curiosity, Griffen Monarch had hardly seemed the kind to have the time or inclination to indulge himself in simple curiosity. No, Chance had sensed that the other man had been toying with something, some idea or plan that he hadn't shared with Chance. That he had been, in some way, testing him.

Apparently, he had passed the test.

They'd met a half-dozen times since then, and Griffen Monarch awed Chance. He was everything Chance longed to be: handsome, sophisticated, a well-educated, savvy and respected businessman. He possessed the things Chance longed to possess: fine, expensive clothes; a Porsche that cost more than Chance would earn in the entire year; and the by-product of all those things, power.

Chance had also decided that he liked Griffen. That he respected him.

Another surprise. Chance hadn't expected to. He had expected him to be like other men he had known in the business world who had been fathered and grandfathered into fortune—cocky, shallow and more than a little lazy. Made that way, he supposed, because they hadn't had to work, to sweat and claw their way to whatever exalted position they held. They hadn't had to earn their position of power.

None of those men had impressed him. Typically, they did as little as possible to get by, depending on the backs and ingenuity of their hungry underlings. They lacked the creativity and drive that had fed their ancestors, the ones who had built the companies that kept them in such fine style now. Chance had found that most members of the Lucky Sperm Club didn't give a shit about anyone or anything but themselves.

His own father had been like that. A rich kid who had been given everything he had ever wanted, a spoiled, selfish man who had cherished nothing. And no one—certainly not the love of the pretty little nobody he'd met in a bar or the son he refused to admit he'd sired.

Not so with Griffen. Griffen valued family. And people. Nor was there anything lackadaisical about him; he took nothing for granted. He made it a point of being involved in every aspect of the business, from working the sales floor to controlling the executive boardroom.

He was smart, dangerously smart, with a razor-sharp intelligence and a keen wit. He had an almost uncanny ability to predict moves, to anticipate both questions and responses.

Chance had seen him lay business rivals out with little more than a few words. Chance hoped they always played on the same side, because the other man would make a formidable enemy.

Chance sat at his desk, eyebrows drawn together in thought. Sometimes, when he looked Griffen directly in the eye, he had the feeling that the man knew more about him than he had ever told. Sometimes he had the feeling Griffen knew everything about him.

It felt strange. He didn't like it.

As if his thoughts had conjured him, the receptionist announced that Griffen Monarch was on the line.

Chance picked up. "Griffen. What can I do for you?"

"Got a question. You have plans Friday night?"

Chance cleared his throat. "My calendar's clear. What's up?"

"Granddad's having a thing. There're going to be some players there. Some big money. I thought you might get a kick out of it."

"Sounds great. Where and when?"

"The Astor Street house. At 8:00 p.m. See you then, Chance buddy, gotta run."

For long moments, Chance held the receiver against his ear, listening to the dial tone. *Surprise number three. An invitation to a social function, one being given at the Monarch family home.*

Chance shook his head. He didn't know what to make of Griffen Monarch. The man hadn't offered him any business yet, though they had met and discussed the possibility several times.

Considering Griffen's position, the invitation was unusual. What was the other man thinking? Chance wondered, setting the receiver back into its cradle. What did he want with him?

Chance realized what he was doing and made a sound of disgust. It really didn't matter if Griffen Monarch had some sort of ulterior motive—Chance smiled at how ridiculous that sounded—this invitation would open doors for him. He was going to grab it with both hands and not look back.

39

Griffen watched Chance as he made his way through the crowd of Chicago's movers and shakers. He smiled to himself, pleased. Everything was proceeding according to plan. Tonight, he would learn for certain whether this Chance Mc-Cord was the one he sought.

And if he was, Griffen would do whatever necessary to learn everything Chance knew about Grace.

Grace. She was close now, so close. He could all but feel her presence. If he closed his eyes, he could imagine the sound of her breathing, her smell, the feel of her skin under his hands.

She would have changed. When he had last touched her, she had been a baby. Velvet-soft and unspoiled. She had smelled of baby powder; her voice had been high and sweet, like springtime.

Then Madeline had stolen her away. And now she would be different, not so soft or sweet. Touched by others, spoiled.

He controlled the fury that wanted to rush over him, holding it back, away from spying eyes. Over the years he had become adept at harnessing his emotions, then twisting them to fit whatever situation he found himself in.

Griffen shifted his attention back to Chance. Griffen knew he impressed the other man—who he was, the things he had. He saw the admiration—the longing to be those things himself—in the other man's eyes.

Because of that, manipulating Chance McCord had been easy. Griffen had something he wanted, and wanted rather desperately. Griffen could open many doors for Chance and his pathetic little company. He could close many, also.

He had the power to make—or break—Chance McCord.

Griffen nodded at something the woman across from him was saying, hardly listening. The wife of one of Monarch's corporate attorneys, Louella Peterson was as vain as she was boring. She had, however, made it obvious to him on several occasions that she would be more than happy to sneak off sometime and fuck his brains out. That he and her husband were business associates was the only thing that would make that rendezvous interesting to Griffen, and he hadn't yet decided when—or if—he would take her up on her invitation. Perhaps immediately before a round of golf with her husband.

Griffen's mouth curved up. Wondering if the other man could smell his wife on him would be more pleasurable than the act itself. It might even improve his swing.

Griffen returned his attention to Chance, noting that he had finished his first drink and had started another. As he watched, Chance stopped and spoke to the mayor, introducing himself to the other man. Griffen shook his head, amused. Nothing shy about his boy Chance.

No, Chance was a smart guy, he was confident, ambitious, motivated. Actually, he was all those things to a fault. Those qualities made him easy to read; they made him even easier to control.

Time to say hello, he decided. Kissing Louella on the cheek, he whispered something provocative in her ear, then excused himself.

Moments later he was across the room. "Chance, buddy. Glad you could make it."

"Happy to be here." Chance smiled and gestured with his nearly empty glass. "Quite a place you've got."

"Home sweet home. What can I say?" Griffen motioned to the bar, where his grandfather was surrounded by a group of his admirers, bankers mostly. "Have you met Granddad yet?"

"Not yet."

"Let me introduce you. Come on. And while we're there, I'll buy us a drink."

As they crossed the room, Griffen nodded to various people they passed, stopping to greet a few, introducing Chance when he did, though careful to keep the introduction simple and noncommittal. When they reached the bar, Griffen led Chance through the throng around his grandfather, stopping before him. "Granddad," he said, smiling. "Chance McCord. Chance, Adam Monarch."

"Mr. Monarch." Chance stepped forward, hand out, expression almost reverent. "It's a pleasure to meet you."

"Same here." Adam shook Chance's hand heartily, then slapped him on the back. "Griffen's told me about you. He says you're good."

"Thank you. That's great to hear."

"Get yourself something to eat. It drives me crazy, I pay a fortune for food and no one eats."

Griffen laughed. "That's because everybody's too busy drinking. Including Dad."

Adam's expression tightened, and he shifted his gaze across the large room. Griffen's father had obviously had more than his limit and was acting it. He was an embarrassment to the Monarch name and Griffen used every opportunity to point that out to his grandfather.

Griffen saw Chance's gaze follow his grandfather's. Griffen smiled. And now Chance knew it, too. He tucked that away. One never knew what might someday come in handy.

"Excuse us, Granddad. There are some people I want Chance to meet."

As they moved away, Griffen leaned toward Chance. "You look impressed."

Chance laughed. "How could I not? Adam Monarch's a legend in Chicago."

"Quite so." Griffen paused, then murmured, "Sorry about you being in on that family thing. That's my father over there. Pierce Monarch, reigning family embarrassment. He's not supposed to drink. He has a heart condition and has already had two major attacks. It's really hard on Granddad when he gets like this, especially in public."

Griffen made a sound of disgust. "As you can probably tell, there's no love lost between me and my old man. Actually, Granddad was more a father to me growing up than my own. I suppose the thing that bothers me most is the way Dad's behavior affects Granddad."

Griffen shook his head. "Enough of that. There's Daniel Conrad, general manager of the Drake. I want to introduce you."

For the next forty minutes, Griffen took Chance around, introducing him to the party guests, telling everyone what a great new talent he had discovered, all but outright calling McCord Public Relations and Special Events the new firm of record for Monarch's Design and Retail.

Griffen saw the speculative looks. The curiosity. He saw the subtle shift in expressions, autopilot cocktail chitchat becoming sharp-eyed assessment, pleasant disinterest becoming pointed appraisal.

Chance was being considered worthy of their interest—because of *his*, Griffen Monarch's, entrée. Because of *his* word, it would be accepted that Chance McCord was good at what he did, that he was a comer to be taken seriously.

Finally, Griffen left Chance on the pretense of needing to do some business. He backed off and watched Chance, curious to see what he would do, laying odds that he went back to the biggest plums he had met tonight and struck up conversation. He would lead the conversation around to business—their businesses and how he could help them. And by the end of the night, Chance would have collected a half-dozen business cards and probably set up a couple tentative meetings. He would be half in the bag and riding an adrenaline high of biblical proportions.

Griffen smiled. Then he would approach Chance about Grace. The timing couldn't be more perfect.

Several hours later, as the party began to break up, Griffen found Chance again. "Hang around, man. There are a few people I need to say goodbye to, then I'd like us to rap."

"Great." Chance swayed slightly on his feet.

It's been a big night for the little man. Griffen smiled. He supposed he might have had four martinis, too, had the situation been reversed.

"Five minutes," he said. "I'll meet you in the library."

Ten minutes later, Griffen headed to the library, anticipation crackling along his nerve endings like sexual arousal. The library door was half-closed. Griffen pushed it the rest of the way open and stepped into the room. Chance was standing in front of the fireplace, studying the row of framed photographs that lined the mantel.

"What did you think of our little party?"

Startled, Chance swung around, his expression almost guilty. "I didn't hear you come in."

"I move like a cat." Griffen smiled and crossed to where Chance stood. "At least that's what Nanny used to say. She always accused me of sneaking around."

Chance indicated a photo of Griffen as a teenager, holding a junior-golf association trophy. "Is there anything you don't do well?"

Griffen laughed. "Do you play?"

"I flail at the ball as best I can, if you call that playing." Chance bent to study another photo, one of him and baby Grace, standing in front of the Christmas tree in Marshall Field's Walnut Room restaurant.

Griffen had prepared himself for this. He knew that Chance would eventually learn about Grace. The trick would be to make sure he never connected Grace to Skye.

Griffen bent, as if also studying the photo. "That was my sister. Half sister, actually. Grace. She...died."

"I'm sorry."

"So are we." Griffen straightened. "I had two half sisters, I lost them both. This family..." He cleared his throat. "We've had our share of tragedy. Money can't protect you from life's big fuck-yous. The little ones, maybe. But not the big ones. Remember that, Chance." He dragged a hand through his hair. "I think I need a drink. A brandy. Join me?"

Chance smiled ruefully. "I think I've had more than enough."

"It's Friday night. Cab home." Griffen poured them both a brandy. He would rather Chance's head thick, his reactions slow. Happy and drunk and much more likely to talk, Griffen thought, crossing to the couch and handing Chance the drink.

The other man gazed at it a moment, as if uncertain whether he had said he wanted it or not.

"I don't usually go for these things. I'm a beer man, usually. That or a glass of good red wine."

Griffen brought his own drink to his lips. "A beer and burgers kind of guy, huh?"

"What can I say?" Chance laughed. "Throw a ball game into that mix, and I'm in heaven. Life just doesn't get much better than that."

"We'll have to catch a Cubs game one day." Griffen took a seat across from Chance. "Make any good contacts tonight?"

Chance shook his head as if to clear it. "Unbelievably good contacts. I have a pocketful of business cards and a couple tentative meetings."

Damn, he loved being right. Griffen took another sip of brandy. "Where are you from, Chance?"

"Everywhere. Nowhere."

"Great answer, buddy. I'm serious, where are you from?"

"California originally. Los Angeles."

"And then?" Griffen brought the brandy snifter to his lips, but this time he didn't drink.

Chance leaned back against the overstuffed leather sofa. "And then to Pennsylvania to live with my aunt on her Amish farm."

Griffen laughed and shook his head. "No shit? You? On a farm?"

"No shit."

"So, how did a boy from California get to Chicago via an Amish farm?"

Chance laughed. "The story gets weirder."

"I'm up for it."

"A traveling carnival. A two-bit piece-of-crap carnival, complete with a fortune-teller and a rickety roller coaster. Marvel's Carnival," he mused aloud. "Old man Marvel kept us all in line with a baseball bat. What a strange few months those were."

Marvel's Carnival. That was it, the name of the show Madeline and Grace traveled with that summer.

Griffen breathed deeply through his nose, struggling to keep his triumph from showing. If he tipped his hand now, it would ruin everything.

He leaned forward, smoothing his expression. "No kidding? A fortune-teller and everything?"

Chance's smile faded. "And everything. But that was a long time ago." He stood and crossed to the bar and set his untouched drink on it. "Left the show, bummed around for a while. And ended up here."

"I like that story, Chance. I like it a lot."

"Yeah?" Chance met the other man's eyes. "And why's that?"

Griffen arched his eyebrows. "It's different. A lot less boring than my life story, that's for sure." He lifted his shoulders. "Look at this place. I grew up here, in this house, in Chicago, and I never left. Went to university in Evanston, for Christ's sake."

"I see what you mean." Chance laughed. "Boring."

Griffen got to his feet. "How would you like the exclusive contract to handle all PR for Monarch Design and Retail? We'll see how you do, and depending on the way things go, we might add some of our other ventures, as well."

Chance shook his head, as if not quite grasping what Griffen had said. Griffen laughed. "Yeah, I'm offering you the contract. I think you have what I need, what Monarch's needs. So, Chance McCord, former carny, you want it?"

"What do you think? Hell, yes, I want it."

"You've got it, then." Griffen held out his hand. "Welcome aboard."

Chance took his hand, his expression stunned. Griffen smiled again, thoroughly enjoying himself. "I told you I'd surprise you."

"That you did, Griffen. Though *surprise* is a rather mild word to describe how I feel. Truthfully, you've blown me away."

"Chance, buddy, you haven't seen anything yet. I promise you that. The best is yet to come."

40

The Old Chicago Brew Pub was located on Lincoln Park, across from the zoo. Noisy, packed with the young-professional, after-work crowd, it lived up to its name, boasting fourteen different beers and ales, all brewed on sight.

Griffen sat alone at a small table to the back right of the bar, a position that afforded him a clear view of everyone who came or went. He never sat with his back to a room, a habit he had learned from his grandfather and one that had served him well over the years.

Griffen checked his watch. He had been waiting exactly ten minutes for Chance, and he didn't like it. Nobody kept Griffen Monarch waiting, especially not some little upstart nothing like Chance McCord.

Griffen brought his beer to his lips, then set it back down, untouched. He worked to get a grip on his frustration. Since the night two and half months ago when he had confirmed that Chance was, indeed, the same boy who had known Grace and Madeline, he had learned nothing more that might lead him to his half sister. In fact, it seemed to Griffen that Chance had been particularly unforthcoming with information, and it was starting to piss him off.

His P.I. needed something to go on—a place, a name, a date, even. Short of outright asking and blowing his cover, Griffen's hands were tied.

He lifted his mug again, and this time drank. The dark ale was strong and full-bodied, one of the house specialties. Over these past months, he had carefully cultivated his relationship with Chance. At first they had met only on the pretense of discussing business. Little by little, Griffen had began to inject personal tidbits about himself and his life, requiring Chance to return in kind. He had invited Chance to several business-related social functions, they had met for drinks and dinner; they had gone to a Cubs game together.

He had done it all in the hopes of learning when and where Chance had last seen Grace or, rather, as he knew her, Skye Dearborn. He had done it to earn Chance's trust, to make the other man believe they were friends.

That part had worked. The other man thought they were friends. Just as Griffen wanted him to think. Griffen's lips lifted. And Chance thought he was Mr. PR. At least a half-dozen new accounts had come Chance's way, the man was damn near preening at his success.

He narrowed his eyes. He, Griffen, had given Chance those accounts. He had used his connections, his reputation, his standing in the community—allowing those bones, those carefully selected bones, to be tossed Chance's way. He was responsible for the way Chance's business had grown.

It had been fun to watch. It had been fun to see doors open for Chance, fun because he could close those doors as easily as he had opened them. Fun because he knew he could bring the other man down as quickly as he had brought him up.

And he would, when Chance had outlived his usefulness. Now the time had come for Chance to give him what he wanted.

"Hi, gorgeous."

Griffen lifted his gaze. A blond woman wearing a denim miniskirt and a tight white tank top stood beside his table.

"I'm Trixie."

He smiled and moved his gaze slowly over her, finally meeting her eyes once again. "I'm sure you are."

"You looked kind of lonely. I thought we could keep each other company for a while."

"Actually, Trixie, as much as I hate to say this, and I really do, I'm expecting a business associate. He'll be here any minute."

She pouted. "Darn."

"Darn, indeed." He skimmed his gaze over her chest, spilling out of the tiny knit top. "Rain check?"

"Sure." She leaned across the table and plucked his Mont Blanc pen from his breast pocket, then caught his hand and opened it, palm up. She wrote her name and phone number across his palm, then closed his hand over it. "I hope you use it."

"I'm looking forward to it."

She tucked the pen back into his pocket, blew him a kiss, then turned, nearly running into Chance.

"Excuse me," she said, ducking around him and walking away.

Chance watched her go, then slid into the seat across from Griffen. "Yeow. Hope my arrival didn't mess up a good thing."

"Not a problem." Griffen grinned and held up his hand, palm out. "I'm covered for later."

Chance laughed. "Man, you're amazing. What is this thing with you and women?"

"Hummingbirds to nectar," Griffen murmured. "Moths to flames. Bees to flo—"

"I get it." Chance signaled the waitress. "All I have to say is, I never want to compete with you for the same woman. You'd kick my ass."

"That's right, buddy-boy." Lips twitching with amusement, Griffen brought his beer to his lips. "And don't you forget it."

The waitress arrived and took Chance's order. After she walked away, Chance turned back to Griffen. "Sorry I'm late. I was on the phone with *Vanity Fair*. We got cover confirmation. February. Demi Moore, wearing Monarch's jewelry and little else."

"Way to go. She pregnant, by any chance?" Griffen asked, referring the famous *V.F.* cover where she had posed nude and very pregnant.

Chance laughed. "Not that I know of. Though, I wish she were. That cover was an attention-grabbing knockout."

Griffen saluted Chance with his beer. "Good work. Granddad and Dorothy will be pleased. Now, if we can just round up something befitting the occasion."

"I'm sure Monarch's has a more than ample selection of pieces to choose from."

"Sure. But it would be nice to have something knockout for the cover. Something really new and fresh. Unfortunately, Dorothy's not up to it."

Chance drew his eyebrows together. "Is Dorothy ill?"

"No, she's just old." Griffen frowned. "Too old to be doing what she is. She's easily fatigued, and her creative abilities seemed to have diminished with her energy. Her work is—" The waitress returned with Chance's beer and a basket of warm-from-the-oven pretzels. Griffen waited until she was out of earshot to continue. "Her work is dated. She knows it and it's depressing her. We're all concerned. Especially Granddad."

"Have you started looking for her replacement yet?"

Grace. He had never stopped. He never would.

Griffen met Chance's eyes. "Dad started looking for one thirteen years ago. Grandfather refused to even consider it. You see, a Monarch has always headed up the design studio. Always. It's more than a tradition with us, it's more than a desire, it's—"

Griffen bit the words back, thinking of Grace, of Madeline and of how she had stolen their girl away from them. From him. His mouth twisted. "We no longer have another choice."

"Wish I could help, man." Chance took a swallow of his beer, his expression thoughtful. "I knew a jewelry designer once. A long time ago."

"Give me her name, I'll call her."

Chance laughed. "She wasn't even in the same league as Dorothy, more of a crafts artist. She taught adult-ed classes at N.I.U. Nice lady. She had a big heart."

"Northern? In Dekalb?"

"Yeah." Chance's lips lifted. "But the most talented artist I ever knew was a kid. She was amazing."

The blood rushed to Griffen's head. "A kid?" he repeated. "What do you mean, a kid?"

"You know, a child. To this date, I've never seen anyone better. Here——"

Chance retrieved his wallet, opened it and slipped out a folded piece of paper. Thin and frayed, it looked to Griffen as if Chance had been carrying that paper around for years.

He handed it to Griffen. "She drew this for me."

It was a fragment of a drawing, a detailed and lyrical rendering of a frog wearing a crown.

"She was only twelve when she did that."

Twelve. Grace would have been twelve that summer they had almost found her.

Griffen worked to hide his excitement, a difficult task, considering that his hands were shaking. "No shit," he murmured, handing the drawing back. "She was good. What's with the frog?"

"It was me."

Griffen arched an eyebrow, and Chance laughed. "Long story."

"Yeah, well, I've got nowhere to go." He leaned back and lifted his beer mug. "I'm up for it."

Chance proceeded to narrate the story of his first days with Marvel's Carnival and of how he had met Skye, the girl who had done the drawing. "She was following me around, making my life a bigger living hell than it already was, and finally nearly got me creamed by this group of carny thugs."

Chance's mouth lifted into a half smile and Griffen could tell the other man was amused by the memory. "In total frustration, I picked her up, tossed her over my shoulder and carried her home. Man, was she pissed. Her mother was pretty pissed, too, but at Skye, not me.

"Anyway, she did the drawing as an apology. After that, the three of us became friends. We kind of hung out together for the rest of the summer."

Grace. Dear God, he had found his Grace.

"They didn't really fit with the other carnies," Chance continued, cocking his head in thought. "And neither did I." He lifted his shoulders. "And there the story ends."

"But it can't end there," Griffen said, leaning forward, heart thundering. "What happened to the girl and her mother?"

Chance hesitated, then shook his head. "I've never told anyone what happened next, never talked about it. Though I don't know why. It can't matter anymore. It all happened so long ago."

"Now you've really got my attention," Griffen murmured, turning a book of matches over and over between his fingers. It was the only outward sign of his nervous excitement that he allowed himself. "It sounds like you were involved in some sort of intrigue."

"Intrigue," Chance said softly, as if deep in thought. "I suppose you could call it that. One stormy night, Claire— that was Skye's mother's name—asked me if I could watch Skye while she ran into town to make a phone call."

He continued, telling about how Claire had returned, soaking wet and obviously terrified, and begged Chance to watch Skye until a friend came for her in the morning. He told Griffen that the woman never showed, but when a private investigator did, asking a lot of questions, he ran with Skye to protect her.

Griffen stared at Chance while he talked, hardly able to believe what he was hearing. All this time, all these years, they had been searching for Madeline and her daughter. A mother with her child.

Madeline had accomplished what she had set out to do—
she had fooled them, she had kept them from finding Grace.
For thirteen long years.

No more. Now he had found her.

"I left her in Dekalb, with the jewelry maker and her
husband. Sarah and Michael Forrest. I had to, she needed a
life. A real family."

Griffen dropped his hands to his lap, squeezing his hands
into tight fists. "What's she doing now? Did you keep up
with her?"

"No. I felt it was better for us both if I didn't. But I did
call once, a few years ago. I don't even remember what urge
prompted me to do it. Skye answered. I recognized her voice.
And then I hung up. I knew she was okay and...and that's
it."

Griffen digested what Chance had just told him. After a
moment, he cleared his throat. "Did you ever learn what the
mother was running from?"

"Nope." Chance pushed away his beer. "Truthfully, I
sometimes wondered if I'd done the right thing. I wondered..." He swore and looked away. "It crossed my mind
that the mother had set me up, that there never was a friend
coming, that Claire had never meant to come back for
Skye."

"But you don't believe that?"

"I knew how much Claire loved her daughter. She
wouldn't have left her unless...unless she was afraid for
Skye. She was definitely in some sort of trouble. And that
P.I. did come around with some lame story about a family
inheritance."

"Maybe it was true. I mean, nobody has nobody," Griffen
murmured, feeling Chance out, trying to ascertain whether
he had been completely honest with him. "Surely this girl
had an aunt or a grandparent or somebody."

"They didn't. At least that's what Claire wanted Skye to
believe. She'd told Skye that her father was dead. And Skye

had no memory of anything before her fifth birthday. Nowadays they call it repressed memory syndrome. It really bothered her that she couldn't remember. She always thought her mother was keeping something from her."

Madeline had been keeping something from her daughter, all right.

Griffen bit back a smile. *If Chance was telling him the truth, this couldn't get any more perfect.*

Grace didn't know who she really was.

"You're yanking my chain about this, right? Repressed memory?" Griffen made a sound of disbelief. "If you're not, it's like the plot out of a paperback novel."

"Or a TV movie of the week." Chance held up his hands, grinning. "But every word is true. I swear."

Griffen laughed, feeling almost giddy. His P.I. wouldn't have a problem locating her now, he was certain of it. Name and last known address, current as of a few years ago. "You, my friend, have had an amazing life."

"Truth is stranger than fiction."

"In your case, for sure." Griffen longed to ask more, he longed to grill Chance with questions about Skye—what she looked like, her likes and dislikes, what made her laugh, what made her cry, if Chance had any pictures.

Of course, he asked none of those things, because to do so would reveal him. So he changed the subject to the Cubs' chances at making the series, then the *Vanity Fair* cover. But the minutes ticked agonizingly past. Sitting there pretending interest in anything Chance had to say was torture. He wanted to laugh, shout, howl at the sky.

Grace was coming home at last.

41

The egg was priceless. Made of tricolored gold and studded with diamonds, it opened to reveal a brilliant blue enameled interior and trompe l'oeil painting of a monarch butterfly. It was Grace's egg, fashioned by Dorothy and her team of artisans to celebrate her birth.

Every Monarch had an egg, though none was so beautiful, so perfect, as Grace's. Griffen smiled to himself. Appropriate, as no Monarch was or had been as beautiful, as perfect, as she.

He took the egg from its pedestal and cupped it lovingly in his hands, stroking the gem-encrusted surface with his thumbs, imagining cupping her, stroking her. He brought the egg to his nose and breathed deeply, imagining her scent.

Soon, he would have to imagine no longer. Soon, she would be home. He had found her. He had seen pictures of her.

Almost home. Almost his.

Hands trembling, Griffen set the egg carefully back in the display case, back on its delicate gold pedestal. Hers sat next to his in the cabinet. Appropriate again.

They would remain side by side forever.

Once Chance had given him her last address and the names of the people she had been living with, it had been simple. Now he knew everything about her—her likes and dislikes, her favorite foods, music, color; he knew her beliefs, her aspirations, her dreams.

Yes, he knew everything about her, he thought again, smiling. Down to the kind of panties she wore.

Griffen trailed his fingers along the display cabinet's smooth, cool glass front, thinking of his Grace, of the things he had learned. She had graduated from Dekalb High with honors. She had studied art at Northern Illinois University, again graduating with honors, and earned a scholarship to the Rhode Island School of Design.

She had few friends, no lover and kept to herself. She was a good student and a gifted artist. Indeed, she had racked up an impressive list of exhibitions already, including one at the Museum of Modern Art.

Griffen had sought out her designs; he had even called to inquire about her work. Her qualifications.

Her faculty adviser had practically salivated all over himself in his praise of her and her work. Just talking to the man about her had aroused Griffen. And not in a small way. No, this had been the boner to end all boners. After he had hung up, he'd gone into the executive bathroom and jacked off, his orgasm incredibly intense.

Grace was everything he had fantasized her being, more, even. Beautiful, brilliant, a shining talent, one equal to Dorothy at her creative zenith.

"Mr. Monarch, can I help you find something?"

He looked over his shoulder. The housekeeper stood in the dining-room doorway. He smiled. "No, thank you, Beatrice. I already found what I was looking for."

She hesitated a moment, clearly not understanding his amusement, then nodded and moved on. Griffen turned back to the cabinet, to the row of jeweled eggs.

Griffen hadn't been surprised to learn the depth of Grace's talent, or that she had channeled that talent into jewelry design. After all, destiny—like truth—could not be denied.

Poor delusional Madeline. She had thought she could take Grace away from her destiny; she had thought she could alter the future. His. Grace's.

She had been wrong. Some things could not be altered; they could not be denied.

Grace was *his* destiny. She belonged to him, she always had. Madeline nor anyone else had been able to change that.

Almost time. Almost his.

Now, what to do with Chance McCord? That was the question. Griffen drew his eyebrows together in thought. Had he outlived his usefulness? Or did he still need him?

Perhaps he did. After all, he knew Grace—Skye, he corrected himself—better than anyone. From what the investigator had learned, and her faculty adviser had confirmed, she kept to herself. She didn't have many friends, didn't date or socialize. She was totally committed to her work, the adviser had said.

Maybe he would need Chance's assistance controlling Grace. For a time. Before long, he was certain, he would have no trouble controlling Grace without assistance.

Griffen laughed softly. Besides, the higher he allowed Chance to climb, the farther, and harder, he would fall when the time came.

Little man was so full of himself. It had been fun to watch how Chance had puffed up a bit more with each new account, how cocky he had become. How self-satisfied.

As if any of it had been his doing.

Griffen chuckled. He had given Chance success, he could take it away, too. A few calls, a few carefully placed stories and down Chance McCord would tumble.

And all the king's horses and all the king's men wouldn't be able to put little ole Chance together again.

"Griffen. Could I see you for a moment?"

Griffen dragged his eyes from the row of Monarch eggs and looked over his shoulder at his father. He swept his gaze over him, disgusted. His father was stooped and gray and weak. It seemed impossible to him that this man was his father. It seemed more impossible still that once upon a time he had been frightened of him.

Griffen smiled thinly. "I'm not in the mood right now. Thanks anyway, Dad."

His father's face mottled. "It wasn't a request, son. Now. The study."

Pierce turned and walked away, expecting his son to follow like an obedient little puppy. Griffen took his time, knowing how angry it would make the old man. He relocked the display cabinet, then carefully, meticulously, wiped his fingerprints from the glass.

Griffen smiled at his reflection, holding his plans close, wondering what his pathetic father would think of them.

Not that he cared, of course. He could deal with his father. Turning, he went to join him in the study.

His father was waiting, pacing. Furious. He swung toward the door as Griffen stepped through. "You little shit," he said. "How dare you."

"What's that, Father?" Griffen closed the study door behind him. "Don't you like being kept waiting?"

"That's not it, and you know it."

"Really? I do?" Griffen slipped his hands into his front trouser pockets. "Then you'd better refresh my memory."

"I don't know how, or where, you got a key to my personal files, but I want it back. You're not to go in them again."

"So, your pitbull finally tattled. Or has it just taken you so long to work up the courage to confront me?" Griffen laughed and clucked his tongue. "Her loyalty astounds me. Really. What could you have done to earn it?" He cocked his head. "Does she know you the way I do, I wonder? Does she know all your dirty little secrets?"

Pierce ignored him. "And furthermore, I'm still president of Monarch's. I make policy, not you. I approve all changes. You're not to make any without consulting with me first." Pierce threw back his shoulders and puffed out his chest, though Griffen found his father's attempt at strength laughable. "Do you understand?"

"What changes could you be referring to, Father? It must have been something big to get your panties in such a wad."

His father looked as if he was going to explode, he was so mad. He crossed to stand nose-to-nose with Griffen. "You may not fire our PR firm, the same firm who's been doing our work for twenty years without consulting me. You may not hire some nobody nothing without first—"

"But, that's exactly what I've done."

"Listen to me, you little bastard—"

"No, you listen to me. I'll do as I please with company policy. I'll make the changes I deem necessary." He bent his face close to his father's. "As for your precious, fucking files, the reason you don't want me in them is because you kept records of things you shouldn't have. Things that were illegal. Immoral. Things that were really fucked up. You're one sick bastard, Dad."

Griffen picked up a curio, an elephant carved out of ivory, then set it back down, aware of how his words were affecting his father. He could all but feel his father's heart beginning to thunder, his blood beginning to career through his veins. "But I bet what you're most worried about are the things that might tarnish your sterling reputation in the industry."

His father paled. "That's ludicrous. I don't want you in the files because they're mine. They're none of your concern. Period." His father held out his hand. Griffen noticed it shook like an old man's. "I want the key. Now."

"What's curious to me," Griffen murmured, moving past his father, "is why you've kept the things you did. Didn't you think someone would eventually go through them? Really, Father. Very sloppy. Stupid, even."

"The key."

"And talk about ludicrous." Griffen swept his gaze over his father again, making a sound of derision. "Look at you. You're out of breath. Standing still and breathing like a horse who's just run the derby. Oh, I forgot. You've been put out to pasture. No good to anyone anymore."

"That's not true. *I'm* still president of Monarch's—"

"Look at the way you're sweating," he continued, chuckling as his father brought a hand self-consciously to his forehead. "It's disgusting. You make me sick."

"You can't talk to me this way. You can't—"

"Oh, but I can, Father. And I will." Griffen circled his father, laughing, enjoying the man's helpless fury. "What are you going to do about it? Fire me? Or do you want to hit me? The way you did when I was a kid? Think you can still take me?"

Pierce's face went nearly purple with rage. "You... You..."

"What, Father? What am I? The son you never wanted? Your whipping boy?

"Funny thing about daughters," Griffen continued, "the way they come and go, that is. Terrible how your little bitch daughter drowned. I never liked her, you know." He leaned toward his father. "Who needed her, anyway? She didn't have the gift, Grace got it all. Every fucking bit of it. And you just...let her go."

Griffen crossed to the window and glanced out at the bright day beyond, then back at his shaking father. "But then, accidents happen. Isn't that right? Just as wives run off with daughters and money. And gems."

His father's face went ashen and Griffen laughed. "What was it that made you keep records of those nice little transactions? Your bloated ego or your tiny brain? Buying gems that had been smuggled into the country." He wagged his finger at his father. "Not a bad deal for Monarch's. We don't pay customs, we get more than our allotted share, we undercut our competitors. Very slick. Though you didn't plan on Madeline making off with a stash of them. You couldn't collect on insurance because they didn't exist. You couldn't file a criminal charge because, again, the gems didn't exist. Boy, that must have been tough to swallow."

"I could kill you now," Pierce managed to say, his voice

thick. He flexed his fingers and took a faltering step toward Griffen.

"Could you? Try, Dad. Give it your best shot. I won't even hit you back." Griffen strode across the study, stopping a couple feet from his father. "Scout's honor."

Pierce took another step; he drew his arm back as if preparing to hit him, then stopped dead. A look of utter surprise crossed his face, then of complete pain. He clutched his chest. His eyes bulged; his face drained of color.

"Oh, dear." Griffen cocked his head. "Are we having a coronary event?"

Pierce's hand went to his shirt pocket. Gasping for air, he fumbled for his nitroglycerin tablets. The tiny box slipped from his fingers and clattered to the floor.

He looked at Griffen, begging. Griffen smiled and slipped his hands into his trouser pockets. "Sorry. No can do."

"Dear...God. You're my...you're my...son."

"God has nothing to do with this. This is between you and me. Payback time, old man."

Pierce lurched toward the phone, hitting the side of the stand, knocking it over. The phone and lamp crashed to the floor, Pierce with them.

Face twisted with agony, Pierce clawed his way toward the box of pills.

As his fingers brushed against the box, Griffen nudged it with the toe of his Bally loafer, putting it just out of his father's reach. "Sorry, Pop, but you see, everything is going so well for me. It really would be better if you died."

Pierce inched across the floor; again Griffen tapped the box out of reach. "I'm proud of the old college try you're giving it, though. Good for you, Dad."

Griffen squatted beside his father, watching his contortions, studying him. He had never seen a man die before. "You see," he said, his tone conversational, "I've found her. Grace. My Grace."

His father stopped writhing and looked at him.

"She's everything we knew she would be. An incredible artist. Every bit as good as Dorothy was at the same age. Maybe better. And she's beautiful. Brilliant. She's perfect. Absolutely perfect.

"You know how I found her? That nobody you were talking about earlier, the PR guy. Chance McCord. Found his name in those personal files of yours."

He laughed with delight, the sound high and youthful. "I'll let you in on a little secret." He leaned down, close to his father's ear and whispered, "Madeline wasn't crazy. You were blind. Just like she said."

A sound escaped his father's lips, part agony and part fear. For his father had realized that his time had finally come. And only hell awaited.

"Unfortunately, you'll be gone. You won't be able to tell my little secret or become reacquainted with your long lost daughter. Such a shame." He laughed again, all but giggling with delight. "But don't worry, I've taken care of everything. Within a month, she'll be calling Monarch's home."

Griffen curled his lip, hatred welling inside him. "Aren't you even going to congratulate me? Are you just going to lie there, clutching your chest and gasping for air? You always were such a selfish bastard. Never could say, 'Job well done, son.'"

Griffen leaned toward his father, then drew back, the smell of death wretched on the other man. "You want to hear the best part? The very best? She has no memory of us. No memory of her distant past. She suffers from repressed memory syndrome. Isn't that a hoot?"

Griffen tipped his head heavenward for a moment, then focused on his father once more. "I always knew she and I would be together again. And now I know how. We'll be husband and wife, Dad. Isn't that perfect? Mr. and Mrs. Griffen Monarch.''

For one moment, the fear and pain twisting his father's features was replaced by pure horror.

And then he was gone.

42

Skye couldn't believe her luck. The call from Griffen Monarch had come out of the blue. The powers that be at Monarch's Design and Retail had seen her work in the MOMA exhibit and had been impressed. They were looking for a new designer, Griffen Monarch had said, and they would like to see her portfolio.

After sending it, she had waited two and a half nerve-wracking, nail-biting weeks for word on what they thought. It had gotten so bad that she had leaped every time the phone rang. By the end, she had decided she would even welcome bad news, just so long as she could stop wondering.

During that time, she had told herself all the things a level-headed person would—not to get her hopes up; that she was an unknown; that they were undoubtedly looking at other artists, ones with a reputation, with experience, with something to bring to the party besides ambition and determination. It had been an honor, she had told herself, a thrill, just to have her portfolio requested by an atelier as old and as acclaimed as Monarch's.

Even as she had told herself all those sane, smart things, she had wished and prayed and agonized. She wanted the job so badly she had been able to taste it.

Then, her wildest dreams had become a reality. Griffen Monarch had called again, this time to arrange for a personal interview. Two days later, here she was in Chicago, being whisked down Michigan Avenue in a pure white limousine that was nearly as big as her living room.

The car had been a surprise. She had scraped together all the money she could, expecting to take a cab to and from the airport. Instead, a uniformed driver had been waiting at her gate, holding a placard with her name printed across it.

Skye ran her hand along the buttery-soft leather seat. Being in this car made her feel like a celebrity. Like royalty. Smiling, she leaned her head against the seat back. She could get used to this. Oh, yes. No problem at all.

Her lips lifted. She supposed she needed a reality check about now, something like—*Don't get your hopes up, Skye. Starving artists did not suddenly turn into princesses. Not ever. Period.*

"Almost there, miss." The driver met her eyes in the rearview mirror. "That's the old water tower on your right. That and the building across from it, the old pumping station, were nearly the only buildings left standing after the great Chicago fire. Watertower Place is there, on the left. Lots of fine shopping, if you're interested. Great food court, too. Like nothing you've ever seen."

"Thanks." Skye smiled. "But I won't be shopping. It's a quick business trip."

He nodded and returned his attention to the traffic, which had slowed to a near crawl.

Skye took a deep breath, realizing that she hadn't in quite some time. She shook her head, amused. Kind of hard to breathe, with ambition burning in the pit of her gut the way it was. She needed to relax, to enjoy this and to accept that becoming the acclaimed designer she longed to be would take time. Despite the anxiousness clawing at her, she was willing to wait, to pay her dues.

It would happen, she thought fiercely. She would get the job that would give her her start. She knew she would.

If not this time, the next. Or the time after that.

Skye took another deep breath and lowered her eyes to her lap, to the envelope she clutched in her hands. If nothing else, Griffen Monarch's call had given her a piece of her past. She took the letter from the envelope and carefully smoothed it. At the left of the envelope the Monarch's logo stood out boldly in relief.

An ornate, curvy "M."

Her "M."

Skye's heart began to thrum. She trailed her index finger over the embossed "M," excitement squeezing at her. When she had opened the letter and seen the logo, she had been stunned dumb. She had stared at it, her entire life, for that split second, coming into focus. Others, the outside world, had ceased to exist. Her universe had consisted of that logo and the unfathomable blackness of her past.

Then she had gotten a grip on herself. She had taken out one of her old drawings and compared the two "M"'s. They were nearly identical. *Nearly.*

So what, she had asked herself, did it mean? The answer had been painfully obvious—exactly nothing. The two "M"'s could be totally unrelated. They probably were. And she was indulging in speculation and fantasies that could hurt her chances of getting this job.

Skye frowned, the beginning of a headache pushing at her temples. She hadn't told Griffen Monarch about recognizing his company's logo from the hundreds of times she had drawn it as a child, of course. He would have thought she was some sort of a nut. A real head case. She would have been able to kiss this interview—and any hopes of a job offer, present or future—goodbye.

No, she hadn't said anything about the "M," and she wouldn't. Not ever. She stuffed the letter back into the envelope, then the envelope into her purse. The time had come to put all that nonsense behind her, anyway; she needed to let go of the past and embrace her future. Starting now.

The driver eased the vehicle to a stop. "Here we are, miss."

Heart in her throat, Skye peeked out the window at the

store's magnificent limestone facade. It was just as beautiful as she had dreamed it would be, she thought. Even more.

She moved her gaze up, taking in the winged Nike, then beyond, to the upper floors where the design department/production studio was located. She swallowed hard, the enormity of what was happening hitting her full force. She was here for a job interview. *At Monarch's.* The place where so many of the creations she had admired and studied had been created. If she was hired, she would have the chance to put her mark on the world of jewelry.

The driver opened her door. People stopped to stare, hoping, Skye knew, to get a look at a celebrity. She smiled to herself, both self-conscious and tickled, wondering what they thought when they saw her, instead—a woman wearing dime-store sunglasses, a secondhand Timex and the latest in business attire from her neighborhood Sweet-Repeats shop.

Skye alighted the vehicle at the same moment Monarch's grand front doors swung open and a man stepped out. The sun spilled over him, shooting his dark hair with chestnut highlights. Long and lean, he wore a suit that was as unmistakably European as it was expensive. It fit as if it had been tailored especially for him, which, she realized, it probably had.

Skye's mouth turned to dust. He was the most handsome, most sophisticated, man she had ever seen.

And he was smiling at her. Walking toward her.

For a moment Skye thought he had her confused with someone else. Then she realized who he must be.

The man stopped before her and held out a hand. "Skye? Griffen Monarch."

"Griffen." She took his hand, shuddering slightly at his touch. "It's a pleasure to meet you."

"A bigger one for me, I assure you. I'm quite a fan."

"Of mine?" she repeated, her cheeks heating. "I don't think anyone's ever said that to me before."

"Well, get used to it." He tucked her arm through his.

"I'm just the first in what I'm sure will become a long line of admirers. Speaking of, Dorothy is anxious to meet you. She's been pacing all morning, and that's not at all good for her blood pressure."

Dorothy Monarch was anxious to meet her? Skye marveled, not quite able to believe her ears. One of the greatest jewelry designers of the last half century, anxious to meet her?

As if Griffen could read her mind, he laughed again. "The time for modesty is over. You, Skye Dearborn, are an incredible talent."

She laughed, beginning to relax, finding him to be as charming as he was handsome. "If *the* Griffen Monarch says so, I guess I have to believe it."

"I like the way you think." They started for the store's entrance. "If only the rest of my employees felt the same way."

Skye kept her excitement in check, though barely. *"The rest of his employees"* implied that she was one, too. But she had not officially been offered the job, and until she was, it would not be wise to take anything for granted. This man was obviously a seasoned businessman, a man adept at working angles and deals. He had also, she was certain, blown wind up plenty a girl's skirt in his time; he might even be testing her in some way.

Still, Skye hung on to those words as Griffen took her through the store, introducing her around, stopping at various cases to point out particular pieces, series, stones.

"We've only just begun carrying the work of other designers." He indicated a case with several pieces by Paloma Picasso and a few by Angela Cummings. "But only the best and only when their creations are far from our own milieu."

He moved on, stopping before another case. "Some of our older designs have remained our most popular." He indicated a matching pin and earring ensemble, styled in a dramatic, vertical swirl. "I'm sure you recognize Dorothy's Tornado."

"Of course. It's part of her Wind series, one of my favorites." Skye bent to get a better look at a pair of pavé-set diamond earrings, a single, simple drop of gold and diamonds. "Classic never goes out of style," she murmured. "Neither does quality."

"True. But we're hoping to put some energy in new directions. After all, classics cannot become so until they spring from the mind of the artist. Our studio hasn't come up with much that's dramatically new lately. And one can't rest on their laurels forever."

"Although, if one must rest, that's a fine place to do it." Skye smiled. "I'd like to earn a few laurels myself."

"And I have no doubt you will." He pointed her toward the elevator. "We were excited by some of your less traditional work. You seem to have a great understanding of what's contemporary, especially in your combinations of materials and techniques. I was particularly taken with the titanium pieces in the MOMA show."

"Thank you." They stopped before the elevator's stainless-steel art deco doors, and he pushed the call button. Skye faced him. "So if I'm hired, I'd be allowed to pursue some experimental avenues?"

"Allowed?" He met her eyes, his alight with amusement. "No, Skye. You would be required to."

Skye could barely contain her excitement. Working for Monarch's would be a dream come true, even if she had to temporarily put her personal creative expression on hold. But to work for Monarch's and still be able to push the edge of the design envelope, well, that would be heaven on earth.

The elevator arrived and they stepped onto it. The doors slid shut, and Griffen turned toward her. Mere inches separated them. Skye saw that his eyes were an almost amazing ice blue. Lighter than hers, even.

"I'm serious when I say Monarch's is actively searching

for new classic designs. We want to return to the bold, visionary work that made us who we are.''

Skye struggled for a deep breath, the elevator feeling suddenly too small, closed in and airless. Suddenly, Griffen Monarch seemed alarmingly big, he seemed to tower over her.

He didn't notice her distress, and continued talking. "Dorothy has headed Monarch's studio for almost fifty years. And she's done an incredible job. But she's tired. In recent years, her health has begun to slip. She's ready to turn over her creative reins to someone younger and more energetic." He looked away. "My father's recent death was hard on her."

Skye swallowed and took a step backward, needing space, air. "Wha...what did you say?"

He turned back to her. "My father. He died a few weeks ago. A heart attack. He was only fifty-five. We all took it hard, but Dorothy—" Griffen drew his eyebrows together and leaned toward her. "Skye, are you all right?"

"Not really." She managed a shaky laugh, fighting the panicky sensation that settled in the pit of her gut. "I'm feeling a bit...claustrophobic."

"Does this happen to you often?" he asked, his expression concerned.

"Never before." She managed another laugh, feeling like an idiot. That made a lot of sense—she had never been claustrophobic before, so it decided to pay her a visit today, the most important day of her life. Right. He probably thought she was a liar as well as a nut job.

"It's just nerves," he murmured. "Relax. Take a deep breath and let it go." The elevator stopped; the doors slid open. "Aunt Dorothy's a real sweetheart. She's going to adore you. Just wait and see."

Skye hurried out of the elevator, the panicky sensations receding as she did. She took a deep, calming breath. He was right; she was nervous. After all, she was about to meet *the* Dorothy Monarch. The woman responsible for the creation of at least a half-dozen designs that had become a part of global consciousness, designs so in tune with their time that they had defined an era. No small feat. One accomplished by only a handful of decorative artists anywhere. Louis Comfort Tiffany. Jean Schlumberger. Elsa Peretti.

Dorothy Monarch.

And she, Skye Dearborn, was about to meet her.

She would simply be professional, Skye decided. After all, they were both artists, both women. They both had to eat, sleep, go to the bathroom. Dorothy Monarch wasn't a god, after all.

The moment Griffen introduced his great-aunt, all Skye's plans to be coolly professional went down the tubes. She gushed. She couldn't help herself. She went on about Dorothy's Wind series; about the pieces she had done during the Kennedy years; about her use of enameling and semiprecious stones in fine jewelry, a most avant-garde direction for their day.

When she finished, Dorothy hugged her. "Thank you, my dear. What high compliments you've just paid me. I believe you've made my week."

Dorothy Monarch wasn't what Skye had expected. She was a petite woman, though her high cheekbones, Joan Crawford eyebrows and wide, mobile mouth, gave her a larger-than-life presence that belied her size. She wore faded blue jeans and a deep purple silk blouse. As she talked, her chin-length, wavy gray hair fell across her face. When it did she would push it away with a graceful gesture that reminded Skye of a butterfly flapping its wings.

It was interesting to look at the great-aunt and nephew together, as they were so dissimilar physically. Griffen was tall, six-three, Skye guessed; Dorothy was five foot one, if Skye was generous. Too, Dorothy was animated, gesturing when she spoke, every bit the creative bohemian; Griffen was still, contained in the way of the predator, a way that suggested he saw everything and missed nothing, the urbane businessman from head to toe.

But they were both handsome people, polished and self-confident. Both with those unusual blue eyes and strong, angular features.

"Let me show you around our facility," Dorothy said, motioning to their right. "Our group consists of two teams, research and development, of which the designers are a part, and production. The production team consists of the bench workers, quality control, inventory and trafficking. Sales and marketing come under retail's auspices, that's Griffen and his crew's baby, though the design team is a part of their decision-making process." She shot him an affectionate smile. "He likes to 'meeting' us to death."

They turned down a hallway, lined on both sides with small offices, belonging, Skye learned, to the six artists in research and development, all of whom were presently at a trade show at McCormick Place.

"As lead designer," Dorothy continued, "I'm ultimately responsible for the look of everything that leaves this studio. I hear all problems and all ideas, I make all the final decisions. Conference room—" she pointed dead ahead, then slightly to the right, "break room. I insist the staff keep the coffee, Coke and any other edibles in there or their individual office.

"That's the software room." She pointed again. The woman working there looked up, smiled almost shyly, then returned her attention to the beads she was stringing. "All beads, seed pearls, cord and the like are stored and applied there. Stone setting is the room beyond that. By the way, we use the store's gemologists and buyers to provide us with our gemstones. And we don't do any lapidary."

She turned left. "The raw safe. Here you'll find all the various gauges of silver and gold wire, as well as any findings you'll need. Inventory is supposed to stay on top of it, but if you discover we're out of something, let Ted know."

She opened the safe and indicated a chart on the inside door. "This will tell you exactly where what you need is. I'm a fanatic about having an orderly studio, so be sure to put things back where you found them." She shot Skye a smile. "Order is a must when your memory is as bad as mine. Gemstones are kept in the store's vault."

Turning, she indicated the room's vertical-filing system. "We have production instructions on every piece of jewelry that's ever come out of the Monarch studio, even Anna Monarch's first pieces. Nothing's been permanently retired yet, except, of course, for the one-of-a-kind and special-order pieces.

"We send all our casting and plating to a production foundry, but do all finishing work in-house. We use mostly vulcanized rubber-injection molds, they're durable as hell and we get exact wax models every time. No smoking from here on."

"I don't smoke," Skye said quickly.

"I do," Dorothy countered. "Like a chimney. And I don't want to hear a word about it." She glared at Skye, then Griffen. He shrugged, as if with resignation.

As they moved through the facility, Skye noticed the bench workers kept their eyes and attention on their work. Occasionally Dorothy would stop to check someone's technique, offer a compliment or advice.

"Bench workers are assigned according to their talents and experience," she continued. "Only my designers can move from one finishing area to the next." Dorothy quickly pointed them all out. Buff room. File and solder room. Electra stripping area. Enameling room.

As they started back the way that they had come, Skye could tell that the tour had fatigued the other woman. Earlier, Skye would have guessed her to be thirty years younger than her seventy years, now she seemed every one of those—plus some.

Dorothy led them into a large front office, obviously hers. The walls were lined with awards, framed medals and photographs of Dorothy with famous faces. She went immediately to her desk and pack of cigarettes. Lighting one, she sank with an audible sigh to her chair.

"Sit." She waved Skye toward one of the chairs that faced her desk. "I want to talk to you."

Skye did as the woman asked, though she noticed Griffen didn't move from his position in the office doorway. Predatory, she thought again. He looked like a cat waiting for the perfect moment to spring.

Dorothy studied Skye through a haze of smoke. "So, what do you think of our little playpen?"

Skye laughed, liking the other woman more with each passing minute. "It's the most fantastic facility I've ever seen."

Dorothy sucked almost greedily on her cigarette. "You being fresh out of school, I'd be interested to know what you think the current trends in jewelry are."

Skye didn't have to pause to think; she, her faculty adviser, and several of the other grads had had this discussion just days ago. "Eclecticism, definitely. If nothing else, the nineties has been about anything being possible. There's also been a no-holds-barred exploration of materials and mediums. Consumption is in, which is always a good environment for the decorative arts to flourish.

"Recently, however, I have seen a return to the classics. Silhouettes have become slimmer, chunky and gaudy are out, sleek and simple are in. Personally, I think that's part cyclical swing and part reaction to society's frenetic pace and the almost constant bombardment on our senses by new stimuli."

Skye leaned slightly forward in her seat, warming to her subject. "But to be quite honest, I don't believe in following trends. People never make their mark by following the leader. To stay ahead, you have to set the trends. Get out on a limb, take risks. Be the leader.''

Dorothy arched her eyebrows. "So, you're saying, know the trends then ignore them?"

"Basically. Leave that to the mass production and costume houses."

"Very artsy-fartsy of you," Dorothy murmured. "But what about our retail business? Our clientele doesn't want tomorrow's favorites, they want today's."

Skye smiled. "It's the age-old conundrum between artist and patron, between creation and starvation. To stay alive, to grow, you need a balance between the two."

"I see." Dorothy's lips twitched, though Skye wasn't certain whether with appreciation or irritation. "And what about *our* balance between crass commercialism and lofty creation? What do you think about how we're doing?"

Skye sat back in her seat, realizing how neatly she had been cornered. "I'm really not familiar enough with your recent work to comment on—"

"Bullshit." Dorothy stamped out her cigarette. "You're one smart cookie. Smart enough to do your homework before showing up here today. Let me have it, both barrels."

Skye tilted her chin up, her gaze never wavering from the older woman's. "Weighing in a bit heavy on the commercial side these days. Just my opinion."

Dorothy cackled. "You're a spunky little thing, aren't you? For myself, I think I would have lied."

Skye held her head up, though her spirits sank a bit. "I speak my mind. Some have considered it a fault."

"I don't. I like it." Dorothy rocked back in her chair. "I get pretty sick of all the yes ma'ams and ass kissing that goes on around here. That's not what I need." She stood and came around the desk, stopping before Skye, looking her dead in the eye. "As I'm sure you know, my day as a leading-edge designer has come and gone."

"That's not what I meant," Skye said quickly. "You're a legend, one of the great—"

"Save it. That was yesterday's news. I've been at this a long time. I've done some great work, and I've had a lot of fun doing it. But I'm old now. I'm not as willful as I once was. Not as creative. And not as strong. I have a great love of the new and innovative, but I have no affinity for it. I need bright, strong-willed people around me. I need people who'll tell me the...the..."

Dorothy frowned, her forehead creasing as with confusion. Griffen took a step into the room, his expression concerned. "Aunt Dot, are you okay?"

"Yes, but I... What was I saying? I've gone completely blank."

He shook his head. "Dorothy, you're getting so forgetful."

"I know that, dammit!" She glared at him. "What I don't know is what I was saying."

"That you need bright, strong-willed people around—"

"That's right!" She smiled at Skye. "It's a bitch getting older, my dear. Remember that and enjoy every moment of your youth. Anyway, as I was saying, I like your work, Skye. I like it a lot. And I like you." Dorothy glanced up at Griffen, as if sending him a silent, guarded message, then back at her. "I'm going to enjoy having you on board. You'll be the perfect addition to my team."

"You mean, I have the job?" Stunned, Skye looked from Dorothy to Griffen. "Really?"

"Really."

"I don't know what to say. I...I'm thrilled."

Griffen crossed to stand beside his great-aunt. He smiled. "Then 'yes' would be the most appropriate response. And the one we're hoping for."

Skye laughed, delighted. "Yes, then. Of course, yes."

Griffen smiled and held out his hand. She took it and he drew her to her feet. "Welcome to the Monarch family, Skye

Dearborn. We are very happy to have you with us." He looked at Dorothy. "Aren't we?"

"Yes. Absolutely delighted." Dorothy caught Skye's hands and kissed both her cheeks, the smell of smoke clinging to her. "You're part of the Monarch family now. Welcome home."

Home. Family. Skye could hardly believe it was happening. She couldn't believe the way they were accepting her. It was like a dream come true. "But…I…when do you want me to start?"

"As soon as possible." Griffen smiled. "After all, we don't want to give you a chance to change your mind. You're ours now, Skye Dearborn. And we don't intend to lose you."

43

Within two weeks Skye and Mr. Moo had moved themselves and everything they owned to Chicago. Skye had talked to Griffen almost daily. He offered to take care of everything for her, and true to his word, he did. He had found her an apartment in one of his family's many properties, a fabulous two-bedroom on the Near North side, only three blocks from Lake Michigan. He had arranged to have it painted, cleaned and aired out for her arrival, and had the phone and utilities hooked up.

Skye had decided that Griffen Monarch was the most wonderful man she had ever met. He was attentive. Easy to talk to. Gorgeous. One night, they had stayed on the phone for two hours, swapping stories, talking about their likes and dislikes, their views on the world. It was almost uncanny, they had so many things in common, from favorite foods, authors and artists, to their views on politics.

It was as if there was this connection between them, this psychic tie. As if they were two pieces of one whole, meant for each other.

Whenever she caught herself thinking such over-the-top things, she scolded herself. She was being a ridiculous romantic. A softheaded, starry-eyed fool. People were not "meant for each other." People did not have "psychic ties" that bound them to each other.

But still, she couldn't quite stop her thoughts, and that frightened her. As did the way she felt around him, giddy and sort of breathless. She was too smart for that kind of behavior, too world-wise.

The thing that scared her the most, however, was the way she found herself wanting to trust him. To depend and lean on him. To believe in him. It had been so long since she had allowed herself that luxury.

Thirteen years, to be exact.

She thought of Chance and stiffened her spine. Luxury left you soft. And vulnerable. She knew that. When you depended on someone, when you trusted them, they could hurt you. Most often they did.

Griffen could hurt her. Badly. He was her boss, president of Monarch's, Inc. He was rich, handsome, sophisticated. He could have—and probably had had—any girl he wanted.

It wouldn't do to be making eyes at him; it wouldn't do to be thinking of him as anything other than her boss and friend. She had better remember that.

Starting now. Today. Her first day as a member of Monarch's research and development team.

Skye stopped in the middle of the sidewalk and gazed up at the building. People streamed around her, some of them sending her a curious glance, but most too hurried to take the extra moment to do even that.

She pressed a hand to her stomach, to her butterflies, and drew in a deep breath. *This was it. Way to go, Skye.*

Releasing the breath, she crossed to the door, prepared to ring for the security guard. Before she could, he was there, opening the door for her, all smiles. "Good morning, Miss Dearborn. Go right in. Mr. Monarch alerted me that you were starting today."

"Thank you—" she read his badge "—Ed."

"Good to have you with us, Miss Dearborn. Have a great first day."

She thanked him and started for the elevator, thinking how nice everyone she'd met had been. She had always heard that people in big cities were cold, that most of them would rather spit on you than lend a hand. That certainly wasn't proving to be her experience. If people got any nicer, she would start to suspect she had somehow fallen into the twilight zone.

The elevator was waiting and whisked her to the fifth floor. No one else was about. She had purposely arrived early so she could explore and gaze wide-eyed at everything before the others arrived. Dorothy had called the night before to say hello and to make sure she had received the agenda she had forwarded via fax.

Skye had received it. Which was precisely the reason she had arrived early. She had a get-acquainted coffee-and-pastry thing with Dorothy and the rest of the studio staff at nine; at ten-thirty the research and development team would be looking at ideas for a Holiday collection; at noon, a lunch meeting with the head of sales and marketing. Afternoon off to meet her moving truck.

Skye wandered through the studio, wanting to look it over while it was empty. She circled around, saving her office, the best, for last.

She reached it, and a lump formed in her throat. Her name was on the door. She ran her hand across the nameplate, fighting the ridiculous urge to cry. She opened the door and the scent of flowers assailed her. A huge arrangement of fresh flowers waited on her desk, a combination of all her favorites—orchids, birds of paradise, tea roses, daisies. She laughed softly at the unconventional but exotic combination, pleased, knowing who they were from without having to read the card.

She wanted to anyway. With shaking fingers she opened it.

Welcome Home. Griffen.

Home, she thought, bringing the card to her chest. That was the second time a Monarch had said that to her. She shook her head, surprised to realize that, odd as it was, this did feel like home already. It felt as though she belonged here. She moved her gaze over the room, soaking it in. The room was outfitted with the usual desk and PC, but also with a jeweler's bench complete with a flex-shaft and bench pin, a drawing table, a viewing board…it even had a window.

It was perfect. She bent her head to one of the blossoms and breathed in its fresh, sweet scent. Just perfect.

"Hi."

She made a sound of surprise and whirled. Griffen stood at her office door, leaning against the jamb, watching her, his expression pleased. She felt her cheeks heat. "Hi to you."

"I see you got the flowers."

"They're beautiful. Thank you."

"Is the office okay?"

"It's wonderful."

"And the apartment?"

"Wonderful, too. Empty, but great." She laughed nervously, holding his gaze a moment, uncertain how she should handle this. How could she keep a professional distance when he was looking at her so intensely, as though she were the only, the most special woman in the world? When he was sending flowers and giving her gifts and making her feel about sixteen years old?

"When does your furniture arrive?"

"This afternoon. What there is of it."

"You'll need a hand with some of the heavy boxes. I'll stop by."

"That's not necessary, Griffen, really, you've already done too much."

"Funny, to me it seems like I haven't done enough." When she tried to protest more, he stopped her. "I want to. Besides, I can't wait to meet this Mr. Moo of yours. I'm sure he and I are going to be very big buddies."

She smiled and capitulated. "All right. I'd like that."

"Good." He smiled. "Until tonight, Skye Dearborn."

44

Griffen arrived shortly after the movers left, his arms loaded with bags of takeout, a bottle of wine and a bouquet of flowers. He smiled. "I thought you might be getting hungry about now."

"Actually, I'm starved! Here, let me help you." She laughed and took the bags from his hands. "It smells fabulous."

"It's Thai. I hope you like spicy."

"I love spicy. Thai's my favorite." She nudged the door open wider with her hip. "Come on in. As you can imagine, I'm in a bit of disarray right now."

As she led him to the kitchen, she sidestepped one of Moo's huge rawhide bones, then nudged aside a half-emptied box of studio supplies. "I can't thank you enough for getting me this place. I adore it."

"I was glad to help. It was just sitting here, empty."

"That's hard to believe. I'd have thought a Prairie style at this price would have been snapped up right away." She deposited the bags of food on the counter. "There's something you're not telling me, isn't there?"

"Excuse me?"

"Am I going to hear clanking chains and the howls of the dead in the middle of the night?" When he continued to gaze blankly at her, she laughed and shook her head. "You know, ghouls, ghosts and things that go bump in the night."

"You mean, is it haunted? Not that I know of." Griffen

glanced around. "Where's this Mr. Moo I've heard so much about?"

"Moo! I forgot all about him! I locked him in the bedroom when the movers were here because he kept wanting to help them unload the truck. Excuse me, I'll get him."

Mr. Moo did not like Griffen. Not one bit, evidenced by the way he hung by Skye, pressed against her legs, glaring at Griffen, growling deep in his throat. Every time Griffen moved, so did Moo's gaze. He never took his eyes off him.

"I don't understand," Skye said, distressed, holding on to his collar, afraid he might lunge at Griffen. "He's usually so friendly."

"He's had a few big days," Griffen said easily. "He's in a new home, the last thing he needs right now is a stranger hanging around."

"But the movers were just here, and he didn't—" She bit back the words, flushing. "I'll lock him up again."

"No, don't. He'll hate me forever."

"He adores fortune cookies," she said. "Maybe he'll warm to you if you give him one."

"It's worth a try." Griffen dug a cookie out of the bag and unwrapped it. Moo's eyes went straight to it; he began to drool.

Skye released this collar. "Okay, boy. You can have the cookie but not the fingers. Gentle…good dog."

Stupefied, Skye watched as he slinked over to Griffen, took the cookie and dashed right back to her side. She had never seen him act like this. She shook her head. "Maybe I should lock him up, I really have never seen him this way."

"Give him a few minutes. At the worst, he'll take a chunk out of me, at the best, we'll become friends."

Skye nodded, appreciating Griffen's willingness to try, though she didn't feel entirely comfortable with her decision. "How about a glass of wine. I'm ready."

Skye went to one of several boxes marked Kitchen Stuff and dug through it, coming up with a corkscrew. Smiling, she handed it to him. "Success. I think my wineglasses are in that one," she said, indicating another box.

Sure enough, she located one of the glasses, unwrapped it, then went rummaging for another. "Ow!" She snatched her hand back. Blood streamed from a long cut across the ball of her hand. "I think I found a second glass," she said weakly, cupping her sliced hand. "Unfortunately, it's broken."

"Jesus, Skye." Griffen grabbed her hands and led her to the sink. He flipped on the cold water, then drew her hand under it.

She winced. "That stings."

"I'm sure it does." Using a bit of dish-washing liquid, he washed the cut, then gently probed it.

She turned her head away. "How bad is it?"

"It could be worse."

"I don't...need stitches, do I?"

"I think you're okay without them." He shut off the water, then patted her hand dry. "Are your first-aid supplies unpacked?"

"Yes, Dr. Monarch." She laughed shakily. "I did the bathroom first. You know, girls and their essentials. I'll be right back."

"But I haven't performed the most important part of the treatment."

He brought her hand to his mouth and gently kissed her cut. Their eyes met. His lips lingered. Her stomach did a funny little something, a lurch or flip-flop. Skye's knees went weak, she went hot then cold.

"You'd better get that bandage."

She drew her hand away. "Yes, I...yes. Excuse me."

She practically ran to the bathroom. Shutting the door partway behind her, she crossed to the sink. Leaning against it, she gazed into the mirror, taking in her flushed cheeks and sparkling eyes. What was she going to do? At first she had thought he was simply being nice, but now she wondered if he was…interested in her. No, she didn't wonder. She knew he was.

And how could she keep a professional distance when he looked at her that way—as though she was beautiful, special, exciting? When he kept sweeping her off her feet with take-out food and flowers and endearing little kiss-make-betters?

She couldn't, that was the problem. She squeezed her eyes shut. This was happening too fast. She didn't know him. He didn't know her. He was her employer, for heaven's sake. He—

"Are you all right?"

She opened her eyes. He stood in the doorway, holding a glass of wine, his expression intent. She forced a smile. "I'm fine…thanks. I'm just…it's just that…I feel a little dizzy."

He held out the wine. "I found another glass."

"Thanks again." She took it, brought it to her lips and sipped. The liquid warmed her as it slid down her throat. "I found the bandages." She set the glass of wine on the edge of the sink. "I'll be out in a minute."

"You're sure you don't need any help?"

"I'm sure." She smiled again, anxious for him to leave the bathroom. It felt too small with him in it. "But thanks."

Ten minutes later Skye emerged from the bathroom to discover that Griffen had found plates and utensils, candles and holders and made them an intimate table on the floor in the middle of her living room.

He lit the candles. "You still hungry?"

"I think so." She curved her arms around her middle, feeling strange about his having gone through her boxes without asking. She shook the feeling off, telling herself that he had only been being nice.

"Have a seat. I'll bring the food."

She did as he suggested, noticing Moo for the first time. He hovered near the kitchen doorway, his gaze on Griffen. He looked almost frightened. "Moo's stopped growling, I see."

At the sound of his name, Moo started toward her, giving Griffen a wide berth.

"He and I had a talk. He's agreed to tolerate me."

"That's good." She drew her eyebrows together and stroked her dog's head. "He's acting so strangely. I wonder if he's sick." She touched the animal's nose to check his temperature, noting that it seemed fine, cool and damp.

Griffen returned with the food. They ate and though it was delicious, Skye couldn't really enjoy it. Her stomach felt funny, jumpy and nervous, and she couldn't seem to stop thinking about the way he had just walked in and taken charge. And the way she had let him.

"God, you're beautiful."

Her fork slipped from her fingers and clattered to her plate. Her cheeks flooded with heat.

He laughed softly. "You are, Skye."

She dropped her gaze to her lap, uncomfortable with the way he was looking at her, as if he wanted to swallow her whole.

He reached across the table and touched her hand. "I'm direct, I know. It puts some people off. I would hate to do that to you, though. It's important that I don't scare you off."

She searched his gaze, looking for something, some clue to what he saw when he looked at her, some clue to why he seemed to want her. In that moment, as she studied him, she thought she knew him—from sometime before, in her distant past. She caught her breath, as in the recesses of her mind a door seemed to open, then quickly shut.

"What's wrong?" he asked, his expression puzzled.

"For a moment, I thought... Could we have ever met before? I mean, sometime...a long time ago? I don't know, for a moment you looked so...familiar."

"I don't think so." He curled his fingers around hers. "In fact, I know we haven't. Because no way would I have forgotten it."

"You're sure, then." She caught her bottom lip between her teeth, troubled. "I must be more tired than I thought."

"I have another explanation."

"You do?"

"Perhaps it's your heart that recognizes me."

A lump formed in her throat, and she drew her hand away. "I don't think we should do this, Griffen."

"Do what?"

"You know—" she spread her hands helplessly "—this."

"What?" His lips lifted. "Wine? Thai? Compliments?"

"You're my employer," she said, flushing. "It could get complicated—"

"Messy, even."

"Yes. Messy. And awkward."

He stood and came around their makeshift table, stopping beside her. He caught her hands and drew her to her feet. He looked her in the eyes, almost with challenge, as if daring her to try to look away.

"Yes, I'm your employer. And yes...I want to be more. Much more."

He laced their fingers. "I've waited a long time for you, Skye Dearborn. A long time. I know I should go slow, but I'm so...hungry for you."

The blood rushed to her head. She actually felt faint. She couldn't drag her gaze from his, as much as a part of her wanted to.

He brought their joined hands to his mouth and kissed her fingers, one after the other, lingering over them, feasting as if they were a rare delicacy. He moved on to her knuckles, her palms, the inside of her wrists.

Her knees went weak; she swayed. He caught her and eased her against him. "Do you believe in love at first sight?"

"No...yes." She shook her head, at the moment uncertain what she believed. "Maybe...I don't know."

"Well, I do. I believe in love at first sight, because I loved you the moment I saw you.'' He cupped her face in his palms and gazed into her eyes, his burning with an almost fevered intensity. ''Is that corny? Does that make me less of a man in your eyes? Does it make me weak?''

She couldn't speak. She tried, but no sound came out. She shook her head.

''Good, because I looked at you and I knew, I *knew* you were the one for me. The one I wanted forever.''

''Forever,'' she repeated, her voice no more than a throaty whisper. Nobody had ever said things like this to her. Nobody had ever made those kind of promises; nobody had ever wanted her that much.

Forever.

The headache started suddenly, at her temples, taking her by surprise. She fought past it. ''But you...you don't know me, Griffen. I don't...know you.''

''I know you, Skye. I do.'' He captured her hands again and brought them to his heart. ''And you know me. Look deep inside your heart, and I'm there. You've been waiting for me, too.''

She had. She had been waiting for a man who would love her on sight. The man who would love her completely, fiercely. Forever.

''I'll give you everything, make your every dream come true.'' He bent his head to hers and caught her mouth, softly at first, then with growing passion. She flattened her hands against his chest, reeling from his words and kiss, reeling from the headache that pressed in on her.

When he lifted his mouth, she could hardly breathe. ''I'll wait for you. I'll give you time. But I mean what I say, Skye Dearborn. I intend for you to be mine.''

45

A monstrous dark bird stalked her. Hovering, its shadow fell over her, obliterating the sun. Skye ran, but not fast enough. Her breath came in small, desperate gasps; sweat poured from her. She knew she wouldn't be able to keep up this pace for long. A part of her wanted to look back, turn and face the monster at her heels. But she was too afraid. Only by running, she knew, could she escape it.

Yet the faster she ran, the closer it came.

From the corners of her eyes she saw the bird's long, razor-sharp claws. In a moment those claws would close around her. And then, the monster would have her.

"Mom! Help!"

Skye sat bolt upright in bed, her scream still echoing in her dark bedroom. Breathing hard, drenched in sweat, she looked around her, confused, disoriented.

Something moved at the end of the bed, then whimpered. Moo, she realized, shuddering. It was Moo. "Come here, baby," she whispered, patting the space beside her. "Come on." He inched up on his belly, then laid his head on her lap.

She bent and buried her face in his fur. Seconds ticked past, becoming minutes. Her heart slowed, her breathing with it. Her head began to clear.

Only a bad dream, she told herself, straightening. Just a nightmare. Nothing to be scared of.

But it had been terrifyingly real. She passed a trembling

hand across her forehead. She had all but felt the dark beast's breath on the back of her neck.

She threaded her fingers through Moo's thick fur, comforted by his presence. Where had the nightmare come from? she wondered. She was on top of the world, all her wishes beginning to come true. She had landed the job of a lifetime; she had a great apartment in a fabulous new city. She had a dream-man professing to be head-over-heels in love with her.

Be careful what you wish for…

It just might come true.

The fortune-cookie warning ran through her head, and a nervous laugh bubbled to her lips. She was turning into a silly, superstitious twit. The next thing she knew, she would be planning her day according to the newspaper horoscope and calling 1-900-Fortune before making a decision.

Moo whimpered again, and Skye realized she had him in a choke hold. She relaxed her grip and snuggled down beside him in the bed.

She had been through a tremendous amount of change in the past two weeks, the nightmare was the result of stress. That, or it had been caused by taking the headache tablets just before bed. Everybody had nightmares sometimes.

Sure they did.

But as she lay awake, staring at the ceiling, she couldn't help thinking about wishes and warnings and monstrous dark birds that threatened to swallow her whole.

46

Over the next two weeks, Skye's nightmare, like her head-aches, became chronic. If not for them, those two weeks would have been perfect. As it was, they were incredible. Magical.

Thanks to Griffen. He had taken her to the theater, to jazz clubs, to restaurants so fancy she couldn't even pronounce most of the dishes on the menu. Night after night, they had talked until the wee hours, sharing their lives, their hopes and dreams for the future.

With each passing day, Skye had become more convinced that he was her every dream of a perfect man coming true. How many times had she wished for a man who would love her so much, so completely, he would be able to see no one and nothing but her? How many times had she dreamed of a desperate, passionate, perfect love, a love that transcended the mundane of the here and now?

That's the way Griffen said he loved her.

Said?

Skye dropped her sketching pencil and brought the heels of her hands to her eyes, tired from the long day. She wanted to trust him. She wanted to believe in him, in his words of love. But something held her back. She didn't know what it was. Maybe it was just that it was too soon, that they were going too fast.

Maybe she feared, deep down, that he would change his mind, realize he was mistaken, that he didn't love her. And then he would leave her behind.

And she would be destroyed.

Skye sighed. What did he have to do to prove his devotion? He said all the right things, all the things she had waited a lifetime to hear. He did the things a man in love should, looking at her and treating her as if she were the only woman on earth. What was wrong with her? Why couldn't she trust him?

She turned her gaze to the window and the approaching dusk. She rubbed her temple. It was almost as if Griffen had crawled inside her head and learned her deepest secrets, her innermost fears and longings.

How did he know her so well?

Soul mates. Is that what they were?

Griffen thought so. He believed there was one ideal person for everyone, one ideal mate, a mate chosen from beyond this world, before birth. Griffen believed that's what they were: soul mates. He had told her so.

Was Griffen why she was here in Chicago, now? Was this, was he, what her whole life had been leading to?

Skye turned her gaze back to her desk in time to see Martin, one of the other artists, walk past her office door, leaving for the day. As he did, he sent a venomous glance her way.

She sighed. She and Martin had not hit it off, and the other artists had welcomed her with varying degrees of warmth. For some reason, although she had only been on board two weeks, word had started circulating that she was Dorothy's favorite. That she was the one Dorothy would hand over the creative reins to, when she retired.

It was ludicrous, really. She had only been a part of the Monarch's family for two weeks. Handing over control to her would be fantastically unrealistic, as well as unbusinesslike. And neither Dorothy nor Griffen could be called either of those things.

As for being Dorothy's favorite, she didn't know about that. Dorothy had taken her under her wing, personally showing her the ins and outs of the design department. And she did feel that she and Dorothy were in sync creatively and that the woman liked her a lot.

But that did not make her next in line for the throne.

Nor did her romance with Griffen, word of which had spread like wildfire through the department. Skye didn't doubt that little tidbit had cost her even more points with the other artists.

Knowing that worrying about her relationship with her colleagues wouldn't accomplish anything, Skye turned her attention to the sketches she had been working on. She tilted her head to the side, studying them.

Her first research-and-development-team meeting had been a disaster. Beforehand, she had decided to keep her comments low-key, her opinions—for the most part—to herself. But when she had seen some of the team's ideas, her plans to ingratiate herself with silence had gone down the tubes. She had been extremely vocal, opinionated and critical. So much for winning friends and influencing people.

But the proposed designs had been worse than pedestrian, they had been deadly dull, uninspired. She had said so.

And earned Dorothy's approval and her fellow artists' dislike and, she suspected, their terminal resentment.

But she hadn't been able to contain her excitement any more than she had been able to hold her tongue. She had jumped in with both feet, making suggestions, changes, additions.

Dorothy had been delighted with her ideas. A couple of the artists had been inspired by her enthusiasm and had rushed forward with her. Thank God. Doing this job without any allies at all would have been nearly impossible.

"Hey there."

Skye looked up. Terri, one of the designers who had accepted her, stood in her office doorway.

Skye smiled. "Hi. I was just thinking about you."

"You were? What's up?"

Skye spun her drawing pad around. "What do you think?"

Terri crossed the office, her expression hesitant. Skye held her breath as the woman gazed at her sketches, at this point little more than a combination of bold lines and angles.

"I thought I'd call the series City Lights," she said.

When Terri still remained quiet, Skye quickly filled the silence, self-conscious. "So far I'm just playing with line and angle, trying to capture the movement, energy and landscape of a city. It's got a long way to go, I know, but—"

"No, I like this direction. I like it a lot." Terri tilted her head. "What are you thinking about in terms of materials?"

"A combination of white and yellow gold, some surfaces textured, some polished to a high shine. I see fiery gemstones. Emeralds, rubies. Yellow topaz."

Terri perched on the edge of the desk, obviously warming to the idea. "We could create a signature piece for different cities. Chicago, of course. London, New York, San Francisco. Each could capture the essence of that particular city."

"I like that."

Terri tapped one of the sketches. "It would be great for a holiday line. The perfect gift for the woman who has everything."

They were silent a moment, both caught up in their own thoughts. Terri broke the silence first, clearing her throat. "I have some ideas. Mind if I put them to paper? It'll still be your baby."

"I'd love that. We're a team, after all."

"Good." Terri smiled. "This is going to be fun."

The receptionist stuck her head into the office. "There you are, Terri. Call for you, line one. It's Will. He says it's important."

Terri frowned. "Thanks." She turned to Skye. "Can I use your phone?"

"It's all yours." Skye stood. "I'll just go get a cup of coffee."

Terri waved her back to her seat even as she greeted the person on the other end of the line. Although Skye tried not to eavesdrop, it was impossible not to notice the anger and bitterness in Terri's voice as she spoke to the person on the other end of the phone.

Within moments of picking up, she dropped the receiver back into its cradle. "Perfect," she muttered. "Just perfect."

"Is there anything I can do?"

Terri met her eyes, then looked quickly away. Skye saw that the other woman's eyes sparkled with tears. "I wish there was. Will's my husband. My soon-to-be ex-husband, actually. He's such a creep."

"I'm sorry."

"Me, too." She looked away, then back. "I might as well tell you, everybody in the department knows. I caught him screwing around on me. Turns out it was far from an isolated incident, if that makes any difference. My life's been a nightmare ever since."

Skye didn't know what to say, so she said nothing.

Terri laughed, though the sound was choked. "It wouldn't be so bad if it weren't for Raye. That's our four-year-old daughter. She misses her daddy. She wants to know why I won't let him come home." Terri twisted her fingers together. "I don't know why, the bastard wasn't home that much as it was. He didn't have the time. He was too busy with his girlfriends."

"Does he want to come back?"

"Yeah, he does." She lowered her eyes to her lap. "But I can't let him come home, not after what he's done." She searched Skye's gaze, looking, Skye knew, for understanding, for approval. "Forget trust and respect. Forget breaking my heart...what about AIDS?" She brought the heels of her hands to her eyes. "I went and got tested. I had to, just in case."

"Oh, Terri. How awful."

"I feel like I'm living every woman's worst nightmare...one minute in a supposedly trusting, monogamous relationship, the next I'm having to deal with a broken heart and an AIDS test. It was negative, thank God, but I have to go back in six months.

"How can I let him come back?" She looked at Skye again. "Am I wrong? Am I being selfish?"

"You're the only one who can make that decision, Terri. But I'll tell you this, you don't deserve to be treated like that."

The other woman gazed at her a moment, then smiled. "Thank you. I appreciate your saying that."

Skye returned her smile. "You're welcome."

"Want to see a picture of my little girl?"

"I'd love to."

Terri wore a locket around her neck with Raye's picture in it. She opened the silver heart and leaned across the desk so Skye could see the photo. Her daughter was adorable. Skye told her so.

"She is, isn't she?" Terri gazed at the photograph a moment, then snapped the locket shut. "Speaking of, I need to take off. That's why shithead called. He said something had come up and he couldn't get Raye at the baby-sitter's. More like *someone* came up, no doubt." She crossed to the door and looked back at Skye. "I'll see you tomorrow?"

"You bet. Terri?" The woman stopped at the door and looked back at her. "Thanks. For being so nice to me. You're definitely in the minority around here."

Terri hesitated a moment, then smiled. "You're easy to be nice to. Besides, you were right. Those other designs sucked."

47

The house was magnificent. The kind of house people only dreamed of living in. A house listed on the national register of historic places, one on the Chicago Architectural Society's tour, three stories of brick, limestone and Italian Renaissance ornamentation.

Skye gazed up at it, heart thundering. "Do real people actually live here?"

Griffen laughed and draped an arm across her shoulders. "I take it you like the place?"

"It's like a castle. The kind of place a princess would live."

"A princess," he murmured, sweeping his fingers rhythmically back and forth across her upper arm. "I like that. Although I always just thought of it as home."

Home. She shivered. She didn't think she could ever call this place home. It was too grand, too cold. She didn't know why, but for all its size, she had the sense it would press in on her, smothering her.

"Come on. I've told Granddad so much about you, he's anxious to finally meet you."

She hung back. "Do we have to do this?"

He looked at her, surprised. "What do you mean, do we have to do this? Granddad's expecting us for dinner. Dorothy's coming, too."

"I know. I—" She passed a hand across her forehead. "I...I feel so strange suddenly. Dizzy and a little...queasy."

"Just nerves." Griffen bent and kissed her. "I promise you that's all it is. Come on."

He propelled her up the walk. Lit from within, the double, beveled glass front doors sparkled like a wall of diamonds.

Skye counted each step. The closer to the house she got, the more her unease grew. With each step, the greater her urge to run.

"Relax." Griffen squeezed her hand. "Granddad won't bite. You'll see."

True to Griffen's promise, Adam Monarch did not bite. Instead, he greeted her with a big, warm hug. As though she was a long lost member of the family, or someone he had been waiting a lifetime to meet.

"My, you're pretty," he said, looking her over, beaming. She flushed under his scrutiny. "Thank you."

"Isn't she a prize, Granddad?"

"That she is. Beautiful. Talented and smart, too, I hear." Adam Monarch and Griffen exchanged glances. "She's so perfect, one might almost think she's a Monarch."

"She will be, if I have my way." Griffen caught her hand and laced their fingers. "It was love at first sight, and I don't intend to let her get away."

Skye squirmed, uncomfortable, embarrassed and pleased all at the same time.

"It's about damn time." Adam chuckled and met her eyes. "He's a catch, lassie, but slippery. Hold on tight, I don't want him slipping off the hook."

Griffen snorted with amusement. "No chance of that, Granddad. She couldn't get rid of me if she tried."

Skye looked from one man to the other, warmed by their relaxed and affectionate relationship. For a moment, she let herself bask in the fantasy that she was one of them, one of their charmed circle. Theirs was the kind of family she had always dreamed of being a part of. Affectionate. Close-knit. United.

What would it have been like to grow up here, in this

mansion, with the Monarchs' sense of history and community, with their roots, the kind that were so rare these days?

She swept her gaze from Griffen to his grandfather, smiling to herself. It would have been nice, she decided. It would have been very nice.

As if reading her mind, Adam met her eyes once more. "We're a temperamental lot, I know. Demanding. Critical. Overzealous. But, we're fiercely loyal to our own. Once you're one of us, you'll know you're part of a family. We'll never turn our back on you."

The front bell pealed. "There's Dorothy," Adam said. "Get our girl a drink, Griffen. I have a good cabernet open on the sideboard. I need a moment alone with my sister."

Griffen nodded and led Skye to the dining room. The table, which could have easily accommodated forty, was set on one end with china, silver and flickering candles.

"It's beautiful."

"Thank you." They crossed to the sideboard and Griffen poured them both a glass of the wine. He handed one to Skye. "There was a time when the house was always filled with guests, the table set to capacity, night after night."

She brought the glass to her lips, sipped and made a sound of appreciation. "What changed?"

"The times. Mother got ill. Our family shrank." He shrugged. "The table will be filled again. Everything moves in cycles."

Skye indicated a large oil painting above the sideboard. "Who's this? She looks like Dorothy."

"Anna Monarch. The talent who started it all."

"And the man with her? Is that her husband?"

Griffen moved to stand behind and rested his chin on the top of her head. "No. That's Marcus. Her brother. Together they started Monarch's." She felt his smile. "With her artistic gift and his business savvy, they were quite a pair."

"As Dorothy and Adam have been."

"Yes. And after them, Marcus's children, Rita and Jonathan. Unfortunately, the brother-and-sister teams ended with my father. He was an only child, and I—''

He bit back the words and she twisted around to meet his eyes. "You never had any siblings?"

He drew a careful breath, his expression sad. "I had two sisters. They both died…young."

"I'm sorry."

"So are we." He smiled, though the curving of his lips looked forced to Skye. "I guess those are the breaks."

She touched his cheek. "That doesn't make it any less painful."

"No, it doesn't." He closed his fingers over hers. "Come, I want to show you something quite extraordinary. But first, close your eyes."

She did as he asked, though she felt more than a little silly doing it. Taking her hand, he led her across the room. "Okay," he said, "you can open them."

She did. And caught her breath at what she saw. She stood in front of a lighted display cabinet, its glass shelves lined with Fabergé-style jeweled eggs of various size and decoration.

"My God," she murmured, stunned, completely taken with the creations. Peter Carl Fabergé's Imperial Easter eggs, created for the Russian royal family, were some of her favorite objets d'art of all time. She had always been drawn to them, even as a child. When she'd gone to college, she had done a paper on them, traveling all the way to New Orleans to see a special exhibit at the museum there.

Skye tilted her head. These were every bit as opulent as those, but they were more contemporary in design, incorporating a modern sensibility in their use of shapes, colors and materials.

"I know they're not Fabergé," she murmured, "but who?"

"Monarch." He opened the case and carefully took one of the eggs off its pedestal and handed it to her. "Monarch artisans created an egg to celebrate the birth of every new Monarch. You're holding my egg.''

"Incredible.'' The egg was a deep, opalescent blue enamel, studded with even deeper blue sapphires and wrapped with white gold wire.

"They all open. Look.''

Griffen unlatched the top, and in the way of a jack-in-the-box, a jester popped out. Only this jester had jeweled butterfly wings. Skye made a sound of surprise. And pleasure.

The little creature was at once ugly and beautiful, evil and angelic. And accordingly, she found herself both repelled and drawn to it. She tapped the figure and he bounced, the light catching and reflecting off his jeweled wings.

"Strange, isn't it?'' Griffen laughed. "Dorothy was feeling particularly creative that year. He bent so their heads were together. "I used to think,'' he murmured, "that the eggs contained the souls of all the Monarch children. I wondered what would happen if I dropped and broke one of them. I wondered if the children would escape...or die.''

Skye met his eyes, chilled. She could imagine Griffen as a young boy, gazing at the eggs and thinking of children's souls trapped inside. She shivered. "That must have been frightening for you.''

"Frightening,'' he repeated, drawing his eyebrows together in thought. "I don't know about that. It was...it just was.''

She returned her gaze to the eggs, unsettled. "Some are so much more elaborately decorated than others,'' she said. "It looks almost intentional, as if there was a sort of pattern at work.''

Griffen took the egg from her hands and set it back on its pedestal. "It's quite simple, actually. The birth of a girl child was more highly celebrated. The artist's job was to create an egg befitting the occasion.''

He said it so matter-of-factly, as if she should understand without asking, that she laughed. "You're joking, right?''

"Not at all. Why would you think that?"

"It's just…unusual, that's all. The whole notion of putting more value on one sex than another is foreign to me, but to value girls over boys? That's even odder. In some parts of the world, they don't even want their girls. They throw them away."

"Well, we want ours," Griffen said softly. "The Monarch girls are our treasures. They're the ones who possess the gift."

Gooseflesh raced up Skye's arms. "The gift?"

"You look almost frightened." He trailed a finger along the curve of her jaw. "All I'm saying is, the creative geniuses in our family have always been girls. That's all I meant. First there was Anna. Then Rita. Now Dorothy."

"But one of the boys could someday have the gift," she said, turning back to the display cabinet. "It just hasn't happened yet."

"Of course." He rested his chin on the top of her head, his hands on her shoulders. "We haven't always been a happy family, Skye. We've had our share, more than our share, of tragedy. But we've stuck together through it all. And we've never forgotten what's important. It's made us closer, stronger."

He was talking about his sisters, she knew. And his beloved mother, who had died when he was young. Too young, she thought.

She turned in his arms. He needed her. This family needed her. Resting her hands lightly on his chest, she lifted her gaze to his. She could help heal him. She could help heal them all. They needed love, and she was so hungry to love someone she was safe with. Someone who needed and wanted her.

"I think you're an amazing man, Griffen Monarch."

His lips lifted. "Do you?"

"Yes." She slid her hands up to his shoulders. "I really do."

He bent his head close to hers. "Does this mean I have a chance with you?"

"Yes," she whispered, lifting her face to his. "Definitely, yes."

With a sound of triumph, he kissed her.

His lips were cool against hers, his technique expert. Skye pressed closer, wishing for a little heat, a little fire. Wishing she would melt at his touch. She scolded herself for her thoughts. Some fires took time to build into a roaring blaze, and that was okay. Not okay, she corrected. It was better. Much better.

Flash fires burned out quickly. They were hard to control, they did a lot of damage. No, a slow, steady building of heat was the way to go. Besides, his touch felt good. It felt nice, comforting and sure.

Behind them, Adam cleared his throat.

Griffen laughed softly against her mouth. "Busted," he murmured.

Skye wriggled out of his arms and, red-faced, turned to find Adam and Dorothy, standing not three feet from them, beaming with pleasure.

"Don't let us interrupt you," Dorothy said airily. "It's about time the boy brought someone home to meet the family. I was beginning to think he never would."

"I was waiting for the perfect woman, Aunt Dorothy."

"And now he's found her," Adam said. "And we're all delighted."

"Delighted," Dorothy repeated, crossing to Skye, hands out. "Hello, dear." She kissed both Skye's cheeks. "How wonderful to have you here with us. Have you seen the house?"

"I thought I'd take her on a tour after dinner," Griffen said.

"Good idea." They began taking their seats at the table. "Be sure to show her the nursery." She looked Skye straight in the eyes, hers amused. "It's quite special."

"Really?" Skye glanced at Griffen. "How so?"

A glance passed between the two men. Griffen smiled easily. "It has a magnificent stained-glass window. Floor-to-ceiling."

"An angel," Dorothy said. "To watch over all the Monarch children. It was designed by a well-known Chicago glass artist. Frank Dewitt. Have you heard of him?"

Skye shook her head. "No, I'm afraid I—"

"The nursery's been closed awhile," Adam interrupted. "It'll be awfully stuffy. And dusty. I hate to have Skye around all that—"

"Nonsense," Dorothy said, smiling as the housekeeper brought in the first course. "I'm sure Skye won't be bothered by a little dust. She's a studio artist, after all."

"That's right," Skye said, intrigued. "I'd love to see it."

That settled, their attention turned to the meal, which was delicious. Baby field greens salad with creamy Roquefort dressing. Roast pheasant. Rice pilaf. A rich amaretto custard for dessert.

During the meal, their conversation was lively. They talked jewelry and other designers. They discussed the anticipated increase in the price of gold. The wine was superb, and Skye drank just enough to be encased in a warm glow.

After dinner, as promised, Griffen took her on a tour of the house. As they moved from room to room, her warm glow cooled. Her earlier unease returned, with it the sense that the house was pressing in on her, smothering her.

She fought to keep her rising panic from showing. This was getting ridiculous. First her claustrophobia in the elevator, then the nightmare, now this. What was wrong with her? She was turning into a neurotic.

Or maybe she was ill, she thought, bringing a hand to the back of her damp neck. Getting the flu. It was going around. Terri's daughter had had it last week.

Skye shook her head slightly, to clear it, trying to focus on what Griffen was saying. The house was amazing. An architectural wonder within as well as without. Around every corner was another painting, or artifact or antique, one that she would normally exclaim over.

And all she could do was count the seconds and pray the tour ended soon. She wanted to go home. She wanted her pajamas and Moo and bed. And she wanted never to set foot in this house again.

Dear God, she had completely lost it.

"You still with me?"

"Sure." She cleared her throat and forced a smile. "There's just so much to see."

"The nursery's down the hall. You're sure you're not too tired?"

She lied, saying that she wasn't and letting him lead her to the nursery's closed door.

"Voila." He threw open the nursery door and flipped on the light. Adam was right; it was dusty and smelled stale. She swept her gaze over the room. White iron baby bed, white rocking chair in the corner, tiny table and chairs, shelves stacked with books and toys and games. At the room's center, a nearly life-size teddy bear sat on the thick, braided rug, his soft belly looking as if it had taken years of children's heads resting on it.

And then she saw the angel. She appeared to be hovering above the room, arms spread, expression celestial. Skye caught her breath. It was magnificent.

"In the morning, the sun streams through the window, bathing the room in jewel colors." Griffen took a step into the nursery, then pointed. "We always put the cradle over there, so the infant can be directly under her watchful gaze."

Skye realized she was sweating. It beaded on her forehead and upper lip. But her mouth was dry, so dry it tasted like ash. She caught her bottom lip between her teeth and dragged her gaze from the angel to the floor.

A pool-like dark stain marred the pickled-oak flooring. As she stared at it, she realized in horror what it was. Not a stain, blood. Bright red. Wet. A cry raced to her lips, and she took a step backward.

"Skye? My God, what's wrong?"

"That...on the floor. It's...it's—"

He looked at the floor, then back at her as if she was crazy. "I don't see—"

"That!" Her voice rose; she turned and pointed. "It's—"

It was gone. The light-colored floor gleamed brightly, not even a shadow darkening its surface.

She blinked. "But I thought— I saw..."

She was losing her mind.

"Skye, sweetheart, are you all right?"

"No." She shook her head, her stomach rushing up to her throat. "No...bathroom, please."

He pointed across the hall; she turned and ran, making it just in time. She bent over the commode and threw up her entire dinner, retching until she had nothing else to lose. Retching until her sides ached and her throat burned.

As she clung to the porcelain bowl, feeling as though she were dying, a dozen different thoughts went through her head, not the least of which was how she was going to face Griffen and his family again. She was embarrassed, ashamed; she felt foolish. Ridiculous.

And she was afraid, she acknowledged. Bone-deep frightened, for the first time in as long as she could remember. The problem was, this time the monster didn't have a name. This time, she feared the monster was inside herself.

48

Even though Chance had a dozen last-minute details to take care of before the Chicago Preservation Society's patron party guests began arriving, he watched the door, anxious for Griffen's arrival.

Except for business, he hadn't seen the other man lately. In several weeks, actually. He had a new woman in his life, he had told Chance. Someone special.

Griffen had been secretive, refusing to tell Chance more about her than she was The One. Chance had snorted his amusement—and skepticism—to his friend. Griffen, Mr. Bees-to-Honey, one woman? Right. And the Cubs were headed for the World Series.

But Griffen had been adamant. This woman was it, he'd insisted. The one. The Real Thing. Then he had knocked Chance's socks off by saying he intended to marry her.

He was coming to the party tonight. And he was bringing the mystery woman.

This was one woman Chance couldn't wait to meet. If what Griffen told him was true, she must be one hell of a special lady.

"Chance!"

He turned. Lisa, his assistant, was rushing toward him, round cheeks pink with exertion. She stopped before him, nearly overbalancing on her high heels. "The caterer's in a snit about where we want him to set up. He refuses to continue until he speaks with you."

Chance smiled calmly. He considered Lisa a real find—

she had experience and an abundance of both energy and enthusiasm for her work. Unfortunately, with both of those came a tendency to excitability. "I'll speak to him now."

"Good, I'll go check on—"

She was already spinning away, preparing to rush to another detail. He caught her arm. "Lisa?" She met his eyes. "Take a deep breath. Then slow down. Everything will get taken care of."

"But—"

"Trust me." He smiled again and dropped his hand. "Hysteria never accomplished anything fast."

She laughed, then nodded, took a deep breath and started off at a half run before she had completely released it. Chance watched her go, a smile tugging at his mouth. No one would ever say that Lisa Johnson didn't take her work seriously.

Chance went in search of the caterer. He found him, listened to his concerns, made a suggestion, an allowance, and was rewarded when the man, all smiles now, launched back into his work.

This event was the first Chance had handled for the society, and he wanted everything to be perfect. And so far, everything had gone without a hitch. No early fuck-ups or last-minute snafus: the caterer's dilemma was now solved, the jazz ensemble had arrived and was setting up; both the *Tribune* and *Sun Times* had confirmed a photographer; *Chicago* magazine was an almost sure thing, and not one of his "celebrity waiters" had pulled a last-minute cancellation on him.

Chance took a final assessing glance at the caterer's work, then went to have a word with the florist. From there, he spoke to Martha, the society's director, and Robert, her assistant. He told them to be on the lookout for the press. He had to make sure the society's most important patrons got into the paper, preferably photographed with one of the celebrities. After all, they wanted something more for buying an entire table than a two-thousand-dollar tax deduction, a mediocre meal and one too many watered-down cocktails.

He had gotten the Drake Hotel to donate their grand front lobby for the party tonight, even convincing them to agree to an outside caterer to provide the tidbits—typically a hotel taboo. He had landed some big stars for the event, including Michael Jordan, Mike Ditka and Oprah, among many others. His biggest coup had been convincing Cindy Crawford— who, he had been tipped off, was home visiting her family in Dekalb—to make an appearance.

It was for an important cause, after all.

Chance smiled to himself. Martha had been delighted with the concept of celebrity waiters from the beginning. At two hundred dollars a person, one hundred percent tax deductible, of course, the opportunity not only to mingle with a favorite sports, movie or television star, but to be served a meal by them, was just too inviting to pass up.

Indeed, they had not only sold out the two-hundred-dollar-a-person tickets, they had sold twenty of the special-sponsor, two-thousand-dollar tables.

Griffen had bought a table; the historical society was one of the Monarch family's charities. Thinking of his friend again, Chance shook his head. He simply couldn't imagine it. Griffen in love? Getting married? Only a matter of weeks ago he had been collecting phone numbers on any number of body parts.

If this was for real, Chance was happy for him. Griffen had been a real friend, the best buddy he'd ever had. He had Griffen to thank for this account, among numerous others. His personal recommendation had gotten him through the society's front door and into the director's office.

Of course, he'd done the work from there, but as he'd always known, he needed to look the part to get the shot, and connections were everything.

Griffen made him look the part. The Monarch's account made him look the part. They connected him to this city in a way that even twenty years of doing good business would not.

Chicago was an amazingly small city when it came to industry news. Ever since Griffen had handed him Monarch's Design and Retail, canning Price, Stevenson and Price in the process, the PR community had been abuzz with the news.

Most insiders had been shocked—Chance had a good reputation, but he'd always had Adams and Sloane behind him. But on his own, they said, who knew what he could do?

Griffen, obviously. That Griffen had believed in him enough to hand him the company's favorite child, Design and Retail, well, that had impressed.

The phone had begun ringing.

Five months later, it still hadn't stopped.

The friendship that had developed between him and Griffen had been a nice side benefit. And another surprise. The last thing Chance had ever expected was to become friends with the other man. Griffen was too rich, too powerful, too important.

After a while, their being friends had begun to feel okay. Then it had become easy. And somewhere along the line, Chance had begun to take the whole thing, if not for granted, then as a kind of lucky break. He had begun to feel like one of those fat-cat executives he had always looked at, wondering what it would be like to be them.

Now he knew. It was pretty damn great.

Pretty damn great, Chance thought again, an hour later as he surveyed the party, now in full swing. It was an unqualified success, judging not only by the attendance, but by the excited din in the room. People were having a good time. Special-events coordinators, especially when working for nonprofit organizations, sometimes forgot that part of the equation. Chance considered it the most important part. When people had a good time, they remembered. They told their friends. And selling the society's next event would be easier, not harder.

"You're a genius, Chance." Martha caught his hands and squeezed them. "People have been stopping me all evening, complimenting me on the event. I sang your praises, of course."

"I appreciate it." He smiled. "By any chance, have you seen Griffen Monarch tonight? I need to speak with him."

"Why, yes. I was just talking to him." Martha turned and pointed toward the other side of the lobby. "He was over…yes, there he is. With his charming date."

Chance looked in the direction she indicated and caught sight of Griffen. Thanking her, he started in that direction. He had been too busy to watch for the other man, but now that he had a moment, he was anxious to meet the mystery woman. She stood with her back to him, her arm tucked through Griffen's. She had shoulder-length, velvety brown hair. It fell in full, soft waves, seeming to almost float around her shoulders and upper back.

And quite a spectacular back it was, revealed by her dress, backless save for a jeweled strap that ran from her neck nearly to her waist. Chance arched his eyebrows in appreciation, skimming his gaze over the expanse of creamy skin. So far, impressive. No wonder Griffen had decided he was in love.

Smiling to himself, he worked his way around a tight cluster of Oprah's admirers. As he did, Griffen's date turned slightly in his direction. Chance's heart stopped. His world rocked.

It couldn't be, he thought. Griffen's date bore a striking resemblance to Skye, his Skye—but all grown-up and as beautiful as any woman he had ever seen.

But it couldn't be her. Only a couple of months ago he had told Griffen the story about him and Skye and how they had been on the run together. For her to show up now, on

Griffen's arm, would be too weird. Too much of a co-incidence.

He drew closer. She turned more fully in his direction. He stopped dead in his tracks.

It couldn't be, but it was.

Skye was here.

A rush of emotion moved over Chance: disbelief, surprise, pleasure. It really was her—his beautiful, pesky, know-it-all little Skye. As he gazed at her, his lips lifted into a smile. He recalled their days at Marvel's, the way she had followed him around, the way he had dumped her, sputtering and red-faced, on her mother's doorstep, remembered her thirteenth birthday and how she used to look at him, as if he were the most wonderful person in the world.

No one had looked at him that way before or since; no one had ever trusted and depended on him the way she had.

His throat tight, he swallowed hard. Damn, he'd missed that. He'd missed *her*.

He only realized just how much now. This moment. He wanted to hug her, to laugh with her, he wanted them to talk for hours—so he could find out everything that had happened to her in the last thirteen years and what had brought her here, to Chicago.

He wanted to find out how she had ended up at this event on his best friend's arm.

Griffen. Chance looked to the other man and found him watching him, his expression almost…amused. As Chance's gaze locked with Griffen's, his friend's mouth curved into a small, sly smile. The hair on the back of Chance's neck stood up.

What kind of game was Griffen playing?

He shook the thought off, though not without effort. Griffen could not have known who Skye was, or he would have told Chance. This whole thing was some sort of bizarre co-incidence. Some weird twist of fate had brought them all together. They would laugh about it later.

Sure they would.

Griffen leaned toward Skye and whispered something in her ear, then pointed. Smiling, she turned in Chance's direction.

Her eyes locked with his. For one frozen second she gazed almost blankly at him. Then her smile faded and she stiffened, her face flooding with hot color.

Reality hit him like a thunderbolt. Skye wouldn't be happy to see him, let alone want to stroll down memory lane with him. He had hurt her. She might still be angry with him, she might hate him.

That would pass, he told himself. Once he explained, she would understand. After all, she had obviously done well, that was partly due to the decision he had made to leave her with Sarah and Michael.

He closed the distance between them, scrambling to come up with what he was going to say to her, scrambling for the best thing to say. Griffen took care of it for him.

"Chance, buddy." He put his arm around Skye. "I'd like you to meet Skye Dearborn. She's the one I told you about."

Chance looked at her, his heart thundering. "Skye and I know each other," he said. "Hello, Skye."

"Hello." She looked at him, then away, her mouth set in a tight line.

"You two know each other?" Griffen glanced from one to the other, his expression disbelieving.

"From a long time ago." Chance's words sounded choked, even to his own ears. "You look good, Skye. Really good. I can't believe it's really you."

She met his eyes, hers glacial. "No, I suppose you can't," she said stiffly. "But then, how could you?" She turned to Griffen. "Excuse me. I need to visit the powder room."

Chance watched her walk away, frustrated, a dozen different things he could have said, things he wished he'd said, on the tip of his tongue. He turned to Griffen and found his friend watching him, again. Griffen looked as self-satisfied as a cat who'd cornered a mouse.

Chance narrowed his eyes. "Tell me, Griffen, how did you two meet?"

"I could tell you, but I'm more interested in how you two know each other."

"Are you really?" Chance rested his fists on his hips, spoiling for a fight. "Somehow I doubt that."

Griffen's eyebrows shot up. "Whoa, what's with the attitude? Skye's our new designer. I saw her work at a show in New York, tracked her down, checked out her portfolio, Dorothy and I were impressed and offered her the job."

"And that's it?"

"That's it. Except, of course, that I've fallen in love with her. If you've got some sort of beef with that, I think I'd better hear it now. But I warn you, my feelings for her are not going to change."

Chance stared at his friend a moment, searching his expression. He pushed away his lingering doubts. Griffen had been a good friend to him, he had done more for him than anyone he had ever known. What reason would he have for lying about this?

Chance shook his head. "Damn, I'm sorry, Grif. It's just that this whole thing is such a weird coincidence."

"A weird coincidence?" Griffen repeated, folding his arms across his chest. "Okay, I'm listening."

"Remember, a couple of months ago, when I told you about the carnival and the girl who—"

"The girl whose mother ditched her?"

"Yeah, that's the one. The one who drew the frog." He leaned toward Griffen. "That girl is Skye."

Griffen widened his eyes. "No way."

"She is. Skye is that girl."

Griffen whistled under his breath. "That is too bizarre. Are you sure?" Chance just looked at Griffen, and Griffen held up his hands. "Okay, I believe you, you're sure."

"You see why I was so surprised?"

"Yeah, I see." Griffen turned his gaze in the direction she had gone. "She didn't seem all that happy to see you. What exactly did you do to her?"

Chance followed his friend's gaze. "I left her behind. I had to, but I didn't even—" He bit the words back, not even wanting to say them.

"What?" Griffen urged. "What didn't you do?"

"I didn't even say goodbye. I thought it was for the best. For both of us."

"Excellent move." Griffen chuckled. "Very classy. I guess I shouldn't count on having you over for dinner after she and I are married."

"She's going to forgive me."

"Yeah, right." Griffen didn't hide his amusement. "You, buddy, have one very large set of balls. If I were you, I'd protect them. That's one pissed-off lady."

"You'd like to see that, wouldn't you?" Chance said, annoyed by Griffen's attitude. By his amusement. "You're enjoying this."

Griffen shrugged, though Chance could see it in his eyes. A sly, secret kind of pleasure. Again, Chance thought of a cat toying with a cornered mouse, taking time to play with it before going for the kill.

Chance looked away, unsettled by the image. Sometimes the other man was such a prick. Sometimes Chance wondered if he even knew Griffen Monarch at all.

49

Skye sank onto the powder room's vanity stool, reeling with the truth, struggling to get a grip on her runaway emotions. She brought her trembling hands to her face. When she had turned around and seen Chance standing there, looking at her, it was as if her life had passed before her eyes.

For one traitorous split second, joy had bubbled up inside her. For that minuscule moment in time, she had been thirteen again, and he had been her best friend, her brother, her family.

Then she had remembered. And remembering had hurt. Remembering had made her angry.

Now, as it had moments ago, anger took her breath. White-hot and blinding. She dropped her hands into her lap, clenching them into fists. How could Chance have done that to her? He'd abandoned her, sneaked out in the middle of the night, too cowardly and small even to say goodbye.

She'd been a child, for heaven's sake. She had needed and depended on him. She had trusted him, loved him. He'd left her without so much as a "Good riddance, kid."

He'd broken her heart.

She hated him.

Skye gazed at her reflection, surprised by the ferocity of her emotions. She had thought she'd let him go. She had thought she didn't care anymore, not enough to be angry or hurt, certainly not enough to hate him.

She closed her eyes, breathed deeply and counted to twenty, working for control, for a semblance of calm. She wasn't thirteen anymore. She was a woman now, independent, strong, self-confident. She didn't need him anymore. She didn't have to talk to him if she didn't want to, she didn't even have to look at him. If she wanted to, she could spit on him and walk away.

Or, if she chose, she could hurt him. She could make him regret the way he had hurt her, the way he had left her.

Another of her wishes coming true.

She swallowed hard and thought of their meeting of minutes ago. How dare he simply say, "Skye and I knew each other a long time ago" as if they had been nothing more than acquaintances? How dare he say she "looked good," how dare he be able to look into her eyes with no trace of guilt or remorse in his?

It wasn't right. She wasn't going to stand for it.

Even as she thought of her revenge, she pictured him—as he had been all those years ago and as he was now. He was taller, broader, a man now instead of a teenager. His boy-next-store face had weathered, laugh lines etched the sides of his mouth and eyes, giving his face a masculine lived-in look.

Dammit. He looked good. She had imagined many things over the years—that he had become fat and bald, that he had been disfigured in a fire or maimed in a tragic accident.

Instead, he was handsome and successful.

And he was Griffen's "buddy."

She muttered her displeasure. Talk about bad luck, talk about a sly, mean-spirited twist of fate.

She searched her memory for what Griffen had told her about the close friend he'd wanted her to meet tonight. Not much. Only that he was in public relations and special events and that he would introduce them tonight.

Skye remembered thinking that Griffen was acting secretive, like a person who knew a really juicy secret that he couldn't wait to share.

She frowned. Could Griffen have realized not only that

she and Chance had known each other, but what their relationship had been? She had told him a little about her past, but not about Chance. Not about the specifics of losing her mother or how she had come to live with Sarah and Michael Forrest.

Skye shook her head. Ridiculous. There was no way Griffen could have known. And he certainly hadn't learned it from Chance. Chance had been as shocked as she.

Now, of course, she would tell Griffen everything. He would be curious; considering their relationship, he had a right to know.

She glanced at her watch. She had been in here for fifteen minutes. She was surprised Griffen hadn't come after her already, or sent in reinforcements.

She was a big girl. Too big to be hiding in a ladies' room. Too grown-up to be trembling and crying and feeling sorry for herself. She could handle this.

She could handle Chance McCord.

Skye stood and smoothed her dress. Leaning closer to the mirror, she inspected her makeup. Deciding she looked pale, she pinched her cheeks for color and added a coat of lipstick.

Ready for battle, she thought, recapping the tube and dropping it into her evening bag. Chance McCord had better watch out. If she saw him, she would blow him out of the water. She smiled to herself. She hoped she did see him, she'd been waiting thirteen years to tell him what a creep he was; it was going to be fun.

She got what she wanted. He was standing outside the powder room, waiting for her.

He sprang forward when he saw her. "Skye, wait. We have to talk."

She swept her gaze contemptuously over him. "Good idea. Why don't we start with a discussion about what a complete asshole you are."

"Only if you go first."

She caught her breath, furious with him, with his cavalier

attitude. "You walked out of my life without so much as a goodbye. Without even having the decency to leave me a note. You did that, knowing full well how much I depended on you. Knowing that I loved you. You knew what my mother's leaving me the same way had done to me. You did it anyway, you bastard.

"No thanks to you, I'm doing well. Great, in fact. I don't need you in my life, not anymore. And I don't want you in it, either."

She started by him; he caught her arm. "Do you really think you'd have anything you have now if we had stayed together? Do you think you'd be so well educated? Or that you'd have your fancy new job at Monarch's?"

"Don't hand me that batch of crap and think I'm going to buy it. You didn't leave because you were worried about my future. Oh, no. It was your own precious future you were concerned with."

"I was worried about us both."

"Please, give me a little credit. 'A rock around your neck.' Isn't that what you called me?"

She pushed past him; he followed her, catching her hand, swinging her back to face him. "True, I knew I was never going to make good on my dreams if we were together. But you needed a family. You needed to go to school—"

She yanked her hand free, so angry she shook. "We'd found a family."

"You could stay there, but not me. You were a kid, I wasn't. I had to make a life for myself."

"Well, you did. You've done well for yourself, Chance McCord. Congratulations, I'm happy for you. Now, get the hell out of my life."

50

As the days ticked past, Skye's memory of her encounter with Chance at the patron party became more vivid instead of less, her anger and outrage grew rather than diminished.

She immersed herself in her work, in her relationship with Griffen and her growing friendship with Terri and her little daughter. But still, she had only to close her eyes and there Chance would be, his image taunting her.

Why couldn't she put him out of her mind?

Murmuring good morning to the main-floor receptionist, Skye stepped onto the elevator and headed up to the design department. She lifted her gaze to the floor numbers as they were illuminated, thinking of Chance. She had seen him a couple of times since the party, but only at a distance. Both times she had told herself not to stare, she had told herself to stop gobbling up every detail of his appearance, as if she was starving for him.

And she had reminded herself that she hated him. That she wanted revenge. Problem was, the more she told herself all those things, the more she thought of him.

She wished he would just go away. Get out of her head and life and leave her alone.

The elevator arrived at the fifth floor, the doors slid open and she stepped out.

"'Morning Skye." Louise, the design department's receptionist and all-around gofer, held out several pink message slips. "Message from Mr. Monarch. About lunch."

"Today?"

"Yes, it's all there. Also, Dorothy's called a meeting for this morning. At ten."

Skye shuffled through the slips, noting both messages. "What's up?"

"Don't know. Dorothy was smiling like crazy, though."

"Interesting." She stuffed the memos into her pocket. "Is Terri here yet?"

"Yup. In her office."

"Thanks, see you later."

Skye headed for her office, thinking again of the events of the past two weeks. Griffen had continued to court and woo her. He was attentive and loving and possessive of her in a way that made her feel safe.

Little by little she had begun to believe—really believe— that he loved her. Loved her with the depth of emotion he said he felt. It was in his eyes when he looked at her, in the way he hovered by her side when they were out.

She was beginning to trust him. She was beginning to believe he would never leave her.

She frowned, a hint of a headache starting at her temple. Why did Chance have to show up now? Reminding her how much it hurt to be left behind. Reminding her how risky it was to trust, how frightening. Making her remember how deeply she could be hurt.

And reminding her what it had felt like to be in love.

She shook her head, forcing the thought away. She had been a kid. What she'd felt for Chance at first had been puppy love, then an adolescent infatuation. She hadn't even loved him, not really. At the carnival, he had been different than the other boys. Smarter, cleaner, nicer to her. And later, when she'd had no one else to turn to, he had become her everything—father, brother, friend, hero. It made sense that she had turned all her love and devotion his way. It had been natural for her to adore him. She was becoming a woman, she'd had new, disturbing feelings to deal with, feelings she had naturally turned his way.

It hadn't been him, she told herself again. It had been the situation. She had confused dependence for love.

But that had been a long time ago. A lifetime ago. Now she had Griffen. He was everything she wanted in a man. Strong, attentive, supportive. He wanted to give her the world. He loved her, he would never leave her.

Pain stretched across her temple, and she massaged the place, her vision blurring. *Dammit. Not this morning. She wasn't going to let this happen today.*

Skye realized she was standing outside Terri's closed office door. She drew her eyebrows together. Terri never closed her door, not even when she was deep into a project. She said it made her feel claustrophobic.

Skye tapped on the door, wondering what was going on. She and Terri had fallen into a fast and easy friendship. They had much in common, including having been abandoned by the people they loved. They had begun spending so much time together that even Griffen had commented on it, sounding almost jealous.

Skye supposed she could understand Griffen's feelings, she'd had to refuse several of his invitations because of plans she had with Terri and her daughter, but she was really enjoying having a girlfriend. Someone she could laugh with and talk to. Someone who thought the way she did.

Skye tapped on the door again. "Terri? It's me."

Her friend called for her to come in. Skye did. "Good morning."

Terri barely glanced up. "Hey."

"Big meeting this morning. Did you hear?"

"Heard."

"Any idea what it's about?"

"Nope."

Skye frowned. "Is everything okay?"

Terri looked up then; Skye saw that she had been crying. "Terri, what—"

"Close the door."

Skye arched her eyebrows in question, but did as her friend asked. She crossed to Terri's desk and perched on a corner. "What's going on?"

Her friend hesitated. "I've been getting these calls."

"What kind of calls?"

"Pranks, I guess." She bit down on her lower lip. "At least that's what I thought they were. Now I'm…I'm not so sure."

Skye drew her eyebrows together, concerned for her friend. "If not pranks, then what?"

"Threats."

The word, the way Terri delivered it, affected Skye like a blow. Terri was not one given to melodrama. "Go on."

"At first the calls were nothing but heavy breathing and an even more annoying hang-up. Stuff like that." She drew a deep breath. "Then he progressed to obscenities. This morning he…he called me a bitch."

"Terri, how awful."

"There's more. Then he told me, 'The only good bitch is a dead bitch.' And hung up." She drew in a shaky breath. "He sounded so cold. So determined. I believe he meant it." She met Skye's eyes. "I'm scared."

Skye covered Terri's hand, curving her fingers comfortingly around her friend's. "You called the police?"

"This morning. They're going to talk to Will. They told me to change to an unlisted number, then to notify them if the calls continue. That's about all they can do."

Skye searched her friend's expression. "You think it's Will?"

"I thought so, and I guess I still do, but he denies it. We'll see what happens after a couple of Chicago's finest pay him a visit. At work."

That brought a smile to Terri's face, and Skye squeezed her fingers, then released them and straightened. "Meeting's about to start. I'm going to grab some java. Want some?"

"Thanks, but I reached my limit about three hours ago."

"It's going to be okay, Terri. This is some sick asshole who picked your number from the book, and once you change it, it's going to end."

"What if it doesn't, Skye? What if this guy knows where I live? I've got Raye to worry about. What if he..."

She didn't finish the thought, she didn't have to. It hung between them, ugly, incomprehensible, but there, nonetheless.

What if he hurt Raye?

Skye covered her friend's hand once more. "That's not going to happen, Terri. You're not going to let it, and neither am I."

"Promise?"

"Yeah." She smiled, giving Terri's fingers a supportive squeeze. "Come on, let's go see what Dorothy's so excited about."

51

The conference room began to fill. Chance sat at the head of the table, Dorothy beside him, chatting excitedly about their upcoming project. Even as he listened to her, nodding at the appropriate moments, he watched the door. Waiting for Skye. Anxious for his first look at her, hoping it would break the spell he'd been under since he'd seen her at the preservation society's patron party.

For two weeks now he'd been unable to stop thinking about her, unable to put her out of his mind. He kept picturing the woman she had become, but at the same time remembering the girl she had been. Images of things they had done, conversations they'd had, the way it had been between them, had plagued him day and night. Things he hadn't thought of in years, he could now recall with perfect clarity.

He had become almost obsessed with her. It was nuts. Counterproductive. It made him feel like a jerk.

She was Griffen's woman now. His friend's woman. He had to remember that.

Chance lowered his gaze to his notes stacked neatly on the table in front of him. He had brought them, though he doubted he would use them. It was a thing with him, he always liked to have his hard facts close by, just in case.

He smiled at something Dorothy said, then returned his gaze to the doorway, his thoughts to Skye. He and Skye happened to share a past. It shouldn't be a big deal. So much time had passed, their lives had gone in totally different directions. It shouldn't matter to him that she thought he was a bastard.

But it was a big deal. It did matter to him what she thought.

Dammit. He cared about her. He always had, contrary to what she thought. He wanted her to forgive him, to realize that what he'd done, he'd done for them both.

Skye arrived finally, walking in with another woman he recognized from seeing around the store. They were deep into a conversation and Skye didn't notice him. It gave him a moment to simply gaze at her. She was radiantly, exotically beautiful. She walked into the room and lit it up. She had done the same when she was a kid, only the energy had been different.

Now it was sexual. Now he felt it like a punch in his gut—only dead south.

Damn but he was in deep, deep shit.

Skye caught sight of him and stopped, frozen, her gaze locked with his. He smiled, he couldn't help himself. She stiffened, her face flooding with color. Dorothy cleared her throat. The woman beside Skye nudged her. Still Skye didn't move.

Griffen slipped into the room, coming up behind her. He laid his hands on her shoulders, and she whirled. The connection was broken, and quickly Chance jerked his gaze away.

Everyone took their seats, Griffen selecting a chair beside Skye instead of coming to the head of the table. Chance couldn't help noticing the proprietary way the other man acted around her, the possessive signals he sent to those around them. *Hands off,* his body language said. *This is mine.*

Chance had never seen the other man act that way before. Indeed, Griffen had been mostly indifferent to the women he dated, callously so. This was completely out of character, as far as Chance was concerned. It seemed almost weird.

Dorothy stood. "I called this meeting," she began, "because we have some exciting news to relate to you. I've asked Chance McCord, from our public relations firm, to tell you about it as he's the one directly responsible for this coup. But before I turn the floor over to him, I'd like to take a moment to talk to you about the Milan design festival, in which we've decided to once again participate.''

Chance cocked his head slightly, only half listening to Dorothy, instead using the moments to surreptitiously study Skye and Griffen. They made a handsome couple, no doubt about that. His smooth sophistication and her classy bohemian worked well together. Their coloring was quite similar and they were both unusually attractive people.

He drew his eyebrows together. But still, he couldn't see the two of them together. It felt wrong, off somehow, though he couldn't put his finger on why.

Maybe he simply had a bad case of sour grapes. He frowned. He had never been jealous of Griffen's ability to draw and charm women. He had never wanted to compete with Griffen.

But none of those women had been his Skye.

His Skye?

Jesus, what was wrong with him? Chance lowered his eyes to the table, to his notes for today. She wasn't *his* Skye—or his anything else, for that matter. She hadn't been in a long time.

He needed to get that fact firmly fixed inside his thick skull. And fast.

"And now," Dorothy said, turning to him, "I'll give the floor to Chance McCord. Chance?"

He thanked her and stood. "For over a century," he began, "Monarch designs have been a major force not only in the world of retail jewelry, but Monarch's artisans have always been at the forefront of the American Arts and Crafts movement.

"And yet," he continued, "Monarch isn't a household name. The public knows our designs, however, from pictures of originals on public figures like Jackie Kennedy Onassis and Elizabeth Taylor, from the many mass-market rip-offs over the years, from Monarch's ability to put their finger on the pulse of the nation. Monarch's creations are, quite simply, a part of the American consciousness."

He swept his gaze over the room, hesitating on Skye. For a moment, he lost his train of thought, for that one moment in time he could only think of her, how she looked and moved, how she had smelled the other night, like a sweet, virgin forest, of how she had changed.

Dorothy cleared her throat, and he dragged his attention back to the matter at hand, though it took effort. "For years Monarch's has been, in essence, hiding its light under a bushel. When Griffen hired me to handle publicity and public relations for Monarch's Design and Retail, I promised to get rid of that bushel and let Monarch's light shine. I promised him that people would know the name Monarch the way they know the name Tiffany."

He shot Dorothy a smile, then turned back to the group. "The light begins shining today. The University of Chicago Press has agreed to publish a hardcover, coffee-table book celebrating Monarch's one-hundred-and-ten years of innovative design. They've slated it for a Christmas ninety-eight release."

For a moment the room was completely, breathlessly silent. Then the excited chatter began, the questions and congratulations. He held up his hands. "Dorothy, Griffen or I will be happy to answer each of your questions afterward. First, let me anticipate some of them. Belinda Constantine, curator of arts and crafts for the Art Institute of Chicago, has agreed to write the book's foreword. David Argyle, who art-directed the last Tiffany book, will design both the cover and the interior layout. A photographer hasn't been selected yet, but we're talking to a couple of the best tabletop shooters in the country.

"Dorothy will, of course, oversee the entire project, from

selection of pieces for inclusion, based on historical or design significance, to curating the last section of the book, which will focus on a look forward.

"Don't kid yourself, this will require overtime from everybody. It will be a group effort." He looked at Skye. "For example, as the newest member of the team, Skye, not as much will be required of you in terms of—"

"I'll carry my weight," she cut in stiffly, cheeks pink. "You don't have to worry about me. I'm a quick study."

"I'm not worried." He arched his eyebrows. "I was going to say, not as much will be required of you in terms of historical significance. However, Dorothy tells me you're working on some interesting new things. We'll need them finished. And we'll need more." He shifted his gaze to the other artists. "Plans, sketches, working models. Whatever you've got."

"So, in other words," Skye murmured, sounding angry, "get busy?"

"Exactly." He narrowed his eyes. "You don't have a problem with that, I hope?"

"Not at all. I love my work."

"Good, because you're going to have a lot of it to do." He returned his attention to the rest of the group. "Mickey Spelling is writing the text. You might recognize him from his work on the Frank Lloyd Wright book, among others. He'll be interviewing each of you about your job, your thoughts about working for a company as old and prestigious as Monarch's, things like that."

He drew in a deep breath. "I'll be happy to talk to you about what we're looking for, in terms of your interviews. I'm sending press releases to the *Tribune* and *Sun Times*, as well as the local TV affiliates. We'll probably get some media interest with our announcement of the project, but even more when the book comes out." He smiled. "Now, for your questions."

For the next thirty minutes, Chance, Dorothy and Griffen

answered questions. Dorothy, in particular, was questioned about her ideas for the book's focus and look, and about which pieces she had already decided to include. One of the guys, Martin, Dorothy called him, had asked if the artists' pictures would be included.

Through it all, Skye remained curiously, stonily silent, her arms folded across her chest. He knew it wasn't the book she had a problem with, it was his involvement with it.

Tough shit. He wasn't going anywhere.

As soon as the meeting broke up, he crossed to where she stood talking to a couple of the other artists. He touched her arm. "Excuse me. Skye, may I speak with you a moment?"

"Of course." She smiled politely and let him lead her away from the others. When they were out of earshot, she looked at him, furious. "How dare you single me out that way. I'm a member of this team, an equal member. And I didn't appreciate your implication that you'd have to coach me on what I needed to do or say."

"Still the know-it-all brat, I see. I guess you haven't changed that much, after all."

"I don't have time for this."

She started to move past him; he caught her arm. "We're going to be working together, if indirectly. Can't we bury the hatchet?"

"Only if I can bury it in your back."

He lowered his voice. "Doesn't it bother you at all that people think you got here by sleeping with the boss?" As soon as the words left his mouth, he wanted to snatch them back. Not because he didn't think it a valid question, but because he'd had no right to ask it. He wasn't her big brother, or anything else, anymore.

For a split second she looked as if he had struck her, then she flushed, obviously furious. She wrenched her arm free of his grasp. "You, Chance McCord, are a complete pig." She smiled sweetly at an associate who moved past, then leaned closer to him. "Stay out of my way, Chance," she said softly. "I'm not feeling very friendly."

"What's this?" Griffen said, coming up to them, grinning like a Cheshire cat. "My two favorite people fighting?"

"We're not fighting," Skye said, lifting her face to Griffen's. "I was just telling him to keep the hell away from me."

Griffen laughed and looked at Chance. "Isn't she the greatest?"

"The greatest," Chance repeated, deciding he wanted to puke as she looked up at Griffen in complete adoration.

"Did you get my message?" he asked her.

"I did." She smiled. "That sounds great. I'll meet you in your office. Now, I've got to go."

Without sparing Chance another glance, she walked away.

"So, buddy," Griffen said, turning back to him, "how's it going? Your kahoonas still intact?"

Chance dragged his gaze back to Griffen's. "Barely."

Griffen laughed, the sound almost girlish. "She's crazy about me. Have you noticed?"

"Yeah," Chance muttered, "I noticed. Congratulations."

Griffen leaned toward him, his eyes alight with self-satisfaction. "I told you before, man, bees-to-honey. They can't resist me."

Chance checked his watch, unreasonably irritated. "I've got things to take care of, Grif, if there's nothing else—"

"Actually, there are a few things I need to discuss with you. But I've got to run. Can you stop by my office, noon-ish?"

"Sure," Chance said, anxious to be away from the man. Something in his eyes and tone affected him the same as gooseflesh crawling up his arms. "See you around noon."

Chance was nearly to the door when Griffen called his name. He stopped and looked back. Griffen smiled. "Don't forget what I said. Bees-to-honey, man. You just can't compete."

52

"Hello, Ashley. Griffen and I are going to lunch. Is he ready?"

Ashley smiled. "Hi, Skye. He's on the phone and asked me to tell you he's going to be just a few minutes."

Skye checked her watch, thinking of everything she had to do, her mind still on that morning's meeting and the upcoming international jewelry festival in Milan. Three months was not that far off. "Should I wait?"

"He said yes. He really won't be long." She slid a couple of folders into her briefcase. "Isn't it something, about the book?"

"It's something, all right." Skye wondered if she looked as sour grapes as she sounded, and forced a smile. "Fabulous for Monarch's."

"I tell you," Ashley said, "Griffen's instincts are amazing. He hired Chance, basically, from a cold call."

"Really?"

"And fired the store's existing firm. After twenty years of working together." She snapped her fingers. "Just like that."

The way he had fallen for her, Skye thought, a ripple of unease moving over her.

"He was interested from the moment I handed him Chance's card. Actually, intensely interested." She glanced at the time and stood. "I thought he was nuts, which shows what I know." She laughed. "I've got to go, lunch date. I'm thinking this one might be Mr. Right."

Skye told her goodbye and to have fun, then sank onto

one of the two couches that graced the waiting room, thinking about what Ashley had told her. She drew her eyebrows together. Griffen had been "intensely interested" in Chance from the moment he saw his card.

Just like that. Odd, she thought. Different.

"Penny for your thoughts."

Skye looked up. Chance stood in the doorway, smiling at her. She frowned. "What I'm thinking is none of your business."

"Still as charming as you were this morning." He ambled into the waiting area. "Consistency can be a very good quality in a person. But it can be boring, too."

"Thanks for the warning," she muttered, selecting a magazine and flipping through it. "But I'm doing just fine, thanks."

"Mmm, I see that." He slipped his hands into his trouser pockets. "Where's Ashley?"

"Lunch."

He glanced toward Griffen's closed door. "Griffen wanted to see me. Is he in?"

"He's on the phone. But you must be mistaken, he and I are going to lunch."

"I'm not mistaken. I'll wait."

"It's your time."

"Yes, it is."

She thought she heard a smile in his voice and looked at him. She was right and her blood boiled.

"By the way," he murmured, taking a seat on the opposite couch, "that unprofessional display of yours in the meeting this morning, what was that all about?"

"I don't know what you're talking about."

"Right."

"Screw you."

"Very adult. And congratulations on the dirty mouth you developed. Attractive."

She wanted to hit him, so badly she could picture herself

drawing back, then slugging the hell out of him. "I learned it from you. Don't you remember?"

"You know, Skye, as much as I enjoy this verbal to-and-fro, we're going to be working together. Can't we at least be civil?"

She got to her feet, too angry to sit. She crossed to Ashley's desk and stared down at its uncluttered top a moment, then turned to face him. "Is that all that matters to you? That we can 'indirectly' work together. That we can be civil when we see each other?"

"It would make life easier."

"You're good at that, aren't you? Making life easier for yourself?"

For a moment he said nothing, did nothing. Then he stood and crossed to stand before her. "The time's come, Skye. You're going to listen to me. We're going to talk."

"Guess again."

She started past him; he caught her hand. She tried to tug hers away, but he laced their fingers. "You'd rather go on this way? Angry and hurt? What good is that doing you?"

"Let me go."

"No. You're going to listen to me. For once, you're not going to act like a hotheaded little brat."

She narrowed her eyes, furious. "How dare you. You're the most odious, overconfident—"

"I'm sorry, Skye," he said softly, cutting her off. "I'm sorry I hurt you. I am. And I missed you after I left. I missed you a lot."

His words affected her like a blow. She struggled to keep it from showing. "Sure you did. That's why you never looked back. Why you never even called."

"How do you know I never looked back? You weren't there, you weren't with me." He moved his thumb softly, rhythmically, along the side of her hand. "I looked back a lot. And I wondered how you were doing, if you'd forgiven me. But I couldn't come back, Skye. I couldn't take care of you. It wasn't right for either of us."

"You loved me so much, you left me behind?" she said, her voice thick with tears. "The same as my mother did? That's so convenient, Chance. And it's so wrong."

"I can't speak for your mother, but leaving you hurt like hell. You were my best friend, Skye."

She fought for an even breath. Her heart hurt; her eyes burned. "If you had loved me, you would have fought for us to stay together. To stay a family. Instead, first chance you got, you took off."

"It wasn't like that. Think about those days before Sarah and Michael's. Remember Kevin? Remember what happened that last day in Boyton? Remember how you felt? Can you remember those things and not admit that we couldn't go on together? You were a kid, but you were starting to grow up. I couldn't protect you anymore. But I couldn't keep you locked up, either. Something had to change." He caught her other hand and brought them both to his chest. "Remember what it was like."

She did remember. How she felt, the way he had made her feel—hot and achy and confused. She recalled, too, the way she had tried to kiss him, and how he had pushed her away; she recalled the way his image had filled her head sometimes, in the darkest part of the night, and the way, flooded with a trembling kind of shame and excitement, she had brought her hands to herself, pretending they were his. The way she had exploded, her soft cries muffled by her own pillow.

Those memories swamped her. Bittersweet but potent. More potent than anything she had experienced before, or since. She lifted her gaze to his, remembering...everything.

In that moment, as their gazes met, something changed between them, shifted subtly but cataclysmically. The past fell away and the present became clear.

Suddenly, he was a man. And she was a woman.

Chance tightened his hands over hers. Beneath them, his heart began to thud heavily against the wall of his chest. He lowered his gaze to her mouth. She lifted her face, the breath shuddering past her parted lips.

"Skye…" He brought her closer. Her name on his lips sounded part prayer, part curse. He said it again.

And released her.

She stared blankly at him, not quite able to believe what had just happened. She had tried to kiss him. And he had pushed her away. Again. He had done it to her again.

"I can't," he said thickly. "I just… Damn." He dragged a hand through his hair. "Tell Griffen…tell him I'll call him later."

And then he was gone.

53

Friday night arrived. As had become Skye and Terri's custom on Will's night to have Raye, they went to dinner together. Tonight they chose Scoozi, a popular restaurant not too far from Terri's place. While they waited nearly two hours in the crowded bar for a table, they laughed and chatted with the other singles waiting for tables, drinking too much and fending off the advances of several overambitious men.

Skye was happy to see Terri smiling. It was good to hear her laugh. She had changed her phone number and the calls had stopped. One week had passed, then two. Terri had begun to relax; they both had breathed a little easier, believing the danger past.

When they were finally seated at their table, half-drunk, they stuffed themselves on bread dipped in seasoned olive oil and little Italian dumplings filled with cheese and spinach and drenched in a calories-not-to-be-calculated pink sauce.

Giggling like teenagers, they cabbed back to Terri's place, where Skye had left her car. They alighted from the cab, landing on the sidewalk in front of Terri's rehabbed apartment building.

"You want some coffee?" Terri asked, still giggling, digging in her purse for her keys.

"I can't drive like this, that's for sure." Skye brought her hands to her flushed cheeks. "I can't remember when I've had such a good time."

"Me, neither. Com'on up."

They entered the building and started up the stairs, neither in a great rush. Skye poked her friend in the ribs. "I couldn't believe the way you were flirting with our waiter. You were shameless!"

"Antonio," Terri murmured, stopping and looking back at Skye. "He was gorgeous."

"How old do you think he was?"

"Old enough."

Skye drew her eyebrows together, then at her friend's expression, burst out laughing. "Oh, old enough for *that*."

"He slipped me his phone number when we were leaving."

"He didn't!"

"He did." Terri pulled a cocktail napkin out of her jacket pocket and waved it at Skye. "Eat your heart out."

"That boy was at *least* ten years younger than you."

"So?" Terri sniffed. "I'm a free woman. At thirty-two, in my sexual prime. Why not have a little fun?" She angled an amused glance at Skye. "What's the matter? Jealous he didn't give you his number?"

"Of course not. I have Griffen."

Terri started climbing the stairs again. "Yeah, right. Griffen."

Skye caught her friend's arm, stopping her once more. "What's that supposed to mean?"

"Nothing. It's just that he's not...he's not my type."

"Why not?"

"Forget it."

"No. I really want to know. I won't get mad."

"I've heard that before. A friend says they won't get mad, then they stomp off and never speak to you again."

"But I mean it. I promise not to get mad."

Terri studied her for a moment, then sighed in resignation. "Okay. He's too intense for my taste. He's possessive and controlling, and I'm just not into that."

"Controlling?" Skye repeated. "You think he's controlling?"

"And too possessive." Terri threw up her hands, swaying slightly as she did. "You wanted my opinion. I gave it to you."

"I know, but you'd be a little intense, too, if you'd had his family life. I mean, his mom died when he was only two. Then both his half sisters got sick and died. He's had three different mothers and has recently lost his father."

"I'm not saying he's a bad guy, just that he's not for me. Okay? And that's not what I heard. About his sisters."

"What do you mean?" Skye frowned. "What did you hear?"

"That one was twenty months old when she died. She drowned in her bath."

Skye widened her eyes. "She drowned in...her bath?"

"Uh-huh. The mother left her alone to take a call and when she came back it was too late. Anyway, the mom went nuts after her daughter's death and ended up shooting herself."

Skye felt light-headed and grabbed the banister for support. "What about the other sister?"

"She disappeared. Kidnapped by her own mother. Neither of them were ever seen again." Terri drew her eyebrows together in thought. "She was actually his first half sister. I think her name was Grace."

"Grace," Skye murmured, testing the sound on her tongue. When Griffen had told her he'd lost both his sisters, she'd thought they had died at birth or of some sort of natural causes. This was even more awful, more tragic. "What a terrible story. Poor Griffen. Poor Adam and Dorothy."

Terri patted her shoulder. "Before, what I said about Griffen...maybe *controlling* was a poor choice of words. Maybe it's just that he's so in control. You know what I mean?"

Skye thought about her friend's description and nodded. "But I don't think that's necessarily a bad thing."

"Good, because you're the one who's dating him. Not me." Terri climbed another stair, then stopped and looked back at Skye. "Are you sure you know what you're doing, dating the boss and all? I mean, I would hate it if you got burned. And he does have a reputation as a kind of ladies' man."

"It's not like that between us, Terri. It's not a fling. I don't know why, but he really loves me."

Terri gazed at her a moment, and Skye thought the other woman wanted to say something else about Griffen. Instead, she laughed. "Maybe I'm just jealous. I'd rather have somebody special than the phone number of some young hunk I'd be too afraid to actually get naked in front of, anyway." She shuddered, then laughed. "Scary thought."

"Silly. You're gorgeous."

"But I'm not twenty anymore, either."

"Who wants to be?" They reached Terri's floor. "Twenty wasn't so great."

"Spoken like a twenty-six-year-old."

"Twenty-seven."

"Same thing. Look, somebody left me a package." The box, wrapped in brown paper and addressed to Terri, waited on her welcome mat. "From one of my many young stud admirers, no doubt."

"No doubt." Skye laughed. "You going to open it?"

"Actually, it's probably from my mom. Something of Raye's we forgot at her house last weekend. We're always doing that." Terri dug her keys out of her purse, picked up the package, unlocked and opened the door. Terri tossed the package onto her entryway table. "Come on, I don't know about you, but I've got to have some coffee."

They went to the kitchen, and while Terri started the coffee, Skye leaned against the counter, watching her friend. She didn't know when she'd had as much fun as she'd had tonight. She had never been like this with another woman, silly and serious and...connected. All those years, she hadn't realized what it was like to have a girlfriend. She hadn't known what she was missing.

"Did you have a lot of girlfriends when you were a kid?" she asked. "When you were a teenager and stuff?"

"Sure." Terri took a couple of mugs from her cabinet. "What girl didn't?"

"Me, for one. We moved around a lot. And I was pretty obnoxious."

Terri widened her eyes as if shocked. "Not *you?*".

"Was that a shot?"

"Nah, you're the greatest. You didn't have any girlfriends at all?"

"Not really. No, actually." Skye looked away, suddenly one hundred percent sober. "I learned fast how much it hurts to say goodbye."

Terri covered her hand, then broke into an off-key rendition of "Love Hurts."

Skye snatched her hand away, laughing. "You, my friend, are an asshole."

"Thank you very much." Terri bowed. "But I also make a very good, very strong cup of coffee. Which you need, because you drank too much wine."

"Me?" Skye laughed as her friend filled the two mugs. "What about you?"

"I have self-control. I understand the 'M' word, and I live by it. Moderation, my dear. Moderation."

"Please, I think I'm going to be sick." Skye took a mug and they started down the central hall that led back to the entryway and living room beyond. "What about your package?" Skye said, motioning toward it. "You going to open it? It might be from one of those young studs."

"Yeah, right." Terri laughed, snatched up the box and shook it. Whatever was inside thumped against the sides of the box. "It doesn't sound like crotchless panties or strawberry-flavored love jelly."

"You're gross."

"I know. Gross is an art form for me." Laughing, Terri ripped aside the brown paper, then the bright-colored foil beneath. That done, she lifted away the box top. And made a sound of horror.

"Terri, what's—"

The box slipped from her friend's fingers, hitting the side of the ottoman and tipping over. Its contents tumbled out, red and raw.

A rat, Skye realized, staring at the creature, her stomach heaving. It had been sliced open, and its entrails spilled out of its belly onto Terri's light-colored Dhurri rug.

Skye's stomach heaved again. She choked the sickness back, bringing a hand to her mouth, unable to drag her gaze from the gruesome sight.

"My God," Terri muttered, backing away. "My God..."

Skye looked at her friend and saw how close to hysteria she was. She shut her eyes and breathed deeply through her nose, counting to ten, then twenty, struggling for control. One of them had to think clearly, and judging by her friend's expression, it wasn't going to be Terri.

"It was him," Terri said, beginning to shake. "The obscene caller. He knows where I live."

"You don't know that for sure, Terri. Before we do anything else, we have to call the police."

"It was him." Terri's voice rose. "What if Raye had been here? What if I had let her open the box? What if—"

Skye crossed to the other woman and grabbed her upper arms. "But you didn't, Terri. Raye's with Will. She's safe. And getting hysterical's not going to help this situation. I'm going to call the police now. Where's your phone?"

Terri pointed. A portable, it lay on the floor, only a foot from the rat.

"I'll get it."

Shaking, Skye stepped around the mess, trying not to look at it, but unable not to. As she reached for the phone, she saw that the rat had not been the only thing inside the box.

Whoever had left Terri the package had also left her a note, a folded piece of paper inside a blood-smeared, plastic Ziploc bag.

Skye looked at Terri. The woman looked terrified. Gagging, Skye picked up the bag by a corner, got it open and took out the paper.

The note was brief. Scrawled across the paper, in what looked like blood, was one word.

Bitch.

54

Skye handed her menu to the waiter. "Nothing for me, thanks." The man looked disapprovingly at her, then turned to Griffen.

"We're not quite ready to order," Griffen said. "Two cabernets for now. The Vichon."

The man nodded, then walked away, and Griffen reached across the table and covered her hand with his. "Not much of a dinner. Are you okay?"

"I'm not hungry, that's all."

"Are you sure?" He curved his fingers closer around hers, and she met his eyes. "I'm worried about you."

"You don't need to be, I just—" She took a deep breath. "I just can't stop thinking about that rat." She shuddered. "It was so awful, Griffen. So frightening."

"You've got to let it go, sweetheart. It's over."

"But it's not, don't you see?" She lowered her eyes to their joined hands, then looked back up at him. "Not for Terri. And not for me, either. Because I can't forget."

"Goddammit! What were you doing there? You should have been home. Or out with me. If you had been—"

"Terri would have been alone," she snapped, angered by his attitude. "Is that what you'd want?"

"Of course not." He made a sound of frustration. "I just hate that you were there. That you were frightened."

Her anger faded, and she searched his gaze. "What if that sicko does it again? What if he does something worse? Or something to little Raye? I couldn't bear that."

"Raye's her daughter?"

Skye nodded. "She's such a little sweetheart. If Raye were threatened, Terri would move away, I know she would."

For a moment, Griffen didn't respond. Then he trailed his thumb along the side of her hand. "I love you," he murmured. "It hurts to see you upset like this."

She looked down at their joined hands. And thought of Chance. That had been happening a lot lately, especially when she and Griffen were together.

Griffen was everything she had wished for, everything she had ever dreamed of in a man. What was wrong with her?

"Tell me how I can help her," Griffen said. "I'd do anything to make you happy, Skye. Anything."

Tears stung her eyes, and she curled her fingers around his. "I wish you could make this sick bastard stop. I wish you could make him just go away."

"I can't do that, Skye. Pick something else."

She forced a laugh. "You're so good to me."

He smiled. "You sound surprised."

"I do, don't I?" She returned his smile. "I guess kindness takes some getting used to."

"Go ahead and get used to it. I plan to keep it up. For a lifetime."

Lately, Griffen had been making a lot of references to forever, to them spending their lives together. Although he hadn't outright asked her to marry him, she felt certain he was going to.

Being a part of the Monarch family, a part of Dorothy and Adam, of being connected the way she had always wanted to be, would be wonderful. To know she was with a man who would love her forever would also be wonderful.

Then why did the idea of Griffen proposing scare her witless?

The waiter returned with their wine and a basket of rolls. After they assured him they still weren't ready to order, he disappeared again. Skye turned back to Griffen. "Can I ask you something?"

"Sure, love. Anything."

"I heard that one of your half sisters disappeared. I heard that her mother kidnapped her and no one ever saw them again. Is that true?"

He stiffened. "Who told you that?"

His anger surprised her. Surely, if true, it was both common knowledge and ancient history. "Who?" she repeated. "No one in...particular. I just, I heard it around...work."

"I see." He drew his hand away and sat back in his chair, considering her through narrowed eyes. "Why are you asking me about it?"

"Because I wondered if it was true. You said you had lost both your sisters, but I assumed—"

"They'd died of natural causes?"

"Yes."

He looked away, then back. "It's true. Grace's mother was unstable. One day she ran away with her. Gone." He snapped his fingers. "Poof, just like that and all our hearts were broken. We found out years later that they were dead. Killed in a car accident. The authorities found us through some of the mother's papers."

"Oh, Griffen. I'm so sorry."

"I loved my sister very much. I loved her mother, too. I was only eleven, and I thought...she was like a mother to me. When she ran away it...it hurt like hell."

Skye held out her hand, thinking of her own mother, her own devastation. He grasped it. "I understand," she whispered. "I know how much that...hurts. All grown-up and I still fantasize that my mother and I are reunited."

"So do I," he murmured, meeting her eyes. "You see why we're so perfect for each other?"

She leaned across the table and kissed him, shuddering slightly at the contact. It was an odd reaction to his touch, one that she had been having with increasing frequency. She didn't understand it. His touch wasn't unpleasant. He was gentle, handsome and obviously experienced with women.

But it wasn't a problem with him, she knew. It was her. She had difficulty with intimacy; she had been told that before. She had difficulty sharing herself. That, too, she had been told. Because of her past, because of her fears.

Now, here was a man who wanted to give her everything, share everything. And a man who wanted her to give him everything in return.

She didn't need a shrink to figure that one out. It was pretty obvious.

She wasn't going to allow herself to mess this up, she vowed. Not this time. Period.

"I want you so much," he murmured, tangling his fingers in her hair. "Some nights I can't sleep for thinking of you...of us."

Skye went hot, then icy, clammy cold. She squirmed, uncomfortable, cursing herself. Get over it, Skye, she told herself. Get over it.

He rubbed some strands of her hair between his fingers, smiling. "I know you're not ready, love. You don't have to look so panicked. I'll wait. Don't you know, I want it to be perfect for both of us. Just one more kiss, and I'll act respectably."

Skye closed her eyes. Griffen's lips brushed against hers; she curved her hands into fists. A moment later he drew away, and she opened her eyes.

And saw Chance. At first she thought her mind had conjured him. She hadn't even caught a glimpse of him since that day in Griffen's office, though she had thought of him constantly.

He stood a couple of feet from their table, looking as if he would rather be anywhere but there. No doubt he was remembering the way she had all but thrown herself at him.

"Chance," she whispered, her cheeks hot.

Griffen swung around. "Chance, buddy. What're you doing here?"

Chance smiled and closed the distance between them, though the curving of his mouth looked forced. "Griffen," he said stiffly. "Skye. Sorry for the interruption. Ashley told me I could find you here. She said you wanted to see these releases before they went out."

"Sure did." He motioned toward the table. "Pull up a chair. Have a drink."

Chance looked at Skye, then quickly away. "I don't want to intrude."

"Don't be a jerk." Griffen smiled at Skye. "Sit."

Chance pulled up a chair and sat down. He opened his briefcase, slid out several sheets and handed them to Griffen. "See what you think. If you're happy, I'll have Lisa get them out first thing."

The waiter arrived and took Chance's order. Skye realized she had been holding her breath since he sat down, and released it, feeling like a ninny. She looked at her hands. Griffen loved her, and she had to force herself to sit still for his touch; Chance didn't give a flip about her, and all she could do was think about his touch.

She was impossibly screwed up. Skye tucked her hair behind her ear and lifted her gaze. To find Chance staring at her chest.

Heat climbed her cheeks. "Excuse me?"

He blinked and shook his head. "Sorry. I was looking at your pin. Is it one of your designs?"

Pleased, she brought her hand to the brooch. "Yes, thanks. It's the first piece in my City Lights series. I'm wear-testing it."

"It's really beautiful. Could I see it?"

"Sure." She unfastened the pin and handed it over. "It's really just the metal production model."

"Meaning?"

"That I'm still fine-tuning. Still making changes, adjustments. This piece was cast using a cold mold, which is temporary. Once I have this just the way I want it, the vulcanized rubber mold will be made. It's permanent, exact and will be used many hundreds of times without breaking down."

The waiter brought Chance's beer. He acknowledged it with a small nod, his attention focused on the piece of jewelry. He turned it over in his hands, his expression admiring. "I remember how excited you were when Sarah finally let you cast something. This was made the same way?"

"Basically. Except at Monarch's we don't do the actual casting in-house, a foundry does it."

"It's beautiful and unusual. I've never seen anything quite like it." He handed the brooch back. "You said you're... wear-testing it?"

"Mmm." She refastened the pin. "Wear-testing is an important part of the design process. You need to make sure it feels good on. That it lies right, that it's not too heavy, that it doesn't catch or pull fabric or somehow scratch the wearer. If something doesn't feel good, women won't want to wear it no matter how beautiful it is."

"She's good, isn't she?"

Skye and Chance both looked up to find Griffen watching them. Skye realized she had gotten so caught up in talking about her work, she had forgotten he was sitting there.

"Yeah, she is. She's incredible." His voice deepened and he cleared his throat. "How are those releases? Anything you want to discuss?"

"I made a few minor adjustments." Griffen handed them back. "Double-check those dates with Ashley before you send them out."

"Already done." Chance slipped the papers back into his case, took a swallow of his beer and stood. "Thanks for the brew. Have a good evening."

"Stay, if you like," Skye said. "We haven't ordered dinner yet."

For a moment both men were dead silent. In that second, Skye realized what had happened, what she had done.

"Yes," Griffen said, looking anything but pleased. "Stay."

Chance shook his head. "Thank you, but no. I've already intruded on your evening enough. Good night."

Without a backward glance, he walked away.

55

Muttering a string of mostly self-directed oaths under his breath, Chance left the restaurant. Hunching deeper into his topcoat, he crossed the parking lot. The wind off of Lake Michigan was stiff and cold. The weather forecast called for lake-effect snow tonight, and the unusually mild fall was about to turn into a real bitch of a winter.

Dammit, what had he been thinking, coming here? Had he lost his mind? Since the day of the project meeting at Monarch's, he hadn't been able to stop thinking about Skye and Griffen together. He hadn't been able to stop picturing them together.

And the picture felt dead wrong.

His thoughts ate at him, day and night, until he was certain he was going to go completely, fucking out of his mind.

So what had he done? Knowing full well he would see them together, he had come here. And he had seen plenty—them kissing and holding hands, Griffen looking at her as if he would like to swallow her whole.

Chance reached his car, unlocked it and slipped inside. He started the engine, flipped the defroster on high, then rested his forehead on the top of the steering wheel. What the hell was happening to him? He had wanted to wrench her away from Griffen and drag her out of the restaurant, caveman-style. He had wanted to warn her away from dark-haired, silver-tongued devils. He wanted her in his arms and safe.

Chance laughed, the sound angry and tight even to his own

ears. He wasn't her big brother anymore. He wasn't her protector, or the champion of her honor.

Her honor? Yeah, right. That was a good one. The other day in Griffen's office, he had almost kissed her. And if he'd given in to the urge, he wouldn't have been able to stop with a simple meeting of their mouths. Oh no, he wanted her so badly, he burned with it. The thoughts he'd had about her, the fantasies, were anything but honorable or brotherly.

He wanted her for himself.

He was a complete bastard.

Chance tipped his head back and gazed up at the car ceiling. What was he doing? Trying to screw up his entire life? Trying to lose Monarch's Design and Retail, his biggest and most important account? Trying to alienate his best friend, the man who had single-handedly brought him more new business in a few months than he would have been able to earn in a few years?

Stay away from her, McCord. Keep the hell away, the farther the better.

Get used to cold showers. And to looking the other way.

A couple picking their way across the now-slippery parking lot caught his eye. He looked in their direction, realizing it was Skye and Griffen.

His adrenaline starting to pump, Chance watched as Griffen helped Skye into the passenger side of his Porsche, then went around and climbed into the driver's side. Griffen gunned the engine and then backed out of the spot.

Then Chance did something insane.

He followed them.

He had no idea where they were going—her place or his, back to the store or to another restaurant, so he stayed as close as he could without arousing Griffen's suspicions. It wasn't difficult, traffic was light and they didn't go far. Within minutes, Griffen maneuvered his Porsche into a spot in front of a rehabbed building on Fullerton.

Nice building, Chance thought, watching the two go up

the short flight of steps and inside. Too nice, he would have thought, for somebody just starting out. He moved his gaze over its limestone and brick facade, taking in the oversize arched doorway and ironwork entry lights. A hell of a lot nicer than the building he lived in. A hell of a lot nicer neighborhood, too.

He narrowed his eyes as the lights in the second-floor right unit popped on. But then, maybe she wasn't the one paying the rent.

He hated the thought. It made him crazy. She was making him crazy.

And this was sick, he decided. Sitting outside her building, freezing his nuts off while he wondered what she and Griffen were doing in there. It was obsessive and pathetic.

He rested his head against the seat back and let out a frustrated breath. What did he think they were doing? The obvious, of course. Making love.

Now, there was a picture. Only the man in the picture wasn't Griffen.

Chance groaned. He cursed himself and her and Griffen. To hell with this, he thought, shoving his key back into the ignition. He was out of here.

The slam of a car door and roar of a powerful engine coming to life drew his attention. It was Griffen. And he was alone.

Chance checked his watch, a smile tugging at his mouth. Unless Griffen's nickname was Speedy, he'd been wrong. No lovemaking for Grif-boy tonight, no nookie, nothing but a few quick kisses and a lukewarm good-night.

Chance lifted his gaze to Skye's windows. He caught sight of her as she moved across one, and his heart began to thunder. Without pausing to ask himself what the hell he thought he was doing, he slammed out of the car, jogged across the street and up her steps, fat wet snowflakes clinging to his hair and eyelashes.

A couple emerged from the building just as Chance

reached it. Heads pressed together, they didn't even notice him, and he caught the security door with his foot and ducked inside. He checked the mailboxes, saw that Skye was, indeed, second-floor right and climbed the flight of stairs.

He found her apartment and knocked. A dog began to bark. One that sounded more King Kong than canine.

He heard her admonish the animal; a second later the door swung open. "Griffen, I..." Her voice trailed off. "Chance?" She glanced past him, as if expecting to see Griffen or someone else in the hallway with him. "What are you doing here?"

At least he had the element of surprise on his side, he thought. But for what? He forced an easy smile. "Can I come in?"

She hesitated only a moment, then stepped aside. "Sure. Can I take your coat?"

"No. I'm not staying. I just—" He stopped because he hadn't a clue what "he had just stopped by" for. "Who's this?" he asked instead, squatting to scratch her dog's chest. The dog licked his hand, looking at him in adoration.

"That's Mr. Moo. I think he likes you."

"Well, I like him, too." Chance patted the animal's side firmly, then straightened. "Great dog."

"Yeah, he is." She folded her arms across her chest. "What are you doing here, Chance?"

He met her eyes and decided on honesty. "I don't know."

"You don't know," she repeated, her voice thick. "Well, isn't that just...wonderful."

"It was an impulse." He shoved his hands into his coat pockets. "I left the restaurant and sat in my car awhile, then I saw—" He bit the words back, knowing how they were going to sound.

"You saw what?"

"I saw you and Griffen leaving. I follow—"

She looked completely, utterly, ta

hollowly. "I know it's ridiculous and obsessive, but I...I can't stop thinking about you, Skye."

She glanced away, then back. Moo whimpered. "Why are you telling me this?"

"I don't know." He made a sound of frustration. "I just had to see you, that's all."

Skye shook her head. "How do you expect me to respond to that?" she asked softly. "What can you possibly expect me to say?"

"I don't know."

She looked at the floor for a moment, struggling, he could see, to collect herself. Finally, slowly, she lifted her gaze to his. He saw that she was angry. "Then *what* do you know, Chance? You come here tonight and hand me this load of..." She let the thought go, and shook her head again. "I think you should go, Chance. I want you to leave."

He took a step closer to her. "I hate the thought of you and Griffen together. I think about you day and night." He took another step. Then another. "The other day in Griffen's office, I wanted to kiss you. I still do. That's what I know, Skye."

She met his eyes. Hers were bright with unshed tears. "And I still think you should go."

"Skye—"

"Now, please."

A part of him wanted to refuse, wanted to drag her into his arms and convince her that he was the one she wanted, not Griffen. But she was right, he had nothing to offer her. As he moved past the dog, Moo whimpered again but didn't get up. Chance bent and scratched behind his ears. The dog moved his legs as if trying to get them under him, to stand. But he couldn't seem to do it. Finally, he fell awkwardly onto his side.

Chance drew his eyebrows together and glanced over his shoulder at Skye. She was staring past him and hadn't seen the exchange. "I think there's something wrong with your dog."

"Very funny. He was fine a minute ago."

"I wouldn't joke about something like that. And I know he was fine a minute ago. I'm not an idiot."

"Here, I'll show you." She turned to her pet and clapped her hands. The dog's head snapped up. "Moo, get your leash, buddy. Go on, get your leash."

The dog tried. But it was as if he couldn't get all four legs to work together. Finally, whimpering once more, he clawed his way upright, then tried to walk. He couldn't keep his balance, moving as if he was drunk. He lurched sideways, into a potted plant, toppling it. He took a few more wobbly steps, then his legs just seemed to slide out from under him.

Chance looked at Skye. She was white as a sheet. "Skye," he said calmly, "call your vet. He'll have an emergency number."

She lifted her gaze and met his eyes, hers terrified.

"I don't think we should waste a minute. Get directions to the emergency clinic. I'll get Moo down to the car."

"But...what if the vet says that's not necessary?"

"He won't."

For one moment, he thought she was going to fall completely apart, then she raced for the phone. Chance went to Moo and, crooning reassuringly, scooped the big animal up as best he could.

No wonder Skye loved this dog so much, Chance thought, carrying him out into the hall and down the stairs, he was a sweet animal. Even though he was in obvious discomfort and no doubt scared, he let Chance handle him, only whining in protest.

The snow was coming down harder, making it difficult to see, let alone cross the street with the huge animal in his arms. Chance made it to his car; luckily, Skye w behind him. She ran across the street, rea only a second behind him. "My keys are in my coat pocket," he said.

She dug them out, unlocked the doors and they loaded the dog into the back seat. Skye ran around to the other side and climbed in beside her dog. She stroked Moo's big head which she put in her lap and talked softly to him.

Chance slid behind the wheel and started the car. "Where are we going?"

She met his gaze in the rearview mirror. "Ten blocks up, straight shot. The veterinary emergency clinic's on the right. The doctor said we couldn't miss it."

The doctor had been right. With its big sign and brightly lit front, they spotted the clinic easily. Chance stopped the car right outside the entrance, hopped out and ran around to help Skye with the dog.

The vet was waiting. Skye begged the doctor to allow her to accompany Moo into the examining room. Her dog needed her, she said. He was scared and hurting. She couldn't leave him alone. It took some doing, but the man convinced Skye to wait by explaining that the room was small, and that she would distract him and his assistant from their work.

So, Skye waited. And paced, wringing her hands, obviously near hysteria.

"Skye," he said quietly, "it's going to be okay. Moo's going to be okay."

"But what if—" She pressed her lips together, as if she couldn't bear to say the words. They hung between them, anyway.

What if he's not okay? What if he dies?

"He'll be fine," Chance said again firmly. "Just hold tight, baby. The doctor will be back out soon."

She nodded and resumed pacing. The wait was hell. With each second that ticked past, Chance watched her confidence crumble a bit more. Finally, after thirty, excruciating minutes, the doctor returned, his expression grim.

Skye looked at the man, her heart in her eyes. "Is he...is he all right?"

"I think he's going to pull through." The doctor slipped his hands into the pockets of his lab coat. "If you had waited any longer to bring him in, it might have been too late."

Skye paled. "I can't believe this happened. One minute he was fine and the next..."

"That's how this stuff works."

"This stuff?" Chance crossed to stand beside Skye. He put his arm around her, and she leaned into him. "What exactly is wrong with Moo?"

The vet looked from one to the other. "I thought you knew. He was poisoned."

"Poisoned!" Skye repeated, shocked. "But how—"

"Ethylene glycol. Antifreeze."

"Antifreeze?" Skye shook her head, obviously confused. "But how did he get it?"

"I can't answer that. But it could have been anywhere. Dogs love it, it's really sweet." The vet cleared his throat. "We made sure we got it all out of his stomach, and I've got him hooked up to a vodka IV right now. Antifreeze causes crystals to form in the kidney and, basically, takes out the kidney. The vodka keeps the crystals from forming. Like I said, if you hadn't brought him in when you did, we could have lost him. Frankly, we would have. This stuff works fast."

"When can he..." Skye's voice shook, and she battled to steady it. "When can he come home?"

"About seventy-two hours. I'm sorry, Ms. Dearborn. I know how distressing this must be for you. But rest assured, we're doing everything we can. I'm very optimistic."

Chance tightened his arm around her. "You'll call if there's any change?"

"Of course. And we open at seven-thirty. You can check on him then."

Skye murmured her thanks and they turned and walked toward the door.

"Ms. Dearborn?"

She stopped and looked back at him. "Doctor?"

"A dog the size of Moo would have to drink a good eight ounces of the antifreeze to affect him this way."

She searched his gaze. "Yes. So?"

"So, I'd be surprised if it was an accident. I believe someone deliberately poisoned your dog."

56

Skye huddled deeper into Chance's front seat, her mind whirling with what the veterinarian had said. "Who could have done this?" she murmured, looking at Chance. "Who would want to hurt Moo?"

Chance glanced at her, then back at the road. "The vet said he *thought* someone deliberately poisoned Moo. But he wasn't certain of that. It could have been an accident, caused by simple carelessness." The light ahead changed to red, and he eased the car to a stop. "So in my mind, the question is where and when, not who."

She frowned, not quite following. "What are you getting at?"

"The vet said, antifreeze acts fast. That means Moo would have had to have gotten into the stuff shortly before I got to your place."

"Because he was fine when you first got there."

"Bingo."

The light changed, and Chance started through it. He flipped the wipers on high. Skye watched them move back and forth, sweeping the snow aside, recalling exactly what she had done that evening.

"As you know, Griffen and I left the restaurant just behind you. I had one of my headaches, and I didn't have any of my medicine with me."

"Where was Moo when you got home?"

"At the front door, as always. Eager to go out." She rubbed her chin with her index finger. "The building has an enclosed garden courtyard. It has a patch of yard, and at night I usually put him back there when I first get home. That way he can get some immediate relief and I can take my time checking the mail, changing clothes, stuff like that.''

"And?''

"And that's what I did. I put him out, took a headache tablet, and Griffen and I talked for a few minutes. When Griffen left, I let Moo back in. And that's it.''

"Then, that courtyard's the place. Let's check it out.''

Her building in sight, Chance took the first parking place he came upon. They climbed out of the car and crossed the snow-slippery street.

Skye touched Chance's arm. ''There's only one entrance from outside. All the tenants have a key, and it's supposed to stay locked.''

"Let's try it and see if it is now.''

She nodded and led him down the driveway beside the building. The courtyard was surrounded by an eight-foot-tall brick wall, its top decorated with multicolored pieces of broken glass. The gate, also eight feet tall, was locked tight.

Chance tried it a second time, really rattling it. It still didn't budge. ''Unless one of the tenants left it open earlier, then came back to relock it, I doubt a stranger was inside messing with your Kong-dog.''

She made a sound of distress. ''You think one of my neighbors did this?''

"It had to happen out here, Skye, unless you keep open containers of antifreeze inside your apartment.''

"Not hardly.'' She frowned and fitted her gate key into the lock. ''Come on, let's look around.''

They did. And found what they were looking for. A coffee can, tipped onto its side, looking completely out of place in the neatly tended courtyard. Chance picked it up and ran a finger along the inside, then touched the tip to his tongue.

"Sweet,'' he said, turning his head and spitting.

Skye took the can from his hands and gazed at it, heart

hammering. *Folgers. Five-pound can. A Jewel food-store sticker on the bottom of the can.*

She lifted her gaze to Chance's, shivering. "Who did this? Why? I can't even comprehend such a thing. Moo's so gentle."

"Do you clean up after him? Some people get pretty—"

"I'm a fanatic about it." Her teeth began to chatter. "What now?"

"We go inside. You're turning blue."

Skye carried the can up to her apartment and deposited it on her kitchen counter. She gazed at it, still shivering. "I miss him. It's too quiet, it's..." She shot Chance a weak smile. "You probably think I'm pretty silly, being so attached to a dog."

"I don't think you're silly at all."

"Thanks." She tugged off her gloves and tossed them onto the counter beside the can, then ran her hands through her hair, shaking the snow off. "You want a drink or something?"

"I should go."

"Do you have to?" The question just popped out, and she flushed and looked away. "It's only that...I don't want to be alone, not yet, anyway. Could you stay a little while? I'd really appreciate it."

He hesitated, then shrugged out of his coat. "So, where do you want me to put this?"

She released a breath she hadn't even realized she'd been holding. "Thank you." She smiled and held out a hand for his coat. "I'll take it." He handed it to her, and she hung his and hers on the brass tree by the door, then turned to him. "How about that drink?"

"What do you have?"

"Hot chocolate?"

"Perfect."

Minutes later, they sat on her battered old couch, big mugs of steaming hot chocolate fortified with a shot of peppermint schnapps cupped in their hands. Curling her legs under her, she angled her body toward his and took a sip of her drink. And sighed.

A smile twitched at the corners of his mouth. "I remember how much you used to love hot chocolate."

"I still do. It's comforting, though I'm not sure why." She shook her head. "My mother used to make it for me even in the middle of July."

"Maybe that's why it's comforting."

She met his eyes, thinking for the first time of what would have happened if Chance had left without noticing Moo, or if he hadn't come at all.

And thinking, too, of what had brought Chance to her door in the first place, of how he had admitted following her and Griffen, and of how angry she had been.

Her cheeks heated as she acknowledged she didn't care why he had come, she was just glad he had. And not only because of Moo.

"I haven't thanked you yet," she murmured. "Without you, Moo might not have made it."

"You would have seen something was wrong. I just saw it first."

She wasn't as sure as he, but didn't argue the point. "You were so certain Moo was really sick. How did you know it was as serious as it was?"

"Common sense. He declined so fast, I knew whatever was wrong, it was bad."

She brought her mug to her lips, but didn't sip. "I didn't know you had experience with animals."

"I don't, not really. But it works that way with humans, too. That's the way it was with my mother. One day she was fine, four weeks later she was dead. She had a fast-growing malignancy."

"I'm sorry."

"Ancient history."

Skye sipped then, studying the man she had once thought

she knew so well, thinking that perhaps she hadn't known him so well, after all. "In all the time we were together, you never talked much about your mother. Will you tell me a little about her?"

He almost refused. She saw it in his eyes, in the way he stiffened, the way he opened his mouth with a denial that sprang to his tongue. But then he surprised her. He told her about his young and pretty mother, about how they had lived. He told her, too, how he had always been alone, even when he was with her because she had spent her life looking outside of them, looking at all the things she longed for but didn't have.

And, finally, he told her about her illness and death. "My old man refused to take me, so they shipped me off to my aunt Rebecca's farm. You know the story from there."

Skye was silent a moment, thinking about all he had said, moved by the emotion she heard behind his words. "It sounds like you loved her a lot."

"She was my mother. We didn't have anybody but each other." He drew his eyebrows together, his gaze directed to a place beyond Skye. "I always knew, though, that she was more important to me than I ever was to her."

"I'm sure she loved you very much."

"Not enough to make her happy. She was never happy." He shook his head, as if trying to rid himself of a bad memory, then grinned at her. "So, how did you and that big mutt of yours hook up? You guys seem pretty attached to each other."

"We are." She smiled. "He was a puppy. I found him abandoned at the side of the road. It was pouring rain, he was drenched, muddy and pathetic-looking. The poor thing, I couldn't not pick him up. Nobody else would have."

"You're a soft touch, Dearborn." He set his half-full mug on the coffee table. "So, you gave him a home, and he pledged his eternal devotion in return."

She laughed. "How did you know?"

"Lucky guess."

"More like good instincts. You always had good instincts, Chance McCord."

He laughed and they talked then, cautiously at first, easing into the events of their last thirteen years. Little by little the caution slipped away from them, and they became the essence of what they were: two people who had shared in a year what most never share in a lifetime, two people who had lived and almost died together, who had, for nearly a year, depended on each other for everything.

Two people who had once meant the universe to each other.

Skye laughed at a memory, scooting down in the plump cushions and resting her head against the sofa back. She closed her eyes. "I had forgotten about that. Was I ever really so young?"

"You were." She heard his smile, felt the sofa shift as he leaned toward her. "I also remember the time you tried to kiss me."

She opened her eyes, cheeks warming at the memory. He was above her, and as she gazed up at him, she realized everything about his face was familiar, familiar in a way that felt really good.

She returned his smile. "That one I hadn't forgotten. I was so jealous of that other girl... What was her name?"

He thought for a moment, then laughed. "I haven't a clue."

"Good." Skye swept her gaze over him. "I fancied myself in love with you. And I wanted to prove to you that I was a woman, too."

He trailed a finger along the curve of her jaw. "You were beautiful even then."

"I was a silly, confused little girl who was trying to become a woman. I was also a major pain in the ass."

He laughed loudly. "I'm glad you haven't changed."

She batted her eyelashes, playing the coquette. "The way you do go on, Mr. McCord. It just sets a girl's heart aflutter."

He didn't laugh at her joke, didn't even crack a grin. Instead, he searched her gaze, the expression in his doing just what she had teased him about a second before—setting her heart aflutter.

Even as she called herself a fool, she reached up and cupped the back of his neck. "You're right, you know. I don't think I have changed."

"I'm glad. I've missed you, Skye."

She tangled her fingers in his hair. "Can I ask you something?"

"That depends."

"On what?"

"On whether I'm kissing you or not."

"Funny...that's what I was going to ask you. If you would—"

He caught the last with his mouth.

And passion exploded between them. Just like that. Like a bomb going off. White-hot. Earth-shattering. She made a sound of surprise. Or was that his?

He drew away, his expression dazed. Then he kissed her again, deeply, erotically, as she had never been kissed before. As she had dreamed of being kissed all those years ago.

She arched up to meet him, pressing her body against his, trembling. He thrust his tongue into her mouth, seeking, stroking. She answered each stroke with one of her own, her body humming, control spinning crazily out of her reach.

Somewhere in the back of her mind, she knew she shouldn't be doing this with him, that it was wrong. But for the life of her, she couldn't think why. It didn't feel wrong. It felt right. And good. Incredibly, deliciously good.

Wanting to feel his skin against her, she tugged at his tie and struggled with his shirt buttons. They broke apart long enough for him to yank her sweater over her head and toss it to the floor.

"We can't do this," she said, pushing his shirt off his shoulders and running her hands over his muscled chest.

"We can't..." He groaned and buried his face between her breasts. "You feel like heaven."

She shuddered and arched against him. "That feels so good. Don't stop. Don't—"

The phone rang; once, then twice. On the third ring, the machine picked up and Griffen's voice echoed through the room. They froze.

"Hi, sweetheart, just wanted to make sure you were all right. Sweet dreams. I love you."

They looked at each other, then separated.

Skye grabbed her sweater and tugged it over her head, sickened by her behavior. What was wrong with her? Griffen loved her. How could she have been so disloyal? So dishonest?

Chance swore and dragged a hand through his hair. "I feel like such an asshole."

"You?" Skye curved her arms around her middle, not able to meet Chance's eyes. "I'm so embarrassed. I don't know what came over me."

"It's my fault," he said, his voice tight. He collected his shirt from the floor and tugged it on. "I shouldn't have come here."

She made a choked sound. "This was hardly a case of date rape, Chance. I practically...I all but threw myself..." She cleared her throat, unable to finish the thought. She pulled her hands through her hair, noticing that they trembled. "It was a mistake. Everybody makes mistakes."

He was silent a moment, then looked her in the eyes. "Was it a mistake, Skye? Are you sure?"

She jumped to her feet, too agitated to sit still. She crossed to the fireplace, then swung around to face him again. "Of course I'm sure. We need to forget this happened. I was upset. Because of Moo." Her voice quivered, and she bit down on her bottom lip, feeling like both a liar and a fraud. "It won't happen again."

Chance got slowly to his feet, his expression unreadable. "Whatever you say is okay by me." He shoved his necktie into a pocket and went to the kitchen for his topcoat. He returned a moment later, coat on, and headed for the door. "Let me know how Moo is."

"I will."

He reached the front door, hesitated, then jerked it open. Only then did he look at her. "You and I both know this had nothing to do with Moo. But keep telling yourself that it did, Skye. Keep telling yourself to forget it happened. Maybe if you say it often enough, you'll even believe it. And God help me, maybe I will, too."

57

But Chance and Skye didn't forget. They couldn't. Unrelieved sexual tension clung to them like potent perfume to a flower. It crackled in the air around them.

Skye thought about Chance, and about sex, all the time. She existed in a constant state of heightened awareness. As her silk blouse fluttered against her skin, she thought of his hands and mouth moving across her breasts. As she stripped out of her jeans at night, she would remember the feel of his rough skin against her, the rasp of his cheek against the side of her neck, the tip of his tongue trailing over the curve of her shoulder.

They saw each other constantly, as if the fates had contrived to taunt them. They avoided looking at each other, so studiously Skye feared those around them would notice and begin to wonder about them. She had no choice but to keep her gaze averted; should she actually allow herself the pleasure of gazing at him, everyone would know. It would be that obvious. That transparent.

When their gazes did happen to meet, she found she couldn't drag hers away. She found herself becoming aroused. Her nipples would harden, her juices flow. And she would ache.

For him to touch her. Everywhere. In every way.

She had taken to crossing her arms over her chest, to hide his effect on her. He knew, anyway. He felt the same. She saw the sexual heat in his eyes, the longing. The frustration.

What had happened between them had nothing to do with

Moo having been poisoned. They both knew it. They both knew, too, that it was only a matter of time before something happened between them again.

Skye gazed blindly at the drawings on the board in front of her. She was embarrassed by her feelings. Guilty over them. She hated herself for being such a fool. It was Griffen she really wanted. Griffen who was right for her. Griffen who promised her all she had ever wished for in a man and a relationship.

Griffen loved her. Chance did not.

Then why did Chance make her feel this way? She curved her fingers into fists. And why did Griffen's touch turn her cold? Why did it unsettle her? Lately, when Griffen kissed her, she had the strongest urge to run. As far and as fast as she could.

Skye brought a hand to her temple. She had a lot of other things she should be thinking about, things more pressing than her sex life. Milan was not that far off. Only four weeks. Dorothy hoped to enter the first pieces of City Lights in the show. They were in the final stages of production; Skye expected the delivery of the cast pieces, ready for finishing, today or tomorrow. She had several more in the metal production-model stage.

Dorothy had been turning to her more and more, for her opinion, her expertise, her friendship. She had begun having Skye take care of many of the day-to-day details and decisions that she didn't have the inclination—or physical wherewithal—to handle.

Skye frowned. She was worried about Dorothy. She was so forgetful. And so easily fatigued. The older woman had scared her the other day by telling her how she had a craving for a deviled egg and had fallen asleep while the eggs were boiling. She had awakened to a smoke-filled house and the most horrible scorched smell. She had burned the eggs completely out of their shells.

Dorothy had been annoyed with the smell and mess; Skye

had been thankful for both. What if she hadn't awakened? Skye had demanded. What if there hadn't been smoke or a smell to drag her out of sleep?

Dorothy had only laughed. Sometimes she exasperated Skye. Sometimes she behaved so childishly.

"Skye?"

Chance. She lifted her gaze. Chance stood at her office door, his hungry gaze upon her. Her mouth went desert dry, her heart began to thrum. "Yes?" she managed to say.

"May I speak with you for a moment? About your interview with Mickey Spelling?"

"Of course." She stood, clasping her hands in front of her, the blood rushing to her head. She felt dizzy and weak. And wet. Unbearably, achingly wet.

He closed the door behind him. He took a step toward her. "I heard he was by to see you this morning."

She took a step toward him. "Yes."

He drew in a shuddering breath and moved closer. "How did it go?"

"Good." Without conscious design, she closed the remaining distance between them, stopping so close, if she swayed slightly, her breasts would brush against his chest. She wanted to, so badly it hurt.

"How's Moo?"

"He's good. Came home and was immediately back to one hundred percent."

"That's great." He moved his gaze hungrily over her face. "I know how happy you must be to have him home."

"I am." She breathed deeply through her nose, feeling awkward and too vulnerable. Wishing she could take that one tiny step closer to him. That was all it would take, she thought. Then they would be together.

"Any luck finding out who poisoned him?"

"No. I talked to the other tenants. They were shocked. The other pet owners were frightened. Everyone's watching closely, making sure the gate's locked. Things like that. Lulu

Green said she had the gate open that afternoon. She lives on the first floor and was bringing groceries in the back way. She didn't see anyone, though. And she didn't see the coffee can, either.''

"Do you think any of them could have done it?"

"I can't imagine. They all seemed so upset when I told them."

He lowered his eyes to her mouth, and her nipples hardened. Just like that. Spontaneously.

He swore and looked away. "We need to talk. About what happened."

She didn't have to ask what he referred to; she knew. They both knew. "Yes."

He returned his gaze to hers. "Dammit, Skye. Stop looking at me like that."

She wet her lips. "Like what?"

"Like you want to eat me up."

But she did want to. God help her.

She swayed toward him. He cupped her face in his palms, searching her expression. "What the hell are we doing?"

"I don't know." She closed her eyes. "I hate this."

"Me, too." Chance trailed his lips up the side of her neck to her ear. "I can't sleep for wanting to touch you. I think about you, us, all the time."

"Me, too."

"Stop seeing him," he whispered thickly. "I need you to stop seeing him."

She froze. *Stop seeing Griffen. Give it all up—her dream of love, a family, a forever. And for what?*

She laid her hands on his chest and tipped her face up to his. "I have to know...what do you feel for me? Besides lust, that is?"

He didn't answer, and heat burned her cheeks. The truth was, she knew, he felt nothing for her but lust. He wasn't even pretending to offer her more than sex. She supposed she should appreciate his honesty, but at the moment she wasn't in a particularly appreciative mood.

"You want me to stop seeing him so you can fuck me and not feel guilty. So you can enjoy yourself and not feel like a total shit for screwing over your friend. Isn't that right?"

"It's not like that, Skye. I don't know what's happening between us, but I know it's strong. And I know I can't bear the thought of you with him. I can't bear the thought of his hands on you."

"Stop it."

"I know you feel the same way."

"I know what I want. I know what I need."

"And Griffen's it?"

"Yes." She fisted her fingers; beneath them his heart thundered. "Yes."

"Then why do you turn to fire when I touch you?" He covered her hands. "You're looking at me that way again, Skye. And it's driving me crazy."

"I'm not."

"You are." He lowered his voice. "Go ahead, eat me up."

She wanted to, wanted so badly she ached. But she couldn't throw away everything she had ever dreamed of. She wouldn't.

She made a move to swing away from him. He stopped her, bringing their joined hands to her breasts, to her nipples, pressing against the silk. He trailed his fingertips across the silk, so lightly it felt like the brush of butterfly wings.

She shuddered and swayed, a small sound of pleasure slipping past her lips.

"Stop seeing him," he whispered, resting his forehead against hers, breathing hard. "I want to be with you. See how much."

He guided her hand to his arousal. For one heady moment,

she curved her fingers around him, reveling in the fact that she had done this to him just by standing close.

Shivering, she dropped her hand. "I can't, Chance. I'm sorry."

"Can't? Or won't?"

"Same thing." She retreated to her desk, legs shaking so badly she could hardly stand. She slid into her chair, not able to meet his eyes for fear if she did, she wouldn't have the strength to do what was best for her.

"Griffen loves me," she murmured. "He wants to be with me for more than a night. I've waited all my life for someone to love me like that. I'm not going to throw that away."

For a long moment Chance said nothing, simply looked at her, his gaze measured. "Then that's that."

"Yes. I suppose it is."

He walked to the door, then turned back to her. "Seems to me, you're asking yourself the wrong question, Skye. Do you love him? That's what you should be asking yourself."

She opened her mouth to say that she did, but the word wouldn't come out. She couldn't say it, not to him or to herself. Her cheeks burned, and she felt suddenly, ridiculously close to tears.

"That's what I thought. See you around, kid."

Chance opened the door.

Griffen stood on the other side.

58

Griffen sat in the dark. Naked. Shaking with the force of his fury. The bathroom's tile floor was hard and cold, the wall behind his back damp. Shards of the shattered mirror lay scattered about him, winking in the darkness.

He looked straight ahead, staring at nothing, his thoughts darting, rabbitlike, from one thing to another, landing on a word, an image, a memory. An impulse.

Some of the impulses were strong. And fierce. More animal than human. Like the impulse to protect what was his, to take out an enemy any way he could.

Griffen's mouth twisted. He had smelled the sex on them. Chance had opened Skye's office door and run smack into him, reeking of pussy. Skye's pussy. He hadn't trusted himself not to kill Chance then and there. But killing him would have ruined everything. So he had smiled and exchanged a few words with the two, then walked away.

Griffen picked up a piece of the broken glass. Long and jagged, he turned it over in his hands. As he did, he alternately saw flashes of his reflection—an eye, a section of his nose, the slash of white that was his mouth—and nothing at all, just blackness.

Griffen dragged the glass across the flat of his belly. Skye was his. She belonged to him. He had found her, brought her here. He had given her everything she had.

She was his prize. His.

Hatred and rage boiled up inside him. He moved the piece of glass again. Skye had always belonged to him. Always.

No two-bit, backstabbing, piece-of-shit nothing was going to take her away.

Griffen squeezed his eyes shut, grimacing. He had been a fool. How could he have missed it before? It was so obvious. Like two animals in heat, sex charged the air around them. They avoided looking at each other, yet their bodies strained toward each other's.

He narrowed his eyes, thinking of all the times he had *thought* he'd seen something pass between them, a silent message, a spark of heat. He had told himself he was imagining things. He had told himself Skye despised Chance, that the heat he saw was the heat of hate. He had told himself that she wouldn't bother looking at a man like Chance when she had him, Griffen Monarch.

He tightened his hand into a fist around the sliver of mirror. He had been a fool for his arrogance.

The rage built. Bitter, burning like acid. He had been soft. More like his father than his grandfather. He had been too lenient with Skye. He had failed to show her who was boss.

When they were children, he had shown her. He had controlled her. And when someone or something had gotten in his way, he had taken care of them. His penis stirred at the memories, becoming semi-erect. He smiled, thinking of those times, remembering how he had sneaked into her room and watched her while she slept, awakening her with a jab or a poke or a pinch—to anyplace he chose to touch.

The glass slipped from his fingers, and he grasped himself and stroked, remembering the times he had forced her to watch him do things, to her toys, to her pet, to himself. And then there were the times, few though they were, that he had forced her to submit to him.

He had been in charge. He had controlled her.

Impulses.

His head lolled back against the wall, his breath coming harder. She was weak, of course. The way all the Monarch women had been. The way all women were, easily seduced, quickly spoiled—like fruit left too long on the vine. She needed guidance, direction. She needed to be controlled.

Griffen slowed his hand, though it was agony. He had given her too much time and space. That, too, had been his mistake.

He had allowed himself to be swept away in his own heady feeling of power, of excitement. When he had finally had her near, it had been the culmination of his every wish. He had allowed himself to celebrate too long.

Unfortunately, he had to punish her now. Even though he was partly to blame. He hated to hurt her, he loved her, after all; but she had left him no choice. He had to teach her a lesson. He had to show her the way. This time he would take care of that ridiculous mutt of hers, once and for all. He would take care of Terri, too. And her little bitch daughter.

When she had no one else, she would understand how much she needed him. He would make her understand.

He increased his pace again, heart thundering. Oh, yes, she would understand. Chance was nothing. No one. He meant nothing to Skye.

Griffen arched his back. A sound bubbled to his lips, part rage, part howl of completion. Skye was his prize, his possession. His destiny.

Spent, he brought his hands to his face. They were sticky with blood and come. He smeared the mixture across his mouth and nose, its taste raw, its smell earthy. His senses filled with both, and he smiled. He and Skye would be together at last. Forever. And it would be good. So very, very good.

Griffen stood and calmly crossed to the sink. He peered into the fragment of mirror that remained. His hands were covered with blood, as were his chest and stomach. The blood stained his face, like a grotesque imitation of a painted woman's mouth.

He turned on the cold water and bending, rinsed his face and hands, the water sluicing down the drain in a pink swirl.

Yes, Skye would understand. Soon, she would see that they were each other's destiny.

And as for that nothing little prick, he thought, splashing water on his belly, he had just outlived his usefulness.

The time had come to take away all that he had given Chance.

59

What the hell was going on? Chance sat at his desk, staring down at the three letters of termination in front of him.

A week ago, everything had been fine. His clients had been happy. He had been considering hiring a third person, he was so busy. Then he had received the first letter, from the Campbell Consumer Group. Then the second, from Michael Reese Hospital and Medical Center. Then the third, from the Drake Hotel.

Previous to terminating him, all three clients had expressed their satisfaction with his services. He'd had projects in progress for all three, projects they'd all canceled, midstream.

Chance searched his memory, trying to recall anything he might have done or said to incur these terminations. If he had screwed up, he wanted to know how. Then he could kick himself in the ass for doing something stupid, promise himself he wouldn't be such an idiot again and pull himself back up.

Instead, he felt as if someone was pulling the rug out from under him and shouting, "Surprise!" And he didn't like the feeling, not one damn bit.

Chance stood. He crossed to the window and gazed out at the cold, gray day, at the sky, heavy with the threat of more snow.

He slipped his hands into his trouser pockets. He had been riding so high, feeling so good. He had been on top of the world. Everything he had wished, worked and longed for had been at the tip of his fingers.

Now, it was all slipping away. And he could do nothing but stand by helplessly and watch.

"Chance?" Lisa tapped on his open door. "The mail just came."

He looked over his shoulder at her. He could tell by her grim expression that she had bad news. "Another one?"

She nodded and brought it to him. He scanned the mercilessly short letter. Bennings and Bolton regretted to inform him that his services were no longer required.

He crushed the letter and tossed it on his desk, then swung back to the window. Just fucking great. If this kept up, in a week there would be nothing left.

"Chance?"

He didn't turn. "Yeah?"

"What's...going on?"

He emitted a short bark of laughter. "Hell if I know, Lisa. I wish I did, maybe then I could do something besides stand here getting screwed from behind."

Lisa cleared her throat. "I want to assure you, the last time I saw these people, everything was fine. None expressed dissatisfaction with any of my actions." She spread her hands. "In fact, Vincent from Campbell's sang your praises only days ago."

"I don't think this has anything to do with you, Lisa." He glanced over his shoulder at her. "The way things are unfolding is too weird. Business doesn't work that way. I'm pretty sure this has to do with me. If I just knew what was going on around about me, or if I knew who was responsible, then maybe I could stop it."

The phone rang; they both swung toward it, startled. Lisa snatched it up. "McCord Public Relations and Special Events. Lisa speaking."

Chance watched her, heart thundering, a sour feeling in the pit of his gut. "Sure, Martha," Lisa said. "He's right here. Hold a moment."

Lisa punched the hold button, then held the receiver out.

"Martha, the preservation society. She sounded strange, Chance."

He nodded, took the phone and released the line. "Good morning, Martha. What can I do for you today?"

The woman hesitated a moment, then cut right to the point. "I've got some bad news, I'm afraid. The society's cutting back."

Chance's stomach sank. He lifted his gaze to Lisa's; her face fell and she sank onto one of the chairs in front of his desk.

"We can deal with that," he said, forcing calm. "We'll simply scale back on some of our plans."

"Wait," she said quickly, before he could continue. "What I'm saying is, we're going to have to terminate our relationship with McCord Public Relations. I'm sorry."

He sat down hard on the edge of his desk. "Martha, I understand the plight of nonprofit organizations such as yours, believe me. I know how tight money is, especially in a conservative economy. But special events bring in dollars. The cost of an event, compared to what it reaps in donations—"

"I'm sorry, Chance," she said again, firmly. "We will no longer be working with your firm."

"I see." Lisa groaned and dropped her face into her hands. "Can I ask, Martha, have you been disappointed with our performance? In any way?"

She hesitated. "Your performance had been excellent. As I said, this is strictly a…a fiduciary decision."

Her slight hesitation gave her away. *She was lying. Why?*

"I can see I'm not going to change your mind, Martha. I hope you'll think of us for your future special-events needs."

"Of course. Good day, Chance."

She hung up. And just like that, he was down another client. Chance set the receiver carefully in its cradle, swallowing against the bitterness and frustration that rose in his throat. He had always thought that hard work and a job well done would earn loyalty.

Just went to show what he knew about anything. That was just bullshit.

"Did she say why?" Lisa asked.

"Money troubles."

"But our celebrity-waiter event brought in forty-two thousand dollars!" Lisa cried, jumping to her feet, shaking with outrage. "After expenses! She said it was the highest-grossing, smoothest-running event they'd ever had!"

"I know." He plucked his suit coat from the back of his chair. "But I guess that was yesterday's news. Today's news is, thanks, but no thanks, your services are no longer required." He started around the desk, heading for the door. "I've got to get out of here for a while. I'll check in for my messages."

"Wait!"

Chance stopped and looked back at his assistant.

"I need to know, should I start looking for another job?"

Her question hit him square between the eyes. She was right to be worried. "You don't have to, not just yet, Lisa."

"Not yet? What does that mean?" She twisted her fingers together. "I support myself, Chance. I can't afford to be unemployed."

"Then start looking." She caught her breath, and he made a sound of regret. "I'm sorry, I don't want to lose you, Lisa. But I can't make any promises right now. If you can hang on a few days, until I get a handle on what's happening and what I have left, I'd appreciate it. If you can't, I'll understand."

"It might be over?" she offered hopefully. "Martha might be the last to drop out."

"Maybe." He tossed his jacket over his shoulder. "But I don't think so. I have a feeling that whoever's fucking me is just getting started."

60

Griffen seemed different tonight, Skye thought, pushing away her dinner plate. On edge, almost kinetic. He darted from one subject to another, sometimes not meeting her eyes, other times looking at her with such intensity she squirmed in her seat. He had brought her here to Morton's, his favorite restaurant, yet he had eaten hardly a bite, instead drinking nearly the whole bottle of wine himself.

They hadn't spoken much since the day Chance had opened her office door and he had been standing there. She had wondered how much of their conversation he had heard, and several times she had given him the opportunity to bring up the subject. He hadn't.

She decided to try again. She reached across the table. "Griffen, what's wrong with you tonight? You seem upset about something. Is it me? Something I've done?"

"You, sweetheart? No." Her curled his hand around hers. "But I have to tell you something. About Chance. I'm afraid it might upset you."

"Upset me?" she repeated, swallowing hard. "About Chance."

"Yes." For a long moment, Griffen was silent. Then he swore softly and met her eyes. "In the past, Chance and I have...competed for women. No, that's not really right. The truth is, Chance has competed with me for my women."

Griffen looked away, then back, his expression troubled. "It's kind of sick, really. He wants what I have. Money, power, fine, fancy things. That want has extended to women

I've dated. He does his damnedest to seduce them, to steal them away from me. He's been successful several times.''

Skye felt ill, physically ill. She took a sip of her water, noticing that her hand shook.

"The thing is," he continued, "once he has them, he doesn't want them. He tosses them away. Like so much garbage. It never...mattered so much before. But with you..." He bit the words back. "This is upsetting you."

She swallowed hard, afraid, so afraid that Griffen would see everything, that he would figure out why she was upset. That he would know what had occurred between her and Chance.

She felt like a liar and a cheat. She felt like a fool.

She wet her lips. "No, it's just that we were once...close. I hate to think of him that way. It's so shallow and ugly."

"I understand," he murmured, tightening his fingers over hers. "Especially considering your past relationship. You weren't lovers, but he tossed you away so easily. I guess he hasn't changed. People's feelings mean so little to him."

A cry rose to her throat, she swallowed it, though not without effort.

Griffen shook his head. "What turns a smart, likable guy like Chance into such a cold, selfish bastard? Envy, I suppose," he said, answering his own question.

"Envy," she repeated, dizzy, nauseated.

"Sure, a kid like Chance, who came from nothing. Ambitious, hungry. I've given this a lot of thought." He looked her straight in the eye. "I think he wants to be me."

His words affected her like a slap. Chance wanted to be Griffen. It was true. It fit everything Chance had ever told her, about his mother, about his dreams, his plans for the future.

She had never been a part of those dreams and plans. She still wasn't. Love wasn't.

But Griffen wanted her to be a part of his future. His life. Griffen believed in love.

How could she have been so stupid? How could she have jeopardized her future that way? What was wrong with her?

"I'm glad I can trust you, Skye," Griffen murmured. "I'm glad I know you can't be fooled or seduced by him. I don't know what I'd do if I lost you. I might even go crazy."

Long after Griffen had brought her home and kissed her good-night, Skye still reeled from what he had said about Chance.

She could hear Chance in her head. *I can't stop thinking about you, Skye. I want you. Stop seeing him.*

She had played right into his sick little game.

That night the grotesque bird visited her again. Only this time, she was a butterfly. And no matter how hard she flapped her wings, she couldn't escape.

She woke up to the sound of her own scream.

61

Skye stood at her bathroom vanity, staring at her collection of perfumes and lotions. She frowned. Something about the arrangement was different than when she had left that morning. She tilted her head. It was as if someone had picked them all up, then put them back in *nearly* the same spot.

This wasn't the first time she had experienced this sensation. Last week she had come home and been certain the fan of magazines on her coffee table had been changed. Twice before that, she had opened her underwear drawer and been struck with the feeling that someone had been into her things, that they had carefully sifted through the drawer. And taken her sexiest pair of panties.

Skye turned away from the vanity and went to her bedroom to change out of her work clothes. She was seriously starting to worry about her mental health. Headaches. Nightmares. Panic attacks.

Now these delusions about strangers in her apartment, going through her things—her undies, no less. A shrink could have a field day with her, no doubt about it.

She slipped into a pair of leggings and a big, comfy sweater and started for the kitchen in search of dinner, when the phone rang.

It was Terri. She was crying. "He did it again," she said. "Only this time...this time..." Her friend's teeth began to chatter. "Skye, he threatened Raye. He said he was going to...to hurt her."

"Raye?" Skye sat down, alarmed. "Have you called the police?"

She said she had, then asked if Skye could come over. "I need some company, I can't bear the thought of being alone right now."

"I'll be there in fifteen minutes."

When Skye arrived, Terri, who was white as a sheet, was frantically digging through old coat pockets and kitchen drawers in search of a cigarette. She found a crumpled, half-full pack and shook one out. She lit it, though it took her three tries, her hand was trembling so badly.

"Where's Raye?"

"Asleep." She sucked on the cigarette, then exhaled a cloud of smoke. "My mother's coming. Raye's going to stay with her for a while."

Terri passed a hand over her face. "I lived through the breakup of my marriage without picking up a cigarette, and look at me now. Damn."

"Tell me what happened."

"He left a message on the machine. For Raye. He called her by name, Skye. He said...he said he was going to—" She choked back the words. "I can't even say it."

"Did you save the message?"

She nodded and crossed to the recorder. She rewound it, then hit play. The man's voice, deep, gravelly yet cultured, slithered through the recorder's speaker, filling the quiet room. His words were vile; the act he described a crime against nature, against all that was good and pure in the world.

Skye stared at the recorder, sweat beading her upper lip, her heart beginning to pound. She struggled for breath, a heaviness pressing in on her, a black, inescapable weight.

With a squeak of terror she sank to the ottoman.

The room was filled with colored light. There was a weight on top of her, another body pressing her down. Bigger, stronger, the body held her captive no matter how she

*pleaded and squirmed. She couldn't breathe, and she thought
she might be sick. She opened her mouth to scream, but no
sound—*

"Skye? Are you all right?"

Startled, she looked up. Terri stood above her, her hand
on her shoulder, her expression concerned.

"Are you all right?" she asked again.

Skye brought a hand to her face and realized she was
crying. She swallowed hard, afraid. That she really was losing her mind. That one day she might wake up and find
herself caught in this dark, paranoid world she seemed to be
creating for herself.

She wiped the tears from her cheeks. "I'm okay," she
managed to say, her voice shaky. "I guess I kind of freaked
just then. That man's voice, what he said...it was so evil,
Terri. So horrible."

"I'm scared, Skye. For me. Now for Raye. I can't take it
anymore. I can't."

Skye reached up and caught her friend's hand. "What did
the police say?"

"Screw the police! They haven't helped me one bit." Terri squeezed Skye's fingers, then let them go. "I need another
cigarette."

Skye watched her friend, sensing that the other woman
was keeping something from her, or that she was working
up the courage to say something unpleasant. Something she
knew Skye wouldn't like.

"Spit it out, Terri. Whatever it is you're thinking but not
saying."

She met Skye's gaze and sighed. "I've come to a decision.
My sister lives in Phoenix. She has room for me and Raye.
She wants us to come. I'm leaving Chicago."

"Phoenix, Arizona?"

Terri nodded and Skye clasped her hands together, working not to cry. She understood. If she were in Terri's position, she would do the same thing. But understanding didn't

stop it from hurting. Terri and Raye had become like a family to her. She didn't know what she would do when they left. She would be so alone.

Once again, she was being left behind.

"I'm really sorry, Skye. I'm going to miss you, too."

Skye lifted her gaze to her friend, her vision blurred with tears. "What about your job, Terri? You love it."

"I love my daughter more." Terri sat on the ottoman beside Skye. "I can't take the chance that this nut case isn't for real."

"You could move in with me and Mr. Moo...? It'd be fun. And you'd be safe."

"Right. Until my sick friend found me there and started leaving dead rats on your doorstep."

"But, Terri—"

"No." Terri covered Skye's clenched hands. "I've made up my mind. I'm going to miss you so much, Skye. You're the best friend I ever had."

"And you're mine. You're—" Skye looked away, willing herself not to cry, determined to find a way for Terri to stay. "What about Griffen? Maybe he could help? He has so many resources, maybe he could do...something."

"I don't think so, Skye."

"Why not? He—"

"Are we good friends, Skye? Good enough to say anything to each other?"

"You know we are."

"Good." Terri tightened her hands over Skye's. "This thing with you and Griffen, it's got me worried. It's been so sudden and there's something about Griffen...about his feelings for you that seems odd. He's more than possessive—sometimes, when he looks at me, I think he would like me...gone."

"Gone," Skye repeated. "Like how?"

Terri laughed nervously. "Like out of the picture. Out of your life. Like what's happening."

Skye frowned. "He always speaks well of you, Terri. Always. And he knows how much you and Raye mean to me."

"That's exactly it. I mean, he *knows* how close we are and maybe he's—" Terri bit back the words and looked at the floor, then sighed. "Please, don't get mad, but I have to ask you this. Do you think...has it ever crossed your mind that...maybe Griffen could be the one...you know, the one behind all...this?"

For a full ten seconds Skye stared at her friend, stunned. Then she jumped to her feet, cheeks hot. "No, Terri, I haven't. That's crazy. How can you even say that?"

"It's just that, when I catch him looking at me that way, I wonder how far he'd go to have you all to himself."

"Well, you can stop wondering. That's nuts." Skye shook her head. "All along, you've known in your heart that it was Will, punishing you for not letting him come back. All along—"

"It's not Will, I know that now."

"How can you be so sure? After all, he has motive and—"

"Because he loves his daughter. That's how." Terri stood. "He adores Raye. He wouldn't do this. He couldn't, not even to scare and punish me."

"Then it's some stranger, some nut who—"

"Knows where I live. And what my daughter's name is. And where she goes to pre-school."

"It's not Griffen."

"All right. I'm sorry." Terri let out a breath, sounding frustrated. "I guess I'm just trying to make sense of this. Please don't be angry with me."

"I'm not angry." Skye hugged her. "But I promise you, Griffen is not the one who's doing this. The police will get the guy who is, and you'll see. It's not Griffen."

62

Terri and Raye left early the following Saturday morning. Skye went to say a final goodbye and to help Terri with any last-minute packing. Only, her friend had taken care of everything already; there was nothing left to do but face the goodbye.

Skye felt as if her heart was breaking. "I hate this," she said softly, swiping a tear from her cheek. "It's not fair."

"I know." Terri hugged her. "You be careful, okay?"

"Don't worry about me." Skye held her friend tightly, not wanting to let her go, but knowing she had to. "You and Raye be safe."

Terri took a step back, sniffling. "We will."

"You'll call me?"

"You bet. And I'll e-mail you at the office. I want to hear everything that happens with City Lights."

"It's your series, too. And don't you forget it."

Raye tugged on her sweater. "Why you crying, Aunt Skye?"

"Because I'm going to miss you so much." Skye squatted and hugged the little girl.

Raye touched Skye's wet cheeks. "You can come, too. Mommy will let you."

"I can't, sweetie. I wish I could."

Raye frowned. "You going to come see me in 'Zona?"

Skye smiled at her abbreviation of Arizona, and brushed her soft, dark curls away from her face. "Can I bring Moo?"

"Sure." She nodded for emphasis. "Moo's my friend."

"Come on, Raye," Terri said quietly, "we need to go."

Choked with tears, Skye watched as Terri got her daughter situated in the car, then made sure she had everything for the long drive, putting off the inevitable, Skye knew. Finally, there was nothing else to do but climb into the car and go.

After a last, tearful hug, Terri did just that.

Skye watched them drive away, waving goodbye, not dropping her hand until they were completely out of sight.

Alone again. Left behind again.

Chance.

His image popped into her head, with it the need to see him. To talk to him. Even as she told herself the need was nothing but an emotional knee-jerk reaction to Terri leaving, she crossed the street to the corner grocery store to see if they had a phone book. They did. Chance was listed.

She jotted down his address, then without planning what she would say, without considering the early hour or the consequences of her actions, she climbed in her car and drove to Chance's building. She parked and went inside, located his apartment and knocked on the door. When he didn't answer, she knocked again, then pounded.

"Okay...okay. I'm coming."

He swung the door open. He had been sleeping, she realized, and was still barely awake. He wore a pair of loose-fitting, gray sweats and a wrinkled T-shirt. His feet were bare, his hair tousled, his cheeks rough with his morning beard. He looked masculine and sexy and more than a little surprised to find her standing at his front door.

"Terri left this morning," she said, voice quaking. "For good."

Wordlessly, he swung the door wider. She stepped inside, glancing around. It looked like a guy's place, nothing quite matched, furnishings had obviously been picked for durability and comfort rather than style; a pizza box and a couple of beer cans decorated the coffee table.

"Sorry, I'm not much of a housekeeper." He yawned and

motioned for her to follow him to the living room. He led the way, picking up articles of clothing as he did—a tie off the back of a chair, a dress shirt in a heap on the floor, sweat socks and athletic shoes from in front of the couch.

"Have a seat. I'll get us some coffee."

He dumped his armload on an empty chair and went to the kitchen. A few minutes later, he returned with two steaming mugs. "I didn't know how you take your coffee."

"Black's fine."

"Good thing. The milk has lumps." He handed her a mug, then took a seat in the overstuffed chair across from her. "Okay, kid, what's up?"

His use of her old nickname brought tears to her eyes. She blinked them back and told him about Terri and her daughter and how close the three of them had become. She told him about the threatening calls, the dead rat and that last, frightening threat to Raye.

"Damn." Chance ran a hand over his stubble-rough face. "That's some sick bastard."

"The police weren't any help. So she…left. She has a sister in Arizona who offered them a place to stay."

"Do you blame her for wanting to leave?" Chance asked, taking a sip of his coffee. "This guy might really have hurt one of them."

Skye shook her head, tears stinging her eyes. "I know. And I do understand. It's just that it…" She dug in her purse for a tissue, found a crumpled one at the bottom and immediately began shredding it. "They'd gotten to be like family, you know? Terri was my friend, and little Raye was so sweet. We spent a lot of time together, and—"

She sucked in a deep breath. "I thought I didn't need anybody. I told myself I didn't. It was easier that way. Safer." She met his eyes, then looked away. "Then I let them in, and I liked having a friend. I liked having them in my life. I started to really care about them."

"And now they're gone." He took another swallow of coffee.

"Yes." She swiped angrily at her tears. "You know, Chance, I'm getting pretty sick of this shit."

He arched his eyebrows, his gaze intent. "Exactly what shit is that, Skye?"

"Getting left behind."

"That's life, babe. Get over it."

She jumped to her feet, hurt. Angry. "Thanks a lot! I suppose that's what I get for thinking *you'd* understand. Mr. Loyalty himself. The last of the all-time deserters."

"Why exactly did you come here, Skye? Because you thought I'd understand about Terri or did you want something else?"

"I hate you."

She started past him; he reached up, grabbed her and tumbled her into his lap. "It's okay, baby."

She struggled against his grasp, furious. "Let me go, you son of a bitch! Let me go or I'll scream!"

"Shh." He put his arms tightly around her, pinning her against his chest, much as he had all those years ago when she had awakened and found her mother had left her.

He pressed his cheek to the top of her head. "I do understand, Skye. I was there, I know how much it hurt when your mom left. I know how much my leaving must have hurt. If you want to cry, I'm here, love. I'm here."

The fight went out of her, and she dissolved into tears. For long minutes she sobbed, clinging to him like a baby, lost in her feelings of emptiness and loss. Her loneliness.

Finally, her sobs abated, becoming small mews of despair. "You broke my heart," she managed to say, her voice choked. She balled her hands into fists on his chest. "How could you do that to me? I loved you. I needed you. You were my everything, Chance."

"I'm sorry, baby. I am." He pushed the hair away from her face, though tendrils stuck to her wet cheeks. "I loved you, too. I didn't want to hurt you. But I didn't know how not to.''

She wiped her nose with the back of her hand. "You did hurt me. I almost died, I almost curled into a ball and died.''

"But you didn't, Skye. You're here.'' He kissed her then, softly, rubbing his mouth against hers. "You're strong, a survivor. I knew that about you.''

"How did you know?'' She shuddered and brought her hands to his face, kissing him back, opening her mouth, her heart. "I didn't. I still don't.''

"Forgive me, love,'' he whispered, bringing his hands under her sweater and stroking her back. "Forgive me.''

She did forgive him, she realized. In a way she had been unable to before. In a way that felt good, freeing and right. She turned more fully to him, straddling his lap. His erection pressed against her, and she rocked her pelvis, rubbing herself against him, growing aroused herself.

"Make love to me, Chance,'' she murmured against his mouth. "I want you so much, make love to me.''

Without a word, he did as she asked. Caressing and kissing her, touching her in ways and places she had never been touched before. He brought her along slowly, exquisitely, until her entire world consisted of his hands and mouth, his voice in her ears as he murmured words of encouragement and arousal, the taste of him, his texture, his sounds.

He stripped off her clothes, and she his. Being naked with him felt good. Right. She fit against him in a way she had never fit with any man. She ran her hands across his chest, stopping on the long, thin scar that ran diagonally across its center. She lifted her gaze to his. "Kevin?'' she whispered, her heart hurting.

He nodded and she brought her lips to the scar and pressed tiny kisses along its length, remembering, aching.

"Come here, baby,'' he murmured, bringing her face to his. "Let me make you happy.''

And he did. He seemed to know all her secret spots,

seemed to know just how and when to touch her that pleasured her most. She arched up, whimpering, needing more, wanting everything. He gave it to her, moving his hands, then mouth, until her body exploded in a shower of color and light.

While she still throbbed with her release, he fitted her on top of him. She gasped as he entered her, at the way it felt to have him inside her. She hugged him, using her muscles in a way she hadn't known she could, holding him as tightly as she could. She never wanted to let go. He was hers. This was as it should be.

He was hot and hard and painfully ready for her, she could tell by the way he trembled at their joining. For one moment he allowed her to hold and milk him, then with a groan he began to move, slowly at first, then with increased passion. Skye exploded with orgasm again, almost violently, crying out his name. He caught his name with his mouth, shuddering with his own climax, his mouth open, wet; he was completely vulnerable to her. As she was to him.

In that moment, for once, there were no barriers between them.

She had never known the joining of two people could be like this, intense yet tender, shocking yet sweet. She hadn't known that together a man and a woman could come this dizzyingly, exquisitely close to heaven.

She'd had sex before, but she had never made love. She saw that now. She saw, too, that she would never be the same.

Afterward, she snuggled up to him in the big chair, moving her body against him, cooing her contentment. She trailed her mouth across his shoulder, kissing, nibbling. "Delicious," she murmured, all but purring. "I feel absolutely...delicious."

She did purr then, playfully, deep in her throat. He didn't respond, and she suddenly realized that he hadn't said a thing, that he had hardly moved since their mutual climax.

She had been so lost in her own euphoria, she hadn't noticed the way he had cooled.

"Chance?"

He opened his eyes and looked at her.

"You're so quiet."

He gazed at her a moment, the expression in his eyes sending her hopes plummeting, her euphoria out the window. What had happened in the space of minutes that caused him to look at her that way?

"What would you like me to say?" he asked, his voice thick. "Or are compliments what you're fishing for?"

She caught her breath, hurt. "I'm not fishing for anything. Forget it."

"No, really, I'd be happy to help you out. You're an incredible lay, Skye. One of the best I ever had."

"You bastard." She slapped him as hard as she could, then scrambled off his lap. She grabbed her sweater and pulled it over her head, suddenly feeling naked and too vulnerable. She swallowed hard, past the hurt, the disillusionment. A minute ago she had felt wonderful, like a million bucks, now she felt like less than nothing. She felt like a cheap lay, one of what had no doubt been dozens of others.

Chance wants to be me. He's competed for my women. And once he had them, he didn't want them anymore. He throws them away, like so much garbage.

She squeezed her eyes shut, wishing she could deny the words, their truth. Wishing she didn't hurt almost more than she could bear.

Griffen had tried to tell her, had tried to warn her.

She was as disloyal as she was foolish.

She had no shame when it came to Chance McCord. In all the years that had passed, nothing had changed. She was still throwing herself at him, and he was still rejecting her.

She jerked her chin up, and swept her gaze over him. His right cheek bore a rosy imprint of her hand. "You want to tell me what just happened here, Chance? Want to clue me in?''

"You showed up crying at my door, Skye. Not the other way around."

"Oh, I see," she said, voice quivering. "This was a mercy fuck. Is that what you're trying to tell me?"

"Don't be so sanctimonious, Skye. You know what this was."

"No, I don't. Tell me." He said nothing and she looked away, hurting, she thought, as much as the day she had awakened and found him gone. She snatched up her panties from the floor. "It was nothing, right? Just one of many other lays, though I'm one of the better ones. Well, thank you very much, asshole!"

"No, dammit!" He jumped to his feet, grabbed his sweats and yanked them on. "What I'm trying to tell you is, I have nothing to offer you. My business is crumbling around me. I've lost almost every client I acquired in the last six months. I had to let my assistant go yesterday. What do you want from me? As you've told me many times before, Griffen can give you everything. He's offered you everything, the world, you said. Take it, Skye. Take it and get the hell out!"

She yanked on her leggings, the task almost impossible because she shook so badly. "I guess what Griffen told me about you was true."

"Yeah? And what was that?"

"That you're jealous of him. That you want to be him."

Chance looked as if she had struck him. "Griffen said that?"

"That's right. He also said you were so fixated on your desire, you would stoop to stealing his woman. That you had before."

"Steal his woman," Chance repeated, furious. "Baby, I'm not the one who showed up at your door, practically begging to be fuc—"

"Don't you say it, you son of a bitch!" She snatched one

of the beer cans from the coffee table and threw it at him.
He ducked and it sailed past his head and hit the wall.
"That's not what happened and you know it!"

"Tell me, Skye, why would I even think you needed a
'mercy fuck,' as you so delicately phrased it? You have Griffen. I would imagine he keeps you pretty well satisfied."

She felt as if he had slapped her. Compared to all else that
had passed between them, that hurt the most. Without even
looking at him, she gathered together the rest of her things
and stalked to the door.

Once there, she stopped and looked back at him. "I
haven't slept with Griffen," she said softly. "But now that
you bring it up, I don't know why I've been waiting."

63

Griffen was going to ask her to marry him. Tonight. Skye was certain of it.

Two days ago he had called and invited her out for tonight. He had a surprise for her, he'd said. Something really special. Now, here they were, at the Ritz Carlton dining room, champagne chilling, soft music playing, a single, exquisite red rose laid across her plate.

If only she knew what her answer would be.

The maître d' eased the table away from the banquette and Skye slid onto the upholstered bench, looking questioningly at Griffen. He had been acting strangely lately, warm and demonstrative one moment, cool and withdrawn the next. It was almost as if he were two different people.

She picked up the rose and held it to her nose. She had wondered if it hadn't been him at all, but her, a reflection of her own confused feelings toward him. She wanted Griffen, she wanted the love and security he offered; she wanted a family and stability. And she knew, with her head if not her heart, that he was right for her.

But she couldn't stop thinking about Chance. She couldn't stop remembering the way her body had come alive at his touch, or the way she had felt afterward. Like the world was hers.

He'd gotten her, now he didn't want her anymore.

She lowered her gaze to her lap. She had been such a fool. What was wrong with her? Chance had nearly destroyed her once, why was she so intent on giving him the opportunity to do it again?

"Skye, sweetheart. To us."

She jumped, startled, then laughed self-consciously and brought her glass to his. "To us," she mimicked, then sipped.

"You looked a million miles away a few seconds ago. Anything you want to talk about?"

"No," she murmured, forcing a smile. She indicated his bandaged hand, changing the subject. "How's your hand? Still aching?"

He glanced at it, then back at her. "It's fine, almost as good as new."

She shuddered. "Fifty-two stitches, I can't imagine how much that hurt. It's hard to believe a broken glass could do so much damage."

He shrugged. "I was distracted, not paying attention to what I was doing." He smiled slightly. "I was lost in space, I guess. Just as you were a moment ago."

"Me?"

"Mmm. Thinking about Terri and her cute little daughter. Don't try to deny it. I know how much their leaving hurt you. I know you miss them."

Something about his expression when he spoke seemed off, inconsistent with his words and tone. She sensed a kind of amusement. Or pleasure.

Skye searched his gaze, but whatever she had thought she'd seen was gone. He was the picture of loving concern. She took another sip of the wine, scolding herself for her thoughts. How could she even think such a thing about Griffen? He had been very supportive of her feelings, very understanding.

She cleared her throat. "I have thought about them a lot, but I wasn't just then."

"How are they?"

"Doing well. Settling in."

"Such a shame, that thing that happened to them. There are so many sick people in the world."

"Yes."

He brought his wine to his lips, drank, then set down the glass. "And how's Moo doing? No more near-death experiences, I hope?"

She shook her head. "No."

"Ever find the guy who poisoned him?"

She looked away, uncomfortable. "He's still out there."

"That's frightening," Griffen murmured. "He could do it again."

Skye's hand began to shake, and she put down her champagne, afraid she might spill it. "I'm being more careful. I never let him out alone."

"That's good." He reached across the table and caught her hand, using his left instead of right because of his injury. "Your hand's so cold." He curled his fingers around hers. "Darling, I haven't upset you, have I?"

"No, of course not."

He rubbed his fingers along hers, gently massaging. "What you've been going through has really made me think about life and what's important. One minute you can have everything, the next nothing. But family is always there. When you're part of a family, you're never alone. Family never leaves you behind."

She thought of her mother and tears sprang to her eyes.

"They don't, Skye," he said, as if reading her mind. "Not when they love you. Your mother didn't deserve that title. She didn't deserve your love. And neither did Chance."

This time, she couldn't hide her distress. A tear rolled down her cheek, despite how she fought it.

"Now I have upset you. I'm sorry, sweetheart, I wanted tonight to be special."

"You're right, though. That's the thing." She swiped at a second tear, then a third. "I don't have anybody, Griffen. I'm all alone."

"You have me." When she made a move to pull her hand away, he tightened his fingers over hers. "No, you do. Skye, you know how I feel about you. I haven't made a secret of it."

She met his eyes, her heart in her throat, knowing what was coming next and wishing she knew what her answer would be.

"I want to take care of you, sweetheart. I want to love and cherish you, I want us to be side by side forever. Skye, I want you to be my wife. Will you marry me?"

Skye gazed at him, choked, thinking of Chance. Thinking of his magic hands and how he could make her body sing. She cursed her thoughts. She cursed him.

"Before you answer, consider this. You'll never have to be alone again. I promise to give you everything you ever dreamed of, love, a real home, a family. Granddad and Dorothy love you, too. We need you. Monarch's needs you." His voice deepened. "I need you."

She began to shake. She didn't know what to say. He was offering her everything she had ever wanted, and yet she couldn't seem to get "yes" to form on her lips.

She brought a hand to her temple, her head beginning to hurt. "This is such a big step," she murmured. "I'm stunned. And flattered."

His lips curved into a triumphant smile. He dipped his hand into his suit-coat pocket and pulled out a violet-colored velvet ring box. He set it on the table in front of her.

When she only stared at it, he laughed softly. "Go ahead, Skye. Open it."

With trembling fingers, she snapped open the lid. Her breath caught as she saw the magnificent diamond solitaire inside. It caught the light and winked at her. "Oh, my God."

She brought a hand to her throat. It was the most beautiful diamond she had ever seen: oval-cut, full of fire, huge. At least five carats. "It's too much."

"Not for the woman I adore. Try it on." He slipped the

ring from its satin nest and held it out for her fourth finger.
She lifted her hand; he slid the ring on. It fit perfectly.

"We know everything about each other, Skye. We have
everything in common, more than you even know. We would
have a perfect life together. Imagine, rich, powerful, beautiful. Side by side, we'll run Monarch's and raise a new batch
of little Monarchs. We'll be unstoppable, Skye."

What about passion? she wondered. *What about love?*

That wasn't fair. He loved her, he had told her so, many
times. And she...she loved him. She did.

Just not the way she loved...Chance.

Tears flooded her eyes. She blinked against them, horrified. With her thoughts, with the truth. She was in love with
Chance. She had been since they were children.

No. She couldn't love Chance. She couldn't. He didn't
love her. He had left her behind once, he would most certainly do it again.

But she did love him—the way she wished she loved Griffen.

"Hey." Griffen tipped her face up to his. "I hope those
are tears of happiness."

"They are," she lied, feeling awful. "I'm overwhelmed.
I—"

"Is that a yes?"

She struggled for the right thing to say, the best thing.
"Griffen, I don't...this isn't a good time..."

He stiffened and dropped his hand, two bright spots of
angry color staining his cheeks. "So, is it a no?"

"Absolutely not." She caught his hand. "I need some
time. I'm just not...I'm not ready."

"Well, I am ready," he said stiffly. "It seems pretty simple to me, Skye. Either you want to marry me or you don't."

"I wish I could be like you, Griffen, so certain of my
every step. But this is forever. And that's scary. I've been
hurt before, and I'm afraid."

"I'm not like your mother. Or Chance, the prick." Griffen

all but spit the words. "I would never leave you. I would never stop loving you. You belong with me, I know it. I believe it. We were destined to be together."

She lifted her gaze to his. His eyes, as if alight with an inner fire, were hot and bright. She had never seen him look quite this way. She shivered. "I can't give you an answer now. I'm sorry. I want to say yes, Griffen. I do. But I can't. Not right now."

"I see." He drew away from her, obviously furious.

"Please," she begged, "try to understand. I want this to be perfect. For us. There's so much going on, and with the upcoming trip to Milan and…and everything. Please, Griffen. Don't be angry with me. Just give me a little time."

He said nothing for a moment, then nodded curtly. "All right, Skye. A little time. But I'm not going to wait forever."

"I wouldn't expect you to. I'll give you my answer when I get back from Milan."

"Two weeks it is, Skye. I'll be waiting."

64

Skye found Chance at his office. He stood facing the window behind his desk, his back to the door. He looked tired, she thought. Something about his stance, about the angle of his shoulders, lacked his usual look-out-world confidence and boundless zest for life.

Apparently, he hadn't heard her arrive, as he didn't acknowledge her presence in any way. Skye caught her bottom lip between her teeth. She could go now, she realized. She still had the opportunity to turn and walk away without facing him, without humbling herself. Without all but begging. He would never know she had been here.

She couldn't do that, as much as a part of her longed to. She had nothing to lose. He had already broken her heart.

If she didn't do this, she would always wonder.

"Chance?"

He stiffened, then turned. He met her eyes, but didn't speak. She clasped her hands in front of her. "How are you?" As soon as the inane question passed her lips, she cursed herself for it.

"How am I? Well, I have three clients left. I even lost one I brought with me from Adams and Sloane. I don't exactly feel like dancing a jig." He swept his gaze over her. "And how are you, Skye?"

She searched his expression, her heart hurting for him. She knew, probably more than anyone, what success meant to him. "I'm sorry," she said softly.

"Yeah, me, too. Sorry as hell."

"You still have Monarch's. They're happy, I know they are."

"So were the others." He shook his head. "Why are you here?"

"Griffen's asked me to marry him."

"Has he?"

"Yes." She cleared her throat. "He says he…loves me. He promises me he'll never leave me. That he'll give me the world."

"Sounds like a hell of a deal, kid," Chance said, his voice gravelly. He turned back to the window. "You took it, I hope."

She felt as if she were being torn apart inside. She took a deep, fortifying breath. What did she have to lose by humbling herself to him? By baring her soul?

Nothing she hadn't lost already, a long time ago.

"Chance, I… Look at me. Please."

He turned slowly. He was closed to her; she saw it in his expression, in the rigid way he held his body, in the way he looked at her, as if he didn't even see her.

"I told him I needed some time."

"I see." Again, he swept his gaze over her. "Did you come for my blessing or to ask if big brother would give you away?"

She looked away, then back, fighting tears. "I want you to tell me not to do it, Chance. I want you to give me a reason…to tell him no."

For a long moment Chance simply gazed at her, as if drinking in every nuance of her appearance, as if this were the last time he would ever see her. She was looking at him the same way, she knew. Eating up everything about him, wanting to hold him so badly she ached.

"I can't do that, Skye," he said finally. "I'm sorry."

A cry of despair flew to her lips, and she brought a hand to her mouth. She steeled herself against the hurt and disappointment. The feeling of betrayal.

"Would it change anything if I...what would you say, if I...if I told you I love you?"

He stared at her a moment, his expression stony, then he shook his head. "Don't love me. Love Griffen. He's offered you the world, Skye. Seems to me a smart girl like you would take that offer."

She opened her mouth, prepared to beg, then shut it. He didn't love her, he never would. No amount of begging would change that. It would only make them both feel bad.

They both felt bad enough already.

"All right, then. I have my answer." She folded her arms across her chest, struggling not to further humiliate herself by crying. "I guess this is goodbye."

"I guess it is," he said, his voice thick. "Next time I see you, you'll be promised to Griffen. I hope you're really happy."

He turned to the window. She stared at his back a moment, then walked away.

As his office door shut behind her, she heard him say something, heard him call her name.

She didn't go back. She never would.

65

Griffen shut Dorothy's office door behind him, then leaned against it, studying his aunt. She looked a wreck. "You rang, Auntie-dear?"

She waved him into the office, sucking greedily on a cigarette, a habit he abhorred. It was bad enough that she smoked, did she have to nurse on the things, like a baby at a teat?

"We have to talk," she said.

"So I assumed by your frantic voice mail." He slid into the chair opposite hers and crossed his legs. "What's the big emergency?"

"Skye told me about your proposal."

Griffen narrowed his eyes. "And what did you say to her?"

"I told her I would love having her as a member of the family." She stamped out the cigarette. "Of course."

"Good." He brushed a piece of lint from his sleeve. "So, what's the problem?"

She opened her mouth as if to answer, then widened her eyes. "My God, Griffen. What happened to your hand?"

He looked down at his bandaged right hand and shrugged. "I had a little accident in the bathroom. It required some stitches. It's nothing." He met her eyes once more. "Back to your little crisis, Aunt Dot."

She shifted under his gaze, agitated. "I can't continue this. I just can't, Griffen."

"Pardon me?"

"I can't keep lying to her. I can't keep pretending—" She began to shake and fumbled around for another cigarette.

He made a sound of disgust. "Calm down. You're acting like a hysterical old fool."

"I can't help it!" She lit the cigarette on the third try and inhaled deeply, pulling almost desperately on it, as if it would somehow save her life instead of take it. "I hate this. It's not right. I've come to care about her, Griffen."

"I care about her, too, Aunt Dorothy. I love her. We all do."

"But how can you... Griffen, you're her brother. It's wrong, what we're doing. You cannot marry your sister."

At her words, he felt a pinch of annoyance and pressed his lips together. "Dot, dear," he said quietly, using a tone one would to address a recalcitrant child. "Do you really think this is the appropriate time and place to be having this discussion?"

"I don't care! I'm telling you, I'm ending this charade!"

Weak. She was weak and stupid. But he would control her.

He stood and crossed to her desk. He laid his palms on it and leaned toward her, looking her dead in the eye. "We've talked about this before," he said evenly. "Before Skye ever came home, we talked about this. We decided this would be the best way. We're into it now, Aunt Dot. We can't get out so easily."

"But we must, don't you see? We have to find a way." His great-aunt looked at him, pleading. "She means more to me now than just her value to Monarch's."

He snorted, not hiding his disappointment in her. Or his mounting irritation. "Easy to say now, isn't it, since the pressure's off?" He leaned closer. "We need her, Dorothy. You need her. Monarch's needs her."

She crushed her cigarette and immediately grabbed for another. "I've thought about this. We could explain it all to her. She's such a sweet girl, she'll understand. She will."

"Sure she will." He straightened, crossed to the window and looked out at the splendor that was the Magnificent Mile.

After a moment, he turned back to his aunt. "Do you remember all the reasons we did this? Do you remember your reasons, what you said when we made our decision?"

She brought a trembling hand to her head, already back-pedaling, he saw. Typical, weak female maneuver. Any moment she would begin to whine about how she couldn't remember or that she had been confused.

"I can't...quite remember, Griffen. You know how forgetful I am. You know how confused I—"

"You thought it would be fun," he interrupted her. "A kind of adventure. Ringing any bells now, Auntie-dear?"

She flushed and guiltily slid her gaze away. "Yes, but...but we were all so angry with Madeline for taking our girl, I thought...I didn't see—" She lit her cigarette; he saw that her hands trembled. "I didn't know her then, Griffen. She wasn't real then."

"Fun," he repeated. "I'm sure Skye will feel warm and generous toward you when you tell her that's why you lied to her. Because you thought it would be *fun*."

"Oh, dear. I didn't think of it that way."

"How do you suppose she'll look at you when she learns the way you lied to her mother? When she learns it was you, Dorothy, who alerted Pierce of her whereabouts and caused Madeline to run, leaving Skye behind?"

"She wouldn't have to know that part. She—"

"But she would find out. She would end up knowing everything." He circled her desk, enjoying her trapped expression. "Recall, Aunt Dorothy, that we feared, when Skye learned the truth, she would side with her mother. She loved her very much, you know. Very much. Remember, too, how desperate you were before she came back to us, how overwhelmed? Remember what it was like to see Monarch Design, your love, your baby, slipping into mediocrity?"

Griffen stopped and faced her. "We needed our girl. We

needed the one with the gift. If she were tied to me, we were certain she would never leave. No man would come along and steal her away.'' He leaned closer. He could all but smell her panic. ''We had all decided this would work. That it was the best way.''

She shrank back in her chair. ''I've changed my mind, Griffen. When I didn't know her, it was easy to see that what you were saying made sense. She wasn't real, she wasn't really one of us. In a way, I didn't even believe she was real.'' She brought a trembling hand to her head. ''I thought maybe you were wrong about her. But she really is our Grace.''

He made a sound of disgust and straightened. *There always had to be a weak link. Always had to be a spoiler.*

''How exactly are you going to tell her, Aunt Dorothy? Just outright say that we planned to trick her? Will you just blurt out how you had planned to stand by and allow her to marry her brother? For the good of Monarch's?''

The woman paled. ''It does sound bad, but we must stop this now, before more damage is done. Before there's no turning back. Besides, once she knows, she'll be partial owner of Monarch's. Who would turn that down? Who would turn down the chance at wealth and position and power?''

''That's right. And angry, she could take it and walk.''

Dorothy went from pale to deathly white. ''What do you mean, take it and—''

''Once we reveal to her that she's a Monarch, she has a right to claim her birthright. We could fight her, of course, but we could lose. We probably would. That was always one of the dangers. And one of our concerns. Remember? It played a part in our decision.''

Griffen moved his gaze over his aunt. ''The only man you ever loved deserted you, Dorothy. Remember? He deserted you because you were barren. So you had no love and no babies. But you always had Monarch's. It's been your baby, your love. Your everything." He paused for emphasis. "She could take it away."

"Dear God." Dorothy brought a hand to her chest, her breathing fast and uneven. "Griffen, what are we to do? I can't go on this way, but I...I can't lose Monarch's. It would...that would...I just can't!"

"I know, darling." Griffen returned to his chair, a smile tugging at the corners of his mouth. "You leave for Milan tomorrow."

"Yes, Adam and Skye and I."

"Good." He steepled his fingers. "That will give me some time."

"What are you thinking?" She sat forward, her eagerness almost childlike.

"That you may be right, Aunt Dorothy."

"Thank God!" She brought a hand to her chest. "Thank God. I was so afraid of what you would say. So afraid you'd be angry with me. That you and I would have to fight over this."

"Dot, love, you're my great-aunt. I would never fight you. Your feelings are important to me." He crossed his legs again and folded his hands on his knee. "Don't say anything yet. We must handle this delicately."

"You're right."

"We can't lose her. And if we handle this badly—" He snapped his fingers. "She'll be gone, just like Madeline was. Only she'll take Monarch's with her."

"You're right," she said again, crushing her cigarette in the already-overflowing ashtray.

She was an emotional wreck, he thought with distaste, God, how he despised weakness. Why was it his burden to be surrounded by such people?

"While you're in Milan, I'll get everything in place. When you return, we'll talk. Just you and I." He stood. "How's that? Does that put your mind to rest?"

"Oh, yes." She made a sound of relief. "Thank you, Griffen. You are such a love. I can always count on you."

"Can I count on you to keep silent until you get back? Not a word, Aunt Dot. It's important."

"Yes." She nodded. "You can count on me. I've grown to love and depend on her. I couldn't bear to lose her."

"I know just what you mean." He walked to the door, stopping and looking over his shoulder at her. "Don't you worry about a thing. I plan to take care of everything."

He opened the door and smiled back at her. "No loose ends, Dot. Just you wait and see."

66

The bar was dark and smoky, filled with biker-types and artists. Not Griffen's usual choice of place for drinks, Chance thought, glancing toward the door. But then, nothing about Griffen's behavior had been usual of late. The other man had seemed strange, off-center slightly, like a mirror image of Griffen, only distorted. Chance wished he could put his finger on what was different about his friend. He had tried, he had given it a lot of thought. Still, all he knew for certain was that lately, Griffen affected him the way fingernails on a chalkboard did.

Chance checked his watch. He had been waiting twenty minutes already. Could be Griffen wasn't going to show. Could be, Chance thought, he was being stood up. He took a swallow of his beer, the brew bitter on his tongue. Could be another fuck-you in two weeks littered with those charming little gems of life.

Could be Griffen knew about him and Skye.

The thought chilled him. He had always known Griffen would be a dangerous enemy. If Griffen knew about him and Skye, he would be an enemy.

Skye. Chance shook his head. She was in Milan, he knew. Due back in a couple of days. Which was for the best. It had kept him from calling her, from going to see her.

To say what? he wondered, scowling at his own thoughts. Skye had asked if he could give her any reason she shouldn't marry Griffen. He couldn't then. He couldn't now.

"Chance, buddy." Griffen breezed up to the table. "Sorry

I'm late, man, I got hung up in traffic." He slid into one of the chairs, motioned the waitress to bring him whatever Chance was having, then turned back to Chance. "Interesting place, yes?"

"It's fine."

"Hmm." Griffen rocked back in his chair, a smile tugging at his mouth. "Looking a little glum, my friend. Anything to do with the rumors I've been hearing around town?"

Chance looked up sharply. Griffen was particularly jovial tonight, oddly so. "What rumors are those, Grif?"

"Rumors that you fucked up, actually. Rumors that your clients are bailing at the speed of light."

Chance stared at the other man, stunned by his cavalier tone, thinking about what Skye had said that day after they'd made love. That Griffen thought Chance was jealous of him. That Griffen thought Chance wanted to be him.

Griffen chuckled. "The industry's just buzzing with how the newly mighty has fallen. Man-of-the-hour to loser-of-the-year in a matter of weeks. You've given the mill plenty of grist, buddy-boy. Congratulations."

"Fuck you," Chance said tightly.

"Lighten up. Jesus, Chance. It's only business."

"Easy to say when your business has been given to you."

Griffen's eyebrows shot up. "You got a problem with that, buddy?"

"I have a problem with your attitude."

"Considering that from what I hear, I'm one of few clients you have left, I'd suggest you cool it. Seems to me, I'm not the man to pick a fight with."

Chance sucked in a deep breath, realizing that Griffen was right: he was picking a fight. He wanted to get in the middle of a knock-down, drag-out, black-eyed, bloody-nosed fight. And he wanted to get into it with Griffen.

Griffen was also right about the stupidity of picking one of his last clients as the one to go to war with.

Chance smiled stiffly, though he couldn't bring himself to

apologize. "Bad call, man. It's been a hell of a couple of weeks."

"Cool." Griffen smiled. "I suppose Skye told you our news."

Chance met the other man's eyes and played dumb. "I haven't talked to Skye in a while."

"The news that I popped the question. Skye and I are getting hitched."

"No shit?" Chance brought his beer to his mouth. "If you're getting hitched, she must have accepted."

The muscles in Griffen's face stiffened, almost imperceptibly, but enough for Chance to know that she had not. Not yet, anyway.

"Of course she did."

"Congratulations." Chance lifted his beer in a salute, the thought of Skye marrying Griffen repugnant. "You'll make a handsome couple."

"We already do." He grinned. "But you don't sound so happy, buddy."

"Don't I?" Chance downed his beer, wishing he had cause to. "I'm thrilled. Truly."

"Funny," Griffen murmured, bringing his beer to his lips, "for a while there, I was thinking you wanted Skye for yourself."

Chance's blood ran cold. "And what would have made you think that."

"Things." Griffen lifted a shoulder. "But then I said to myself, why would Chance compete when he knew he couldn't win? Why would he do that when he knew how angry it would make me?"

Chance narrowed his eyes, not liking the threat implied in Griffen's words. "Are you starting something with me, Grif?"

"You tell me. Am I?"

"I'm not competing with you for Skye, if that's what you're asking." Chance pushed away from the table. "In case you haven't noticed, I'm not in the mood for bullshitting tonight. Did you want to talk about anything in particular?''

"Nope. I haven't seen my buddy much lately, and I thought we'd have a drink. For old-time's sake.''

Chance thought about begging off, about claiming work or an early day tomorrow, instead he let Griffen order him another beer. They talked and swapped stories, the atmosphere strained between them. Chance pretended not to notice, pretended to be amused by things Griffen said, pretended that he didn't feel Skye between them, as surely as if she had been sitting in the middle of the table.

Finally, Chance had had enough. "Look, Grif, I'm beat. I'm going to call it a night.'' He stood, dropped a few bills on the table and took his coat from the back of the chair.

"I'll walk you out.''

Within moments, they were on the street. The night was clear but cold, the sky starless.

"Where are you parked?'' Griffen asked, stopping beside his Porsche.

"Just up the block.''

"See you around the store.''

Chance nodded, hunched deeper into his coat and crossed the nearly deserted street. His car, he saw when he reached it, was just as he had left it. With one exception. All four tires had been slashed.

Chance swore and dragged a hand through his hair. And in the middle of nowhere, too. What next?

Griffen pulled up beside him, window lowered. "Problem, buddy?''

Chance met Griffen's eyes, narrowing his own in suspicion. His friend looked tickled pink. "Somebody did a number on my tires.''

"Bummer.'' Griffen smiled. "Hop in. I'll give you a ride.''

After making sure his car was locked, Chance went around to the passenger side and climbed in.

They rode in silence. Griffen handled the little car expertly, cutting down side streets, heading away from the city's heart rather than toward it. While he drove, he smiled to himself, every so often flexing his fingers on the steering wheel and making a sound of amusement.

"What's the deal?" Chance jerked his thumb in the opposite direction. "The Loop's that way."

"Got a shortcut." Griffen's lips curved into a smirk. "Just sit back and enjoy the ride."

Chance sat back, but he didn't enjoy. He didn't want to take his eyes off Griffen; something was seriously out of whack with the guy. Chance drew his eyebrows together. Weird, Chance thought. Griffen was acting weirder by the moment. It was as if the other man was charged with a strange sort of energy, as if a switch of some sort had gone haywire inside him.

Griffen took a curve too fast, and Chance fastened his safety belt. "Want to slow it down a bit, Grif?"

Griffen laughed. "Something wrong? Am I making you nervous?"

"If it's all the same to you, I don't particularly want to die tonight."

Griffen laughed, though the sound was almost childish, like a giggle. "Considering the state of your business, that's saying something."

"What's with the attitude tonight? You're being an asshole, even for you."

He laughed again. "I'm glad we have this chance to talk. There are some things I've been wanting to tell you."

"Yeah?" Chance muttered, deciding he didn't like Griffen Monarch, and that he wished he was anywhere but inside this car with him, even standing beside his own car in the cold.

"Yeah." Griffen giggled again. "It was so easy, really. A few calls, a few complaints. The suggestion of fiscal impropriety, of dissatisfaction, of inappropriate behavior."

Chance looked at Griffen, his heart beginning to thud. "What are you talking about?"

Griffen looked him dead in the eye. "Why, your business, of course." He smiled. "Or current lack thereof."

Chance stared at Griffen, his words, their meaning, sinking in. "You called my clients?"

"Surprise, Chance."

Chance felt sick. He had known something weird was going on, something that didn't make sense. He had suspected that someone was sabotaging him. And doing a damn good job of it. He had figured it might be someone from Adams and Sloane. Or even Price, Stevenson and Price.

But Griffen? His friend?

"You son of a bitch." Chance fisted his fingers. "I ought to kill you, now."

Griffen laughed again, unfazed, obviously relishing his story. "Some were more difficult to convince than others. Of course, that only made it more fun. Martha put up the biggest fight." Griffen made a sound of disgust. "Loyal little bitch. She was so impressed with you, with what you had done for her, she told me she didn't care how you had allegedly performed for your other accounts, your performance with her had been spectacular. Damn nonprofits, they're such idealistic assholes.

"I finally had to explain the facts of life to her. She either got rid of McCord Public Relations and Special Events, or she lost Monarch's sizable support. And, of course, anyone I could bring with me. Money talks, buddy-boy. Bullshit walks."

"You son of a bitch," Chance said again, flexing his fingers. "Stop the car now. I swear to God, I'm going to kill you."

"Yeah, right." He lowered his voice to a thready, sarcastic whisper. "You're too nice to kill me, Chance. Too much a by-the-rules kind of guy."

Griffen laughed, the sound high and thin. And crazy.

Chance looked at the other man in dawning horror—it wasn't just the liquor talking, it wasn't just your run-of-the-mill nastiness. Griffen was unbalanced.

"I have to say, you've been a hell of a date, Chance." Griffen roared around a slower vehicle, jerking the wheel so sharply the Porsche fishtailed. "I don't know when I've had more fun. Watching you, little by little puffing up with your imagined success, thinking that you were some sort of Mr. Big. Knowing all along that I could take it all away." He snapped his fingers. "Anytime. Anytime at all."

"Why?" Chance managed to say, gripping the strap of his safety belt, the blood rushing in his ears, so furious he could hardly speak, too furious to be frightened.

"You even have to ask?" Griffen cut him a glance from the corners of his eyes, his mouth tightening into a grim line. "Skye, of course." He shook his head. "What did you think you were doing, messing with my woman? Did you think I was blind? Huh, you little prick?" His voice rose. "Did you really think she would ever want *you,* when I wanted her? Me, Griffen Monarch. Please, it's pathetic."

"Then why are you so worried?" Chance shouted to be heard above the roar of the engine. "Why all this?"

"Why all this? I'll show you why!" Griffen hit the accelerator again, and Chance watched as the speedometer inched from eighty to eighty-five, eighty-five to ninety.

"You're losin' it, man!" Chance shouted, gaze fixed on the speedometer. "Slow the fuck down! You're going to kill us both!"

"I can give her everything. Money. Power. Success. I can give her Monarch's! Do you have any idea what that means? You're nothing! By the time I'm finished with you, you'll have nothing left. Not even a pot to piss in. Just like when I found you, a pathetic nothing."

"You crazy son of a bitch! She doesn't love you! She never will!"

Griffen tilted his head back and howled, the sound wild,

primal. Out of control. "She's mine! My possession, my prize. Don't you get it? She always has been. I own her."

"You're out of your mind. She'll never love you."

"No?" Griffen turned to him, completely calm suddenly. Eerily calm. A chill raced up Chance's spine, and he stared at the other man, fear penetrating his fury.

He might not live through this. Griffen might kill them both.

"If I can't have her, nobody will. Remember that, Chance. You heard it here first."

Griffen turned back to the road. Up ahead it curved sharply. Beyond the road lay an elegant estate, protected by a brick wall. With a grim smile, Griffen tightened his fingers around the wheel and floored the Porsche, aiming the car directly at the wall.

Chance realized what Griffen meant to do and yelled for him to stop. The car took off like a jet. The wall raced up to meet them.

Chance threw his arms across his face.

Griffen slammed on the brakes and yanked sideways on the wheel. The car went into a wild spin; Chance was thrown against his door, his head against the window, cracking it. The car's back end smashed into the brick wall; the seat belt snapped tight, knocking the wind out of him.

Chance struggled free of the belt, wrenched the door open and stumbled from the car. Dizzy, sick, he doubled over, heaving up everything he had. *He had almost died just now. Dear God, Griffen had tried to kill him. He had almost killed them both.*

When he caught his breath, he went around to the driver's side and yanked open the door. For a moment he thought Griffen was dead, he sat so still. But he wasn't dead, Chance saw. He was laughing. Silently, softly, with great pleasure.

The son of a bitch was out of his mind.

Chance grabbed him by his shirtfront and dragged him

from the car. "You could have killed us, you crazy bastard!" he shouted, shaking him. "What the hell's wrong with you?"

Griffen knocked Chance's hands away, a small, satisfied smile curving his mouth. "Go to hell, buddy-boy," he said evenly. "Go right to hell."

Without another word, he slid back behind the wheel, started the car and drove off.

67

The image of the brick wall rushing up to meet him haunted Chance. As did the almost otherworldly quality of Griffen's laughter. After four days, it still rang clearly in Chance's head, causing him to shudder.

He had never come so close to death before. He had never looked into the face of pure evil before.

He had now. And he was frightened. For Skye. Griffen held himself accountable for nothing and to no one, not God or man. He believed himself all-knowing, all-powerful and without flaw.

Rich, powerful and twisted. A deadly combination. A dangerous one.

Dangerous to anyone who crossed Griffen's path. Or to anyone who refused to give him what he wanted.

And Griffen wanted Skye. He didn't love her; he was incapable of the emotion. He was obsessed with her, Chance realized. He thought of her as some sort of prize, as something that belonged to him.

If I can't have her, nobody will.

Those words, that threat, had played over and over in Chance's head. As had possible explanations for Griffen's bizarre behavior. Medication, for one. Or illegal-drug use. Or perhaps an undiagnosed physical illness of some kind.

None of those rang true. No, Chance sensed that Griffen had simply decided to reveal himself to Chance.

Chance felt stupid. And vain. He had completely fallen for Griffen's line. He had believed in their friendship, had believed that the other man was impressed with him and his abilities. Everything that had come his way, he had thought to be the result of his own hard work, his ingenuity and knowledge.

But Griffen had simply given it to him. All of it.

Then he had taken it away.

Chance stood in front of his office window, gazing out at the sunset and gathering dusk. The sky had turned a deep violet hue, the last fiery glow reflected off the side of the John Hancock and Nine Hundred North buildings. The image stirred him, reminding him of the way he had felt his very first days in Chicago, filling him with the memory of his excitement and ambition. Reminding him of his belief that in this city, this beautiful, ugly, vibrant city, he could make all his dreams come true.

He narrowed his eyes. He had been a fool. A dupe. Cocky, arrogant and too ambitious. He had never really asked himself why Griffen Monarch had initiated that first meeting, had never questioned why the other man would up and fire his firm of twenty years and hire him, a virtual nobody; he had never examined why Griffen had come on so strong and so friendly.

Because he had wanted what Griffen offered him. Because, as Skye had said, he had wanted to be Griffen. To have what he had, to be what he was. He had wanted that so badly, he had been blind to everything else.

Chance rested his hands on his hips, watching as office lights in the adjacent buildings began popping on. In the days since facing death at Griffen's hands, he had asked himself all those whys.

And when he did, he kept coming back to the only thing he and Griffen had in common: Skye.

Skye. Chance frowned. He had always thought it too co-incidental that Skye had shown up here in Chicago, on Griffen's arm, only weeks after Chance had told him about her.

Chance cocked his head, trying to fit all the pieces together. Griffen had been interested in his past, he had led the conversation around to it several times. But he hadn't been *too* interested. Just enough to keep Chance talking, but not so much that he found Griffen's curiosity out of the ordinary.

But how did it all fit together? What could Skye and Griffen possibly have had in common before she came to Chicago?

He didn't know, though he had thought about it day and night, sleeping little. And he had thought about his business, what was left of it, anyway, what his options were. He had made a decision.

He may have stupidly fallen for Griffen's twisted game, but he wasn't so stupid that he didn't learn from his mistakes. He wasn't going to just roll over. He wasn't going to let some demented, spoiled little rich kid take away what he had worked so hard and so long for.

He was fighting back. Starting now.

Chance checked his watch, then went to his desk. He dialed the preservation society, then asked for Martha. Moments later she picked up.

"Martha? Chance McCord."

"Chance?" He heard her surprise. Her reluctance to speak with him. "How are you?"

"Look, I'm going to get right to the point, Martha. I know what Griffen did. He told me."

He had her attention then, and he continued, "He also told me you refused to go along with his little smear campaign until he threatened pulling Monarch's annual donation."

"I'm relieved you know," she said. "I feel terrible about the whole thing. The bastard forced my hand, Chance. I'm sorry. You did a damn good job for the society."

"I appreciate that, Martha. That's why I'm calling. I need your help."

"I don't know what I can do."

"Start by just hearing me out. I have a proposal for you, one that I think will work to both our benefit."

She hesitated. "All right. But I can't promise to do more than listen."

Chance outlined his plan. All Martha had to do was make a few calls, starting a rumor of her own—telling how a jealous colleague had set Chance up, telling how nothing that had been going around had been true and telling all that she had rehired him.

"I'd love to, Chance, but there's the little problem of the Monarch family donation."

"I'm prepared to donate my services to the society. The money you save paying a public relations representative and special events coordinator will go a long way toward making up for the Monarchs' lost donation. Also, you'll be your own boss again."

She was quiet for several minutes, considering, he knew, all he had said. "That slimy little bastard really pissed me off," she said finally. "I don't enjoy being threatened. I resent being blackmailed, and I abhor an abuse of power. If it was just me, I would jump on this opportunity. But I have to act in the society's best interest. Let me think about this overnight, Chance. Let me crunch some numbers. If there's any way I can help you, I will."

Chance thanked her, hung up and, smiling, turned back to the window and its view of downtown Chicago. While he had been on the phone, the fiery oranges and reds had begun to fade as the sun dipped lower, setting on Lake Michigan. But not on his dreams, he vowed. No way was he going to give up and die now.

With or without Martha's help, he would go to every client he'd had and lost. He would convince them, at the least, to hear him out. At the best, to take him back. Griffen would see who the best man was.

That started tomorrow. Tonight, he was going to find Skye.

He had to warn her about Griffen.

68

Griffen waited for Dorothy. He sat on her couch, alternately still and agitated. A sense of urgency pressed at him. A sense that others conspired against him. One wrong move, he knew, no matter how small, and they, the others, would descend on him. And like vultures, they would rip the flesh from his bones. They would tear Skye from him.

He would not allow it. Not now. Not ever. Soon he would have everything under control, the way he always did.

The calm settled over Griffen once more. He checked his watch. Dorothy was due home any moment. Her plane, a direct flight from Milan, had landed on time, one hour and ten minutes ago.

By now, Skye was already home. He pictured her, checking her mail, talking to that disgusting dog of hers, already retrieved from the neighbor's. He could see her move to her bedroom, could see her standing in front of her closet, selecting her garments for their evening, then beginning to disrobe. He shuddered, imagining her naked, imagining the curve of her buttocks, the way they would feel cupped in his hands, the way her nipples would harden as he sucked at them, the way she would buck against him as he drove himself into her.

Tonight, he would have his answer. Tonight, he would make her completely his. Tonight, he would finish what had been begun so many years ago.

Then he would have to imagine no longer.

Griffen dropped a hand to his lap, to his erection. He toyed with it, with himself, barely brushing against the bulge, allowing himself to imagine it was Skye's hand, Skye's cry of frustration at having to wait.

He sucked in a sharp, steadying breath, willing himself to stop. He had waited a long time for the main course. He was not about to spoil it by having a snack first.

He heard Dorothy at the front door. Heard her key, her muffled oath, the door swinging open, then clicking shut.

"Hello, Dorothy," he called softly. "I'm in here."

She appeared in the doorway between the foyer and parlor, squinting in the dim light. "Griffen, darling, is that you?"

"Yes, Aunt Dorothy." He reached up and turned on the light by the sofa.

She dropped her keys on the entryway table, blinking at the sudden brightness. "Don't you look handsome. I do so admire a man in a tux."

"Thank you. Tonight's the benefit for the new museum."

"That's right, you're meeting Skye there." Dorothy flipped through the stack of mail her housekeeper had left for her, the junk mail already weeded out. "She's quite excited."

"How was the show?"

"Marvelous, but exhausting. We won a gold for City Lights. Adam was beside himself."

"Yes, I know. He called."

"My bags are still in the car. I'm too exhausted even to try to bring them—"

She stopped suddenly, as if realizing for the first time that it was odd she would come home and find Griffen inside, waiting for her. She looked at him. "But Griffen, love, why are you here?"

"Aunt Dot," he chided. "You didn't think I'd forget, did you? I made you a promise before you left for Milan. I'm here to fulfill that promise."

"You thought about what I said? About Skye?"

"I thought about little else. And I said I would take care

of everything, and I will." He patted the couch. "Come. You're tired. Sit down."

She crossed to the sofa as he instructed and sank onto it with a sigh. "You've thought of a way to make everything right?"

"I have." He stood and plumped a throw pillow for her. "Lie down, I'll get you a cup of tea. We'll talk some more."

"That would be lovely." She slipped out of her shoes and stretched out on the couch. "These trips are getting too difficult for me. I'm too old."

"I know, darling." He took the throw from the sofa back and tucked it carefully around her. "Luckily, now you have Skye to take them for you."

"She's such a blessing." Dorothy sighed. "She has the gift. Just like we all knew."

"She does."

"Thank goodness you thought of a way. You take such good care of me, Griffen. Of all of us, really."

"Because I love you, Aunt Dorothy." He brushed his lips against her forehead. "I'll get that tea now."

"Don't forget," she said sleepily. "The pilot light is out. You have to use a match."

"I won't forget, Aunt Dot." He smiled at her. "I haven't forgotten."

Griffen went to the kitchen. He filled the teakettle with water, then set it on the back burner. He got out her favorite teacup and her chamomile tea, and set them by the range. He turned the burner on high, heard the hiss of the gas pouring through the valves, smiling as the sweetly noxious smell stung his nose.

He ripped a paper towel off the roll and carefully wiped the teakettle's handle, the range and knob and anything else he had touched. He folded the paper towel and slipped it into his pocket.

He went to the parlor doorway and looked at her, deeply

asleep already. "Aunt Dorothy," he said softly. "Your tea is almost ready."

She didn't stir. He tried again, this time loudly.

Still, she didn't move.

He smiled again and started for the foyer and the front door beyond. In the doorway, he stopped and looked back at her. "Sleep well, Aunt Dot. I love you."

69

Skye let herself out of her apartment and descended the single flight of stairs to the building's main foyer. Her trip to Milan had been exciting, exhilarating, exhausting. She would have loved every minute if not for the confusion of her thoughts. About Griffen and his proposal. About her feelings for Chance. She had promised Griffen his answer tonight. Though she had thought about it night and day, she still wasn't sure what that answer would be.

As if her thoughts had drawn Chance to her, there he was, right outside her front door, waiting for her, shoulders hunched into his leather bomber jacket, face red from the cold wind.

Skye's steps faltered. She didn't want to see him, not tonight. Not when she had the biggest decision of her life to make. Not when she was already confused.

Before she could back away, he turned. Their eyes met. There was no sneaking out the back way now, Skye acknowledged. Taking a deep, steadying breath, she let herself out of her building, the security door automatically locking behind her.

He looked like hell, disheveled, cold and desperate. She denied the way that tugged at her emotions. "You could have buzzed me," she said.

"Would you have let me in?"

"No." She shivered and pulled her light wrap closer around her, neither it nor her beaded evening gown much protection from the cold January night, wishing she hadn't lost her last pair of gloves. "But you wouldn't have had to stand out here in the cold for nothing. I suggest you go home."

She started down the steps; he followed her. "We need to talk, Skye."

"I don't think so, Chance. I think we've said everything to each other that there is to say. And more than once." She edged past him, descending the last steps to the sidewalk. "I have a party to go to."

"Have you decided, Skye? Are you going to marry him?"

She stopped and looked back over her shoulder at him. "That's none of your damn business. Good night."

He came after her then, catching her arm and turning her to face him. "I have to know, Skye. It's important."

"Why? Have you decided now that you want me for yourself? Is that why you were lurking around outside my building?" She could tell by his expression that he didn't, and she tugged against his grasp, furious. With him. With herself. Would she always play the fool for this man? "I thought not. Let me go, Chance. I'm late."

Instead, he caught her other arm. Her keys slipped from her fingers and clattered to the sidewalk. "He's crazy, Skye. He's obsessed with you."

"Obsessed?" she repeated, her voice quaking with the force of her anger. "Give me a break. Maybe you've never encountered it before, Chance, but it's called love."

"It's not love." When she tried to pull away, he tightened his grip. "Listen to me, Skye. He tried to kill us."

The blood rushed to her head. "What?"

"The other night. He was out of his mind." He quickly described the harrowing drive in which Griffen had deliberately spun his Porsche into a brick wall.

"You're lying." She shook her head. "That's nuts."

"Exactly. Skye—" He lowered his hands to hers, clasping them tightly. His were ice cold. "He's behind it all. My business, my clients terminating me. He called them all, he told them lies about me and my actions. For fun, Skye."

"My God." She took a step backward, searching his expression, understanding suddenly. "Now I see what you're doing."

"I'm trying to warn you, that's all. Griffen's dangerous."

"No." She shook her head again, the truth hitting her with the force of a wrecking ball. "Your business is crumbling and you want to blame someone else. You want to punish Griffen because you're so…because you're so jealous."

"That's not it. Skye, how can you say that? You know me."

"No, no, I don't. I thought I did." She backed away. "But I don't."

"He's unbalanced, Skye. He said if he couldn't have you, nobody would. I think he meant it."

"You're the one who's unbalanced. I offered you my heart, Chance. You threw it back in my face. *'Stay with Griffen,'* you said. *'Love Griffen, not me. Griffen can offer you everything.'* Now you want me to do the opposite?"

Tears stung her eyes, and she cursed them, determined that they wouldn't fall. "Really, Chance, at least you could keep your lines straight. Or are you really that confused?"

"I'll tell you I love you to keep you from marrying him. Skye, I'm frightened for you."

She stared at him, his words a blow to her ego. Her heart. In that moment, she made her decision. Her answer to Griffen was yes. Chance really did have nothing to offer her.

"You'd even tell me you love me? What a great and terrible sacrifice, Chance," she said softly, voice cracking. "How noble. I guess you played my big brother and protector for so long, it's hard to shake the role." She bent and snatched her keys off the sidewalk. "But I've got a news flash for you, I'm all grown-up. And I can take care of myself. I've been doing it a long time."

She turned and walked away. He called after her.

"You don't love him, Skye. I know you don't."

She stopped and swung to face him. "Don't you get it? He loves me. He's devoted to me. I know he'll never leave me."

"That's obsession, Skye. Not love."

"Maybe so, but you know what? That's what I need. That's what's important to me. I need forever, Chance. That's why I'm going to marry him."

This time, when she walked away, he didn't come after her.

70

Lakeshore Drive was nearly deserted. Skye sat in the passenger seat of Griffen's Porsche, hands folded in her lap, staring straight ahead. The ring on the fourth finger of her left hand felt too heavy. Foreign and wrong. She twisted it, wishing she could take it off but knowing she couldn't. Not ever.

Griffen reached across the seat and covered her folded hands. "Skye, my darling, you've made me the happiest man on earth."

"I'm glad." She lowered her gaze to the ring. The stone was magnificent, the artist in her couldn't help delighting in its brilliance, its icy fire. She just wished she could admire it on somebody else's finger.

Guilty for her thoughts, she turned her face toward the side window and looked out at the vast darkness of Lake Michigan as they sped past. She should be happy. She should be about ready to bust with pride and pleasure; she should want to shout her good fortune from the top of the Sear's Tower, loud enough for all Chicago to hear. Instead, she felt like whimpering.

What was wrong with her?

Chance. The things he'd said tumbled through her head, undermining her confidence in her decision, ruining a moment that should be one of the best of her life. He'd said Griffen had tried to kill them, that he'd rammed his car into a brick wall. Yet here she was, riding in that same Porsche, a car that was running so well it purred like a kitten.

"Penny for your thoughts?"

"I was just thinking how well the car's running." Her cheeks heated at the lie. "Has it been in the shop?"

"Nope. Just out and about in Chicago."

She let out a breath she hadn't even realized she held. "Oh."

"You sound disappointed. Would you like me to put it in the shop?"

Chance had lied. About everything, all along. Tears stung her eyes. She called herself an idiot for wanting to believe him, for holding on to that hope.

"No. Of course not." She forced a smile. "Only an observation."

He cut her a quick, concerned glance. "Are you all right?"

"Fine, just tired. I must be suffering from jet lag."

She pushed away thoughts of Chance. She would focus on the future, her future, her forever with Griffen.

She had everything now. Her every wish had come true.

Be careful what you wish for...

"Tonight's the night, love. The night you become completely mine."

Griffen covered her hands again, and she felt his tremble. Something about that small quiver made her uneasy.

"I've waited so long," he continued. "You can't imagine, darling."

His words proved a prophecy. Skye couldn't have imagined the horror of his hands on her. Their lovemaking took on the quality of a distorted, surrealistic nightmare. She found the act almost unholy, dark and frightening, although he was not rough with her.

Indeed, the opposite was true. He held himself taut, controlled; she felt it in the way he quivered, like a bow stretched to the limit, felt it in the thin line of sweat that ran down his spine and beaded his upper lip.

Almost unable to bear his hands on her, Skye squeezed her eyes shut. When she did, strange images played on the back of her lids, images that she recognized somehow, but couldn't make out. They mixed with the sounds he made, low and feral, frightening her on a level someplace far below the surface. She felt ill, smothered by his weight on top of her.

The pain in her head became almost unbearable. It felt as if there was a balloon in her brain, expanding, pushing at her skull, ready to explode. And when it did, she would shatter into a million pieces.

He moved his lips, sucking at her breasts, her abdomen, between her legs. A scream welled somewhere inside her, in the place that knew all her secrets. She held as still as she could, eyes squeezed shut, praying it would be over soon. But still, the darkness pressed in on her.

Dear God, she prayed, what was happening to her?

He began to pant. Like an animal. Her stomach heaved; she curled her fingers into the bedsheets, clutching them for dear life, certain they were the only thing that kept her anchored to this world, to her sanity.

He finished, and she launched to her feet and ran to the bathroom, slamming the door shut behind her. She barely made it to the bowl before she was violently sick.

She stayed in the bathroom a long time, clinging to the commode, resting her cheek on the cool porcelain, crying silently.

What had she done? Dear God, what had she done?

Finally, she made it to her feet, rinsed her face and mouth and hands and returned to the bedroom.

Griffen lay stiffly on the bed, not looking at her when she entered the room. He was, no doubt, angry. And hurt. Her heart ached. She could only imagine how he felt right now.

She clasped her hands together. "Griffen, I'm...I'm so sorry."

"Don't apologize," he snapped at her. "Jesus."

"It wasn't you." At his look, she said it again, wringing her hands. "It wasn't. How could it be? You were... wonderful. I'm lucky to have a lover who's so gentle and considerate."

"Sure." He sat up, his face pinched with fury. "That's why you ran as quick as you could to the bathroom to puke after we made love."

He was right, her reaction to him had not been normal. There had to be an explanation for it, there had to be.

She crossed to the bed and sat carefully on its edge. "I probably ate something that was bad. Or I'm suffering from jet lag. I'm so tired, Griffen. I'm sorry I ruined our night."

For a moment he said nothing, then he held out his arms for her. "I shouldn't have expected perfection tonight. Next time will be better."

She moved into his arms, refusing to acknowledge his words, the thought of a next time. She couldn't even bear the thought of *this* time. He closed his arms around her, holding her closely. Tightly.

Too closely. Too tightly.

Skye trembled, feeling trapped. Suffocated. She squirmed slightly, needing air, wishing he would relax his hold on her.

He wouldn't Not ever.

She had made a terrible mistake. One she had to think of a way out of.

After a while, Skye feigned sleep, thinking Griffen might relax his grip on her. When he did, she planned to slip out of bed. But even in sleep, he held her possessively, tightly.

She slept eventually, she knew that because the phone awakened her. Light streamed through the window. She reached for the receiver, wincing. She ached as if she had been beaten during the night. She heard the water running in the bathroom. "Hello."

"Skye? Is that you?"

"Adam? Yes, it's me." Skye sat up in bed, bringing the sheet with her. He sounded as if he was crying. Griffen appeared at the bathroom door, his expression concerned. "Adam, what's wrong?"

"There's been an accident, Skye. Dorothy's dead."

Part VI

Horizon's End

71

Chicago, Illinois,
1997

From the moment Claire's plane touched down at O'Hare International Airport, thoughts of Skye flooded her mind. With them came a sense of urgency, of impending disaster.

Something terrible was going to happen. It was going to happen here, soon.

Claire walked down the jetway, working to shake off the feeling and clear her mind. She had been called to Chicago to help the police with the case of a girl abducted from a slumber party at a friend's home. The police had no leads, and the public outcry had been so loud it rocked city hall.

Claire had agreed to come to Chicago, though she had thought long and hard before doing so. She feared she wouldn't be able to help with this one. She had too much history here, too much of her own psychic trauma to be able to pick up on that of others. But they had begged her, and she had agreed. Now here she was, back in Chicago for the first time since escaping Adam and Pierce twenty-one years before.

Her contact, Detective Baker, met her at the gate. She recognized him instantly—she had spent so much time around cops that spotting one was easy.

He smiled and held out his hand. "Ms. Dearborn, thank you for coming."

She took his hand. "I hope I can help."

"Let me carry that."

She handed over her garment bag gratefully. "Thank you."

After exchanging the usual meaningless pleasantries about her flight and the weather, he filled her in on the case.

"As I explained on the phone, we've got another Polly Klaus here. Nine fourteen-year-old girls having a slumber party. Nice, quiet neighborhood. An affluent neighborhood. When they all fell asleep, everybody was accounted for. When the girls woke up the next morning, one was gone."

"Becky Williams."

"Yes." The detective touched Claire's elbow, directing her to bear right. "At first the girls thought she had gone home. Apparently, Becky and one of the other girls had gotten into it the night before. A fight over some boy."

"Obviously that's not what happened."

"Obviously. When the host mother learned Becky was missing, she became understandably concerned. She organized a search of the house, just to make sure the girl wasn't playing a sick trick on her friends, then she called the other mother."

"And all hell broke lose," Claire murmured, empathizing with all concerned.

"To put it mildly." They stepped onto the moving sidewalk. Above them, neon tubes of brilliantly colored moving light provided a spectacular, if dizzying, show. "We've followed every lead. We checked out both fathers, the neighbors. We even considered that, in a fit of pique, Becky had decided to walk the block and a half home."

"She could have been abducted on her way," Claire murmured. "It was the middle of the night; the streets were deserted."

"Right. Ruled that out. Her coat was still in the front closet. Middle of January, she would have taken it even if she had been pissed as hell at the other girls."

"The house was locked?"

"Nope. Front door wasn't. Neither were several first-floor

windows." He fumbled around for his cigarettes, then, as if remembering that the airport was designated smoke-free, swore and slipped the pack back into his jacket pocket. "As I said, we're talking a safe neighborhood. Low crime. Involved neighbors. Anticrime watch. The whole bit. This thing's thrown the entire community into turmoil." They stepped off the moving walkway, and the detective made a sound of frustration. "We have nothing else to go on."

Nothing else to go on.

Skye.

Claire brought a hand to her head, vivid thoughts of her daughter, like images composed of emotions, pressing in on her.

Her daughter needed her.

"Ms. Dearborn?"

She started. The detective was several steps ahead of her, looking back, his weathered face marred by a frown. "I'm sorry, Detective. I'm a little tired."

"I asked, what do you think?"

That people could disappear in the blink of an eye and never be seen again. "It's too early. I'll need to surround myself with her things, some of the last things she touched, her pillow and sleeping bag. I'll also want to tour the house. I'll need phone books and newspapers. Every one from a few days before Becky's disappearance until now."

"Shall I take you directly to the station?"

"Like I said, I'm tired, Detective." She smiled. "It helps when I'm fresh and well-rested."

"Of course." They stepped onto the escalator, going down. "We have a suite for you at the Knickerbocker, downtown. It's a classy old hotel in the historic Streeterville section of town."

"I know the Knickerbocker. I'm used to more modest accommodations."

"The hotel donated the suite. The community has really pulled together on this one."

"How many people know I'm here? You did remember,

Detective, that I insist on a low profile? As I explained, I'm not one of those Hollywood-type psychics who likes the limelight. I need quiet and solitude. Distractions block the process for me.''

''Not to worry. Only a few people know you're here, even within the department. The G.M. of the Knickerbocker is the girl's uncle.''

She inclined her head. ''Thank you.''

He cut her a questioning glance. ''You say you know the hotel? You must be familiar with Chicago.''

''I used to live in Chicago, Detective Baker. But that was a long time ago.''

He smiled. ''It's a homecoming of sorts, then.''

''A homecoming,'' she repeated, remembering the past, seeing Adam above her, eyes bulging as he tried to squeeze the life out of her. His blood spilling across the gleaming oak floor; Skye screaming.

Claire rubbed the chill from her arms, feeling strongly that her daughter was alive and needed her, that something terrible was going to happen.

She looked at the detective. ''I hadn't thought of it that way, but maybe you're right. Maybe this will be a kind of homecoming, after all.''

72

Dorothy's funeral was held at Cathedral of the Holy Name on Wabash. The church was filled to overflowing, the number in attendance stood testament to how much Dorothy Monarch had been loved and respected. After the Mass, she was laid to rest in the Monarch family mausoleum at Graceland Cemetery. The weather cooperated, the February day was bitterly cold but the skies clear and bright. Those closest to the family were invited back to the Astor Street house to express their personal condolences and share a meal.

Through it all, Skye was numb. Devastated. Over the past months, she had grown to care for Dorothy; she had been both mentor and friend; Skye had started to think of the woman as her aunt, too.

Through the entire ordeal, Griffen stayed by her right side, Adam by her left. Both men leaned on her, destroyed by grief. She had never seen either of them so, and she ached for them. Two deaths in less than a year, first Pierce, now Dorothy. They were a proud, clannish family, to see their number shrink to so few must be as frightening as it was heartbreaking.

"I need a drink," Adam said hoarsely as they closed the door behind the last mourner. "Anyone else?"

Without a word, Skye and Griffen followed Adam to the library. He fixed them all a drink, pouring himself a stiff whiskey.

"I should have insisted she hire full-time household help." Adam tossed back his whiskey, grimaced and poured another. "This wouldn't have happened."

"No, it wouldn't have," Griffen murmured, lounging on the sofa, gazing at the ceiling. "But we all knew how forgetful she had become. We're all to blame."

"Stop it," Skye said, eyes burning. "Both of you. Assigning blame isn't going to bring her back. It was an accident. A tragic, terrible accident. Even the police said so."

Griffen threw an arm across his eyes. "I can picture her, going to the kitchen to make a cup of tea, then lying down to rest until the kettle whistled. Of course," he added, his voice strangely choked, "the kettle never whistled. She never awakened again."

"What are we to do now?" Adam sank heavily to the big, leather armchair, looking his age, Skye thought, for the first time. "What's Monarch's to do?"

She crossed to the older man, bent and hugged him. "It's going to be okay," she murmured, heart hurting for him as he clung to her. "Everything's going to be okay."

"That's right." Griffen sat up. "Monarch's has Skye now. She's the future of Monarch Design, just as she's my future. She'll take Dorothy's place."

"Oh...Griffen, no." Skye shook her head, almost embarrassed by his suggestion. "I'm not ready. I don't have enough experience. I don't have enough knowledge. Dorothy did so much more than just create, she ran the entire—"

"Griffen's right," Adam said, his voice suddenly strong. "You have the creative gift that's the lifeblood of Monarch's. The rest you can learn."

Skye couldn't believe what they were suggesting. "But others in the department have seniority. They would have a much better understanding of how to keep us running smoothly. Or you could hire an established designer from—"

"The outside?" Adam cut in. "Never!"

Adam's adamance took her by surprise. "But Adam, only a few months ago, I *was* from the outside."

"But you're family now. Period."

Skye glanced imploringly at Griffen. "I'm not ready. It doesn't make any sense for me to take over."

Griffen stood and crossed to her. He took her hands and drew her to her feet. "Darling, it does make sense. You're the one with the gift. And this was what Dorothy wanted. She talked to me about it. She talked to Adam about it. When she passed away, she wanted you to take the creative reins. She was even more convinced of that after the trip to Milan."

Skye returned her gaze to Adam, only to find his on Griffen. He looked almost...frightened. "Adam?" she whispered, a prick of unease moving up her spine.

His expression cleared. "I agree. It's what she would have wanted."

"We need you, Skye," Griffen murmured. "You're family now. You're one of us. We need you to do this."

Family.

The thing she had always longed for, to be a part of people who needed her, who loved her, people she could call her own. But how, after the other night, could she continue her engagement to Griffen? How could she remain one of them?

As the days since making love with Griffen had passed, the horror of the experience hadn't dimmed. It had clung to her like the aftereffect of a terrifying dream. She had begun to wonder if she hadn't been sick, as she had suggested to Griffen. What else could have caused such a strange and horrifying reaction in her? It wasn't natural.

She brought a hand to her temple. It had been as if he'd been raping her. Why? She didn't find him disgusting or ugly; he hadn't been cruel, hadn't used even a hint of force.

Adam stood, he took one of her hands and curled his around it, bringing it to his chest, his heart. "You're not going to leave us, are you, Skye? I don't think I could bear that now."

"Of course she's not," Griffen said, taking her other hand. "She's family now. She wouldn't break our hearts that way. Would you, love?"

Both men looked at her. A fluttery, panicky sensation settled in the pit of her gut. Trapped. She was trapped. After all, what could she say? Now was not the time to express her real feelings, her fears and uncertainties. How could she? Both men were in pain; both men needed her.

Instead, she concurred, speaking to Adam, unable to meet Griffen's gaze. "Of course I won't break your heart. And if my running the design department is really what you want, I'll try."

Adam hugged her. "That's our girl. Isn't she, Griffen?"

"Our girl," he repeated, hugging her, too. "Always our girl."

73

The hemorrhaging of McCord Public Relations and Special Events had finally stopped. Chance owed Martha a huge debt of gratitude. She had helped him, refusing, she said, to allow Griffen Monarch to hold her hostage another moment. Nobody was going to blackmail her, she had decided. She'd had enough.

Once Martha's story began to circulate, Chance had been able to convince several of the clients he'd lost due to Griffen's smear campaign to come back. And working day and night, he had also managed to acquire a few new accounts.

During it all, Chance had realized some things. The first being that he, Chance, had built his own business—with ingenuity, hard work and his reputation for getting the job done, and done right. Griffen had not given it to him, Chance had earned it.

The truth of that had been freeing. It had brought him back to life. Brought back his will to fight and win.

But still, those realizations paled in comparison to another.

He couldn't allow Skye to marry Griffen. And not because he feared Griffen was unstable. But because he feared he couldn't live without her himself.

That was why he had come here, to Monarch's. To Griffen's lair, as he thought of it. He took the elevator up to the design department, greeted the receptionist, announced that he had popped in to say hello to Skye and, not giving the woman time to question his right to do so, he strode boldly down the hall.

Luckily, Skye was in her office, alone. She was at her

jeweler's bench, her head bent over her work. She was using what Dorothy had called a flex-shaft, and she didn't hear him over the machine's low hum.

He closed the door behind him. "Don't marry Griffen."

Her hands stilled. She turned off her buffer and hung it on the hook at the back of her workstation, then slipped off her safety glasses. Only then did she face him. "What did you say?"

"You asked me once to give you a reason not to marry him. I am. I'm here. Don't marry Griffen."

"I'm buried in work here, trying to keep a studio that's been thrown into complete turmoil running smoothly. Trying to keep up with a job that I don't have enough experience to handle. And you want to play a competitive, sick little game with me. I'm not interested, Chance."

He strode across the room, stopping before her. He caught her hands and drew her to her feet. "This isn't a game. This isn't about Griffen. It doesn't have anything to do with anything but you and me."

He brought their joined hands to his chest. She wore Griffen's ring. Seeing it affected him like a punch to his gut. He wanted to yank it off her finger. "I don't want you to marry Griffen. Because of me. Because of my feelings for you."

He tightened his hands over hers. "I can't let you slip away, Skye. I think about you all the time. I can't imagine living without you. But I want to be honest with you. I can't promise you forever, not yet, anyway. I can't promise you a perfect love. Hell, I don't even know what that is. But I think I love you. I want to give us a try."

She searched his gaze, looking suddenly, impossibly vulnerable. She pressed her lips together for a moment before speaking. "The last time we saw each other, you told me that to keep me from marrying Griffen you'd even tell me you loved me. Now you've done it. Are you really that jealous of him?"

"I'm not jealous of him," he said, realizing that he meant it, realizing how good it felt. "Look, Skye, I've spent my whole life working to be better than I was, different, more important. I spent my life looking at the Griffen Monarchs of the world and wanting what they had, wanting to be what they were. I'm sure there's some psychobabble bullshit reason for it, but I don't care about that. That's over, I don't want to be Griffen Monarch or anyone or anything besides who and what I am. But I do want you. I want to give us a try,'' he repeated.

For what seemed like forever she said nothing, simply stared at him, her expression frozen. Then she yanked her hands free. "If that were true, if I could believe that some epiphany had brought you here instead of your competition with Griffen, what would you want from me? How am I supposed to respond to your little halfhearted commitment? Am I supposed to fall down in a faint of joy? Am I supposed to be... What? Honored? Grateful? Please. I'm not an idiot. And I'm not desperate.''

"I'm being as honest as I know how to be.''

"Bully for you.'' She strode to her desk, stared at it a moment, then whirled to face him, furious, he saw. "Griffen has promised me his undying love and devotion. He's promised me forever, a perfect love for always. You start off with a disclaimer about not being able to offer anything.''

"Don't you get it?'' Chance asked, as angry now as she. "When are you going to grow up? There's no such thing as perfect love, there's no such thing as forever—''

"Because you can't make a commitment,'' she shouted. "Because you're too afraid to let yourself love anyone.''

"I'm afraid?'' he said, disbelieving. "I'm not the one marrying someone I don't love so I can feel safe.''

"Get out. Get the hell out of my office before I call security and have you removed.''

"Do it,'' he said, moving closer. "See if I care. You're pissed off because all I can do is offer to try. Don't you see that's all there ever is? Two people who love each other and are willing to try.'' He looked her dead in the eye. "And you don't love Griffen.''

"Two people trying," she mimicked sarcastically. "For how long, Chance? Until they don't feel like it anymore? Until they get the itch to take off?"

"Back to that well, Skye? My leaving you with Sarah and Michael was the best thing I could have done for you. And you know it. Or you would if you'd ever stop thinking like a thirteen-year-old and start thinking like an adult."

She grabbed for the phone, he yanked it away and caught her to his chest. "You want me to promise I'll never hurt you, I can't do that. No one can. Being hurt is part of being a fallible human being, surrounded by other fallible human beings." He pulled her closer, until she was pressed so tightly against him he could feel the wild beat of her heart against his. "You don't love Griffen," he said fiercely. "You don't."

"How do you know?" she whispered, her voice thick. "I'm madly in love with him. Wildly, passionately in love with him."

"You're not." He cupped her face in his palms. "You're in love with me."

"I'm not." She wedged her hands between them and flattened them against his chest, though she didn't try to push him away. "I refuse to love you. I refuse to allow myself to be—"

He caught her words with his mouth, kissing her deeply. He moved his hands to her hair, freeing it from its clip. The clip clattered to the floor; her hair tumbled to her shoulders. He tangled his fingers in it, the strands, soft and silky against his skin.

But instead of pushing him away, she made a sound deep in her throat and pressed closer, curling her fingers into his shirt as if holding on for dear life.

He kissed her again and again, one dizzying exchange after another, moving his tongue in and out of her mouth, wet, open, wanting. A true imitation of the sex act. She mimicked him, as hungry as he, as desperate.

"I've missed you," he muttered against her mouth. He

inched her backward, until she was pressed up against the wall.

She arched slightly, bringing their pelvises into stunning, breath-stealing contact. It was all he could do to keep from making love to her now, against this wall, not giving a damn who might hear them.

He slid his hand under her skirt and up her thigh. "You're so wet," he whispered.

She bit back a moan, trembling. He curved his hand around her and she came. Just like that, almost spontaneously. Silently, for he caught the sounds of her pleasure with his mouth and tongue.

And then he let her go. She met his eyes, disoriented, still caught in the throes of her release. Her chest rose and fell with her labored breathing, her cheeks were flushed, her eyes heavy-lidded with arousal. He was so hard he hurt.

"You see how I know?" he asked softly. "You don't love him, Skye. If you did, your body wouldn't respond like that to me. All I did was touch you."

He crossed to the door, stopping and turning back when he reached it. "Grow up, Skye. I'm sorry I hurt you all those years ago. But you're not a kid anymore. Get over it."

74

Claire couldn't shake the sense of foreboding that pressed in on her, the feeling that Skye needed her, and that something terrible was about to happen. Those feelings had dogged her every moment since she had arrived in Chicago. She had slept little. She had eaten even less. She was exhausted and jumpy, on the verge of falling apart.

She had spent the past days buried here at the hotel, surrounded by police evidence, leaving only when desperate for fresh air or at the police's request. She had picked through the evidence with excruciating care; she had visited Becky Williams's home and neighborhood, she had visited the home of the slumber party and had talked with the girl's parents and friends.

So far, she had come up with nothing.

She shouldn't have come here; she shouldn't have agreed to try to work on this case. Claire realized that now. She wasn't even certain whether her sense of foreboding pertained to future events or were simply remnants of the past, come back to torment her.

Claire brought the heels of her hands to her eyes, working to clear her head, to focus. She hated this. She hated when she picked up nothing. Because of the parents, the friends of the family, the police. They were all counting on her, all hoping against hope for a lead, an answer—even if that answer meant facing the most awful truth.

She dropped her hands. That morning, the police had delivered the newspapers she had requested: back issues of every paper within the metro area, from a week before the abduction until now. She went to the first stack of *Tribunes,* checked the dates—she always started back and moved forward, and had asked they be delivered that way—took the first three papers and went to the desk, sat down and began flipping slowly through.

The minutes ticked past. The pages crackled as she turned them. The first paper revealed nothing. She moved on to the second. Then the third.

Claire went slowly, scanning every page. She never knew what was going to trigger a vision. Once it had been a coupon for Puppy Chow. The child had wandered off to "help a nice man" search for his missing puppy. With her help, that child had been found, and found alive.

That case had taught her something about herself, about her ability—not to take anything for granted, not to think she understood how her sight worked, or what made it work. She had been sick with a cold, she had been tired and anxious to go home. She had almost skipped the annoying mountain of coupon circulars. She hadn't, thank God. But she had always wondered what would have happened if she had skipped them. She had always wondered if that child would have been lost.

Claire turned another page, skimming her gaze over the society news, the advice columns, the engagement announcements. A photo caught her eye. She stared at it, at the picture of a smiling couple, the blood beginning to thrum in her head.

She lowered her gaze to the caption.

Griffen Monarch and Skye Dearborn.

A sound of horror, of realization, slipped past her lips. Now, she knew the source of her foreboding. Now she understood her feeling of urgency, of impending disaster.

Skye was here. In Chicago.

She was engaged to marry her brother.

Claire leaped to her feet, so suddenly her chair fell backward, crashing into the wall. Every moment counted. She felt that as surely, as clearly, as she had ever felt anything.

She raced to the desk and retrieved the Chicago-area phone book.

Nearly hysterical, she flipped through, ripping the delicate pages as she went. She found the D's. Shaking, she ran her index finger down each column of names, crying out in frustration. She closed the book.

No Skye Dearborn.

She had to find her daughter; she had to warn her. Claire looked around the room, searching frantically for something, a way, an answer. Her gaze landed on the phone books Detective Baker had brought this morning. She looked at them, then back at the one before her.

It was a year old.

Claire scrambled across to the stack, rifling through it, finding the one for metro Chicago. She opened it and went to the D's.

Dearborn, Skye.

She sank to her knees, tears of joy filling her eyes, spilling over. Her baby, her Skye. She was alive; she had found her. At long last she would see her daughter again.

Claire went to the phone, clutching the book to her chest. Heart beating so wildly she could hardly breathe, she dialed the number. It rang once, then twice. The wait was agony. Claire squeezed her eyes shut, praying Skye was home, praying she answered the phone. After all these years, she didn't think she could wait another second.

A recorder picked up. Claire almost cried out her disappointment. She left a garbled, half-hysterical message, her words tripping over each other, her breath coming in shallow gasps. As she was begging her daughter to call her, the machine cut her off.

Claire dropped the receiver back into the cradle and began to pace, wringing her hands. What now? She couldn't just sit here and wait, doing nothing. What if Skye and Griffen were getting married today, this moment? Or tonight or even tomorrow?

She had to stop this. She had to find a way.

Gooseflesh crawled up her arms, and she rubbed them. She couldn't wait, she couldn't take the chance that—

Chance.

She stopped, frozen. The last time she had seen Skye, she had been with Chance. She swung her gaze to the phone book, still open to Skye's number. It was a long shot but maybe they had come to Chicago together.

She raced to the book. And found a listing for Chance McCord. She called and got his recorder. Much as she had with Skye, she left him a message, telling him where she was and that she had to see him as soon as possible.

She didn't know what to do now, but wait.

Claire went back to the newspaper and gazed at the black-and-white photo, her eyes flooding with fresh tears. She had found her daughter. Her precious daughter. It felt as if she had found a piece of herself; she felt whole for the first time in fourteen years.

A tear landed on the photo, and Claire wiped it carefully away, drinking in her daughter's image. She had grown into a beautiful woman, just as Claire had known she would. She could recall, with perfect clarity, the first time she had held her baby daughter in her arms, could recall how small and utterly sweet she had been. She could recall her first smile, her first day of school, the way they had laughed together.

Tears choked Claire. She wished she had been with her to see her grow. To help her. Just to love her. They had missed so much.

Heart aching, Claire lightly touched the photo. Now they would get a second chance. Finally, they would be together again.

If Skye would let her. If she could understand and forgive her.

She should have told Skye the truth, should have told her about the Monarchs and Griffen. And she should have kept them together, no matter what.

Claire shifted her gaze to the blurb beside the photo, realizing that she hadn't even thought to read it before this. As she skimmed the words, as they penetrated, the breath left her body. Her hand went to the gem-filled talisman around her neck. Her world seemed to shift on its axis, and she sank to the floor.

Skye worked for Monarch's. She was a designer.

Just as Adam and Pierce had always wanted. Just as they had always planned. How had this happened? Claire wondered. She had taken her daughter away; now here Skye was, twenty-two years later, completely entangled with the very people Claire had tried to free her from.

Something terrible was about to happen.

Skye needed her.

Claire stood and went to the phone. She called Monarch's and, voice shaking, asked for Skye Dearborn.

"May I ask who's calling?"

"No, it's…personal. But it's an emergency. I must speak with her."

"I'm sorry," the woman said. "She's in a conference. Perhaps if I could tell her the nature of the emergency?"

Claire heard another voice, a man's voice, in the background. She began to shake. Her voice rose. "I need to talk to her! It's an emergency! Tell her it's her mother."

"Skye's mother?" The woman paused. "I tell you what, give me your number, and I'll see she gets the message immediately."

"Thank you! Thank you so much! I'm at the Knickerbocker Hotel, suite two-twelve." Claire recited the phone number, then thanked the woman again.

"You're welcome, Mrs. Dearborn, I'll see Skye gets—"

"Griffen Monarch here. Can I help you?"

Claire couldn't speak. Fear took her breath, her voice, her ability to think. Hearing his name spoken out loud, the sound of his voice, sent her hurtling back twenty years. Adam was above her, eyes bulging as he tried to choke the life out of her. Skye was screaming. Screaming—

"Hello? Is anyone there?"

Claire slammed down the phone, a strange rushing sound

in her ears. Her heart raced; she began to sweat. A darkness settling over her, a feeling of impending disaster.

Her legs began to shake. She brought her hands to her talisman, dropping to her knees. Her vision blurred, then cleared. Her head filled with an image, one she recognized from many times before, of a dark white forest. This time she saw two figures, one fleeing, the other tracking. A game of cat and mouse, one the hunter, the other hunted. She heard a cry for help and strange, high laughter.

She doubled over, the images slamming into her. She saw an icy lake, glittering in the moonlight, saw a body struggling, then being pulled down into its cold, dark depths.

The vision shifted, then changed. Music. Jazz. Old buildings laced in curling ironwork. She saw a girl. And a young man. They were holding hands. And laughing.

It shifted yet again. She saw hands clawing desperately, saw a figure fall, rag doll–like to the floor. Claire couldn't breathe. Her eyes popped open. She was afraid. For herself. For Skye.

But not for Becky Williams. Wherever she was, she was laughing.

Skye needed her, Claire knew. She needed Claire's talisman; she needed the gems. It wasn't over yet, but it soon would be.

She had left her hotel and suite number with Monarch's receptionist. Griffen would come for her.

Fatalism settled over her, a sense that every event of the past twenty-six years, since the day in the nursery when she'd had the icy vision for the first time, had been leading to this moment.

Something terrible was going to happen. She didn't know if she could stop it.

She might never see her daughter again, after all.

Claire went to the desk, sat down and dialed Detective Baker at headquarters. When he answered, she described her vision, and what she thought it meant, in detail. That done, she took out some hotel stationery and began to write.

Skye had to know everything. She should have known long ago. Claire wished she could look into her daughter's eyes while she told her, she wished she could hold her.

But that might not be possible. She had to do this now, before it was too late.

Claire poured her heart out, telling her daughter everything—about the day in the nursery that had started it all, about Griffen's obsession and the abuse she had witnessed, about Adam and Pierce's threat to take Skye away, and about her vision and lifting the gems. She told her about Susan being killed and about her own desperate search for Skye afterward. She shared with her daughter the events that had brought her back to Chicago, of how she had spent the last fourteen years of her life, and how many parents and children she had helped, and that she had never given up hope that she would someday find and be reunited with her own daughter.

But above all, Claire let her daughter know how much she loved her. She had never stopped. She never would, she promised. Not even in death.

As she wrote, time slipped away; her sense of approaching doom growing with each passing minute.

Claire folded the letter and took the gem-filled talisman from around her neck. Emptying a box of police evidence, she tucked the letter and gems inside, retrieved Skye's address from the phone book, then wrote it on the top of the box.

Heart hammering, she glanced at her watch, picked up the box and headed down to the concierge to have it hand-delivered to Skye.

75

As she had known he would, Griffen came for her. Claire opened the door and acknowledged that she had not been wrong about him. He was the same as he had been twenty years ago only smarter, more powerful. More corrupt. When she looked into his eyes, she saw a monster. She saw a man who had no soul.

As she stared into his dead eyes, her mind tumbled back to that day in the nursery, shortly after Skye had been born. *"I'm going to marry baby Skye when I grow up,"* he had said.

He was making good on his promise.

The monstrous dark bird of her nightmares hadn't been Pierce, after all. It had been Griffen.

A squeak of terror slipped past her lips. "You can't do this."

He smiled. "I don't like it when people tell me I can't. You should know that, Mama Madeline."

She took a step backward, hand to her throat, going instinctively for her talisman. The gems were gone, she remembered. On their way to Skye.

Thank God she had done that. Thank God.

"We always recognized each other, didn't we, Madeline?" He followed her into the room, closing the door behind him. "No one else has ever really seen me. Did you know that?"

She took another step backward, frightened, struggling for words.

"I've always wondered, what's it like?" he asked. "Having the sight?"

When she didn't reply, he arched his eyebrows in question. "You're so quiet." He laughed. "I know. Confronting one's past can be so difficult. Poor Skye, she hasn't been able to do it yet. Though she has these annoying little flashes of the past. And those ridiculous headaches of hers. They only succeed in upsetting her."

He shook his head, pleased. "Repressed memory, that must have been quite convenient for you. And I have to thank you, Madeline, it's been most convenient for me, also."

"You're completely mad," she whispered, seeing the phone from the corner of her eye, inching for it. "Insane."

"Ugly words. And quite untrue. The great ones are often misunderstood."

"She's your sister!"

"She's my destiny. You tried to take her away, from me, from Monarch's. But you failed. Because it was meant to be this way."

"Listen to reason, Griffen. You'll want children. Heirs to carry on the Monarch name. A brother and sister, the gene pool—" her voice rose, the thought of it making her sick "—they won't be right, Griffen. What will Monarch's do then?"

His expression remained passive, save for the small smile that curved his lips. Claire tried another tack. "Skye will find out, someday, somehow. Her memory might even come back. What will she think then? She'll hate you. She'll leave you and Monarch's forever. Griffen, listen to me!"

He clucked his tongue. "You're being silly and melodramatic now, Maddie. Skye and I are soul mates, we're each other's destiny. None of those things will be a problem. You're just wanting everything your way. As you always did."

"I won't allow this."

He laughed again; the sound chilled her to her core. "And how will you prevent it?"

She turned and lunged for the phone. She had it in her hand, her finger on the O, when he snatched it from her. With a cry, she watched as with a swift tug, he ripped it from the wall.

He shook his head and set the instrument carefully on the sofa. "That wasn't nice."

"I won't allow you to do this," she said again. "I won't keep silent. I'll kill you if I have to."

"No," he murmured apologetically. "You see, I'll have to kill you before you stop me."

She darted for the door. He caught her easily, dragging her back. She twisted and scratched. With a grunt of pain, he released his grip and she scrambled away.

She got to her feet, stumbling for the door. She reached it; her hand closed over the knob, she opened her mouth to scream for help.

He caught her from behind, his arms going around her like a vise, one at her throat, the other at her middle, knocking the wind out of her.

He lifted her off the ground, surprising her with his strength. Claire struggled, kicking, clawing at the arm at her throat. Griffen lifted her higher. Stars danced at the edges of her vision.

Skye...baby, I'm here. I love you.

Claire squeezed her eyes shut, praying, trying to reach her daughter, trying to speak to her with her mind. Wanting to let her know...wanting to tell her...

The mantel clock chimed 4:00 p.m. Claire's eyes popped back open.

With a grunt of exertion, Griffen snapped her neck.

76

Now, what did she have to go and do that for?

Griffen gazed blankly at Claire, crumpled in a rag doll-like heap on the floor at his feet. The blood beat frantically in his head, muddying his thoughts. He wiped a hand across his forehead, realizing that he was trembling, that he was sweating.

He'd had to kill her, he'd had to. She'd been about to ruin everything. She'd meant to take his Grace away from him, the way she had before. He'd had to stop her, of course. He glanced around the room, his gaze darting from one thing to the next. But why here?

He wiped his mouth with the back of his hand. The stupid bitch. If only she had stayed away. She, more than anyone, should have understood the lengths he would go to keep Grace by his side.

But she had decided to come back and fuck everything up anyway. She had decided to stick her big nose where it didn't belong. He looked at her, annoyed. And where had it gotten them?

Her dead and him in a whole shitload of trouble.

Griffen sucked in a shuddering breath, wishing he could think clearly, wishing the rushing sound in his ears would stop. He had to clean away the evidence. He had to think, to plan. He couldn't be caught; that wouldn't do, not at all.

He would find a way out of this, he decided, looking the room over. He was in control. He could fix anything. He always had.

He narrowed his eyes. What had he touched? The doorknob. The back of the chair. The doorjamb. Nothing else. He stepped over Claire and went to the door. He took out his handkerchief and carefully wiped the doorknob, then the jamb.

He moved to the chair and wiped it. Smiling, he went to tuck his handkerchief back into his jacket pocket. As he did, his sleeve pulled up slightly, revealing scratches on his hand. He pushed the sleeve up farther and saw more scratches. Bloody ones. He lowered his gaze in dawning horror. Drops of blood, his blood, stood out in bold relief on the white carpeting, on her pale blue blouse.

The police would scrape her fingernails and find his skin and blood under her nails. His DNA. Griffen's mind raced. He had ridden in the elevator with a man and woman who would be able to identify him. He had seen an old business associate in the lobby. The man had nodded at him from across the room.

Griffen shifted his gaze to the phone. Claire had called the store; the hotel and telephone company would have records of that call. When he had heard the receptionist say Claire's name, he had taken the phone from the woman's hands. She had been startled by his actions; she was not likely to forget it.

Claire would be traced to the Monarch family. The police would learn that she was Madeline Monarch. That Skye was really Grace Monarch.

He would be caught. He would go to jail.

No. That wasn't the way it was supposed to go. Griffen pressed the heels of his hands to his eyes, working to focus his runaway thoughts. But no matter how he tried to think of a way out of this, his thoughts kept coming back to the same thing—Grace. When he was caught, she would turn to Chance. McCord, that *nothing*, would have her then. As would Monarch's. And his grandfather.

No. Never. He wouldn't allow it. Grace was his. His prize. His possession.

She was his destiny.

Of course. Griffen dropped his hands, calm now, his direction, his path, clear.

If he couldn't have Grace, nobody would.

77

Skye made a sound of distress. It slipped past her lips, chill bumps racing up her arms.

The woman standing beside her in the elevator, probably a customer, looked at her in concern. "Are you all right?"

"Yes." Skye rubbed her arms, cold. "I just had the strangest sense that..." *That someone needed her. That someone she loved was hurting.* She wasn't about to say that, and let the thought trail off, smiling weakly at the woman. "I'm fine, thank you."

The woman returned her smile. "Do you know what time it is? My watch stopped."

"Sure." Skye looked at hers, then back at the woman. "It's four. A couple minutes after, actually."

The elevator shuddered to a halt; the doors slid open. Thanking her, the woman stepped off.

Skye rubbed her arms again, thinking of her mother. She had been all afternoon, ever since Chance had left her office, though she couldn't say why.

Perhaps it had been his words.

Grow up, Skye. Get over it.

Those words had rung in Skye's head all afternoon. As had the way she'd responded to his touch, the way she longed for him. The way she thought about him all the time.

She couldn't marry Griffen. She didn't love him.

She loved Chance.

She had known that for a while now, since the awful night she and Griffen had made love. But she had been too afraid to admit it, too afraid of being hurt to let go of her dream of perfect love.

No such thing existed. Chance had been right about that. The only forever that life guaranteed was the forever of death.

She had to break it off with Griffen. As soon as possible. Tonight. She hated to hurt him. She hated to hurt Adam. She had no choice. She had let this go on too long already.

Her decision scared the hell out of her. Griffen offered her everything she had ever wished for; Chance offered her nothing but a promise to try. He had hurt her once; he might hurt her again. She didn't care. The thought of living without him was more frightening than anything she could contemplate.

The time had come to grow up. Chance might hurt her, but being hurt was a part of life.

With the realization came a giddy sense of freedom. Kowtowing to the past, to fear, was a ridiculous way to live. She was done with it. Now, this moment, she began anew.

It brought, too, thoughts of her mother. Not bitter or angry ones for once, but sweet thoughts, happy memories. Skye smiled, thinking of the way her mother had loved her, recalling the way she had shown that love day in and day out.

Her mother had loved her, Skye realized, suddenly feeling as if her mother's arms were around her now, holding her, filling her with the most incredible sense of peace and well-being. Skye closed her eyes, holding on to the moment, the feeling. Holding on to her mother.

The elevator reached the first floor and Skye stepped off. She called goodbye to the downstairs receptionist, wished her a good weekend and left the store.

It was clear and bitterly cold, and she stuffed her bare hands into her pockets, wishing the gloves she'd ordered from Marshall Field's would arrive. She started up Michigan Avenue, heading for the parking garage where she had a monthly contract, the wind, thankfully, at her back.

Twenty-five minutes later, she was home, slipping into a parking spot less than a block from her building. This time the wind was against her, and she bent into it, trudging the rest of the way home, imagining snuggling up in front of a fire with a cup of hot chocolate and Moo.

She reached her front steps at the same time a deliveryman did. She glanced at the package and saw her name. *Her new gloves. Finally.*

"Excuse me?" She touched the young man's sleeve. "I'm Skye Dearborn. Is that for me?"

"Yup." He grinned. "You sure you're her?"

"Yeah, I am." She smiled. "You want ID or something?"

"Nah. You'll have to sign, though." He held out the clip-board. "You got lucky. I had to circle the block a couple of times. Can you believe that jerk parked by the fire hydrant? That was my spot."

Skye followed the kid's gaze to the hydrant directly across the street. A black Porsche 911 was parked in front of it. She lifted her gaze to her apartment. That looked like Griffen's car. What was he doing here?

"Lucky break for you, though. I would have missed you." He handed her the box. "Have a good one."

She thanked him, let herself into the building and climbed the flight of stairs to her apartment. She stopped at the top landing, her heart beginning to thrum. Her door was partially open. She heard the sound of someone moving around inside.

She swallowed hard and crossed to her door. With just the tips of her fingers, she pushed it open. Griffen's back was to her, he was squatted down by her coffee table, leafing through a pile of mail. *Her mail.*

Fury took her breath. "What do you think you're doing?"

He launched to his feet, whirling to face her. "Grace!"

"What did you call me?"

"I mean, Skye. You startled me."

"I startled you?" She shifted the box from her right arm to her left. "What are you doing in my apartment? How did you get in?"

"I came to get you." He looked strange, hardly like himself at all. He was pale, out of breath and sweating. And he was acting strange, too. Wired and jumpy. Usually immaculately groomed, his suit was rumpled, his hair untidy.

She shifted her gaze to his hand. He had cut himself, blood marred the cuff of his white dress shirt.

"I thought we should go away," he said. "Up to the family retreat at Horizon's End. I packed you a bag."

"Away?" she repeated, noticing her overnight bag at his feet. He had entered her apartment without her permission, he had gone through her things. Unease crawled up her spine. She didn't like this, not at all.

"How did you get in here, Griffen?"

"We need to go." He wiped his upper lip with the back of his hand, his gaze jumping from one thing to another. "It's getting late."

"Griffen?" She took a step backward, toward the door. "Are you all right? You don't look well."

"I'm fine. Anxious to go, that's all." He dragged a hand through his hair; she saw then where the blood on his shirt had come from—the back of his hand was marked by a row of vivid gouges, as if he had been clawed. "This thing with Dorothy," he continued. "We're all feeling the stress. We need to get away, relax a little. Be together."

She shook her head. "I don't think so, Griffen. In fact, I've been doing a lot of thinking about us, and I—" She bit off the words, suddenly realizing that Moo was missing.

"Where's my dog?"

"Moo?" He swiped at his lip again. "He's with Granddad."

"Adam?" She struggled not to panic. "What do you mean?"

"I forgot to tell you. Adam's meeting us there. He's already left." Griffen picked up her bag. "I knew how much Moo would enjoy running in the woods, but there wasn't room in the Porsche."

She frowned, rubbing her temple. *Something was wrong. Terribly wrong.*

"Moo and Adam are on their way?" she asked. "You're sure?"

"Of course." He smiled, suddenly looking like the Griffen she knew and trusted. "How could I not be sure about that?"

Her every instinct warned her not to go. But how could she not? Adam had Mr. Moo. Once they were all together, as painful as it would be, she would break the news about the engagement to them both.

"All right. Did you get my headache medicine?"

"And your toothbrush and a bottle of wine." He smiled winningly. "I'm taking care of everything, sweetheart. I always take care of everything. Trust me."

78

Chance listened to the message on his recorder for the third time, heart thundering. Claire? Could it really be her? The message was garbled, half-hysterical. Some of it he couldn't quite make out, even after listening to it three times. She was staying at the Knickerbocker. Room two-twelve. Skye, she said, was in danger. Then she mentioned Griffen's name. She begged Chance to come quickly.

Griffen, Chance thought, frowning. How did Claire know Griffen?

Chance hit Stop, then Replay. He listened to the message yet again, unable to understand what she was saying about Griffen, but growing convinced the voice he was listening to was Claire's.

He reached for the phone to call Skye, then changed his mind. Before he put Claire in touch with Skye, he wanted to find out just where the hell she had been for the last fourteen years. He wouldn't allow Claire to hurt Skye that way again.

Chance grabbed his coat and keys and headed out the door.

Twenty minutes later he pulled up in front of the Knickerbocker hotel. The valet leaped forward, his expression almost panicked. Chance glanced around and frowned. Something big was going down. He counted six police vehicles outside the hotel and spotted a couple of uniforms just inside the hotel lobby.

The valet opened his door. Chance stepped out of the car

and handed the kid his keys. "What's with all the cops? Somebody snuff out one of the guests?"

The kid paled. "No, sir. Nothing like that." He handed Chance a claim ticket, his hands shaking.

The hairs on the back of Chance's neck stood straight up. "Hey, I was only kidding. Don't get rattled."

The boy laughed self-consciously. "No, sir. I'm not rattled."

Chance headed into the hotel. He caught the elevator, sharing it with a couple of Chicago's finest. The two said nothing; their silence spoke volumes.

Somebody had been murdered.

The detectives alighted on the second floor, and Chance followed them off, a sick feeling in the pit of his stomach, Claire's words ringing in his head.

Something terrible has...Skye's in danger. Come as quickly as you can.

As he followed the two men, Chance prayed. That they were going to another room. That his imagination was working overtime. That they were investigating a drug deal or a robbery.

His prayers went unanswered. The detectives stopped in front of room two-twelve. They tapped on the door.

Chance slowed. The door opened and the officers slipped inside, just as Chance passed it. He looked. The room was filled with uniforms and guys in cheap suits. A couple of them were squatted down, examining something on the floor. Not something, Chance realized. Someone. A body.

Chance stopped where he was, light-headed. He bent at the waist, hands on his thighs for support. He breathed deeply through his nose, counting to ten, then twenty, reasoning with himself as he did. Maybe it was all a mistake. He could have gotten the room number wrong, or the hotel. Maybe that hadn't even been Claire who'd called.

Not believing his own assurances, Chance headed back down to the lobby, then out to the valet. Sometime between when he had parked and just now, the coroner had arrived. His wagon was parked just up from the valet's station.

"Hey, kid!"

The valet looked his way. Chance held up his claim ticket. The kid jogged over. "Short stay."

"My friend's already checked out."

"I'm sorry to hear that. Your car's right over there." He pointed. "I haven't even had time to park it yet."

"Great." Chance took a twenty-dollar bill out of his wallet. He met the kid's eyes. "Who got killed?"

The boy shook his head. "Nobody."

"The coroner's here. The place is teeming with cops. And I've got twenty dollars for the person who makes my curiosity go away. And somebody *will* make my curiosity go away. It might as well be you."

The valet glanced behind him, then back at Chance. "You didn't hear it from me."

"Of course not."

"I don't know her name, but I heard some of the cops talking. She was some sort of a psychic, here to help the police with a case."

"A psychic?" he repeated, his words choked. "You're sure?"

"I'm sure."

Dear Jesus, no. A psychic? That couldn't be a coincidence. It had to be Claire.

"The G.M.'s about to shit bricks. We've got a Mary Kay Cosmetics convention checking in tomorrow. You with the press?"

"Yeah, I'm with the press." Chance handed the kid the twenty, hurting for Claire, hurting for Skye.

Skye would be devastated.

He had to get to her before she heard it on the news, or saw it in the paper.

From the car, he called Monarch's and learned that Skye had left for the day, almost an hour ago. He made his way to Skye's place, his mind whirling. Claire had called. She had left a frantic message, a message in which she had said Skye was in danger and had mentioned Griffen's name. Now Claire was dead.

What was the connection? He didn't know, but he kept picturing the brick wall rushing up to meet him, kept hearing Griffen's high-pitched laugh and his words: *If I can't have her, nobody will.*

What lengths would Griffen go to hold on to Skye?

Chance floored the car, going as fast as he could without risking his life, taking every shortcut he could think of. He reached Skye's building and double-parked in front of it. He climbed out and raced up her front steps. He buzzed her and waited. Nothing. He buzzed again.

He went back to the car, got the cell phone and called her apartment. He got the recorder. "Dammit, Skye, if you're there, pick up. It's an emergency. Pick up."

He hung on a moment, praying she would answer. She didn't. He ended the call and tossed the phone on the front seat. Dammit, where was she?

Swearing again, he went around the side of the building to the courtyard gate. He eyed the top of the wall and its row of jagged glass, then the sheer expanse of gate. Scaling it would be damn near impossible.

What now, McCord? With a sound of frustration, he tried the gate. It swung open. Glancing around to make sure no one was watching, he slipped inside and up the steps to Skye's back porch. He peered in her window. Her kitchen was empty, her place looked deserted. He didn't even see Moo.

Something wasn't right. Chance looked around him, fighting a growing panic, a strange sensation crawling up his spine. She was out to an early dinner, he told himself. She had gone to a show, or to a neighbor's.

Then where was Moo?

He knocked, softly at first, expecting Moo to barrel into the kitchen from another part of the house, barking his Kong-dog bark. Nothing. He knocked harder, calling out, the knot of fear in his belly tightening. Still nothing.

Just as he was considering breaking a window, he realized where she must be—walking Moo, of course. His knees went weak with relief. She always walked him right after arriving home.

Chance started down the stairs, prepared to go sit on her stoop to wait, when he thought he heard the faint sound of barking. He heard it again, though it didn't sound as if it was coming from Skye's unit—or any of the others, for that matter.

It sounded as if it was coming from the courtyard.

Chance descended the last steps and, frowning, moved his gaze over the small, immaculate yard. It was empty, yet he was sure he had heard a dog.

The sound came again. Along with another, a snuffling, clawing sound.

"Moo," Chance called. "Moo, buddy, is that you?"

The sound came again, this time louder, more insistent. Chance followed the sound around the far corner of the building. There, tucked into a corner where nobody could see it was an equipment shed. And the sounds were coming from inside.

Heart pounding, Chance grasped the padlock, looped over the hasp, but not fastened. If it was Moo in there, Chance would know Skye was in trouble. He would know Griffen had her; that he meant her harm.

Chance removed the padlock and lifted the hasp. He swung open the door and a giant ball of black-and-white fur lunged at him, nearly knocking him down in gratitude.

Now Chance knew. Skye was in danger. He had to find her.

79

Chance went to the Astor Street mansion. He rang the bell, then too impatient to wait, pounded on the door. The housekeeper answered, looking annoyed.

Her expression softened a bit when she recognized him. "Hello, Mr. McCo—"

"Where's Mr. Monarch?"

"Mr. Adam's in his study, but Griffen's not—"

Chance slipped past her and into the foyer. "Which way?"

"You can't—" She scurried after him. "I'll announce you, if you'll just wait—"

"Fuck that." Chance spun to face her. "Which way?"

She pointed, obviously frightened.

"Thank you." He strode in the direction she indicated. Finding the study, he let himself in. Adam sat behind his desk, studying some papers.

"Where's Skye?"

Adam looked up, scowling. "Who let you in?"

The housekeeper appeared at the study door. "I'm sorry, Mr. Monarch. He pushed past me."

"Is she with Griffen?" Chance demanded, ignoring them both. "Is she?"

Adam excused the housekeeper, then got heavily to his feet. He came around the desk to face him. "I know what you're up to, boy. Griffen told me about you, about how you tried to steal Skye from him."

"This isn't about some damned imaginary competition. I think she's in danger."

"From my grandson?" Adam gave a hoot of laughter. "Give it up, McCord. The best man won. Now, get the hell out of here before I call the police."

"I think calling the police is a good idea. But before you do, how does Griffen know Claire Dearborn?"

Adam paled. "Who did you say?"

"Skye's mother. I got home today to find a message from Claire on my recorder. She sounded hysterical. She mentioned Griffen's name and that Skye was in danger."

"Sure you did." Adam made a sound of disgust. "You're pathetic."

"Claire's dead now, Adam. Murdered in her hotel suite at the Knickerbocker. This afternoon."

"That's a lie."

"I wish it were." Chance went to the desk and picked up Adam's phone. He held it out to the older man. "Call the police, find out if I'm lying."

For one moment, the older man simply stared at him, his expression blank. Then he seemed to crumble before Chance's eyes. He took a step backward, fumbling behind him for a chair, then sank onto it. He dropped his head into his hands.

"So, you did know Claire Dearborn," Chance said, his tone harsh, having zero pity for the man.

Adam lifted his head, meeting Chance's gaze. He nodded. "But you don't understand. You have no idea how much we…needed her."

"Who?" Chance searched Adam's expression. "Who did you need?"

"It was Griffen's idea. His plan. We all agreed." He brought his head to his hands again, and Chance had to struggle to decipher what he said. "Me, Dorothy and Griffen. The three of us. We needed her."

A sick sensation settled in the pit of Chance's stomach. He closed the distance between him and the older man, stopping before him. "What plan? What did you decide?"

He lifted his gaze; the old man's eyes were bright, as with

fever. "You see, Madeline stole her away from us. Just like that. But she was the one with the gift, I saw it even when she was only five. We needed her, Chance. We had to have her." Adam balled his hands into fists. "Everything was falling apart, don't you see? This was the only way, the perfect way."

"No, dammit! I don't see. Who was Claire Dearborn to Griffen?"

"His stepmother."

"His step—" This time it was Chance who took the involuntary step backward, Chance who made a sound of disbelief. "But that would mean that Griffen and Skye..."

He let the words trail off, but they hung unspoken between them.

Griffen and Skye were brother and sister.

Now Chance knew what had bothered him about Skye and Griffen as a couple, about the picture they made. Somehow, deep down, he had known. He had seen the familial resemblance. It made him sick to think of it.

"You son of a bitch! You knew. All along, you knew." Chance grabbed the front of Adam's shirt and lifted him to his feet, quaking with fury. "You not only knew Griffen's unholy intentions, you condoned them. How could you do that to her! She's your granddaughter, for Christ's sake! I ought to beat the hell out of you, you old bastard."

Adam began to tremble. "You don't understand. Griffen was all I had. I had to go along with him. We needed Skye, it seemed so right. Everything was as it was supposed to be. A brother and a sister together, running Monarch's. But Dorothy—" He choked on the words, overcome with emotion.

"What about Dorothy?" Chance shook him. "What about her?"

"She was always soft, always ruled by her emotions. She cared too much for Skye. Even if I had known, I couldn't have stopped him."

"What are you saying?" Chance gazed at the other man, realization dawning, horror with it. "My God, are you saying

Griffen...that he had something to do with Dorothy's death?''

"She wasn't part of the plan!" Adam cried. "I didn't give him permission to do that." He looked beseechingly at Chance. "She was my sister. She was a Monarch."

"What about Claire?" Chance shook the old man again, so hard his teeth rattled. "Was she part of the plan?"

"I didn't know anything about her! I didn't!"

Chance released the man, and he fell back to the chair, breathing heavily, cheeks wet with tears. "I knew there were things that...things that weren't quite right about Griffen. But I didn't think he could...and then, when I knew...I was frightened. Don't you see? He was all I had. I needed him. Monarch's needed him. I couldn't send him...away. I couldn't." Adam began to cry again, deep racking sobs of despair.

Chance watched him, unmoved. Adam was as crazy as his grandson. Obsessed with the family and his own twisted beliefs. He hadn't even expressed remorse for what they had done to Skye.

"Where are they, Adam?" Chance squatted in front of the man. "Skye's in danger. I know she is."

"He wouldn't hurt her, I know he wouldn't."

"Listen to me, old man. Griffen told me if he couldn't have Skye, nobody would. He meant that. You know he did. I know he did. He's murdered two people to keep them quiet. But this time he's going to be caught, and he knows it. And when they take him away, he won't have Skye."

Adam met Chance's gaze, the truth of his words registering in the terror that crossed his features.

"Where are they, Adam?"

"Wisconsin," he whispered, his voice thin, broken. "They went to our retreat at Horizon's End." He dropped his head into his hands. "Ask the housekeeper, she'll give you directions."

Chance straightened and started for the door. "Call the police. Tell them everything. I'm going after her."

80

Horizon's End had recently been blanketed in a thick layer of fresh snow. Although well after dark, the light from the full moon reflected off the white world, turning the landscape almost eerily bright, like noontime gone haywire.

The town looked deserted, dark and closed up tight. Skye huddled deeper into the Porsche's bucket seat. "Doesn't anyone live here?" she asked, shivering.

Griffen didn't answer. He didn't glance her way. It was as if he hadn't even heard her. Skye caught her bottom lip between her teeth, longing to arrive, longing to see Adam and Moo. Longing to be anywhere but on this desolate road, alone with Griffen.

His behavior had been more than odd, alternating between brooding and kinetic, between frenzied rambling and suspicious silence. At times, when he'd been rambling, she had wondered if he even remembered she was here.

Skye turned her face to the window, thinking about Chance, remembering the things he had said about Griffen. Now she understood what he had meant, now she understood why he had called Griffen unbalanced. She understood why he had been frightened for her. But surely she wasn't in danger? Surely Griffen wouldn't harm her?

"We're almost there."

Startled, she swung to look at him. He was flexing his fingers on the steering wheel, his gaze fixed straight ahead, a secretive smile tugging at the edges of his mouth.

"It's all worked out so perfectly, don't you think?"

"Pardon?"

"Everything. The way it worked out. For you and me. For Monarch's." He shook his head and continued, not waiting for a response. "Of course, there were little annoyances I had to take care of along the way, but that's to be expected. The important thing is, we're together now."

He sighed. "I suppose the hardest was Dorothy. Sweet Dorothy, she was just so weak. I despise weakness, you know." He looked sadly at Skye. "I loved her very much nonetheless. I hated that she had to go. That really hurt me."

Had to go? What did he mean by that? Skye shuddered and inched closer to the car door. He meant it was a shame that she had passed away. Of course that was what he meant. What else could he have meant?

"Father, on the other hand, didn't hurt a bit. In fact, Father was rather fun. He was a nasty little prick. It's good you didn't know him, you wouldn't have liked him." Griffen drew his eyebrows together in thought, then bobbed his head, as if coming to a conclusion. "Yup, he deserved to die."

Fear made her light-headed. *Two Monarchs had died in the past twelve months. Somehow, Griffen had been involved in both deaths.*

He smiled at her. "Sometimes I even surprise myself. I mean, getting you that apartment was pure genius."

"Pure genius," she whispered. "Why?"

"Why?" he chided. "Because I own the building, silly. Remember?"

She squeezed her eyes shut, struggling to keep a grip on her fear. She recalled the times she had looked at a stack of magazines, or the books on her shelf, or even the contents of her dresser drawers, and thought they had been moved slightly. She had told herself she was imagining things. She had thought she was losing her mind.

She hadn't been.

Griffen had had a key to her apartment. He had been able to come and go whenever he wanted. He had touched her belongings, her private things, ones meant for no one's eyes and hands but her own.

Griffen no doubt had a key to the courtyard, as well. He could have been the one who poisoned her dog. He probably was. She could picture him, slipping in with the coffee can of antifreeze, then slipping out. No wonder he had called later that night; he had wanted to hear her distress. He had wanted to find out if he had done the job.

The son of a bitch. The bastard. She fisted her fingers, outraged and angry, longing to confront him and demand the truth. Skye held her tongue. She didn't know Griffen Monarch at all, she realized. He just might be capable of anything.

"Here we are."

Griffen turned onto a narrow, unmarked driveway, bordered on both sides by thick, white forest. His headlights sliced across the snow-covered roadway, scaring a rabbit and sending it scurrying for cover. The tires made a crunching sound as they cut a path through the virgin snow.

Almost there, Skye thought, relieved. Thank God. In a moment, Adam would be giving her a big hug, and Moo would be barking and running around her in excited circles.

Adam would know what to do. She would pull him aside as soon as she could. He would be able to calm Griffen.

Only, Adam wasn't there. The house was pitch-black, sealed up tight, like a coffin. She should have realized Adam and Moo weren't here from the snowy driveway. She hadn't been paying attention; she had been too busy thinking about how Adam would help her.

With a sinking sensation in the pit of her gut, she acknowledged the possibility that Adam might not be coming at all. If that was the case, she was on her own. Starting now, she noticed everything.

Skye stood on the front porch, teeth chattering while she waited for Griffen to unlock the door. "You said Adam would meet us here."

"He must have stopped to see friends. He knows a lot of people in the area." He smiled at her. "You'll feel better once we get the place warmed up. Let's take the bags upstairs, then I'll get a fire going. They'll probably be here just in time to roast marshmallows.''

When they weren't, Griffen made a show of calling the state police ''just to make sure Adam hadn't been involved in an accident,'' and the Astor Street house, talking to the housekeeper.

A show, Skye was convinced, because Adam wasn't coming. She was certain of it. Just as she was certain that Adam didn't have Moo. Griffen had done something with him.

''See, sweetheart,'' Griffen said, hanging up the phone. ''He's visiting with friends along the way. Just like I said. Everything's fine.''

Skye sat in front of the fire, huddled under a blanket, fighting to get a grip on her rising panic, worrying about her dog and what Griffen had done with him. Worrying what he planned to do with her.

Coming with him had been a mistake, she saw that now. Something about this whole thing was wrong, and not just with this trip—with Griffen's courtship, his feelings for her, the way he had known so much about her. It all rang false. Terri had seen it and had tried to warn her. So had Chance.

Skye drew her knees to her chest and stared into the fire, watching as it consumed everything it touched. She thought of her headaches and nightmares, her sudden bouts of claustrophobia. She had known, too. She had just refused to see.

Because she had wanted her dream of perfect love, a love that came without risk.

He's obsessed with you, Skye. He said if he couldn't have you, nobody would. I think he meant it.

Skye worked at the edge of the afghan, fraying it. Maybe Griffen had figured out that she meant to break off their engagement. Maybe he had decided to make good on his words to Chance.

''Sweetheart? Are you all right?''

A squeak of surprise, of terror, slipped past her lips. She looked up at Griffen, forcing herself to act as if nothing was wrong. As if she wasn't about to crawl out of her skin. "I'm a little tired, that's all. I'm getting one of my headaches."

"Poor baby. Why don't you lie down for a while? I'll make us something to eat."

She had seen a phone in the upstairs hallway. She could call 911. They would send someone.

She smiled, feeling as though her cheeks were going to crack. "Thank you, Griffen. If you really don't mind, I think I will."

He helped her to her feet, then drew her against his chest, holding her possessively. A scent clung to him, something bitter and bad, something like death. She squeezed her eyes shut, her heart racing. She had to get to that phone; she had to get help.

"I couldn't live without you, you know that, Skye? Life would be meaningless." He kissed her then, rubbing his lips against hers, groaning. She curled her fingers into his sweater, feeling sick, praying he didn't try to take the kiss any further, not knowing what she would do. His light caress was already almost more than she could bear.

Her prayers were answered. He ended the kiss and released her. Though she wanted to run, she climbed the stairs slowly, careful not to arouse his suspicion. She counted each step, picturing the phone, focusing on that instead of her fear.

When she reached the top landing, she glanced back at him. He still watched her, though his gaze was unnaturally blank. As if he had somehow managed to leave his body behind.

She started down the hall, heart thundering, gaze fixed on the phone, there at the end of the hall. When she reached it, she nearly cried out with relief. After taking one last glance behind her to make sure Griffen hadn't followed her up, she lifted the receiver and brought it to her ear.

The phone was dead. She jiggled the plunger, then checked to make sure the jack was plugged into the wall. It was.

She jiggled the plunger again. Still nothing.

Griffen had lied about Adam and Moo. He had lied about making those calls. What else had he lied about? Why had he lured her up here?

He meant to hurt her.

Maybe even to kill her.

She brought a hand to her mouth, really and truly afraid for the first time. She had been worried before. Nervous. But she hadn't seriously thought that he would harm her.

She did now.

She had to get out of here as soon as possible.

She dropped the receiver onto the cradle, momentarily forgetting stealth. She ran to the bedroom where their suitcases were, closing and locking the door behind her.

Think. Think. What to do? She moved her gaze around the room, looking for an answer. She stopped on the window. She ran to it and peered out, seeing a short drop to another section of roof, then a bigger drop to the snowy yard.

The snow would cushion her landing. She could do it.

She whirled back around. Her gaze landed on Griffen's coat, tossed with hers across the bed. The car keys, of course.

She crossed to the bed, a desperate prayer playing in her head. That she would find the keys. That she would get out in time, before he came for her. For he would come for her.

She searched Griffen's coat. His keys weren't there. She went to his suitcase then, shoving aside her own coat and the box containing her new gloves. She opened his case and as slowly and as carefully as she could, began searching for an extra key. Nothing. She found nothing.

She would have to escape on foot. She glanced back at the window, thinking of how desolate, how deserted Horizon's End had seemed. But surely someone lived here year-round. The streets had been plowed; she had seen several stores in town, a service station and a café. She would find someone who would help her. At the least, she would find a phone and call for help. She had to. This was her only chance.

She went to her suitcase and opened it. Luckily, Griffen

had packed her things—a pair of jeans and a pair of sweats, a couple pair of woolen socks, a turtleneck and her heavy old cardigan. She would layer them; they would have to do.

A floorboard creaked. Skye froze, her gaze going to the bottom of the door and the strip of light flooding through from the hallway. A shadow moved across it, and her breath caught. Griffen was out there. Just standing in front of her door; she could hear his breathing. She brought her fist to her mouth to keep from whimpering. Moments became like hours, minutes an eternity.

Then, as suddenly as he had come, he was gone.

For several moments she didn't move, afraid he was still there, that he was trying to trick her into believing he had gone. Finally, gathering together her courage, she tiptoed to the door and pressed her ear against it.

She heard the faint strains of music, then what sounded like the clatter of pans from the kitchen. Reassured, she stripped out of her work clothes and into the ones Griffen had brought for her, layering them. She wished for her lined boots, the warm ones she had bought for a ski trip a couple of years ago, trying to decide between the low-heeled boots she had worn to work and her Nikes. The athletic shoes won, though she knew her feet would be cold and wet within minutes. Better, she thought, than breaking an ankle in her heels.

Her gloves. Thank goodness they had come.

Skye grabbed the box and tore it open. Not gloves, she realized, surprised, drawing out a strange-looking necklace. She held it up, wondering what it was and who had sent it, turning it over in her hands. It was a vessel of some sort. A container. It was filled with something.

She found the safety and clasp and snapped them open.

Gems spilled into her hands—diamonds and rubies and sapphires.

She was sitting on the floor while her mother packed their suitcases. Her mommy was upset about something, she knew, though she tried to pretend she wasn't. They were going

*away on a trip. Just the two of them. Her mommy said they
were going to have such fun.*

*Skye inched over to her mother's suitcase and opened it.
Inside she saw a pretty, black bag. Skye took it out and ran
her fingers over the soft, fuzzy fabric, then the shiny, silver
Monarch "M" stamped on it.*

*Skye opened the bag and beautiful little rocks spilled out.
Like the ones Grandfather had shown her down at the store.
"Mommy! Look! Pretty stones."*

*Her mother whirled, then snatched the pouch away, the
jewels scattering across the gleaming wooden floor. "No,
Grace! Bad girl!"*

Skye brought her hands to her mouth, remembering everything, seeing it with her mind's eye as if it were unfolding
before her.

*A man, her grandfather, burst into the room. He and her
mother began to fight, shouting at each other in a way that
frightened Skye. She tried to cover her ears, but she could
still hear. Her grandfather hit her mother so hard she fell.
Skye wanted to go to her mother, but he scooped her up,
meaning to take her away from her mommy. She squirmed
and kicked. "Mommy!" she screamed. "I want my
mommy!"*

*Her mother lunged at him. Skye slipped from her grandfather's arms and hit the floor hard. She started to cry. A
moment later there had been blood everywhere. Splattering
across her while the angel smiled down at her.*

Skye made a sound of horror. The angel. The old stone
mansion on Astor Street. The curvy Monarch "M." The butterfly, of course.

A hysterical laugh bubbled to her lips. Why hadn't she
seen it? All along, her subconscious had been trying to tell
her, trying to warn her. Her headaches. Her constant sense
of unease. The claustrophobia she had experienced, her feelings of being trapped.

Her reaction to Griffen's lovemaking.

Griffen. Dear God, Griffen.

He was her brother. The monster from her nightmares, the one she couldn't outrun. He was the horror her mind had blocked out.

She had never been alone, she remembered, never been safe from him. He had followed and tormented her. She remembered waking in the night to find him beside her bed watching her. Or worse, in the bed with her, staring, his breath hot and foul against her face.

Curving her arms around herself, she rocked back and forth, her mind playing a series of dark, distorted images for her.

Griffen lured her outside. He had her kitten, he said. She couldn't have it unless she came out with him. So she followed him into the back garden and out the gate, to the back alley, where her mother had warned her never to go. There was her kitten, in a cardboard box, mewing and crying. But before Skye could get to it, he brought his baseball bat down on the helpless creature. Once. Twice, then a third time. When she screamed, he grabbed her and shook her. "Tell anyone, and I'll do it to you, too. Tell, and I'll do it to your precious mama."

Skye realized she was sobbing and pressed a fist to her mouth, willing the memories to stop, wishing she could reclose the door, lock it tight for the next twenty years. Maybe forever. But she couldn't control them, and they spilled forth much the same as her tears.

Griffen lay on top of her, holding her down, a hand over her mouth so she couldn't call Nanny or anyone else. She fought as hard as she could, squirming and kicking, but he only laughed. He could do anything he pleased to her. She belonged to him. And just so she wouldn't forget it... He put his hand under her dress then, and pulled aside her underwear. While she cried and silently begged him to stop, stuck his fingers there, inside her, hurting her.

Skye squeezed her thighs together now, hurting, hating him. How could he have done that to her? She'd been a baby. He'd been her brother, her own flesh and blood.

That's why her mother had run with her. No one had believed her about Griffen. No one.

The bastard had found her, somehow. He had tracked her down, laying his trap, much as he had when she was small. Did Adam know who she was? Had Dorothy? She pressed her face to a bed pillow, holding back the sounds of her sobs, afraid Griffen would hear.

She thought back, to glances Griffen and his grandfather had exchanged, to the way they had all welcomed her, as if she was a long lost member of the family; she recalled the things they had said.

"Welcome home, Skye dear."

"You're part of our family now. Now you can never leave us."

"You have the gift. It's right that you take Dorothy's place."

"A brother-and-sister team have always run Monarch's."

A brother-and-sister team... Dear God, they had all been in on this, she realized, scrambling off the bed, panic pulling at her. They were all sick, obsessed with who they were and with Monarch's.

They were sick, but Griffen was a monster. She had to get away from him. To do that, she had to get a grip on herself. If she didn't, she wouldn't last thirty minutes out in the cold.

She grabbed her cardigan and put it on, then slipped into her coat. She wrapped her muffler over her head and around her neck, then tucked it under her coat's collar. Saying a silent prayer for help, she crossed to the window, unlocked it and carefully slid it up.

She looked out, judging the distance, getting her bearings. Before her, she saw an expanse of lawn, then a glittering frozen lake beyond. To either side lay heavily wooded property. She could do it. She would make it to the lawn, then head into the forest to her right, going toward town. The moon would light her way.

She climbed onto the ledge and swung her legs out. She heard a sound at her door, like a key being slid into a lock, then turned. She twisted toward the door, eyes wide, heart hammering. The knob turned; the door cracked open.

Griffen! He had come for her.

Taking a deep breath, she jumped.

81

Skye landed on the section of roof below. She hadn't realized how steeply pitched it was, and her feet slipped out from under her. She landed on her right side and skidded toward the edge. Gasping, crying, she clawed at the icy shingles, trying desperately to stop her forward momentum. The shingles tore at her bare hands, though they provided nothing for her to grab on to. She pictured herself, tumbling over the edge, landing in a heap, too broken to escape Griffen.

He was above her, watching from the window, laughing.

The laugh of a madman.

She twisted her foot, trying for a toehold. She found one. She wedged her right foot in the gutter, wincing as pain knifed up through her ankle.

It stopped her. Only now she was stuck.

"Skye, my love, going somewhere?" Griffen leaned farther out the window, giggling. "No, apparently not."

She fought her way into a sitting position, though with her foot twisted sideways in the gutter, it was agony. Once upright, she tugged at her leg, breath coming in small gasps.

"You can't run away from me, Grace. Oh—" He brought a hand to his mouth in an exaggerated oops. "Now I've gone and given it away. You're not Skye Dearborn at all. Your name's really Grace. Grace Elizabeth Monarch.

"See, that's the thing. You're down there working so hard, and you can't run away from me. Destiny can't be changed any more than it can be ignored. Your mother tried, the silly bitch. But that's all behind us now, isn't it, my pet?"

Skye looked up at him, heart thundering, determined not

to let him see how frightened she was. She refused to play the terrified victim for him, the child he had tormented and controlled with fear. "What do you want from me?"

"Just for us to be together. Forever. The same thing you always wanted. Remember, Grace?"

"Go to hell. I wouldn't want you if you were the last man on earth."

He smiled and rested his elbows on the window ledge. "In a way, I *am* the last man on earth. The last one you'll ever know, anyway." He frowned. "I didn't appreciate your diddling around with that nothing McCord, by the way. I expected more from you, Grace."

"You're not half the man he is!" she shot back, thinking that maybe, if she rattled him, he would do something stupid, slip up somehow. "You only wish you were."

He frowned. "Stop that, Grace. I don't like it."

"That's because it's true. You're just a slimy little bug compared to him. He's better in every way...especially in bed!"

His face contorted with fury, and Skye felt a rush of victory. "I love him," she said. "And nothing you can do will change that."

For a moment he looked as if he was going to explode, then he chuckled. "I know what you're doing, darling, and it's not going to work. You're not going to get me all riled up so I forget my plan and go and do something sloppy. Besides, if I were going to get riled up, I would have done it long before now. Between Chance and Terri, you kept me pretty busy."

Terri. He'd been behind that, too. Of course. "So, you're the one who sent the rat."

"The very one. I also left that charming little message for little Raye." He grinned. "I couldn't have you spending time with her, growing close to her and her little bitch daughter instead of me. I couldn't have it."

"So, how are you going to make it happen?" she asked, looking at him while concentrating on freeing her foot. "Are

you going to kill me, Griffen? Bludgeon me with a baseball
bat, the way you did my kitten?''

He looked almost comically surprised. ''You've regained
your memory, Grace.''

''That's right, and soon enough to realize what a slimy
piece of refuse you are.''

''A surprise, but good. Now you understand how important, how right it is for us to be together. And Grace, *kill* is
such an ugly word. I prefer *joined in death.*''

Joined in death. Terror took her breath; she fought it off.
''How are you going to do it, Griffen? If not a baseball bat,
how?''

He laughed, the sound high, like a child's. ''That's for me
to know and you to find out.''

''I don't think so.'' With an almighty tug, Skye freed her
foot. Fire shot up her leg. She leaped off the edge.

The snow cushioned her fall, though the impact knocked
the wind out of her. It took a moment to get it back. When
she did, she scrambled to her feet and started to run, though
it felt more like wading, the snow was so deep.

From the house, she heard a door slam, heard feet pounding across the deck. ''Grace,'' he called. ''Why are you wast-
ing our time and all this energy? You're not going anywhere.
The nearest house on either side is a mile and a half, and
those homes are closed for the winter. Just like ours.''

She dared a glance back, he was well behind her, but gaining fast, she saw. She turned her gaze back to the line of
trees, fixing on them, pushing harder, each step taking a Her-
culean effort.

''It was so easy, once I found you. We have Chance to
thank for that. I recognized his name from one of the P.I.'s
reports. I hired him, cultivated a friendship, then let him un-
wittingly lead me to you.''

She reached the stand of trees and with a cry of relief,
plunged into the woods. It was much darker, the snow not
as deep. But the going was treacherous. She picked her way
around fallen trees and a labyrinth of thick, dead underbrush.

Griffen made his way into the woods. He snapped on a flashlight and the beam cut across her path. "Little Grace, little Grace, come show your face."

She heard him moving deeper, stopping every so often as if to get his bearings. "I can't believe you're treating me this way," he said, chiding her as he would a child. "After everything I've done for you. I love you, Grace."

Out of breath, drenched with sweat, Skye stopped, pressing herself up against a tree. She listened, straining to make sure he was still behind her. That he wasn't circling around her. The forest played tricks on her ears, bouncing the sound off the trees, making it difficult to get her bearings.

"Do you know what I've done for you, the concessions I've made? Dorothy, for one. She was my aunt, I loved her. But I killed her. So we could be together.

"Then there was little Stephanie, the one they thought could replace you—" He stopped moving, and she saw the flashlight beam sweep back and forth. "I took care of her. For you. No one could take your place, Grace. It was the one time I was disappointed in Granddad. He was hoping *she* would have the gift. He was making noises like he thought she might. How could *she* have it, when you already did?"

Skye brought her hand to her mouth. His little sister, the one who had drowned in the bath. *Her* little sister, she realized. It hadn't been an accident at all. She pressed herself closer to the tree, heart thundering, struggling to get hold of her emotions.

"You know, we're really here because of your mother." He made a sound of disgust. "She's the one who fouled everything up, as usual. She came to town, she found out about us. She tried to find you at the store. She got me instead."

Her mother was in Chicago? Looking for her? The gems, Skye realized, joy blooming inside her. Her mother had sent them, of course.

"Unfortunately, I had to kill her. Snapped her neck, just like that."

"No!" The word raced past her lips. "No! You bastard!" Sobbing, Skye started to run as fast as she could, branches ripping at her face and hands. She tripped on a fallen tree and fell, then dragged herself to her feet.

He'd killed her mother. Dear God, her mother.

She ran until she could run no more, until her lungs burned and it felt as if her heart were going to burst right out of her chest. She took cover behind a tree, pressing up against it.

A twig snapped nearby. Her heart flew to her throat. He was closer than she'd thought. She looked frantically around for a weapon, something to use against him. Her gaze landed on a thick piece of branch on the ground to her left. She bent and as quietly as she could, picked it up. Arms quivering with the effort, she lifted it over her head, waiting. He drew closer. Closer. She held her breath.

He stepped past her hiding place and she swung, hitting him hard in the chest. With a grunt of pain, he stumbled backward. "That's for my mother, you bastard!" She swung again, this time connecting with the right side of his face. "And that's for me!"

His head snapped sideways and he toppled, his expression one of complete and utter surprise. She threw the branch at him and ran.

The trees cleared suddenly, and the lake lay before her, gleaming in the moonlight. She heard Griffen drag himself to his feet, grunting in pain, gasping for air. There was nowhere for her to go but forward, onto the lake. She saw lights on the other side. If she could get across, she would find help.

Holding her breath, Skye stepped onto the lake. It held, feeling solid beneath her. She began to make her way across the slick surface, inch by careful inch, saved only by the fresh snow on top of the ice. Still, her Nikes didn't give her much traction, and she had to go slow or fall.

He was stronger, faster. He had the advantage of snow

boots. She couldn't beat him to the other side, she realized. And on the ice she lost the ability to stop, catch her breath and hide.

For all the good it would do her, she realized. She wasn't going to make it out of this. She was numb with the cold already, exhausted. Griffen was gaining on her with every step. And even if she made it to the woods, what could she do? Hide and freeze to death? Tears swamped her, she fought them, knowing they would only sap the little bit of energy and will she had left.

She changed her direction, angling toward the Monarch place, toward their dock that stuck out onto the lake like a bony, dark finger. She took one last, longing glance at the lights on the other side, trying to memorize their location, when she thought she heard her name.

She stopped and listened, then heard her name again. *Chance. It was Chance. He had come for her.* A moment later, she heard barking. *He had Moo.*

"Chance!" she screamed, almost sobbing with relief. "I'm here! I'm here!"

"Skye! Where are you?"

She saw him then, standing on the Monarchs' deck. She waved her arms and screamed again. "Here, Chance! Here! On the lake."

Chance must have spotted her, because he started to run toward the dock, Moo with him.

"No!" Griffen bellowed. "He won't have you!" Griffen lunged at her, falling, hitting the ice, his fingers brushing against her ankle. Skye screamed again, lurching away from him.

The ice began to crack. She stopped and, horrified, watched as weblike veins shot through the ice at her feet. She looked up. "Chance! The lake! It's cracking!"

"Keep coming!" he shouted. "I'll get you, I promise."

Skye ran, the ice shifting beneath her feet, the crackling and groaning sound becoming louder, more ominous. She could see the movement of the water below.

A cry of despair flew to her lips. She didn't want to die.

"You're almost there, Skye. You're going to make it. You're—"

The ice gave beneath her feet. She went down. The cold paralyzed her. It drenched her clothes, seeming to triple her weight, dragging her down. Her head slid under and for a fraction of a second, she considered giving up, just letting go and allowing the cold to take her. She was so tired. It seemed so hopeless.

Then she heard Chance's voice calling her, and she began to fight, kicking her way to the surface. Gasping for air, she grabbed at the edge of the ice in front of her, trying to get leverage.

Every time she did, the ice broke off.

She heard Griffen in the water behind her, struggling, flailing his arms and legs.

Chance was at the edge of the dock, climbing down the ladder attached to the side. "Come on, baby, you can do it." Holding on to a rung of the ladder with one hand, Chance reached out his other. "Come on, Skye. Baby, grab my hand!"

She reached. Their fingers brushed. With a cry, she slipped and went under. She fought her way up, the layers of sodden clothes dragging at her. She broke the surface; she reached for Chance's hand.

Their fingers connected; his closed around hers. He began to haul her toward him.

Something closed around her ankle. Griffen. He had her ankle, he was pulling her down. She looked back, hysterical. He wasn't trying to save himself, she realized. He wanted her to go down with him.

Forever. They would be together forever.

"Don't let go, Chance! Don't let—"

Her hand slipped from his; her head went under. She was going to die, Skye realized. This was it, the end. She saw Griffen then, below her in the water, looking up at her, his mouth twisted into a grotesque smile.

He thought he'd won.

No! She drew back and brought her heel square into his chin. His head snapped back, and his hand fell away from her ankle. A look of disbelief crossed his features, and he reached out for her as the last of the oxygen bubbled out of him.

Skye dragged her gaze away and struggled toward the surface for the last time, completely spent. She couldn't do it again, she knew. This was it; her last shot at life.

Her head broke the water; she gasped for air. Chance was there, half in the water, arm looped around the ladder, searching for her. He caught her and hauled her out and onto the dock. They collapsed into each other's arms, shuddering, teeth chattering.

"I could have lost you," he said, stripping off her sodden coat and wrapping her in his. "When I realized—"

"I was so scared. I thought I'd never see you again."

He ran his hands over her, as if convincing himself she was with him, that she was safe. "That'll never happen." He kissed her cheeks, her eyelids, her mouth. "I love you, Skye. I love you so mu—"

"Hold me, Chance. Just hold me." She clung to him, coming back to life. "Don't let me go."

"I won't, love. I won't let you go. Not ever."

82

The next morning, Skye awakened in Chance's arms. Sunlight spilled through the window and fell across the bed, doing its best to dispel all traces of the hellish night before. The police had arrived shortly after Chance pulled her from what had almost been her icy grave, alerted by the Chicago police and Adam.

They had questioned her, wanting a detailed account of everything that had happened. She'd had to go over it all again and again; retelling the story brought back her terror, the horror of believing she was going to die. The horror of those last moments, when Griffen's hand had closed around her ankle and he had pulled her under.

She could have died. If not for Chance, she would have.

The police had done a perfunctory search for Griffen's body, though they hadn't expected to find him. They probably wouldn't until spring, they'd said, but planned to bring a team out today for another attempt. She and Chance would be gone by then, on their way home. Together.

Through it all Chance had stayed by her side, his arm protectively around her. It had been he who'd insisted she was finished answering questions, he who had fed her some soup and tucked her into bed, crawling under the covers to hold her until the cold was gone. His tender lovemaking had chased the last of the terror away, only then had she been able to sleep.

Skye snuggled into Chance and he made a sleepy, comfortable sound. She was safe now, she thought, moving her gaze lovingly over his face. In Chance's arms, where she had always been meant to be. Griffen had talked of soul mates. If there was such a thing, Chance was hers. It seemed as if she had loved him forever already.

She would take whatever the future brought them; she didn't expect a perfect love, not anymore. She just wanted two people who loved each other enough to give it their best shot.

She kissed Chance lightly, then slipped out of bed. She padded down the hall, toward the other bedroom, Moo at her heels. There, she found the strange necklace and gems, just as she had left them. And there, she saw the letter she had missed the night before.

Knowing it was from her mother, Skye sat on the edge of the bed, unfolded it and began to read.

Chance found her there, head bent over the letter, crying. He came to her, he took her in his arms. "She really did love me," Skye whispered. "She didn't leave me behind, we only got separated."

Skye cried for a long time, for what she had and what she had lost, she cried for the mother who had loved her as much as a mother had ever loved her child, so much that she had given up everything to protect her. Even her own life.

It would take a long time for the hurt to go away, Skye knew. For the deep ache of longing and regret to fade.

But it would. And when it did, she would be left with just the memory of love.

She had gotten her every wish, she realized. With them had come terrible consequences and the miracle of Chance's love. And through them, she had learned a powerful lesson. She was done wishing for what she didn't have; life was too short, too precious to waste that way. From this moment on she would enjoy all she had been given.

Wearing her mother's talisman, Skye packed her few things, anxious to leave this place, this house. Anxious to leave Griffen and the events of the past months behind her forever. It was time to begin the future, hers and Chance's, free of the taint of the Monarch family, free from the darkness of their sickness and obsession. She wanted nothing to do with them, nothing to do with the things they held dear.

"Are you sure?" Chance asked when she told him her intentions. "Are you sure you want to give it all up? Monarch's and all that goes with it is worth a fortune. Some might even call it your destiny."

Skye shook her head and closed her hand over the gem-filled talisman. "These are my destiny," she said softly. "My fortune. These and you."

He kissed her, then together they stepped outside, sunshine spilling over them, warm and bright.

Without a backward glance, they headed toward their future.

Take 3 of
"The Best of the Best™"
Novels FREE
Plus get a FREE surprise gift!

"Jayne Ann Krentz entertains to the hilt…"
—Catherine Coulter

JAYNE ANN KRENTZ

There is no getting around it once you realize it *is* the

LADY'S CHOICE

After sharing the passion and soft intimacy of his embrace, Juliana Grant decides that Travis Sawyer is Mr. Right. And Travis realizes that his desire for revenge has gone way too far—but he can't pull back. As Juliana gets caught in the cross fire, she discovers that she can also play the game. Travis owes her—and she intends to see that he pays his debts…in full.

Available in March at your favorite retail outlet.

MIRA The brightest star in women's fiction   MJAK1

Look us up on-line at: http://www.romance.net

Bestselling Author

MARGOT DALTON

explores every parent's worst fear...the
disappearance of a child.

First Impression

Three-year-old Michael Panesivic has vanished.

A witness steps forward—and his story is chilling.
But is he a credible witness or a suspect?

Detective Jackie Kaminsky has three choices:
1) dismiss the man as a nutcase,
2) arrest him as the only suspect,
   or
3) believe him.

But with a little boy's life at stake, she can't afford to
make the wrong choice.

Available in April 1997 at your favorite retail outlet.

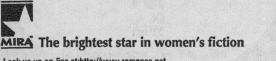

If you enjoyed this captivating story by

ERICA SPINDLER

Don't miss out on these additional titles
by one of MIRA's bestselling authors: